Acclai:

MW01230256

Kendy Pearson's devotion to history and faith shines through every chapter of this novel. Brimming with heart, *When Heaven Thunders* is an emotionally charged journey for characters and readers alike. While addressing struggles unique to the American Civil War, this redemptive story translates well to the inner battles we all face within ourselves. Exploring soul-level choices—between faith and fear, self-preservation and sacrifice, forgiveness and resentment—are themes both timely and timeless. A must-read for fans of well-researched, immersive Christian historical fiction.

Jocelyn Green,
Christy Award-winning author
of *A River Between Us*

When Heaven Thunders is a Civil War romance that beautifully weaves historical detail with deep emotional resonance. The characters are richly drawn, and the narrative unfolds at a deliberate pace, allowing readers to fully immerse themselves in the era and the heart-touching journey of the protagonists. A captivating read!

Lynnette Bonner,
USA Today Bestselling author of
the Wyldhaven series, The Sheperd's Heart series,
the Oregon Promise series, and more.

Pearson pulls back the curtain on war-torn America in this moving story of love and sacrifice. Loyalties are tested, hidden motives unearthed, and danger lurks for more than just the enlisted soldiers in *When Heaven Thunders*. This story will have you rooting for

Fin and Melinda Jane, and on the edge of your seat to see if good will triumph over evil.

Erica Vetsch,
author of the Of Cloaks & Daggers
Regency Mystery series

Kendy Pearson is a gifted author who can bring the past to life with her character development and descriptive scenes. It is refreshing to read a Christian based story line that has the courage to step out of the caricature expectations of faith-based writing and be real about war, human nature, romance and Christian living.

Ken Pratt,
author of the Bestselling
Matt Bannister series

I could not put this book down. I had no idea what I was in for. It was beautiful. It was heart wrenching. It was so perfect! (*When the Mountains Wept*)

Redeeming Lit Podcast

Kendy Pearson brings to life the Kanawha Valley's explosive Civil War history in this multi-faceted jewel of a tale inspired by true events. Endurance, faith, and love shine through *When the Mountains Wept*, the first book in what is sure to be a stellar series.

Laura Frantz,
Christy Award-winning author
of *The Rose and the Thistle*

As West Virginia sat perched between the Union and the Confederacy, neighbors were forced to make difficult choices and kinfolk found themselves across from one another in battle. Gifted storyteller Kendy Pearson makes this scene spring to life with her vivid storytelling, every character so expertly sculpted that I found myself missing them when I closed the cover. Augusta and James stole my heart, and I rooted for them from page one until the very end. Don't miss *When the Mountains Wept*, and I can't wait to see what Pearson writes next.

Karen Barnett,
Award winning author
of *When Stone Wings Fly*
and the Vintage National Park Novels

Kendy Pearson's debut is a stirring look at the people who lived, loved, and lost during the darkest period in our country's existence. *When the Mountains Wept* is a heart-rending romance between Augusta and James that reveals the God who is always there...even when we think all is lost. A story to savor and an author to watch!

Tara Johnson,
author of *To Speak His Name*

When the Mountains Wept takes readers on an emotionally-layered journey, both heart-stirring and redemptive. Pearson pens a moving tale of family loyalty, complex devotions, and hope amid the turmoil. A delight historical fiction fans won't want to miss!

Stephenia H. McGee,
Award-winning author of
The Accidental Spy series

West Virginia: Born of Rebellion's Storm 2

WHEN
HEAVEN
THUNDERS

KENDY PEARSON

Heart
of
History
an imprint of
PEAR BLOSSOM BOOKS

Published by Pear Blossom Books, Dundee, Oregon, U.S.A.

Scripture quotations are taken from the King James Version of the Bible

Publishers Note: This novel is a work of fiction. Names, characters, places, and incidents are either products of the author's imagination or used fictitiously. Because this is a work of historical reconstruction; the appearance of certain historical figures, places, and incidents are therefore inevitable.

ISBN 979-8-9899317-1-2 (print)

Library of Congress Cataloging in Publication Data

Cover Design by Mountain Creek Books LLC

Subjects: Novel / Historical Fiction / Christian Historical Fiction / American Civil War / West Virginia History / Appalachian Historical Fiction / Military Fiction / U.S. History / West Virginia breaks from Virginia / Christian Historical Fiction inspired by true events

It is not the light that we need, but the fire.
It is not the gentle shower, but the thunder.
We need the storm,
the whirlwind,
and the earthquake.

Frederick Douglass
July 5, 1852

1861–1865

Rebellion's tempest swept the land
and a state was born of a nation torn.
West Virginia: a Child of the Storm

One

FAYETTE COUNTY, VIRGINIA

December 1861

"Shake a leg, Hicks. The call of nature wasn't hollerin' from the next county, ya know. A pie-eater like yourself oughta know not to dally." What was taking so long? They only had a four-day pass, but Fin Dabney meant to make the most of it.

He tucked the poke of sowbelly into his saddlebag, stiffening as a too-familiar wisp of cool air brushed the back of his neck. Setting his jaw, he inched the Colt from his gun belt, snugging it between his chest and the bay gelding.

Steadying his breath in a practiced rhythm, he called louder, "You keep lollygagging, you'll find yourself working to catch up to me and Duke." One hand stroked the horse's sleek withers as his trigger finger twitched on the other. His eyes scanned the dense woods pressing in on the narrow trace.

The snap of a twig. Another.

The brush parted, and a shoeless boy prodded Noah Hicks forward with an ancient musket. "You best leave that horse be and step over to that tree, Yankee." He jammed the gun harder into Noah's back, glaring at Fin. "No tomfoolery, now."

1

A fierce expression—more fear than menace—glared from the shadow of the boy's ratty kepi. One eye disappeared behind a hank of straw-colored hair. A threadbare havelock draped over his collar, its edge snagged in a frayed rope tied to his britches.

Fin turned three quarters to the bushwhacker, pistol out of sight. "You don't want to do this, boy. Why, I bet you're no older than my little brother. Reckon Zander would be seventeen now." Holding the young Rebel's gaze, he scrubbed his beard with his free hand. "What do you plan on doing with the two of us?"

"I . . . I'm gonna take them horses. Our band has need of 'em."

Noah raised his thick eyebrows, grilling Fin in silent communication as he lifted his hands higher in a cagy surrender.

Fin offered a half-smile to the boy. "What's your name, son? You from around here?"

"Ain't none of yer business. Just step over there, or I'll sh . . . shoot this'un. Right here and now." His attention darted from Fin to the prisoner.

"I'm pretty fond of ol' Duke here. If you're insisting on taking him, you don't leave me too many options."

"In case ya haven't noticed, I got a gun in yer friend's back." Despite the frosty day, a single glistening trail crept from under the boy's hat, angling its way across a dirt-streaked cheek.

"I see that." *He's so young. Give me true aim, Lord.* Fin gave an apathetic shrug. "Aww, just shoot him. He eats too much anyways."

Hicks played along. "Dabney, I oughta—"

In an instant, Noah dropped to the ground. Fin fired, propelling the boy's cap three feet into the air. He snagged the musket from the Rebel's hands. The boy's eyes gaped wide in shock; his face paled, falling slack as the truth of the moment sank in.

Noah stood, brushing the dirt from his britches, a grin twisting his wheaten mustache. "Took you long enough, Dabney." He yanked the pistol from the boy's waistband. "I reckon this'd be mine."

Fin holstered his Colt. "Gonna have to take you into Gauley, son. Who you with?"

"I ain't talkin'." The boy spat on the ground, scooped up the smoking kepi and crammed it back on his head.

"At least tell me your name."

"Marrs. Seaton Marrs." He drew back his shoulders and pinned a defiant look on Fin.

"You Claude Marrs's boy?"

"What if I am?"

Fin grumbled, slapping his hat against his thigh. He had been taking on the irregulars down on the New River of late, and this was the closest he'd made it to the home place. Holding Claude Marrs's son at gunpoint was not the homecoming he had imagined.

"Your pap fightin' for the Confederacy?" Sadness twisted his middle like bad meat. Most of the folks he'd known all his life were siding with the Secesh. And here he was, back in his own neck of the woods—in a Union uniform, no less.

"No, sir. The Yankees took him away. Said he was a political prisoner." Seaton gave his leg a shake and shifted his weight.

Fin hated this nasty business of war, but if he didn't trust he was in the right, he'd have a hard time living with himself. And sending this boy to a prison camp . . . "We're gonna take you to the Federal encampment at Gauley Bridge, just like any other prisoner, Seaton." He snatched the grungy hat off the boy's head and tossed it into the scrub brush. "But they'll let you go if you and your pap take an oath of allegiance to the Union. Maybe your pap is still there."

He tugged a length of rope from his saddle strap and tossed it to Hicks. "Tie his hands."

A grin tugged at Fin's cheek as he took in the familiar sights. A smattering of white on the upper ridges of the hills, like frosting on a birthday cake, hailed recollections of his growing-up years. Naked sugar trees waved hello, and the roar of the river welcomed him home. Here, the Gauley and New Rivers converged to form the mighty Kanawha, the watery pike of western Virginia.

"Nice to be home, ain't it?" The words sank to the ground, glum as the look on Noah's face.

"Aw, now. You paid a visit to your home place when we made that run through Greenbrier, didn't you?"

"Yep. I'm a-kinda wishin' I hadn't, though. Seems since I left the holler, Bubba Cletus and my cousin both joined up with them Rebel bushwhackers. It'd be a mercy not to meet up with a body I know in *this* county. I'd be coddlin' the mully-grubs for sure." Noah's sigh was as forlorn as they come.

Regret and melancholy swirled together like a river eddy. What an intolerable thing to come up against your kin. Fin heard tell many a story thus far in all his three months of soldiering. Stories of brothers hugging one minute, then taking up arms against each other the next. It stuck in his craw like a spiny bone. Try as he might, he couldn't wrap his thinking around it—a family warring amongst themselves, a mother broken-hearted even before a shot's fired. A father taking up arms against his son.

He yanked off his hat and combed his fingers through matted hair. He'd cut off both legs before he'd take on his brother or his pap, God rest his soul. Jonathan Dabney had been a force to be reckoned with in his day. He'd held the respect of the entire county and always had a knack for figuring the right way through a trouble. *I miss you, Pap.*

And what of Jimmy Lee? His best friend was somewhere off fighting for the Confederacy—most likely far from Fayette County. Least ways, he surely hoped Jimmy Lee was far from here. And still alive.

Seaton Marrs growled from the end of the rope lashed to Noah's saddle. "How much longer we gotta traipse down this road? Seems to me we oughta be there by now."

"It always seems longer when you're the one walking, sonny." Noah slowed his horse on a cue from Fin. "Need a little break, do ya?" He lobbed a canteen.

Even with bound wrists, the boy caught it and plopped to the ground. His Adam's apple bobbed with a long draw of water.

Fin shifted in the saddle. "Almost there, Seaton. I sure hope you find your pap. Albeit you're prisoners, best you be together."

Seaton stood, capping the canteen. "You a Dabney?"

"I am."

"I recollect you helped with our harvest a couple years back." The boy kicked at the dirt as his tongue tripped over the words. "I wanna thank you for that. Mama took to her bed that summer. She died just after harvest. It was a real hard time for all of us."

Fin remembered. Just neighbor helping neighbor. Now it's folks fightin' folks. He snugged his canteen back into place. "Let's get on to the camp." Nudging Duke into the lead, he continued ahead, his mind already on the farm and his family. He'd surprise them for an early Christmas.

His attention bounced between vigilance and imagination for the rest of the journey into Gauley Bridge. Try as he might, visions of family and home crowded his thoughts. He could almost smell the steaming platters of ham, onions, cornbread—and Melinda Jane's cookies. It was so clear in his mind. His brothers' and sisters' faces. And Melinda Jane's enticing grin.

He ached for it all. The inviting kitchen with its grand stove. The sitting room and Mama's settee. He'd have to check the woodpile.

Maybe work with Zander to lay up some more. No such thing as too much firewood.

He reached back and patted the saddlebag with a measure of satisfaction. He'd picked up a few small gifts passing through Charleston, including a pretty hanky for Melinda Jane, folded into a neat square. What a misery it was choosing just the right one to buy.

Now to figure out how to give it to her. He'd like to do it in private, but if he didn't give it to her with the family, they'd all wonder why he didn't get her anything.

"Dabney . . . Fin! You off wool gatherin'?"

Fin straightened in the saddle and studied the rows of tents through a haze of wood smoke.

Noah dismounted and untied the rope from his saddle. "I'm gonna find out where to deliver this boy."

Fin nodded to their charge. "You take care now, Seaton. Give your pap my best."

The boy dipped his chin in a tenuous nod. Pale blue eyes, void of their earlier fire, spoke more than words before he stared at his feet and shuffled off. Young Seaton Marrs was now a prisoner of the United States Army.

Fin struck out on foot for the command tent where a flag on a tall post drooped for lack of a breeze. After tying Duke, he retrieved a thick envelope from his saddlebag and stepped up to the lean, beardless private standing sentry. "I have a package from Ceredo. From Colonel Lightburn for Colonel Moor."

"Send him in, Private," a throaty voice boomed from inside the tent.

He pushed the flap aside. Cigar smoke hung in the warm air, lingering just in front of the short, black stove in the middle of the spacious tent. The camp commander's private quarters formed a nook to the left. A hinged trunk, square table, and a quilt-covered cot took up much of the space. Books overflowed two stacked crates.

Fin saluted and handed the envelope to the sturdy, graying colonel. "From Colonel Lightburn, sir."

"Ja, thank you. He wired ahead that you would be coming. You have a pass also, I understand." His words rode up and down in a crisp fashion.

"Yes, sir. My farm is only five miles down the road, so Colonel Lightburn issued a pass for us. The other courier is taking a prisoner to the stockade."

"You brought a prisoner with you as well?"

"A young man wanted to borrow our horses, and we weren't too obliging, sir." Fin cleared his throat, refusing to cough.

"Well done, then. What direction are you headed, Corporal?"

"Up Gauley Road, sir."

"We are still having run-ins with bushwhackers in that area. Probably best if you head that way tomorrow. Not a lot of daylight left. Seems those nasty animals like to come out just as the sun disappears." He jabbed the cigar into one side of his mouth. "I hope you find your family well, Corporal. Godspeed."

"Thank you, sir." Fin saluted and turned about.

As he watered Duke, troubled thoughts rolled over him. *Bushwhackers.* He quickly snuffed out the notion. Federal soldiers guarded his family and farm. No need to borrow worries. But he'd head out right away just the same.

The horses took the bend in the road at a healthy lope, and Fin swallowed a lump in his throat at the twilight-washed sight. The graceful weeping willow stood watch, guarding the rocky path that led home. *Home.* It had consumed him from the minute Colonel Lightburn gave him this mission.

"This is our lane," he said, gesturing ahead.

"Good thing, too. Don't fancy meetin' up with them critters the Colonel bespoke." Noah stretched, arching his back. "Don't s'pose there's a possibility of sleeping in a proper bed tonight? A body forgets what a mattress feels like after a time. Mayhap you got one of them plush feather mattresses?" His eyebrows wiggled like fat, yellow caterpillars.

"I think I can oblige you. Pretty sure Gus won't mind tossing Zander out of his bed. He'd just as soon sleep in the barn with his horse, anyway."

"Gus sounds like a tough fella."

"Gus ain't a fella," Fin laughed. "She's my sister. Given name's Augusta."

"Ah-guh-sta." Noah drew out each syllable. "Mmm. Sweeter than cornbread and honey. She purty?"

"I reckon so. Strong too. Mothered the younger ones since Mama passed six years ago. But Melinda Jane—now, she's the real beauty."

"I seen her likeness in yer Bible. How can ya live with a woman that comely that ain't yer kin? Don't seem right. Likely there's many a tongue wagging at both ends 'bout all that." Noah shook his head like a wet dog. "Tsk-tsk."

"Nah, it's not that way. We took Melinda Jane in when her folks passed. Shoot. I've known her all my life."

They rounded the switchback and Fin squinted, unwilling to believe his eyes.

What?—No!

An iron hand gripped his gut. He kicked Duke into a sprint, pitching dirt and rocks into the air. "Hyah! Hyah!" Scorched lungs begged him to breathe, but he couldn't. He skidded to a stop at the pump and slid from his saddle, numb.

He staggered forward, shock twisting to anger. Debris lay scattered among charred remnants of the once-magnificent barn—a barn that housed Union soldiers and wounded men when he'd joined up. Not a wall stood, a ghostly reminder of some unknown violence.

He crouched and scooped up a handful of the stale, black crumbles, stirring a hoary powder that seared his heart and nostrils. All the years, all the memories, rendered to . . . this. He shook his head, trying to vanquish the ache that glutted his throat. Standing, he let the grit fall through his fingers, then wiped his hand across his thigh. He stared at the streak it left—dark as the notions spiriting through his mind.

A troubling silence hung in the air. No barked greeting from the old hound, Coot. No hurried steps, rushing to give a welcoming hug. No hollered announcement of his homecoming by seven-year-old Bertie. His innards churned like river rapids as he whirled, charging from the grisly sight toward the house.

Seeing the front door ajar, Fin pulled his Colt and scrambled for the back door. Questions assaulted his mind like angry hornets, and he swallowed down the horror of what he might find.

Instead of fodder shocks, rotted cornstalks lined the garden fence like defeated sentinels. Gus never would've let those spent stalks go to waste.

He nudged open the screen door with the toe of his boot, heart thumping wildly with each metallic groan. Footfalls silent, he entered the back porch, then the kitchen. He touched the stove. Cold. Ears straining for the creak of a floorboard or the snap of a flintlock, he inched forward.

A chair lay on its side near the once-polished oak table, its surface now gashed and blotted with dark stain. Broken jars, emptied of the women's labors, littered one corner. The carved sideboard stood gap-toothed, drawers ajar or missing, contents strewn across the floor.

He winced at the crunch of dried corn and beans crumbling under foot. After a pause, he continued, this time sliding the sole of his boot along the floor, moving on through the debris before edging his way to the parlor.

The room's dimness and shadowed corners drew him forward until the faintest of sounds cut the silence. A familiar groan of the floorboard—*the one beneath the hall rug, just inside the front door.* Slipping into the shadows, Fin waited. Could be Noah. But why was he sneaking around?

Just as he considered moving from the corner, a figure crept into the room. Rifle ready, it advanced slowly, the gun barrel tracing the room's perimeter.

Fin saw his chance and emerged from the shadow. He slammed his pistol grip into the base of the man's skull. Catching the limp body, he lowered the man noiselessly to the rug.

He slipped back into the kitchen, checking to his right, his left. Before he could take another step, the unmistakable snap of a hammer froze his movement.

"Turn around nice and easy there, Yankee. I like to look a man in the eye when his light goes out."

He turned, met with a woolly chest on a human mountain of greasy, rank flesh.

A mouth spoke, buried beneath a grizzled beard. "We leave for a short spell and all kinds of varmints invade this nice place we got here."

Fury gripping his voice, Fin snarled, "What happened to the family that was living here?" Possibilities tore through his mind like demons rising from Hades.

The Rebel chugged out a rough snicker. "Ain't none of yer concern." A sneer bared yellow teeth as he leveled the gun barrel. "Goodbye, Yankee Bill."

Fin dove at the bulky arm, sending the revolver clattering to the floor. It discharged, raising an acrid fog. He landed a kick to the man's shin. The Rebel bent with a grunt, and Fin brought his twined hands down like a sledgehammer onto the man's neck. With a mad-dog growl, the bushwhacker jerked upright and drew back a meaty arm intent on squashing him like a gnat.

Grabbing up a chair, Fin crashed it against the tree-trunk legs. The big man wavered like a drunkard as spittle and foul words sprayed the air. To Fin's dismay, his foe managed to remain upright.

Diving for the worktable, Fin pulled at the curtain covering a shelf. *Please be there!* His fingers curled over the handle of an iron skillet.

The Rebel groaned and bent to pick up his gun. Before he could straighten, Fin brought the heavy skillet down onto the back of his head with a *THUNK*. The giant dropped, sending the floorboards bouncing. Fin waited, chest heaving and skillet poised for another strike.

"I'd pay good money to see all that again." Noah stood in the doorway, a trickle of crimson slithering over one ear. One fist gripped the arm of a scraggy Rebel and the other pressed a pistol to the man's head.

"How long you been standing there?" Fin sidestepped the motionless heap on the floor.

"Long enough, I'd say. Got knocked silly takin' a drink at yer pump, and when I come to, I found this one sneaking in the door real quiet-like. Then I had to come see to all this clatterment." His mouth pinched lop-sided as he perused the room. "Got any rope around here?"

"I'll get it." Fin retrieved a length from the back porch, and before long, the three prisoners were situated in a neat little row against one wall, trussed up like hogs on a spit.

"Too bad one of them buzzards got away. Had a face liked to an eight-day clock—all scarred up like a splittin' stump."

"Scarred?" It couldn't be. "Just one side of his face? Long, gray hair?"

Noah scowled. "That'd be him. You know him?"

Fin swallowed hard as an old fire flared in his belly. The only man on God's earth he had imagined killing with his bare hands.

Maybe he'd get the chance.

Two

"I'm going upstairs." Fin slapped his hat to his thigh, a habit from long years of pent-up words burning a hole in his noggin. He turned back to Noah. "I suppose you best keep a lookout for some of their friends."

He lifted the lantern, glaring at the prisoners, despising the cruel imaginings that flitted through his mind. He'd look for some clue. A note. Anything to ease his fear. Anything to convince him of his family's safety.

The acrid stench of ammonia and human waste floated down from the second floor. Upstairs, dresser drawers gaped, and clothes cluttered the floor. Aside from the full slop jars in each room, the beds were intact, though disheveled and sweat-stained.

The furniture seemed no worse for wear, and he owed that to the ample woodpile out back. Once that ran out, bushwhackers would start burning the furniture for heat. Fin searched through the mess. It was what he didn't find that gave him hope. Absent were the quilts, every one of them, and the carpetbags he knew each of the girls owned.

Neither did he find the journal Melinda Jane kept. She'd told him of it often when they'd been in school, but seldom had she mentioned it over the last year.

Her face filled his mind—her brown eyes and tawny curls. Now, it seemed, there was almost more unsaid between them than spoken. It was his own fault. How could he tell her the yearnings of his heart?

Seemed every time he opened his mouth to speak his feelings, her perfect smile or even the tilt of her head would drive every thought from his thick skull. Just being near her oft set his insides aquiver.

His boots echoed down the stairs, then followed the hallway to his pap's room. Pap had been gone for months now, but it was still Pap's room to him. Mama's quilt was missing from the bed where Pap had passed into glory.

A handful of books littered the room, and Fin's heart sank even more at the breaches in the floor-to-ceiling bookshelf. Only half of Pap's beloved books remained. His gaze rose to the top shelf, settling on the faded green tome of *Gulliver's Travels*, the custodian of his last hope and the revelation he sought.

Propping the lantern on the bedside table, Fin stepped onto a chair and reached behind the book, searching the dusty shelf. Nothing. He smiled. Only two living people knew of the leather pouch hidden behind ol' *Gulliver*, and he was one of them. Surely his sister had taken the money and left with the rest of the family. Now, where'd they go to?

"Lose somethin'?" Noah leaned into the room.

Fin stepped down, the book still in his hand. "You mean besides my entire family?"

Flipping through the pages, he felt a keen lonesomeness for the first time since leaving home. He thought of the rowdy suppertime discourses so often instigated by his thirteen-year-old sister, Will. That girl knew just how to get under a body's skin, for sure.

For certain he'd been missing his family since the day he set-out, but something had changed. This churning in his gut—he thought it had subsided with the first bushwhacker he'd shot dead. He'd lain awake all that night—over a month ago now—just trying to convince himself that taking that man's life was to protect his family. Well, now he needed no convincing.

"He was wrong," Fin rasped, throat aching with the effort.

"Who was wrong?" Noah stepped into the room.

"My pap." He lifted his eyes. "He said this isn't our war to fight. It is. *My* family. *My* home. *My* war." His fingers caressed the ridge of the book's binding, as his vision eased out of focus and his voice claimed his thoughts. "*Blessed be the Lord my Rock, who trains my hands for war and my fingers for battle.*"

The book slipped from his hands, landing softly on the bed.

The morning sun hid its face behind angry gray clouds. How very much the sky mirrored Fin's mood as he guided Duke away from the farm and over the hill toward Ol' Izzy's cabin. His dear friend was sitting at the feet of Jesus now, but his memory was alive as ever his body had been.

To Fin's way of thinking, the two men that taught him the most about being a godly man were Pap and Izzy. He had no intention of letting them down, but hadn't Jesus turned over the tables of the sellers? But Jesus didn't kill his enemies. He loved them.

Sorrow snatched his breath away when the magnificent maple tree came into view. *I shouldn't have come.* He could almost see the rope, the weight of Izzy's bronzed body pulling it into a slow spin. *I'm fighting for you, Izzy.* He squeezed his eyes shut against the burn of sorrow. He never got to say goodbye.

Fin guided Duke toward the little cabin. He climbed down and found it empty.

He was ready now. Ready to go forward. Ready to take back his home. His state. His country. But first, he had to know his family was safe.

The dismal overcast had blown south of the home place and now Fin squinted into the sun, already a ways up from the horizon. He wiped at his brow with a clean kerchief. What a surprise to find a couple of clean ones and folded winter drawers in the dresser this morning. Too bad there wasn't much in the way of food. Even the dried stores were spent.

"You figure we're about ready to head out?" he called.

"I reckon so." Noah tied the lead rope to his saddle. He faced the three prisoners, bound hand and foot, each draped over his own horse. "Ya know, a lesser man woulda just put a ball through yer eye. Lucky fer you, we are men of integrity. And yes, we particularly enjoyed nearly killing ourselves hoisting yer ugly hides onto those forty-year-old, swayback Confederate ponies. You know . . ." Noah rubbed his whiskered jaw in thought. "We're just about in Crook's territory. His men don't take prisoners if'n they come across a bushwhacker. Lucky for you it were us and not them bestowed the good fortune to make yer acquaintance."

"You planning on killing us with all that yammerin', Billy Yank? Just shoot us!" The man-mountain sneered.

"Maybe we should've gagged them, Hicks." Fin said, thinking to use rags since he felt protective over his clean kerchiefs.

"I guess that's still a consideration. I'd rather just clobber ol' Goliath there again. Did you happen to pack that skillet?"

"Very funny," grumbled the big man.

"Uh oh. Where's that skillet?" Noah feigned looking through the packs.

"Let's head out. I'd like to make a stop at the neighbor's before we head into Gauley." Fin nudged his horse forward, scanning the yard. The tall white house stood as a lone reminder of the boy buried deep inside of him. A boy he never quite got to say goodbye to. Life had a way of demanding too much—and a man had to be the one to pay.

Fin led the caravan down the long lane to the willow that only yesterday had beckoned a welcome call—a welcome that had soured and congealed into something bitter churning in his belly.

He moved along Gauley Road toward the neighbors', his thoughts whipping back and forth like a sheet in the wind. One minute he assured himself his family was safe and the next, pictures flashed in his mind, torturing his sanity. *Help me take these thoughts captive, Lord. Help me to trust in what I can't see.* That was his only hope. Not a thing he could do about what already was.

The sun had climbed a little higher in its circuit by the time Fin led the caravan into the familiar yard.

"We've got nothing left here!" A man hollered, stepping into the yard. He motioned with the barrel of a shotgun. "You might as well be heading on along." Hector Dorton's slight frame was bent and his hair, now fully gray, rendered the appearance of a man twenty years older than the one Fin knew.

"It's me, Fin Dabney, Hector." Fin halted, raising both hands in surrender.

"That a Federal uniform you're wearing there?"

"Sure is. Can I dismount?"

"What's all this?" Hector poked the gun muzzle toward the train of prisoners.

"Caught us some bushwhackers. Found them at my place making themselves to home."

"About time somebody nabbed them animals." Hector spit and lowered his weapon. "Come on down."

"Thank you." Fin tipped his head, gesturing toward Noah. "This is Private Hicks."

"You're welcome here too, son. Good to see you, Fin."

"Any idea where my family is, Hector?"

He shook his head. "Everything happened kind of fast-like. Your sister and brother rode in here, asked me to take their stock. A lot of good it did. 'Bout everything with four feet got stole away from me. I managed to keep one milk cow hidden, but everything else is gone. Every chicken gone too—yours included."

"Did they say where they were going?"

"All Gus said was Charleston. Don't know what's there, but that's what she said."

Charleston? "Thank you, Hector." Fin stepped up to Duke, ready to take his leave, then pivoted. "How is your family? Everybody doing all right?"

"We're doin'. No one's been hurt and I surely hope the worst is past." The man's gray eyes dimmed as he massaged his temple. "Had a few close calls . . . We keep to ourselves, staying locked in the house after dark. Kinda hard with the days so short now, ya know?"

"You're doing right by your own." Most folks with some place to go just left. But Fin figured the Dortons didn't have anywhere else to go. Like a lot of families. "It was good to see you. Appreciate the information. We'll be off now."

"You take care of yourself, Fin. Things will get back to normal one of these days soon. You'll see."

Fin mounted and turned Duke around. The days of darkness that wore on the man were not just the sun's doing, that much was obvious. Hector approached and motioned for him to lean down.

"Yeah, Hector?"

"You know that dead aspen tree surrounded by all that laurel between your place and ours, as the crow flies?"

"I know it."

"You didn't hear it from me, but there's been 'bout ten or fifteen bushwhackers camped in the cove east of there for the past couple weeks."

"Much obliged, Hector. I'll take care of it."

Fin led out down the lane. He would see to those bush-whackers with or without help from the post at Gauley Bridge.

Fin stood before Colonel Moor once again. Surely the man didn't expect him back so soon. After all, wasn't he supposed to be enjoying a family reunion? If only that were the case.

"You say you brought in three more bushwhackers, Corporal?"

"Yes, sir. They'd taken over my home place. We delivered them to the stockade." He didn't come to report taking in three scraggly Rebels.

"Well done."

"I wanted to report a group of irregulars, sir. A camp." Fin suddenly wished he had taken the time to ride out there. Even if they were too late, there'd be a trail, and he intended to be the one to track them.

"Where is this camp you speak of?" The colonel's speech was stiff, much like his stance. "How many are there?"

"It's between my place and the neighbor's, sir. Ten to fifteen. Been there a couple weeks."

"Mmmm. And our scouts haven't spotted them. It's these hills." The Colonel sat down at a scarred table. Pushing aside a stack of maps, he scribbled on a piece of paper. "I want you to take this to Lt. Col. Becker. Two tents down." He pointed to his right. "He'll instruct you further. Thank you, Corporal."

"Yes, sir." Fin saluted, turned about face and headed to find Noah.

He didn't have to look far, as he was carrying on with some tall tale about a man the size of Goliath and a frying pan. A crowd of a dozen German Ohio boys stood transfixed as Noah punched the air with his fist, spun on his heel, then flailed his arms, his face racked with mock pain.

Fin motioned him over.

Noah's brow furrowed, announcing his obvious reluctance to leave his performance unfinished. "What now?" He indicated the paper in Fin's hand.

"We need to find Lt. Colonel Becker."

"Fine. You lead, I'll follow. Some of these fellers talk purty funny. You reckon this is one of them German units?"

"Yes, it is. And I'm sure there's plenty of folks who think you talk funny, too." Fin chuckled at Noah's frown. "It's this way."

Three

F in scanned the familiar terrain laid out before him. The
threatening clouds of early morning had surrendered to sunshine, a precious treat for this time of year. He stopped at a dead
tree, enveloped by a mound of laurel. "Just over that rise is the cove
where those irregulars were spotted."

Capt. Schubert looked over his shoulder to the detachment of
twenty. "I'd like to hear your suggestions, Corporal. Wait until
nightfall?"

"Well sir, I'd say now is as good a time as any. If it were me . . ."

"It *is* you, Corporal."

"Well then, I'd have a couple of scouts sneak down there just to
see what's going on and where everybody is. I'd have a few more
scout this area in here on foot." Fin motioned in a wide circle, "And
check the perimeter for pickets."

"Me and Fin can sneak down there . . . ah . . . sir." Noah started
to dismount, then stopped, his look bouncing between the captain
and his friend.

"I like how you think," said the captain, already signaling eight
men to scout the perimeter while Fin and Noah headed out.

"You got a big mouth," Fin whispered as they started down to
the clearing.

"I figured you'd be itching to get yer hands on these ol' varmints
this close to yer farm."

"I said you got a big mouth, I didn't say you're stupid." Fin stopped. "Let's split up. Keep low."

Noah crouched, commencing with what he liked to call his moccasin step. He claimed to be part Indian. Seemed all that yellow hair of his didn't deter his claim in the least.

Fin stepped out, his Colt leading the way while his other hand swept branches aside. He angled toward a waft of smoke. A movement caught his eye, and he sank lower. Sure enough, a pot hung over a campfire and at least five—no, seven men sat nearby. He scanned the area around the camp for any occupied bedrolls, then rotated his torso for a different angle. His foot slipped, nearly sending him sprawling.

He stilled.

Nothing. This wet weather tended to work in favor of sneaking up on a body, but it made keeping one's footing a mite tricky. One bushwhacker was talking, but he couldn't make out the words. He'd work his way a little farther to the left for a better view, then skedaddle back up to the captain.

Noah joined him a few minutes later as they headed back up the hill, taking the path they'd blazed on the way down.

Fin spotted four of the captain's scouts. "Are the others back yet?"

"We will wait for them. What did you find?" the captain asked.

"I counted seven around the fire, one in the tent, and one in a bedroll." Fin turned to Noah.

"I saw the same, but make that two in the tent. There was another one heedin' the call of nature." His nose scrunched up. "A touch of the gripe if ya ask me. I heard them say something about tonight. Couldn't quite make it out."

Two scouts emerged from the brush, each clutching one arm of a staggering bushwhacker. The prisoner's slouch hat looked like something a wagon mashed into a rut, and dingy drawers poked through a gaping hole in the knee of his tight, gray britches.

"Found this one on the lookout, almost asleep. We surprised him good."

Captain Schubert's eyebrows arched. "Just one picket?"

The prisoner spat on the ground. "You tetched? There's another fifty of us got a bead on you boys right this minute." He let go a boisterous laugh—abruptly silenced by a rifle butt to the jaw, sending him slithering to the ground.

A private peered down at the motionless bushwhacker. He passed a sheepish look to his commanding officer. "Sorry, Captain. I didn't want him warning the others of our presence."

Captain Schubert shook his head with a grin. "Well done, Private Fischer." He turned to Fin. "Corporal, what would you do?"

Fin thought for a minute, thankful for this chance. "Sir, I believe we should surround the camp, then once we're within fifty feet, we wait for Noah's signal and close the circle. It's best if your men can make eye contact with one another and take those boys out quietly." Fin flicked a thumb in Private Fischer's direction. "Like this private did just now. Enemy closest to the perimeter falls first, but only by an instant."

Noah threw his hat on the ground and scrubbed his fingers through his hair as if he had cooties. "You take them out with a big ruckus, and it's just an invitation to every guerilla within two miles of here." He stripped off his gear, then his coat. "I'm ready."

"Ready for what, Private?" Confusion marked the captain's eyes.

Noah grinned. "Ready to signal."

"Let's go." Fin motioned for everyone to surround the camp, save three soldiers. "Not a sound. Go slow. Look where your feet fall before you step. Move branches with your hands, not your body." He set out, sending up a prayer for God's favor. So much can go so wrong in so little time. Isn't that what Colonel Joe always says?

Fin waited, crouched on the ground. It had been thirty minutes, plenty of time for everyone to be in position. He gave Noah the go-ahead.

Hicks stood full upright and scrubbed a bit of mud across his cheek. He staggered forward and began singing, softly at first, then louder: "*Old Dan Tucker was a mighty man.*" He wobbled, catching himself with a clumsy lurch.

Fin flanked his friend's position and started forward, knowing all eyes would be on Noah. He stood taller seeking out soldiers of the Twenty-eighth Ohio. He spotted one. Another. Two more. He nodded to each wide-eyed man, willing orders to override their shock.

"*Washed his face in a fryin' pan. Combed his head wid a wagon wheel . . .*" Noah crooned like a drunken fool.

The butt of Fin's carbine came down hard on the nearest guerilla, followed by muffled grunts and thuds as more victims hit the ground.

A groggy Rebel sat up from a bedroll. "Hey. What's going . . ." He never saw the blow.

"*And he died wid a toofache in his heel.*"

They accounted for and bound the bushwhackers, then loaded them onto horses, ready for delivery to Gauley Bridge.

Fin found himself once again in Col. Moor's tent. He stifled a yawn, hoping neither Capt. Schubert nor the colonel had noticed.

Noah and the others had recounted their story a dozen times to the entertainment-deprived soldiers of the Twenty-eighth last night. By then it had been after midnight, and the bugle had them up well before sunup this morning.

Noah scrunched one eye, fighting his woozy state.

"Corporal Dabney, Private Hicks. Here we are again." The colonel pointed to a crystal decanter. "Schnapps?"

"No, thank you, sir."

"I've never tried . . ." Noah caught a glare from Fin. "No, thank you, sir."

Unfazed, the colonel raised his eyebrows, looking to the captain, who lifted a palm to pass on the liquor.

"Gentlemen, the two of you have delivered to me more Confederate irregulars in the last two days than I have managed to round up in the last month. I've been in communication with Colonel Lightburn. He has agreed to a temporary assignment for both of you to this camp. You will be directly accountable to Lieutenant Colonel Becker and myself."

"I don't understand, sir." Noah glanced from the Colonel to Fin.

"A temporary assignment. Just for a month or so. You will be assigned quarters and provisions.

"I've made some successful strides training men of the Twenty-eighth in guerilla warfare." He removed the glass stopper from the decanter. "I believe you will augment that training in a unique way. You will choose ten men to train in whatever way you deem necessary over the next few weeks." The Colonel poured Schnapps into a miniature glass, the likes of which Fin had never seen. "Any questions?"

"No, sir."

"That is all for now then, *Sergeant* Dabney and *Corporal* Hicks."

Ten paces from the Command tent, Fin turned to Noah, "I expect you heard the colonel as I did?"

"Uh huh. I expect I did." Noah stared ahead, furrows multiplying across his brow.

"You okay with being promoted like that? Almost seems you're not too happy about it. I figured you'd let go a holler by now." Fin stopped and turned to his friend.

Noah kicked at the dirt. "I do have a bit of consternation. Seems to me that someone with rank oughta set a good example for the lowly privates that most assuredly look up to such a one as received said rank. I'm just not sure I can do that—set a good example."

Fin threw his arm around Noah's shoulder. "I'll watch out for you—make sure you don't make too big a fool of yourself. You'll do just fine, Hicks. Just so long as you make me look good."

Four

The hills enticed Fin's gaze with their silhouetted memories. A dusting of stars shimmered far from the glare of the camp-fire. Heaviness settled against his heart, but he vowed to center his thoughts on the reason for this little celebration tonight.

It wasn't much, but the mess had served up a special meal of roasted wild turkey and dried apple pie for Christmas dinner. Now a harmonica carried the notes of Silent Night through the crisp air. There was beauty here—in this moment. It lingered and wrapped its frail arms around him like a mother holds her child.

German lyrics faded with their harmonies into the stillness as the last note dissipated.

The Christ Child. The greatest Gift of all time. All eternity. Fin's heart lurched as he thought of the One who made those stars. The One who named each and knew the number of hairs on his head. He asked that same Almighty Creator to care for his family and bring them all together again in safety and peace. *Father, I need your peace. The kind that passes understanding.* He hated this filthy war—and he despised the ways it had changed him in such a short amount of time.

His thoughts went to Melinda Jane. He pulled the small Bible from his pocket and found the picture she'd given him. In the dim glow of the fire, he could only make out her form, but in his mind he saw the golden brown eyes and her spectacular hair. He smiled as he thought of the way wispy curls framed her face when she worked hard and the droplets of sweat beaded on her temples like tiny pearls. Would he ever see her again?

Every morning, when he woke, he knew it could be his last. While he wasn't afraid of death, he didn't want to meet it without telling Melinda Jane how he felt about her. He'd written a few letters home, but not to her. Not *just* to her. What would he say? *"Dear Melinda Jane, if I could tell you how I feel, I'd tell you that you make my heart soar like an eagle and my arms ache to hold you and never let go. But I can't tell you that because I'm a coward. Best regards, Fin."*

Fin stood as the men quietly dispersed amid soft "Merry Christmas" greetings. Each man, no doubt thinking of his home fires.

He'd write a letter tonight. Tomorrow was Thursday. He'd head to the post office.

Duke huffed as Fin dismounted and tied the reins to a weathered post. The tiny Gauley Bridge post office wasn't much more than a lean-to off the side of Old Mr. Pritchard's house, just down from the now-abandoned Jackson's Mercantile. Fin figured Cullen Jackson to have headed up north, as did most of the Union sympathizers in the area. He'd thought the man was on the fence—where his loyalties sat—but his absence made a statement.

The post office door was locked, and after several minutes of pounding on the screen door, Fin figured Mr. Pritchard had high-tailed it too. The Army had taken over the mail delivery, so Fin could collect his forwarded mail at the camp, but he was hoping to find something else here.

He glanced up and down the street. Slipping his knife between the framing boards and the door, he broke the lock. Stepping into the narrow room, Fin's eyes fixed on the cubby marked DABNEY in bold black letters. Sure enough, it held the only three letters he'd sent home. His family must be worried sick, having never received a word from him. He fingered a folded piece of paper tucked into the back of the space. A forwarding address, written in his sister's script. Charleston. An address on Cox's Lane. This wasn't the address of Gus's friend from school. Who had taken them in?

Now, at least, he could put an address on the letter he'd written last night and post it tomorrow. To his dismay, he couldn't bring himself to write the words to Melinda Jane that refused to spill from his heart. But he did include her with the rest of the family in his greeting, hoping she would somehow read between the lines. A coward. He was a coward. A true yeller belly in matters of the heart.

Fin shivered as he plunged cold feet into his boots. The temperature had dropped dramatically overnight. He shoved more sticks into the short black stove, blowing on the glowing embers. Leaving the iron door ajar, he picked up Noah's haversack and tossed it onto his chest. "Rise and shine, Sunshine."

Noah groaned and flipped over. "That's no way to talk to a Corporal, Sergeant."

"You did notice I still outrank you, right?" Fin closed the door on the stove.

"Yeah, yeah. I'm still gonna write home about it, though."

"Speaking of writing home, we need to see about getting our mail forwarded here. I haven't gotten any since we came here. Guess it's just not caught up to us yet."

A knock at the tent caught their attention.

"Come in." Fin stood, tucking in his shirt.

"Lieutenant Colonel Becker wants to see you, Sergeant." A lanky private loomed in the doorway, easily towering over Fin's six-feet-plus. His hooked nose pointed decidedly to a sandy scraggle of whiskers around his lip.

Fin, tipped his head to look the man in the eye. "We'll be right there, Fisher." He turned to Noah. "You've got about ninety seconds to get that carcass up and dressed, Corporal, or I'll have you busted back down to private, ya hear?"

Noah grumbled as he tied his shoes and was still fumbling with the buttons on his uniform as he trotted behind Fin toward the command tent.

Lt. Col. Becker angled his pipe to one side. "Reports came in last night that well over a hundred Moccasin Rangers took Sutton and burned part of the town. Colonel Crook's Thirty-sixth Ohio has taken pursuit—likely sending those bushwhackers scattered to the hills. In thirty minutes, you, Captain Schubert, and myself will each take a detachment to the north, hoping to head off some of the Confederate fringe." He tapped the bowl of his pipe with his index finger. "Colonel Crook's men will not be looking to take prisoners. I can't say I agree with his philosophy. Am I clear?"

"Sir, yes sir." Fin nodded, swallowing down a rumble from his stomach. Another day without breakfast. What he wouldn't give for a pile of Melinda Jane's flannel cakes right about now.

"Dismissed."

Instead of taking the ferry across the Gauley River, Fin crossed his unit farther upriver. After a sharp climb back up the bank, he connected with a wide path that snaked through the trees. Noah followed just behind Fin, and a handpicked group of ten men trailed behind. Men, under his tutelage for only a week, who could be as much of a liability as an asset. Fin breathed a prayer for protection. He'd come to recognize just how fragile and fleeting this life could be. *Lord, go before us.*

"Looks like this here road was surveyed by a cow!" Noah pulled up closer. "I assume you know just exactly where this trace comes out?"

"Of course I do." These are my stompin' grounds, Corporal. "Watch and learn." Fin pointed up ahead. "If any of those Moccasin Rangers are from these parts and heading home, there's about a dozen places real close to here where they could be. All Rebel homesteads."

Duke nickered softly and Fin drew up to a clearing off to the right. He and Noah dismounted while the others watched. "There. Somebody's passed through here not too long ago." Fin glanced up at his men and pointed. "Several rocks overturned, not yet dry."

Noah angled his head off to one side, looking across the clearing. "Here's another two fellas on foot, leading their horses. Looks like a few of yer neighbors comin' home for a spell, Sarge."

Fin willed a witty retort, but truth be known, he wasn't too keen on the idea of following those tracks. As the crow flies, they were heading directly for the Lusher place. Not that he was all that close to J.T. Lusher, but they did come up through school together. He came from a good family—mighty poor, but good folk.

Fin stood straighter, sucking in a chest full of air. "Let's go."

Within minutes, he spotted a spiral of smoke, its lazy path into the clouds marking the Lusher cabin. Fin dismounted and signaled the others to do likewise. "You stay here, Corporal. I'll take Walter with me and scout the perimeter."

"Me, Sarge?" The private was diminutive in stature, but a quick study and a fast runner. His freckled face was more akin to a schoolboy than a soldier.

"Yes, Private Walter. You ready for this?"

"I'm more than ready for this." Walter said, checking his pistol.

31

The Army had met Fin's one request, which was to issue his men revolvers and carbines. They'd had little time for target practice, but they were spunky, the lot of them. He'd watched them as they loaded their packs. To a man, each seemed ready for action. Winter camp could bore a man to insanity. A body could only take so much of tedious chores and endless drilling.

"We're coming at the cabin from opposite sides. Scouting only, got it?" Fin took a knee. "You a prayin' man, Walter?"

"Yes, Sarge, I am. And I been praying ever since you picked me as one of your men."

Fin nodded, and the man bent his knee. "Good to hear. Lord, we don't know what we're going to find up there. Be our strength and our shield. Amen."

"See you back here in twenty minutes or less." Fin turned left and Private Walter right.

Sure enough, as Fin crouched behind an elderberry bush, he could see not only the two horses he'd tracked, but four more, tied to a rail outside the Lusher place. Shutters covered the windows and the front door was closed, no doubt barred on the inside. Keeping cover between him and the cabin, he circled, searching for a lookout.

Fin froze.

Ten paces ahead, a thick man with his back to Fin and overalls rolled to his calves, raised a melon-sized rock to bring down on the head of an oblivious Private Walter.

Fin let fly with a perfect tree frog imitation. In an instant, the spry private whirled and stabbed his pistol into the bushwhacker's gut. "I wouldn't do that if I were you," Walter said, his shoulders heaving slightly. The man froze, the rock still in the air.

"I'd listen to that boy." Fin said, fixing his Colt on the man's temple. "Drop the rock nice and quiet-like or you won't see another sunrise."

Minutes later, Fin tugged on the cord binding the bushwhacker's hands and gagged him with a kerchief. "I'll take our prisoner back down. You stay here. I'll be back with a plan and reinforcements."

"I'll be right here, Sarge." Walter lowered himself into the brush.

Fin moved swiftly, guiding his charge back down to his unit. He returned to Walter's location with all but two of his men. "Any activity, Private?"

"Not a thing, Sarge. What's the plan?"

"Noah is going with you, and you, Private Walter, are going to stop up that chimney." Fin motioned toward the roof. "Those Bushwhackers will not hear a sound, not even a tiny bird hopping on that roof. You understand me?"

"Yes, Sergeant."

"When those varmints in there have had enough, they'll come pouring out right into our obliging presence." Fin nodded to Noah.

"Come on, little one. Follow me." Noah crouched and jogged off, Walter on his heels.

Within fifteen minutes, the front door opened and out came six staggering, coughing bushwhackers, and a woman. The men wiped at their eyes, tears streaming. They brandished their weapons, frantically trying to identify an enemy.

"Drop your guns, gentlemen. You're outnumbered at the moment." Fin stepped into the clearing as the last man laid down his rifle.

A stout, buckskin-clad man shook his head as he raised red eyes to meet Fin's. "Dabney?"

"Sorry to meet up this way, J.T. Afraid I'm taking you in." And he was truly sorry, but folks just couldn't go around burning down towns. And word was these Moccasin Rangers were responsible for a whole lot more than destroying buildings. They'd built quite a reputation as resistance guerillas in this part of the state.

Five

CHARLESTON, VIRGINIA

Melinda Jane willed calm to her insides as she filled her lungs. *Sing to Jesus, girl!* Mama's voice. How she missed her. Embracing the love that coiled around her heart, she let the beloved words flow:

> *For lo, the days are hastening on,*
> *By prophet bards foretold,*
> *When with the ever-circling years*
> *Comes round the age of gold;*
> *When peace shall over all the earth*
> *Its ancient splendors fling,*
> *And the whole world give back the song*
> *Which now the angels sing.*

The rest of the choir joined in to repeat the first verse of "It Came Upon the Midnight Clear".

Preacher Lambert burst into applause as the last word was sung. "Breathtaking, Melinda Jane. You raised the hair on my arms!"

"Now Brother Lambert, I don't believe that was my intention. We were all just singing along together here." She could feel the pink blossom on her cheeks. Melinda Jane smiled timidly, ever at a loss for proper words in the face of a compliment.

"You've had a fine practice tonight, choir. Just one more practice tomorrow night and I believe we will be ready for the Christmas pageant. You are dismissed. I'll see you at seven o'clock sharp tomorrow evening. God go with you."

Melinda Jane collected hymnals, stacking them neatly, the strains of the last song drifting through her mind. Preacher Lambert shuffled his music together, then removed his spectacles, massaging his eyelids with thumb and forefinger. He smiled at Melinda Jane, then turned to the pianist. "Thank you so much for filling in for Mrs. Vandyke, Mr. Price. You are doing an extraordinary job."

"It is my pleasure, Preacher." Anderson Price tugged on the edges of his vest as he stood and reached for his hat. "I'm happy to be of help where I can."

Melinda Jane followed the others toward the door of the church, pulling her cape around her shoulders before tugging on her gloves.

"Don't look now, but here comes that Price feller." Willamina Dabney fluttered her eyes like only a teasing thirteen-year-old would do. She grabbed Melinda Jane's hand and said with a manly voice, "Miss Minard, would you allow me the honor of walking you home this fine evening?" She bowed and doffed an imaginary hat.

Melinda Jane swatted her hands away. "Stop that now, Will. Here he comes."

"Excuse me, Miss Minard?"

"Yes, Mr. Price?" She met his gaze, but not before spying Will feigning a dramatic swoon only two feet behind the man. Careful to school the irritation, she offered her sweetest smile.

"May I have the pleasure of escorting you home this evening?" He tipped his head so that bold hazel eyes met hers from beneath long brown lashes.

A frantic coughing attack suddenly seized Will. Mr. Price turned around. "May I retrieve a glass of water for you, Miss Dabney?"

Melinda Jane wrapped an arm around the girl and turned her toward the door. "I think she'll be fine in a moment, Mr. Price. I best get her home. Thank you for your kind invitation, though. We don't have far to walk. Maybe another time?"

"Of course. Perhaps tomorrow evening. After practice." He donned the bowler hat and opened the door for them. "Ladies."

Melinda Jane practically dragged Will down the church steps, not surprised at her quick recovery from the dreadful coughing attack. "Just what do you think you're doing? That man there was a perfect gentleman—hard to come by these days, with so many going off to fight." Her words convicted her. "I didn't mean that, Will."

The girl halted. Her sad eyes almost brought Melinda Jane to tears.

"I know you're thinking of Fin, honey. So am I." Her heart lifted as she pictured his handsome face—the tousled brown hair and trimmed beard. She missed him sorely, especially at night when she lay in bed having made up conversations with him. Even in her imagination, she did most of the talking, though. And that was the problem right there.

"I don't understand why he hasn't written. I sent him four letters already." Will's lower lip pooched out. "You don't think . . . that . . ."

"Shush, now. We're not gonna think like that. Likely the Army has him moving all over the place and the mail just hasn't caught up to him as yet."

"You don't really like that dandy Mr. Price, do you, Melinda Jane?" Will fixed her attention on the road as they walked. The near full moon swallowed the darkness and the two-story, white house shone brightly just down the block.

"Well, I don't *dislike* him. He's a nice gentleman. He's very handsome. Not that good looks is all that important—it just doesn't hurt none."

They turned up the brick walkway leading to the front porch. A shingle, still suspended above the white porch railing, read: DR. JAMES HILL, PHYSICIAN. Perhaps one day this house would be a haven for those needing a doctor again, but only God knows.

She turned to sit on the top stoop and pulled Will's hand with her. "Let's have a talk, Will."

"Right here?"

"Yes, right here." Melinda Jane spread her skirt, fingering the flowered fabric as she planned her words. "I s'pose it's no secret that I care for your brother."

"Mmmmm." Will dropped her chin into her hand, propping one elbow on her knee.

"I'm thinkin' our relationship is somewhat one-sided. I'd give anything to have Fin walk through the door and sweep me off my feet and ask me to marry him. But I reckon he still thinks of me as a little sister, following him around. Just a nuisance."

"Seems to me if you want his attention, you're gonna have to work a little harder to get it. I know what I'd do if I was in your shoes."

"Will. Stop. You're not in my shoes. Now I've been praying a lot about this. I'm thinkin' if the good Lord spares Fin in this forsaken war, then mayhap we're meant to be together. Until then, I'll just live my life as it comes. Understand?"

"That mean you're gonna up and let that Mr. Price court you?"

"He has only asked to escort me home. That's not courting."

"Well he can't seem to take his eyes off you when you're singing." Will stood, her posture stating her opinion on the matter.

"I'm used to the looks, Will. It's the character of a man that interests me, not whether or not he thinks I'm pretty." She rose, draping her arm around the girl's shoulder. "And I prefer the character of a certain brother of yours, but I just don't know if it's meant to be."

Melinda Jane bounded down the stairs and paused as the stiff scent of pine tickled her nose. Memories of mornings so much like this one flooded her mind, but a pain pricked her heart as she realized so many of those memories included Fin. She raced around the corner to find a tall pine tree stretching to the ceiling.

Mrs. O'Donell stood in the kitchen doorway, her ruddy cheeks spread in a wide smile. "Zander's been out since before the dawn gatherin' trees for his clients."

Melinda Jane laughed. "Clients, Mrs. O'Donell?"

The woman could light up the dreariest day with her melodic speech and way of lookin' at life in general. What a blessing she was. When they were forced to flee their home, God had provided this home—complete with a precious soul to mother them all.

"Aye. Clients—those women he's been helping, doing what their husbands would be tending to if they weren't off to war. He already cut six trees this mornin', he did—this one bein' the grandest, of course."

"He's become quite the businessman, hasn't he?" Melinda Jane looped her arm through the older lady's as she turned her back toward the kitchen. "What say you sit yourself down for a cup of tea while I see to breakfast for everyone."

"Child, yer such a blessin' to me. I'll oblige ya for now, but don't ya be thinkin' you'll take over me bakin' later."

"I wouldn't dream of it." Melinda Jane patted her hand. "I'm gonna rope Will and Bertie into makin' some taffy this morning. After that, we can decorate the tree." She tied on an apron and pulled the box of eggs from the shelf. She still couldn't get used to the idea of buying eggs from a storefront.

"Will ya be attendin' yer musical practice again tonight?" Mrs. O'Donell lifted the teacup to her lips and closed her eyes. A sigh of contentment slipped from her smile.

"Yes, ma'am. Our last chance to practice before the program tomorrow evening."

A rush of cool air drew their attention to the back door just as the old liver-colored hound, Coot, bounded in and headed straight away for his bed by the stove. Zander stood in stocking feet, a grin lighting his red face. He shoved his straight blond hair away from one eye. "I figured after a man's chopped six Christmas trees and set them upright, he oughta have some breakfast before he takes on the chores."

"Just sit yourself down there, and I'll try to fill those hollow legs of yours." Melinda Jane set a cup of steaming coffee in front of him.

"Thank you. Just what a man needs to warm up his bones. I'll take a whack of jacks two tall men couldn't shake hands over." He winked at her and she chuckled. How he'd grown into a man since they'd come to Charleston—taking on so much without complaint. *Fin would be mighty proud of him.*

"The tree, the tree!" The rhythmic thumping of seven-year-old feet bounded down the stairs before Bertie rounded the kitchen threshold. "Can we decorate it now? Can we?"

Mrs. O'Donell laughed at his exuberance. "Well, might ya have some breakfast first, little man?"

Melinda Jane turned a flannel cake, then switched her attention to the boy, spatula in the air. "Breakfast will be on in a few minutes, Bertie. After that there's some chores and something special. We'll decorate this afternoon, all right?"

He scooted up to the table. "What kind of special?"

"It's a surprise. You'll see." Melinda Jane set a glass of milk in front of him. He guzzled it and grinned, spreading his milk mustache wide.

"I'm gonna need a shave," Bertie said, rubbing his chin.

Zander shook his head, his eyes serious. "You don't wanna start that. Believe me. It's nothin' to look forward to, little brother."

"It ain't?"

"Isn't," Melinda Jane corrected.

Zander nodded. "Now that's something to look forward to, though."

Bertie wiped his mustache on his sleeve. "What is?"

"Growin' old enough where you can make it a whole day without a woman correcting your grammar." Zander fired a lopsided smile at Melinda Jane, who promptly snatched back up the stack of cakes she'd just set in the center of the table.

He reached for the plate, but she held it in the air. "Just maybe you don't need any breakfast this morning. Just maybe you've grown too big fer yer britches."

"Aw now, Melinda Jane. You know I didn't mean anything by it." He pouted for several seconds and batted his eyes. "Forgive me?" When Zander's stomach erupted in a loud gurgle, Coot's head jerked up.

Mrs. O'Donell was the first to snicker. "To forgive is divine, lass." Her eyes stayed on her teacup, but a sly smile curled her lips.

"Oh, all right. I forgive you. But mark my words—a woman who doesn't want you to be your better self just isn't worth your time." She set the plate down and spun toward the stove. "My flannel cakes!" Scooping up the ones in the skillet, she sighed. "I guess Will's getting the ever-so-slightly burnt ones."

"I'm not eatin' burnt cakes." A sleepy Will shuffled into the kitchen, her moccasins sliding across the polished board floor.

"Well good mornin' to ya. Aren't you a cheerful las!" Mrs. O'Donell stood and set her teacup beside the pump.

"Willamina Dabney, you are welcome to make your own flannel cakes, but as I said, these are just ever-so-slightly burnt." Melinda

Jane stepped to the side of the stove, presenting the stack of cakes with a flourish.

Will shrugged her shoulders and grabbed up the plate. She rounded her back, dragged her feet to the table, then plopped into the chair. "Humph."

Melinda Jane couldn't help but smile. That girl was either a firecracker or a snuffed-out match. Not much in between.

Six

M elinda Jane sighed and snugged the covers to her chin. Another Christmas season consigned to the past. And another pang of lonesomeness stabbed as she missed her loved ones.

Would the earth stop spinning if she stayed in bed? Her eyes fell on a tattered rag doll on the nightstand. She reached for it, tucking it under her chin. She could easily remain wrapped in the soft quilt and entertain cozy memories of happier times. A time when her parents were still alive. Even her years on the Dabney farm. How she missed her grandpappy Izzy. Never had a sweeter presence walked this old earth—except for the Savior Himself. Izzy's words, rooted in her very soul, often sprang up like blackberry vines, its fruit nourishing her spirit when she needed it.

But regret was a lone hawk, forever circling above. Her last moments with Fin haunted her. She had scolded him like a child, demanding he return to his family. Then she left him standing there—alone. She had run into the house because she couldn't bear the painful rush inside her. She'd wanted to throw herself at him and kiss him for all she was worth, beg him to claim her as more than another sister. All her flirting and hinting had gotten her nowhere. He clearly did not feel the same way about her.

There was absolutely nothing keeping her from moving forward with her life.

Her resolve was short-lived. Fresh tears fell at a phantom vision of Fin, face-down in the mud, a bullet in his back. *Heavenly Father, please protect him. Try as I might, I do love that boy!*

She dabbed at her face with the her nightgown sleeve and flung the covers off. The warmth of the coal furnace never failed to amaze her. Such luxury these city dwellers lived with. How easily a girl could get spoiled.

She pinned the last thick braid in place and then tip-toed downstairs so as not to wake anyone. Coot thumped his tail in greeting as she entered the kitchen. She opened the flue and rattled the coal bin on the stove. As she did every morning, she'd prepare breakfast for the family. Her family. And now Mrs. O'Donell was a part of that family. So this was her home until it was safe to move back to the farm—the Dabney farm, where she'd dreamed for years that she'd grow old with a certain tall, handsome Phineas Dabney.

She waltzed and twirled in a circle before retrieving the grease tin. My, but this yanking' back and forth of her emotions was tiring. She waxed dramatic, waving her hands in the air, "Like a wave of the sea, driven with the wind and tossed." *Lord, I don't want to be double-minded. Please give me the faith I need to trust in You.*

"And who might ya be conversin' with, lass?" Mrs. O'Donell tottered into the kitchen, her steps slow and a hand to the small of her back.

Melinda Jane rushed to pull out a chair for the woman. "Just myself and the Good Lord. Your rheumatism actin' up this mornin'?"

"'Tis naught but a nuisance befriendin' me till I be hoppin' the twig."

"Not exactly friendly-like if you ask me. And you won't be hoppin' the twig on my watch, Mrs. O'Donell. I've lost enough people I care for in my short life." Melinda Jane set a cup of tea in front of the woman.

43

"Sarah Young is spending the afternoon with me, and we're going over to the mercantile. Can we pick up anything for you?"

"I shan't be needin' a thing at the moment, but I'm puttin' together a list for after the Lord's day. You just enjoy yer time with Miss Young. 'Tis a fine family she's from, that one." Mrs. O'Donell sipped her tea and smiled up at Melinda Jane. "'Tis truly a joy to have you all here with me. Sure and another month alone, and I'd be fillin' the rooms with those be needin' better shelter."

"You just reminded me, I best get to finishing up those mufflers I'm knitting for the Finley family. Those Christmas mittens just weren't enough. I intend to outfit as many of those poor folks as I can. That's one of the reasons I'm going to the store today—to see about buying some fabric."

"You are such a dear. We'll make a visit to the poorhouse when we take in our list next week." Mrs. O'Donell rose from her chair, and Melinda Jane gently pushed her back down.

"You stay put, ma'am. I'll have breakfast on in the jerk of a frog's leg." Her mind buzzed with the planning of new sewing projects for the folks in need as the eggs plopped into the sizzling grease.

"Now, this calico would work nicely for a man's shirt or a work dress." Melinda Jane brushed her hand across the bolt of fabric.

"I hope you'll include me in this endeavor of yours, 'Linda Jane. It would so warm my heart to have a project different from church decorations or printing up an invitation list for some party. With Papa gone, the house just seems so empty. Did I tell you he was home for two days at Christmas?" Sarah Young turned from the fabric, her store-bought gray dress billowing like a bell. "I do loathe feeling useless."

"Oh, you won't feel useless once you start helpin' those that need helpin'. The conditions in the shanty town are deplorable."

"Oh, dear."

"What is it?" Melinda Jane grabbed Sarah's hand. "What?"

"My father would never approve of me visiting there with just us women."

"I guess I didn't think of that. Mrs. O'Donell's been callin' on the poor real regular for years now. She said Dr. Hill treated the folks at the poor house and shanty town before the war."

"Well, maybe I can't actually go, but there's no reason I can't make clothes and such. Maybe even some bread or pies?" Sarah's face brightened. "That's what I'll do. I'll help you help them."

Melinda Jane threw her arms around her friend. "Sarah, you're truly a God-send. What say we pay for this fabric then head over to Inman's for a treat?"

"Excuse me, Miss."

The male voice startled Melinda Jane, and she stepped aside, thinking she was in the way.

"I was just wondering if you might point me to the loveliest voice in all of Charleston?" Anderson Price stood behind them, hat in hand, a broad smile lighting his face. He bowed slightly. "Miss Minard. Miss Young."

"Why, Mr. Price, surely you aren't in need of fabric too?" The silly words fled Melinda Jane's tongue before she could stop them. "I . . . I mean, fancy meetin' you here."

White teeth gleamed above a dark spade beard. She detected the faint scent of Macassar oil, no doubt slicked on his head to hold down that too-perfect part in the center of his dark hair. "I only just entered and my eyes were drawn to the two most beautiful items in the room."

Sarah giggled and covered her mouth. Melinda Jane's words caught on the way to somewhere. Her jaw dropped.

"If you ladies are done with your shopping, may I offer you a ride home? Or we can walk if you prefer."

The man had gumption, she'd give him that. "Mr. Price, we were just about to walk over to Inman's for a refreshment. Would you care to join us?" Melinda Jane said, ignoring the way Sarah's eyes grew round.

"Nothing would please me more. I'll wait for you outside." He winked at Melinda Jane, then turned on his heel like a soldier and headed for the door.

Sarah bumped her friend's shoulder. "What do you think you're doing? My heart belongs to Edgar. Am I to be a chaperone here?"

"Something like that, I reckon. He's been after me pretty nearly since I got here, and I've always turned him down. I figured this was a chance for a safe foray to get to know the man a bit." Melinda Jane turned begging eyes to her friend. "Puh-lease?"

Sarah lifted her head high. "I will be the strictest of chaperones!" She marched toward the counter with her bundle of fabric. "And mind you, I'll not tolerate any moony eyes in my presence—lest it's me and my Edgar."

"Your Edgar? You've met twice and shared a dozen letters. You fancy yourself in a wedding dress already?" Melinda Jane giggled, picking coins from her reticule. "I'm sure he's a wonderful fella. Seems this war has put everything on hold and nothing is normal anymore."

She forced thoughts of Fin from her mind and painted on her brightest smile as they emerged from the store. Mr. Price offered an arm to each, guiding them down the sidewalk. *Like a gander and his geese.* Melinda Jane covered a chuckle with her free hand.

Sarah spoke first, dashing aside the half-block-long silence. "Did you hear about that awful execution a couple of weeks ago? Right here in Charleston?"

"Indeed. The first one of its kind in this dreadful war. I dare say there will most certainly be more." Mr. Price paused. "Let's not talk of war. What are your views on the new state?"

Melinda Jane breathed deep, but the distinct aroma of coal smoke and fish floated on the air. "I think it's a right fine idea, Mr. Price." Just a block away, the blast of a steamship sounded, drowning out her escort's voice. "Excuse me?" She tipped her head closer.

"I said, 'Please, call me Anderson.' Mr. Price is my father. The Honorable Cyrus Price, to be exact, and he is far from Charleston at the moment. For that, I am thankful."

"All right, then, Anderson. I think all this palaver about the folks on the other side of the mountains knowing what's best for us is vexing." She met his gaze, trying to determine if a woman who spoke her mind would send him runnin'. Some men wouldn't tolerate such a thing.

Anderson paused and angled his body toward her, both ladies' hands still coiled around his elbow. "What exactly do you mean, Melinda Jane? May I call you Melinda Jane?"

"You may, and I mean that life over here is nothing like what's going on over there. We're not like them. Here we got simple folks and farmers. We got the mountain folk that don't have schools and the old line Sawney who don't take too kindly to folks tellin' them what they can and can't do with their intentions. We've hardly got more than a handful of sizeable plantations like the ones over there."

Sarah nodded. "I agree." She tugged on Anderson's arm, leading the threesome forward again. "I'm kind of partial to the name 'Kanawha' for the new state, but seems the new congress is going with 'West Virginia' instead."

"I agree with both of you. My father is working to make this new state happen. He believes it will give us the new start we need, breaking away from the Old Dominion. I must say, it will take some getting used to, however." Anderson tilted his head to one side. "It may change the entire economy of the state if slave labor is squashed."

A familiar angst rose inside Melinda Jane. "Just another way in which the new state of West Virginia will be different. It's people who make the state what it is, not its economy. No room for codfish aristocracy this side of the mountains. There will always be enough willing workers for the mining and farming. The Good Books says a worker is worthy of his meat. Pay him for his labor and he'll be happy with what he earns."

Anderson paused, his eyebrows raised, then lowered. "Here we are, ladies." He held opened the door to Inman's and then rushed to pull out chairs for them at a small table just inside. "This is my treat." He strode up to the counter, digging into his pocket for coins.

"You sure are testing that fellow," Sarah whispered, leaning close in a conspiratorial manner.

"If'n he's not a man with a solid backbone, I probably shouldn't even consider spendin' time with him." Melinda Jane set the paper bundle of fabric on the floor. "Thank you for going along with this little scheme, Sarah. I didn't give you much of a chance to back out, did I?"

"No, you didn't. This just adds a mite of excitement to my day is all."

"Here we are ladies. Three apple ciders." Anderson took a seat between them. "So, tell me. Have either of you ever been to a minstrel show?"

A minstrel show! Like a child on Christmas morning, excitement bubbled up inside Melinda Jane. "Never in all my born days have I seen such a thing. I am a big fan of Jenny Lind. Sings just like an angel in heaven, some say. Her concerts draw big crowds in New York."

He laid his hand on hers. "I know someone else who sings just like an angel."

"Well, you are very kind." She slid her hand to her lap, suddenly feeling self-conscious. "But there are a number of wonderful singers in the church choir. I . . . I thank you for your compliment, however, Mr. P . . . Anderson." His eyes pulled her in like a fish on a hook.

Sarah set her glass on the table with a bang. Melinda Jane snapped her a shocked look, then turned back to Anderson. "I'd love to see a minstrel show. Is there one coming to this area, Anderson?" She shared a coy smile with him.

"As a matter of fact, there is a show coming to Charleston in June." He cleared his voice and turned his attention to her alone. "I'd be honored if you would accompany me, Melinda Jane. Of course, I hope Miss Young here would be a willing chaperone."

A real live Minstrel show! How could she say no? "I'd be delighted to attend with you. And I'm sure my very dear friend, Sarah, here, will be happy to also." If she smiled like this much more, her cheeks would hurt. The months couldn't pass fast enough!

Seven

FAYETTE COUNTY

"Aw, come on, Mertens. I've just gotta get this telegram sent. If they don't forward my mail from Ceredo, it'll be months before I get a letter." Fin hated to beg. "A favor for a man who's lost his family?"

"Lost your family? Sorry, Sarge. I can't imagine how a man loses his family, but the colonel says the telegraph is only for military use. You need an order from him." The hefty private pushed the piece of paper across the counter back to Fin.

"Tell you what. I'll trade you for the favor." *Leverage.* Surely he had something this boy needed.

The private leaned over the counter, his eyes darting left and right. "What've you got to trade?"

"Well, I've got some extra rations and a nice bandana." Fin's mind whirled. What *did* he have that the others didn't? "You read, Private?"

"Sure do. I love to read. You got a book you can trade? I'm taking a mighty colossal risk here."

"Ever read Nicholas Nickleby?"

"By Dickens?"

"The very one."

"Been wanting to read that one. You produce that book and you got yourself a telegram sent."

"Be right back." Fin headed to his tent, his steps a little lighter. He drew back the tent flap, and Noah's yellow mop of hair just missed smashing him in the face. "The Colonel wants to see us. No rest for the weary."

Fin retrieved the book. He hadn't been clear with Mertens. Was this a borrow or a gift? He wasn't too keen on parting with one of Pap's books, especially since he'd managed to fit only a few into his haversack before leaving the farm. Being hard to come by in the camp, books passed through the hands of so many soldiers that they often fell apart from the rough treatment. He didn't intend to let that happen to these books.

Pap had instilled his own love of literature in all of his children, and his knack for making stories come alive had endeared most of his books to the Dabney youngsters. Over the years, those books, stacked in neat rows clear to the ceiling, wove their way into the fabric of Fin's family.

He patted the buttoned shirt pocket where his greatest material possession rested—Pap's Bible. Yep. That was the thing he most cherished if a thing was to be cherished.

Frustrated with the interruption in plans, he looked about, hoping to find someone he knew. Sure enough, one of his very own rounded the next tent, pushing a wheelbarrow of firewood. "Private Benzinger, I have a brief mission for you."

The brawny man with a sorry excuse for a beard and a head of ash colored hair to match, dropped the load. "Whatcha need Sarge?"

He slipped the message inside the cover and handed him the book. "Drop this by the telegraph tent. Give it to Private Mertens. No one else. Understand?"

"Sure thing, Sarge." The man's eyebrows shot up. "Can I read it after him?"

He should've wrapped it in something.

Wintry pewter clouds had given way to a warm, mid-winter glow. Fin had even shed his outer coat for a time, but considered donning it again as the chill returned with the sinking sun. Once again, he led his men through the dense forests, this time trekking through Nicholas County toward Webster County.

Col. Crook's Thirty-sixth Ohio had scattered the Moccasin Rangers to the wind, retaliating for the group's attack on Sutton. The Indian-fighter Crook's practices were rumored to put the bushwhackers' deeds to shame in comparison. Reports stated that Col. Crook's men had even driven families from their homes, forcing them to watch as Federal soldiers set the houses ablaze.

Fin and his men rounded a bend in the road. The sun sat low enough now that its amber rays stabbed sharply through a break in the trees. Duke's ears twitched and the tension in his withers alerted his rider. Something was amiss. Pulling the horse to a stop, Fin motioned the others to do the same.

Silence.

Too silent.

A fierce cry split the air as horsemen lunged over the rise to Fin's left, zigzagging through the trees. Fin drew his pistol and fired off a shot. He reined the gelding in a tight dance as he chose a new target and fired again.

A movement in the corner of his eye caught Fischer dismounting. The private steadied his rifle across the back of his horse. He took out an attacker, then reloaded and fired again, dropping another.

Noah let go a chilling Indian cry as he dove from his saddle, crushing a bushwhacker who had lost his horse. A tangle of gunfire and smoke unraveled.

Fin was out of bullets. He grabbed his carbine from the scabbard.

"Sarge!" Walter's hoarse scream rent the air.

Fin whipped his head around. Just three feet away, a wicked sneer creased a face that had haunted his nightmares. Puckered, purple flesh masked the side of that face. The click of the trigger in the Rebel's hand barely registered.

A misfire.

Incensed, the man pulled back the hammer again, plunging the pistol closer to Fin's head.

Fin jerked back and swung his rifle, sending it crashing against the apparition. Matted gray hair struck the ground with a thud and bounced. A shot rang out near Fin's leg. He swapped his attention to see a knife-wielding Rebel collapse to the ground.

"You're welcome!" Noah hollered, his face stone as he holstered his revolver and grabbed up his carbine.

"I'm hit!" The cry came from Altizer, the youngest of his men, thrashing on the ground.

Six other bodies lay in the dirt. A half-mounted bushwhacker, clutching a bleeding arm, gave a yell and the others disappeared into the trees. Fin jumped to the ground and rushed over to Altizer.

The boy seemed more scared than hurt.

"It's not so bad, Private. Not enough meat right there in your arm to hold onto the bullet." In a short time, Fin had the boy bandaged up tight, complete with morphine powder for the pain. The months of watching and helping in the Dabney barn-turned-hospital certainly weren't wasted.

"You're not gonna be happy." Noah towered over him.

Fin stood. "About?"

"The ugly one that nearly done you in must've walked off." He pointed to the ground where the Confederate had landed.

Somewhere inside, a taut rope snapped. Fin threw his hat to the ground. "Find that animal!" He screamed the command and his men jumped into action, their eyes round with shock. They scurried into the woods like frightened rabbits.

After all these months, that old fury gripped him again. He was suddenly back in Gauley Bridge, his friend's head in his lap—body mutilated and still. Dead at the hands of that demon. Many a night that hideous face had fueled his hatred—fed his desire for vengeance. How he had struggled, knowing he was supposed to forgive his enemies. Obviously he hadn't.

A hand pressed his shoulder. "You all right, Fin?" Noah's voice carried a weight of concern.

Fin shrugged off the hand. "I'm fine." He pointed to the place in the dirt where the man should've still been lying. "He was on foot. Unless one of the others picked him up, he shouldn't be too hard to find." Fin grabbed his hat and slapped it against his thigh, the sting a welcome charge to his senses.

He reloaded his Colt, then started into the trees. "Let's go."

An hour wasted and still no sign of the bushwhacker with the scarred face. Fin's ire had simmered some, but that face had newly seared itself into his mind. Somebody must've circled back for him. A couple hours of daylight remained for the taking, so Fin would push his men farther east into Webster county before making camp.

"Look sharp, men. These woods have eyes!" Fin led the detachment away from the river, and into a forested patch of rolling ground. They followed a serpentine game trail for over an hour until it opened into a field. Just as Fin eased into the clearing, a shot rang out.

Backing Duke into the trees, he motioned for the others to do the same. "Anybody see anything?"

"Can't say I did. The old boy must not be much of a shot." Noah dismounted. "I'll go take a look."

Young Private Bridger piped up, "Want me to go with him, Sarge?" The boy looked all of sixteen, but his eyes burned with tenacity.

"All right. The two of you scout in opposite directions. You have ten minutes." Fin twisted in his saddle. "The rest of you, keep your wits about you. Keep quiet so we can hear if they aim to sneak up on us. And don't go shootin' before you see what you're shootin' at. It could be one of our own coming back here." Fin heard tell a few stories of friendly fire taking men out of this life. These boys were still mighty green for this kind of action—or even inaction. Like right now.

Within minutes, Noah returned. "I didn't see nothin', Sarge. Bridger back yet?" He scanned the group.

"Not yet." An uneasy notion chewed on Fin's instincts. "We'll give him some more time."

Several minutes passed in silence. Air brushed the back of Fin's neck, and he pulled back the hammer on his Colt. He scanned the woods, searching for anything out of the ordinary. His peripheral vision caught Noah doing the same.

A branch scraped, then snapped as a gagged Private Bridger stumbled into their midst. Hands bound behind him, he fell forward, his knees striking the frozen earth. Blue eyes blinked frantically relaying a message. Two Rebels stepped from the brush, one brandishing a musket, the other a revolver, intent on Bridger.

"Two of your horses for the life of this feller. You got to the count of five—then I'm pullin' this trigger." The bushwhacker spat a string of brown juice, his eyes pinned on Private Bridger. "One. Two."

Fin ground out an order. "Hicks, Fischer, give him what he needs." The men stepped forward, offering up their reins as one Rebel lowered his musket to take them. A wide grin painted his face as he turned, heading back into the woods.

"I thank you, kindly." The other bushwhacker's mouth curled into a dark sneer as he backed into the brush, his pistol still holding Bridger in its sight.

He fired, and the boy crumpled forward into a heap.

Fin squeezed off a shot that found its mark on the bushwhacker's forehead. The smoking barrel blazed a second shot, taking down the other one several feet into the trees. The horses shied as his body dropped to the ground, still gripping the reins.

Fin rushed over to Bridger. A stain crept across the middle of the young soldier's back. He touched his shoulder. Dead.

The blood pounded in his ears as he stood. Angst. Hatred. Remorse. It all twisted together like an oakum cord, pulling his chest tight and quivering his voice. He looked over his men. "This wasn't some battle. This was murder. Cold-blooded, shot-in-the-back murder." He scrubbed his beard with one hand. "You men see if there's any identification on these boys, then bury them real quick-like."

He bent to grab the boy's arm, and Noah joined him. Together, they draped his body over his horse.

The burying done, Fin guided Duke toward the clearing to head out. "We'll push through to Summersville and camp there for the night." One wounded, and now one dead. He wrangled with guilt and a sense of failure. Who was he to lead these men, anyway?

"What about Bridger, Sarge?" Sweat muddied the dirt on Benzinger's face, and he swiped at it with his sleeve, smearing dark streaks across his cheek.

"They'll tend to him at the advance post. We'll head on east in the morning. Let's git."

The heavy darkness pressed in—along with a mighty weight of grief and regret, negotiating with the commitment that put him here in the first place. If he felt this blackness, so did his men. *Lord, help me light a candle. If not for me, then for them.* Tonight he would write a letter to Bridger's mama.

Eight

CHARLESTON

Melinda Jane gripped her seat as Zander guided the wagon over the rutted path. A row of rickety shanties stood like skeletons, their gray, cracked walls and moss-covered roofs echoing the hardships of the occupants. A larger clapboard building to the right was home to several families. Just how many families was a mystery, but at least five she knew of for sure.

Children in tattered clothes, many without shoes, trickled from their homes. Adults followed, their weary eyes colored in hues of a strangled subsistence.

How she longed to gather the children into her arms and take them home. She would feed them heartily and comfort them with a hot bath. She'd sing them a lullaby as they drifted into a sound sleep, tucked between warm quilts in a soft bed.

The aroma of the savory soup in the two big kettles would draw a crowd as usual, but today was different. Today Melinda Jane and the rest came bearing gifts. A fresh loaf of bread for just about every family and dozens of molasses crinkles. If only they had brought milk. The children needed milk.

Her feet just touched the ground when a gentle tug at her arm drew her attention. "Miz 'Linda, you're here! I told Perry you'd be here. I just had me a feelin'." Six-year-old Olivia Penchant beamed a gap-toothed smile. She threw her arms around Melinda Jane's waist, nearly throwing her off balance.

"Well now. I'm feelin' mighty welcomed. Ya gotta know by now if I'm not here today, I'll be here soon enough." She brushed back a shock wooley hair from the delight-filled face, then pressed a paper-wrapped bundle into the girl's arms. "Why don't you take this and share with the other children?" The collection of slippers, mittens, and mufflers had been her very own labor of love for these dear children. She covered every loop and pull of the yarn in prayer. Prayer for better times, for joy and health, and for God's mercy in their harsh lives.

Will helped move the offerings and food to the edge of the wagon bed. "I know we bring them what we can, but it's never enough, it seems."

Angry shouting drew all eyes to the very last shanty. "Ain't no woman gonna lord it over me!" A woman stumbled across the threshold. A hand snatched her back into the house.

Melinda Jane scanned the area for Olivia and her four-year-old brother, Perry. It was no secret how their pap treated their mama. She had begged Nettie to leave her man, but she wouldn't have it. "So long as he ain't beatin' on the young'uns, I'll stay," she would say.

A scream from the end cabin sent a chill down Melinda Jane's back. "I'll not keep to my business!" Lifting the hem of her skirt, she stormed toward the Penchant's shack.

"Melinda Jane, wait!" Zander took off after her.

His boots thumped the ground behind her. She would not wait. She had ignored this horror long enough. Nettie Penchant had nobly claimed the bruises and sprained wrist were only a product of her own clumsiness. This time, Melinda Jane was bent on taking a blow herself, if it meant getting that woman away from her husband.

She pounded on the door and waited impatiently. *I will only count to five. Lord, give me strength and protect your child.* Just as she raised her fist again, the door jerked open and Mr. Penchant's dark frame filled the doorway. Red-rimmed eyes squinted into the light.

"I'd like to see Nettie, please, Mr. Penchant." Melinda Jane gentled her voice, but the words in her head barked angry accusations.

"She don't wanna talk to you!"

A broken sob slipped around him and through the opening.

"I'd like to see her," she repeated. She planted her feet to push past the looming man to see to her friend.

He scowled at her, then at Zander. "Wait here," he growled before slamming the door closed.

"You sure about this?" Zander asked, his fingers tapping on the hunting knife strapped to his leg. "Maybe it'd be better to leave them be."

"I will not. I've kept out of this long enough. Nettie is my friend, and I aim to protect her and those children."

Mr. Penchant jerked open the door and pushed past them, jamming a ratty hat onto his head. "She's all yours. I don't want her no more."

Nettie sat on the dirt floor, arms propped on her knees. With her head tucked beneath her arms, she quivered, choking back a sob. She wiped a dirty apron across her wet face and accepted Zander's hand to stand.

"Thank you," she mumbled, keeping her eyes to the ground.

Melinda Jane threw her arms around the woman. "Oh Nettie, did he hurt you?" She pulled back to look more closely at the woman.

Pained eyes blinked from a tear-streaked face, and just like always, she smiled weakly and said, "I be jes fine, Miss 'Linda."

She helped Nettie to one of the two chairs in the tiny quarters. She turned to Zander. "You can go back out and help Mrs. O'Donell. We'll be all right here."

"If you're sure." Zander glanced around the room, then back to Melinda Jane. "Holler if you need me." Four long strides took him outside.

Melinda Jane offered Nettie a tin cup of water. "You want to lie down?"

"Won't help none. It's my fault this time." She shook her head, swiping at her nose with the back of her hand.

"He's the one to blame, Nettie. Don't you take on guilt just 'cause your man can't hold his temper—or his liquor."

She wagged her head in slow motion. "No. No, this time it's my fault." Her eyes locked with Melinda Jane's. "I got me another baby." She rubbed her belly. "In here. Milo say if'n this happen again, I got to make the baby go away." A fresh tear trickled down her cheek. "I love this baby, Melinda Jane. God give me this baby. I can't do what my husband is askin'."

Nettie leaned into Melinda Jane, her body wilting. "I can't even feed my other two. How we gonna care for this one? Milo say he be leavin.'"

"You hush now. We'll give this to our Father in heaven and let Him carry this burden. You don't do a thing, 'cept trust God, you hear? God is bigger than all our problems rolled into one big riled mess. He'll make a way, Nettie. He'll make a way." She rocked the woman like a child, pulling her head snug into her bosom, willing the fear and heartache away.

A soft tap sounded at the door and Melinda Jane answered without so much as a look. "Come in."

Mrs. O'Donell's head poked through the opening. "The children are wantin' you to sing for them." She wore a mantle of concern but smiled tenderly. "You want me to hold them off a bit longer, lass?"

Nettie wiped her eyes. "Oh, you must sing for them Miss 'Linda. You is such a ray o' sunshine in this dark place."

Melinda Jane looked from one woman to the other. She did what she could, but what they needed was the Lord's light. He's the only One who could make a lasting difference in this sad place of broken dreams and aching hearts.

She squeezed Nettie's shoulder. "I'll go if you'll come get yourself something to eat."

"All right. I'll come." She stood, dabbing at her face and fussing with her hair, tucking errant strands into the gray muslin coiled around her head.

Melinda Jane encouraged the folks to sing with her. The old women, the mamas, the children, and even the few men present. Watching your family starve or die from disease was a hard thing to ask of a man. It was just easier for him to walk away.

After a rousing three verses of "Oh Susanna", "Camptown Races", and then "Rock of Ages", the pots of food set empty. Children flitted around and between adults, showing off their new mufflers and hats.

"Warms the heart to see these dingy smiles." Mrs. O'Donell dabbed at her eye with a hanky.

"I say we hold a big ol' quilting bee with the ladies at church and bring them all the quilts we make." Will pushed the empty pots against one corner of the wagon and plopped down next to them, pulling a blanket over her lap.

That girl is plum full of surprises these days. "Why Will, that's a wonderful idea. Maybe the church women haven't done much yet because they don't know how to help." Melinda Jane beamed at Mrs. O'Donell.

"Don't be gettin' yer hopes up, now. I've tried before to get the women at the Episcopal church to give me a hand. You think yer Methodist ladies to be any different?"

"I pray they will be. Brother Lambert is such a kind man. Surely he can get the ladies to see that quilting for the poor is no picayune affair." Melinda Jane turned at a tug on her skirt. Four-year-old Perry Penchant looked up at her. She squatted down to meet his dark, round eyes, so much like her own.

"We are all out of treats, Perry." Her mind raced to think of some little something she could still leave with this sweet child.

"I know. My mama says I s'pose to say . . . "—he puffed his chest as he inhaled—"thank you, Miz Dabney."

"You are most welcome, Perry. You take care of your sister and mama, now. Ya hear?"

"Yes, ma'am." He nodded several times, then flung boney arms around Melinda Jane's waist, squeezing tight. "Bye Miz 'Linda."

If only I could take you home with me. "Good bye, Perry." She patted his curly head. "I'll see you again real soon." The boy turned and ran to the end cabin where Nettie stood waving, a sad smile on her face.

Zander stood beside the rig, waiting to help the women up to the seat. "Ready to go?"

She turned her gaze away from Nettie at last. "I don't suppose I'm ever really ready to leave these folks. There's so much need here."

As the wagon rolled away, the hollowness in her stomach spread to her heart. How very blessed she was. She had never known real hunger like these folks, and she had never missed a night's sleep for lack of warmth. *Lord, please watch over Nettie and the children. Don't let any harm come to them—or that baby.*

◦◦

"Stop peeking out that window, Will. It's not polite to spy on someone." Melinda Jane stepped up next to the girl, peering through the lacy curtains.

"Now *you're* peekin' out. How come it's not polite for me and it's all right for you?" Will huffed dramatically, her hand on one hip.

"Pfft. I was just makin' sure there wasn't someone in need of help out there, that's all." She flashed Will a disarming smile, then turned back to the window. "You been watching out this window for some time, I noticed . . . Oh!"

"A-yep. It's that Mr. Price from church." Will folded her arms across her chest. "He's been a-sittin' out in that carriage for the longest time. He just stared straight ahead most that time, then he started fussing with his hair and fiddlin' with his tie."

"You leave that poor man be." She fought the grin that tried to erupt. "I wonder what he wants?" she said, more to herself.

"You wonder? That so, Melinda Jane? What do any of those men want when they look all silly and stricken at you? You gonna go out there and tell him to scoot?"

"How's about I tell you to scoot?"

"This could be real entertaining, and you're gonna make me miss it." She hung her head and sauntered off toward the kitchen.

Melinda Jane marched into the big room where the boys slept. Cots lined a wall, once reserved for patients back when the house was Dr. Hill's clinic. She grabbed up the rag rug and promptly marched to the front door. Keeping a smile at bay, she opened the door and leaned over the porch railing, allowing the rug to unfold its full length. Pretending not to notice the conveyance, she gave the rug a firm shake, then let her eyes meet those of Anderson Price. It was all the encouragement he needed.

"Good day, Miss Minard," he said, striding up the brick walkway.

"That it is. And it's Melinda Jane, remember? Miss Minard makes me feel a bit like an old maid, and I'm not there just yet."

"Yes. I mean, no, you're right . . . Melinda Jane." His eyes darted from the door to his buggy, hesitant to meet her gaze. "I wanted to say I enjoyed our short time together last week—at Inman's."

"Why, thank you, Anderson. Sarah and I had a pleasant time also."

"I'd like to spend more time with you. Would you mind if I came calling?"

That hopeful look in his eyes warmed her heart. How could she let him down? "That would be a fine idea. How about you come for dessert tomorrow evening? About eight o'clock?"

"That sounds wonderful. I look forward to it." He bowed slightly. "Until tomorrow."

A lump like cold dough sat in the pit of her stomach. *What did I just do?* She turned to take the rug into the house. *Fin has no intentions on me. Nothin' wrong with a little companionship. It's not like we are sparkin' or something, right?* She stopped inside the door and tipped her head to the heavens. "Right?" she said aloud, wishing for an audible answer.

Nine

Late morning brought Fin and his men across the county line. Only an hour outside of Summersville, the little detachment happened upon a clutch of four bushwhackers breaking camp. After a brief tussle, they corralled all four and took them back to the post, leaving Fin and the rest a good two hours behind schedule, as they started out a second time.

"You boys hear that?" Fin pulled Duke to a gentle stop.

In a few seconds, the clatter of hooves behind him quieted. "What *is* that?" One of the Ohio boys cupped his ear as he spoke.

"That is a little side trip we're gonna take." Fin angled his horse toward the sound, leading the men single file, snaking around an outcropping of gray rock, over a ridge.

Crisp, moist air took on an earthy aroma. A rushing swelled to a roar, and when they rounded the last turn, a magnificent waterfall awaited. What it lacked in height, it gained in ferocity. White water rushed around boulders, colliding angrily, raising mist from the boiling cauldron at the lowest point.

"Isn't that just a thing of beauty?" Walter grinned, standing in his stirrups.

"That it is. That it is." Noah shot a hopeful look Fin's way. "What say we stretch our legs, Sarge?"

"Five minutes, then we're on our way." Fin dismounted and dropped the reins to ground-tie Duke. This place never ceased to bring him to a keen sense of God's power and his own weakness. He filled his canteen with the fresh mountain water. Too bad it wasn't summer—he'd be stripping down for a dunk in his birthday suit.

How could something so wild and beautiful be nestled in the middle of this confounded war? He'd always thought there was a kind of beauty in the way Almighty God's presence inhabits the affairs of men. But, what about men on an open battlefield? Men burning out neighbors? Men skulking behind trees, hoping for a chance to kill or maim the unsuspecting? Where was God in that?

"You look real serious." Noah stepped up next to him, capping his canteen. "What's on that mind of yours?"

"The voice of the Lord is upon the waters," Fin said, half to himself. Then louder, "The God of glory thundereth. The Lord is upon many waters." He pinned Noah with a sober look, before cocking his head to one side. "You asked."

"I did at that." Noah nodded. "You listen real close to what the Lord's telling you. I feel a mite better thinkin' I'm following Him and not just you."

The welcoming smell of a home fire teased at Fin's senses. He signaled his men to halt. "Smell that?"

"Smoke, Sarge?" Fischer piped up.

"What kind of smoke? Where?" Fin asked, his gaze bouncing from one man to another.

"Cooking. Not a campfire. South of here since the breeze is bringin' it." Benzinger offered, refusing to wilt at the inquiry. "Am I right?"

"Good, Private Benzinger. How far you reckon?"

"Less than a quarter mile, I'd say." Pride showed in the big Ohioan's eyes, and one cheek twitched like it wanted to bolt into a smile.

"Right again." Fin pointed to three of his men. "You come with me. The rest of you stay here."

In just a few minutes and a few hundred yards, the tree canopy opened up ahead. Leaving the horses, he signaled the three men to spread out. Fin crept forward, careful not to draw attention. The yard of a ramshackle cabin came into view and something akin to an angry sadness wilted his good mood.

Fin entered the clearing in front of the old cabin, motioning for his men to do the same. A woman bent over a prone body as three small children clung to her faded skirts. Their sobs intermingled, slicing his heart in two.

"Pardon me, ma'am." His voice was gentle, not wanting to startle the woman.

She raised her head, and he saw the bruises forming on her tear-streaked face. Pain masked her eyes, but only for an instant. Then fury sparked.

"You come to finish the job? You Federals think you can do what you want—kill when you feel like it!" Her face buckled as she screamed the words.

Fin holstered his gun and held up his palms. "Whoa now. We didn't do this, ma'am."

"You're all the same. You Yankees think you can lord it over anybody you've a mind to. Take what's not yours. Figure if a man ain't wearing a Federal uniform, he's deservin' of death." She choked on a sob and pulled her children closer.

He stepped forward, his eyes scanning the body. Nothing to indicate the man was a Rebel. In these parts, garb didn't account for much anyway. The sight brought a mighty urge for vengeance just now. "Who did this, ma'am? Maybe we can catch them."

"Another mess of Federals. Came ridin' in here calling out my man. They say he's a bushwhacker. Say he's guilty." She squeezed her eyes shut, waving her hand toward the cabin. Her breath halted as she seemed to imagine the whole ordeal all over again. "I . . . I tried to stop 'em. They brung us all out here to watch while they shot him. Shot him in cold blood." She broke down again, sobbing into the children's hair. "You tell me. H . . . how is that right? My Ernest was no bushwhacker. He's been here mostly with me. We just trying to mind our own business."

Fin widened his stance. Crook's men. He was sure of it. They had taken to their own kind of war. "I am sorry for your loss ma'am. I am not part of the unit that did this to your husband. If you show me where you want it, we will gladly dig a grave." Dig a grave? Is that all he could do for this poor woman and her children?

Not two hours later, the men had dug the grave, chopped up more firewood, and bagged a few rabbits for the family. The woman tended her husband's body in the cabin, and when Fin asked if she was ready to have the body buried, she simply nodded.

He quoted a fitting verse and his men covered the grave. Without another word from the widow or children, Fin left with his men in silence.

They followed a handful of tracks leading from the cabin until dusk. Fin pulled up, taking in the surroundings. "This looks to be about as good a spot as any to make camp."

"You planning on picking up these boys' trail in the morning?" Noah asked, pulling the ties loose on his bedroll.

"Not sure. Wondering if tracking our own soldiers is such a good idea. I need to sleep on this." What he really needed was to pray on the matter.

Already soft snores sounded among the men, and owl hoots serenaded the chilly evening. Fin tossed another broken branch onto the fire and pulled the worn Bible from his pocket. Leaning in toward the firelight, he thumbed the curled cover and ruffled through pages in the middle of the Book. He loved the Psalms. The soothing words calmed his spirit and spun a sweet web of comfort around his disquieted soul. He smiled at Melinda Jane's picture—even thought of putting it to his lips—but such foolishness would only mock his longing. A longing that squeezed his insides against his backbone.

He brushed aside one page after another until his eyes fell on the words he sought. *"Fret not thyself because of evildoers, neither be thou envious against the workers of iniquity. For they shall soon be cut down like the grass, and wither as the herb."*

Well then, that was that. If those Union soldiers chose not to play by the rules, he figured God would make them pay. Did that mean he should ignore it? Was war not supposed to be between soldiers—not families? What if those boys were just acting on orders? He thought of his own colonel. A respectable man. A God-fearing man. Many of his men just called him *Colonel Joe*. He breathed a thank you to the Lord that his commander wasn't some bloodthirsty lunatic without a care for women and children.

Fitful sleep tossed body and thoughts in his bedroll, his mind lingering on what the next day would bring. By the time dawn's ochre glow filtered through the trees, Fin had determined to follow the tracks until noon, then head back to Gauley Bridge.

Best guess was five riders keeping to a game trail. After an hour of riding, they met up with fresh tracks.

"Not far now." Noah stood, wiping the dirty snow from his fingers. "We can probably catch up to them in the next half hour easy enough."

Fin leaned forward in his saddle. "Let's do just that."

Two sets of tracks veered off to the south. Duke whinnied, and another horse answered back. "They're right up here." Fin eyed the tree canopy. "There's a clearing." He signaled his men to hang back as he slowed his pace.

A log barn with a new fence set off to one side of the clearing and a cabin claimed the other side. Two horses with U.S. Army tack were ground-tied in the yard. A woman's scream rent the quiet and Fin sprang from his saddle, drawing his Colt. Noah followed on his heels as they rushed to the cabin. The door was ajar and Noah nudged it open.

"No! No!" A woman crouched on top of a bed, blankets clutched to her chin. Her eyes wide with terror, she gulped down air, screaming in desperation.

A Federal soldier shoveled up hot coals from the fireplace and growled, "I said, get outta here or I'll burn the place down with you in it!"

The woman's eyes bulged, her screams now an incoherent jumble of raspy syllables. Fin watched in horror as the soldier dumped the coals onto the bed. He lunged for the woman, yanking her from under the covers. He scooped her up in his arms as hungry flames enveloped the blankets.

"Are you mad?" Fin yelled, searing his throat from the force of it. *What kind of nightmare did I walk into?*

He whipped around to a ruckus. Noah was trying to wrestle a kerosene can from a different soldier. The vile liquid soaked the floor. In seconds, the flaming bed touched off the entire cabin.

"Noah! Get out of here!" Fin charged through the doorway, the woman clinging to his neck, lost in hysteria. The first soldier barreled through the door, the shovel still in his hands.

Seconds later, a red-faced Noah stomped off the porch, dragging the other soldier from the flame-engulfed cabin. He hurled him to the ground as the man clutched his head with a whimper.

"It ain't lawful to do to you what I ought!" Shoulders heaving, Noah glared at the sniveling private and spat.

Fin eased the woman onto the ground. Shivers racked her body as she huddled in only a thin nightgown. "You're safe now, ma'am." One of his men draped a blanket over the woman's back and Fin snugged it around her. She was likely about the age his mama would've been. "I'm real sorry about this, ma'am. I'll make sure these men are dealt with." Even if he had to go over somebody's head, he'd see to it these fools were punished.

He strode over to the first soldier, his insides quaking with each step. "What's going on here, Private?" He spat the words into the soldier's face, his temper barely controlled.

The man's expression wavered between indignation and humility. "Just following orders, Sergeant."

"Whose orders?"

"Colonel Crook's, Sergeant."

Noah jerked up the second private, shoving him over to Fin. "They were just another piece of rotten meat, Sarge," the man muttered.

Fin shot Noah a look of disgust. "Any more of your unit out here, flittin' around burning out family homes?"

"Our orders were to spread out and take care of bushwhacker homesteads, then get back to camp by dark." The first soldier's eyes flashed, and he shifted his weight, trying to catch the eye of his partner.

"That include beating and burning women, Private?"

"No . . . Yes, Sergeant. If they got in the way, we were told to make them regret it."

"Is that right?" The bile rose in his throat. Helpless. There was nothing he could do. This was not what he signed on for. "You make me sick." His eyes passed to the terrified woman. He could still file a complaint. "Get outta here. Both of you!" It felt good to yell—to vent even a little of the steam building in his gullet.

They sprang onto their horses and bolted like spooked calves.

Noah yanked the blanket from his saddle and offered it to the woman. Still shivering, she clutched it around her, covering the first blanket. "Ma'am, you got any kin close by we can take you to?" His voice was tender, like calming a bull about to charge.

"M . . . m . . . my sister's f . . . family live just over . . ." She pointed with her fist.

"It ain't right just to leave her here like this." Noah scowled, looking off after the two galloping horses, dust still hanging in the air.

Fin had enough practice reading Noah's mind. Words sometimes just got in the way. "All right, then."

Noah scooped up the woman, setting her atop his saddle sideways as best he could, trying to keep her modest. He picked up the reins and started walking toward her kin.

Gauley Bridge

Fin tightened the saddle cinch, then thumped Duke's neck. "That's a good boy." He crooned reassuring words—as much to himself as the horse. Strange how something as familiar as grooming was a comfort. He'd been pretty impressed with the way ol' Duke had handled himself in scrimmages. "Yep, you're a good boy."

Noah's grinning face popped over the saddle. "Why thankee. I reckon you're a good ol' boy, too, Dabney.

"Very funny."

"I gotta take a compliment where I can get it. Even if it was meant for a horse." Noah chuckled.

"Did you get the word out to everyone?"

"Sure did. I've got a surprise for you, too."

Fin raised an eyebrow. "A surprise, huh? Like when you put that copperhead in Walter's haversack? No thank you, Hicks."

"I am sorely wounded, Sarge." Noah feigned a stab to the heart, then produced a bundle of letters, tied with a string.

Excitement rushed at Fin for an instant. But he didn't let on. He leveled his gaze, voice calm. "Are those mine?"

"Indeed, they are, Sarge. A pity you won't have time to read them until we make camp this evening." He handed them over, then walked away, wagging his head like an old hound. "Such a pity."

Fin's eyes followed the flight of a merganser across the rushing gray waters of the Gauley. Its frilled black and white head dipped, then rose slightly, never straying far from the river's enraged surface.

Seemed like just yesterday he was a boy, daring the others to climb the rafters of the great covered bridge that had once spanned this section of the river. Confederates burned it back in July. Even from his farm, he had watched the sky glow amber and red from the fire. But that was in the past, and today brought a celebration of sorts.

The entire Twenty-eighth Regiment, packed shoulder to shoulder, stood on a span and a half of the new bridge. Captain Simmon's battery filled in the rest of the bridge. Music from the band soared over their heads as much of the regiment marched in time. Only yesterday, Captain Shonberg's entire cavalry had marched across the bridge—not once, but several times. All to test this new example of engineering marvel.

"Seems everybody's happy about the new bridge." Fin dismounted and leaned forward, stretching his back. "We might as well wait here 'til it's clear to cross." Fin lifted the saddlebag flap, grabbed the stack of letters, and sat down on a boulder at the water's edge. Six letters in all from his sisters, Will and Gus. And two from Melinda Jane. He decided to open them in order until he noticed one from Gus had a different postmark. Instead of the Kanawha Court House marking, it was stamped WHEELING. *Wheeling?* He would open that one first.

Six letters later, Fin laid back, pushing his hat over his eyes.

Noah leaned over him. "You wanna talk 'bout it?"

With every chuckle or smile the letters pulled from Fin, Noah had put in his two cents worth, speculating on the letters' contents. Fin would have to ask somebody to write to the poor boy. He hardly ever got mail.

"I wanna stew on it some. I'll share with you tonight." Fin bit back a grin. Had Noah been born a girl, he would be one of those gossipy, lip-flapper types—always wantin' to know about everybody else's business. It would drive him plum crazy to wait until this evening to hear the Dabney news.

After an hour, with the bridge testing complete, Fin and his men headed out. Their new assignment involved squelching some guerilla activity in the Mountain Cove area. The going was slow as they headed over the hills instead of taking the normal traces.

"We sure don't have country like this back in Ohio," Fischer said. "You're always moving up or down. Not much flat land around here."

"You know what mountains those are?" Noah pointed toward the east.

"The Appalachians, aren't they?" Walter said, sitting a little taller in his saddle.

"That they are." Noah turned his head back toward Walter. "You know what Appalachia means?"

"Is this some kind of school test? No, I don't know what it means." Walter scowled.

"It's an old Indian word. Means endless mountain range."

"Will wonders never cease?" Fin chuckled. "Hicks, you do occasionally surprise me. You learned that on that one day you attended school, did you?"

"I'm not all learned like you, Sarge, and I may not be the sharpest knife in the drawer, but I know me a thing or two." Noah turned back to the road and his face fell slack.

Fin raised a hand to signal a silent halt.

"Just saw the tip of a musket and a man slippin' behind that tree," Noah whispered. He jerked his head to indicate a burled chestnut tree.

Ten

CHARLESTON

Melinda Jane slid scissors through the paper with trembling fingers. Finally, a letter from Fin after all these months.

Will reached for the letter. "You're slower than molasses in January. Let me do it."

Melinda Jane turned her back, protecting the coveted missive. "I'm just being careful." Slipping the letter from its envelope, she faced the anxious girl. "Let's go sit at the table, and I'll read it out loud. It's addressed to all of us."

Will tromped into the kitchen and dropped into a chair. "Now I suppose we have to wait for Zander." She plunked her elbow onto the table, propping up her chin.

"Wait for me for what?" Zander sauntered into the kitchen, a harmonica in his hand.

Will pulled out a chair. "Hurry up and sit down so we can hear Fin's letter." She bounced on her seat like a child, her pent-up energy barely contained.

"*Now* can we hear it?" Bertie's exasperation made Melinda Jane chuckle.

"We're all here, so I'll read it." She unfolded the letter and smoothed it out on the table.

Dear Family (and Melinda Jane),

I have left Ceredo, and I am back in Fayette County on a temporary assignment. It seems I have a knack for rooting out bushwhackers around here, so I am to remain here at Gauley Bridge under Colonel Moor's command for some time. I went to the farm to surprise you all for Christmas. Imagine my shock when I found the barn burned and all of you gone. An altercation with some unsavory Confederates who were living in our house gave me cause for great concern. After some investigating, I decided you had left on your own accord. I am somewhat flummoxed about the when and why of it all, though.

I have wired for my mail and hope to find some answers to my questions when it comes as to settle my worries. As for news, I have been promoted to Sergeant, and a new bridge over the Gauley will soon be completed. I checked in on the Dortons. They have lost much to guerillas but are holding up. God is faithful to keep me safe. It is both a blessing and a curse to be so close to home. The familiar is as comforting as the war is trying, for the ugliness of this rebellion continues to tear at that which we love, and on our very doorstep.

My love to all of you. You are in my prayers, as I know I am in yours. — Fin

Melinda Jane's heart sank. How she had yearned for even a few words to be for her. Just her. *I am so selfish. Instead of being overjoyed that he's alive and in good health, all I'm thinking of is me.* The ugly truth shamed her. *Lord, thank you so much for watching over him. Please help me accept that I will never be more than another sister to him.*

"He didn't say anything about the letters I sent him." Will stood, her face drooped in a frown.

Zander patted her shoulder. "He just hasn't gotten them yet, sounds like. He will and he's sure to be real thankful when he does."

Bertie's somber stare connected with the floor. "Seems Fin's been gone so long. I hope he don't forget what I look like. Could be I'll be a man before I see him again." He lifted shimmering eyes to Melinda Jane. "I miss him—and Gus."

She squeezed the boy against her. "I'm sure they miss you even more, Bertie. It's just for a season. You'll see. If we just bide our time and try to be patient, we'll all be back together in no time."

"But . . ."—Zander caught her look, warning him to keep his thoughts to himself. He pressed his lips together in a tight line and dropped his gaze.

A long turn of the front doorbell interrupted their silent concern, and Will dashed to answer it.

"I wonder who that could be," Melinda Jane said, smoothing her skirt to head for the door.

Will burst into the kitchen, a wide grin on her face. "Oh, Za-aan-der." She sang the words, then batted her eyelashes. Rolling her shoulders from side to side, she spread her skirt wide like a crinoline. "There's someone here to see you."

That girl could tease the feathers off a rooster. Melinda Jane chuckled when his ears blossomed pink as two roses. "Zander? Well, my my."

"Cut it out. I'll just go out the back door, then you can tell them I'm not here." Zander reached for the doorknob.

Melinda Jane crossed the room. "Oh no you don't, Zander Dabney. If you've got a caller, you go handle it like a gentleman."

Bertie jumped in, "You don't even know who it is yet."

"Yes, I do." Zander's shoulders slumped, and his attention darted around the room like a caged rabbit. "It's the Talbert sisters. They said they were gonna make me some cookies and bring 'em over. I said it was fine, since I wanted the cookies. But now I'm thinking they think I like them and I'm actually gonna have to talk to them." His eyes pleaded with Melinda Jane.

She pointed to the front door. "You go on out there right now and show them that you're a respectable, polite Dabney man, and that you'd never take advantage of a lady's affections." Fin quit the kitchen like a whupped pup, tail between his legs.

"Can I watch?" Will started to follow, but Melinda Jane grabbed her arm.

"Your time will come, honey, and I won't let anybody watch then, either."

Melinda Jane moved each plate an inch to the left. She stood back, surveying the table-setting, then repositioned the pitcher of water and butter dish.

"Sure seems yer doin' a load of fussin'. Do ya really think he'll be admirin' the table service when a lass as fair as yerself is sittin' across that table?" Mrs. O'Donell pulled the shepherd's pie from the oven. Her eyes closed as she inhaled the warm aroma. "Ahh. The smell of home."

"It's just . . . the last time he was here was only for dessert. This time it's a whole meal. Silly of me, isn't it? I've got no need to impress Anderson. He's just a friend."

"Mind you, be sure to be the one answerin' that door when the bell sounds. Will's been in such a sour mood, she's liable to chase him off before he steps foot in the house."

"She has been, hasn't she? In a sour mood, I mean. Her and I just don't see eye to eye where Fin's concerned. He's pretty nearly a hero in her eyes ever since he went off to fight."

She jumped at the turn of the front doorbell and rushed into the parlor. Will raced down the stairs, colliding with her at the door, but Melinda Jane beat her to the knob.

"Now, Will," she cautioned, one eyebrow raised.

"Oh, all right," she huffed, then pivoted and marched into the kitchen, grumbling under her breath.

Anderson Price stood at attention on the porch, with his perfectly oiled hair and his perfectly straight part. He pulled a paper-wrapped box from behind his back. "I wanted to bring you flowers, but it's the wrong time of year, so I chose chocolates instead." He beamed a satisfied smile and offered up the box of candy.

Never. Never had she received a box of confections. Especially not one tied with such a beautiful bow. Her first response was to refuse it, but she grabbed hold of what propriety she owned and took the box from his hand.

"Anderson, you didn't have to go do that." She stepped back to let him pass, and her footing wavered. In an instant, his hands were on her arms, very nearly in an embrace.

"Are you all right?" he asked, his expression and voice much too concerned.

"Silly me!" She pulled from his touch. "I . . . I'm just fine."

She showed Anderson to the kitchen, where everyone but Mrs. O'Donell was seated at the table. Whatever was wrong with her? She wasn't one of those citified women—all weak and swoony, pawing over a man for his attention. She might be on the underside of tall, but she was anything but fragile. Although, it felt good to have a man care; she had to admit.

By way of a miracle, Will managed to keep her mouth quiet throughout the meal. She shot daggers at Melinda Jane a time or two and growled at Zander when he bumped her arm, but all in all behaved herself. Polite table conversation ruled, but the wall between Will and Melinda Jane had grown a couple of bricks taller by the time pie was served.

"My compliments to the cooks." Anderson nodded regally. "I believe it's time I took my leave and let this marvelous meal settle." His dark eyes fastened on Melinda Jane.

Taken aback by the intensity of his gaze, she jumped up, almost capsizing her teacup. "If you'll excuse me, I'll see Anderson to the door."

The dark porch overlooked the peaceful street, providing a modicum of privacy for them. Melinda Jane pulled her shawl snug and gazed up at the stars—the same stars she had admired a thousand times. She searched for words to break the awkward silence, but they seemed as far from her brain as those stars. Funny how she was never at a loss for words with Fin. Just the opposite, in fact. She'd blurt out just about everything that came to mind. Well, not everything. She had deliberately refrained from speaking about their relationship. Just like she had read in *Godey's Lady's Book*: a lady waits for the man to make the first move.

"Did you hear me?"

Anderson's voice brought her back to the present. "I apologize, Anderson. I was off gatherin' wool. What did you say?"

"I said I'd like to see you again. If the weather is agreeable, may I walk you home from church on Sunday?"

"I'd like that." A thought crossed her mind. "We'll be heading over to the poorhouse after church, would you like to come along?"

His smiled widened. "I would like nothing better, but I must decline this time. I'm afraid my father will be in town, most likely demanding my time." He tipped his hat and smiled. A very pleasant smile. Not too big, just right. "Until Sunday. Goodnight."

"Goodnight, Anderson." Melinda Jane watched as he boarded the carriage, wondering why he didn't just ride a horse. Wouldn't that make more sense?

Melinda Jane set the tea tray on the short table between the two chairs. "This is as good a place as any to finish up these stockings." She handed Sarah Young the bundle of yarn and needles. "I hope it didn't get too tangled in the bag."

Sarah pulled the tangle apart. "It's not bad. Hopefully we'll be able to include these with the batch of goods you're planning on taking over Sunday afternoon." An angelic smile spread to her eyes as she tugged at the yarn.

"Sarah, you are positively glowing. Spill the beans." Melinda Jane nudged her arm. "Out with it."

Sarah giggled. "I got a visit from Edgar. He had a two-day leave and came to see me since that wasn't enough time to see his folks in Ohio." Her words tumbled out.

"Slow down, now. Did you have a nice visit?"

Sara's eyes squeezed into half-moons and her voice went up a notch. "I think he wants to marry me." Her hand flew to her mouth. "Oh dear. I said it out loud. I don't want to jinx it."

Melinda Jane laughed. "You look so happy. Did he declare his undying love for you?"

"Not exactly. He said he cared for me and wanted us to be together after the war."

"But he didn't say the words, exactly?" Melinda Jane hugged herself and feigned a male voice. "Words like, 'I love you, Sara Young. Will you do me the honor of becoming my wife?'"

They giggled like schoolgirls.

Sarah pressed her hands to her heart. "I just know I can't stop thinking about him and wishing he was here! I've got this gap in my stomach something awful."

Melinda Jane knew that feeling. Right after Fin left the farm, she prayed day and night that he'd come home to her and ask for her hand. Oh, she still prayed for him plenty, but she had squashed her feelings down for so long now, she wasn't sure what was really there anymore.

"You're quiet all the sudden," Sarah said, setting the knitting in her lap. "You thinking on Anderson?"

She scowled at the yarn on her needles. "Will you look at that! I just dropped a stitch."

The front door burst open, and Mrs. O'Donell waved an envelope. "'Tis from Gus. Where are the children?"

"I'll round them up." Melinda Jane set down her knitting. She found Will and Bertie hovered over a game of checkers in the room they had taken to calling the cot room. Were the house not used as a doctor's office before the war, the room might've served as a formal dining room. For now, it was just an oversized bedroom for the boys, since Will had slept in her older sister's room for the past few months.

"Zander is shoveling coal for Mrs. Overby at the moment. Do we want to wait for him?" The woman looked to the others for an answer.

"My vote is open it now," Bertie said in a very adult voice.

"Yeah. Let's just open it now." Will climbed onto the wine-colored serpentine-backed sofa and stretched out her legs, taking up the entire thing. Bertie pushed her feet out of the way and sat on the end.

Mrs. O'Donell handed the letter to Melinda Jane. "You read it to us."

Melinda Jane slit the envelope and read aloud:

Dear Loved Ones,

I continue to nurse patients wherever needed up here at the Wheeling Hospital. They are happy to have me, it seems. At times, when there is a rush of wounded soldiers, the days run into night, with little time to rest. I spend as much time as possible seeing to James's needs and helping with his therapy. He is healing from his burns quite well and asks that I send you each a fond greeting from him .

Have you heard from Fin yet? I find myself in constant prayer for him, wondering where he is and how he fares. I endeavor daily to trust more fully in the faithfulness of our God. All the talk here in Wheeling is about the new state, West Virginia. I must say I agree with much of the talk about it being the right thing to do, but there are still those who are not so agreeable.

Melinda Jane, how are you holding up? Are the children behaving? I miss your friendship more than I can say. Zander, are you helping where you can? A strong young man like yourself is always needed, with so many men off to war. God will bless your servant's heart for your kindness. Remember to do everything as unto our Savior. Will, are you getting used to wearing a dress? I know you long for your overalls and the farm. Be patient. This is but for a season. Bertie, I hope you have been a big help to Mrs. O'Donell and that you are making friends. Has Coot healed well from his war wound? It is our fondest hope to return to Charleston by February's end. My prayers are ever with you.

Your loving sister — Gus
P.S. I have a big surprise for you when James and I
come home.

"A surprise!" Bertie threw his arms around Melinda Jane's waist. "What kind of surprise do ya suppose it is? Maybe another dog. A pup of my very own. I'd call him Chance, cuz there's a good chance he'd be the best dog in the whole world if I could take him and train him up from a pup."

"Whoa now. Slow down, Bertie." Melinda Jane held him at arm's length. "Don't go trying to figure out what the surprise is. Just might be a possibility of guessing it right, then it wouldn't be a surprise."

"A man can dream if he wants to." Bertie squared his shoulders.

"How 'bout you dream of ways you can make their homecoming a nice one?"

"I don't need a surprise," Will chimed in. "I'm just glad they're finally coming home."

Mrs. O'Donell wrapped a fleshy arm around Will's shoulders. "I couldn't agree with ya mores."

Eleven

FAYETTE COUNTY

The stillness of the woods lent an eerie unrest to the snow-scattered clearing. Snugging his collar against the back of his neck, Fin figured his options. They could keep going, possibly directly into an ambush. Turn and run. Or maybe even-out the playing field a mite.

He pulled his Colt and signaled for the men to follow. Veering off the game trail, he circumvented some fifty yards forward. By providence, he hoped to outnumber the Confederates up ahead and flank them.

There was no hiding the crackle of hooves against the marshy ground strewn with brittle twigs. No matter. Their presence was surely already known.

Noah and Walter dismounted to scout the near side of the path, disappearing into the thick woods.

Moments later, Walter burst out of the brush. Bent over, hands on his knees and chest heaving, he rasped, "Looks like they're on the other side of that trace, Sarge. Couldn't see a one on this side." The words tumbled as he gulped air.

"Where's Corporal Hicks?" Fin scanned the trees.

"Can't say. I lost sight of him."

"Mount up, Private."

Seconds stretched torturously into minutes before Noah strode up from the opposite direction. "We could take them from behind, if they weren't backed up against a ravine. It's too steep to climb and there're rapids below."

Leave it to Noah to cross the trace and scout farther on.

A shot rang out. Then another.

"Looks like we fight right here. Maybe we can push them back to that ravine and force a surrender." Fin dismounted, looping the reins around a young birch. "We're going in, boys." He pulled the carbine out of the scabbard and waited for his men. "You got any idea how many we're looking at?"

Noah shook his head. "They're well hid behind those fallen trees. My guess is anywhere from five to fifteen."

"Ready?" Fin met each man's gaze. The determination and trust he saw in their eyes humbled him.

"You got a word for us, Sarge?" Walter leaned forward like he was waiting for a starting pistol.

A word? *The* Word. Fin closed his eyes and bowed as the words of the psalmist came to him: "My times are in thy hand. Deliver me from the hand of mine enemies, and from them that persecute me. The Lord is my light and my salvation. Whom shall I fear?"

Returning his grave nod, the twelve men walked into the woods. Bodies stooped and sight keen, they anticipated the *whiz* of a Minie ball.

Within minutes, a volley shattered the silence, slicing through the thin line of trees separating them from the trace. The only proper protection this side offered was a boulder and a downed tree. But the tree was enormous—a sanctuary for several soldiers sitting upright.

They hunkered down, trading shots until dusk. As if by some unspoken agreement, the exchange slowed.

Noah crawled through the freezing mud and settled next to Fin. "Mind if I try to talk 'em into a surrender?"

"Hicks, if you really think that flapper of yours can accomplish something besides puttin' a body to sleep, you go right ahead." He grunted, figuring it was good an idea as any at this juncture.

Noah laid down his gun and cupped his hands to his mouth. "Hey Johnny! What say we come to an agreement?" Seconds of silence ticked by, goading the unease that hung in the air. "Did ya hear me? Ya got cotton in yer ears?"

A shot rang out.

Fin shifted, rubbing his shoulder. "I guess that's your answer. You tried."

Hicks wasn't giving up so easily. "Well, we changed our minds anyways," he shouted. "We're not gonna surrender after all."

Fin whirled on him. "What–"

Noah winked and whispered, "Trust me on this."

"What do you mean you're not gonna surrender now?" The voice rang out from the enemy's number. A familiar voice. Fin's stomach flip-flopped.

"Campbell, that you?" Fin yelled, hoping against hope that he was wrong. He wanted to be wrong in the worst way.

"Dabney?"

He wasn't wrong.

His breath hissed through gritted teeth, rising in a vaporous puff. It vanished in the chilly air like the hope he had held close until this minute. He tried to rub away the misery that burned behind his eyes.

"Friend of yours?" Noah hadn't missed a thing.

Fin nodded as a tumble of emotions settled on remorse. He took a breath and yelled, "Jimmy Lee, how you been?"

"It's good to hear your voice, Fin. Too bad it's under these circumstances."

What could he say? He had prayed to never run into Jimmy Lee, and here they were. "Ya ever figure we'd be shootin' at one another instead of some stag or boar?"

"Never would've thought it in a hundred years." The voice paused. "How's the family?"

Just like his old friend. More likely, he wanted to know how Gus was. Always did take a shine to her. Considered himself something of a ladies' man. "I kind of lost them until just recently. Got caught up on the mail, though. They're all doing fine. Mostly in Charleston."

"And Gus? How's she faring? I got a couple of letters from her back in the fall."

"She's up in Wheeling, working at a hospital."

"Do tell."

Silence settled between them for a spell. Fin didn't figure his friend to be any kind of coward, but maybe he would see some sense in a surrender. "This is downright awkward, Jimmy Lee," he hollered. "Maybe you and your boys should just come out of there and surrender to us so's nobody gets hurt."

"I might say the same of you and your boys, Fin."

"You're outnumbered. You'd be wise to throw out your guns." He didn't know about the manpower, but neither did Jimmy Lee—least ways he hoped not.

"Reckon maybe we outnumber you. Guess we'll wait for daylight to see who takes who."

Hang it all. "If that's the way you wanna play it. Truce 'til first light?" Clouds had drifted across the moon, bringing with them an inky-blackness.

"Truce 'til first light." Several moments of silence passed before Jimmy Lee spoke again, his voice hushed. "Good talkin' to you, Fin."

"You too." A bucketful of regret seeped into those words. His friend was clearly in a quandary of his own.

Fin set lookouts in one-hour shifts. Staring into the darkness could drive a man mad. After a while, a body sees all sorts of things that aren't even there. Holding this position would lend itself to a whole day of standoff tomorrow. He had to come up with a plan.

As dawn's first rosy glow touched the darkness and a man could see past his arm, Fin and five others set out to flank the Confederates and attack soundlessly from behind. The rest of his men would return any fire from the other side.

A Rebel lookout hunkered in the snow, his musket propped on a log, its barrel aimed at the Federal line. He rubbed his eyes before scanning the trace both directions. In the span of a gasp, Fin struck the soldier's head with the butt of his carbine and the man slumped, his gun striking the ground. Fin winced, anticipating the blast of a discharge.

Silence.

That was too close.

A muffled groan, somewhere to his left, caught his attention. The creak of a hammer froze his movement. An instant later, Fin felt the pressure of a gun barrel to his back.

"I never wanted it to come to this, Fin." Jimmy Lee's familiar drawl rumbled with emotion.

Suddenly a shot rang out, then another. Jimmy Lee shoved him away from the path, jabbing his ribs with the pistol. "Keep moving," he growled.

Fin scanned the trees as he stumbled forward, hoping to glimpse one of his men. The tempo of fire increased until there was a constant exchange across the trace. "What are you doing with me, Jimmy Lee?"

"You're my prisoner, ya idiot. I'm gonna tie you up to this tree, then get back to what I'm s'posed to be doing."

"Like heck you are!" Fin had not figured on this twist of circumstance. The meanest, ugliest scowl he had ever seen masked his friend's face.

"Shut yer bone box, or I'll have to shoot ya!"

"You'd up and shoot me? We've known each other since diapers."

"Of course I'll shoot ya. Maybe not in the head or chest, but I'll shoot ya just the same!" He nudged Fin closer to the horses.

"I see ol' Midnight is doing all right." Fin tipped his head toward the black gelding.

"Yeah. I reckon he's the best friend I got. Now, anyways." Jimmy Lee glanced away to draw a length of rope from his saddle.

Fin seized his chance. He slapped the gun from his friend's hand and drove his fist into his gut. He turned to run, but jerked back like a fish on a line when Jimmy Lee grabbed the back of his coat. The force spun him around and an iron fist landed a blow to his jaw that sent the trees racing by. He reeled as pain blurred his vision and the ground threatened to erupt. *So this is the way it's gonna be!* When Jimmy Lee bent to pick up his gun, Fin threw his full weight into him. Locking him in a bear hug, he squeezed for all he was worth. Maybe the fool would pass out from lack of air.

They staggered away from the horses, slipping over the slush-covered leaves until Jimmy Lee twisted and hurled himself to the ground. Fin's back smacked the hard earth with the crushing weight of both men, knocking loose his wind and his grip.

Breathe!

He rolled to his side, at last filling his lungs with air.

Jimmy Lee rose up on his knees like an enraged bear, taking another shot at Fin's jaw. But Fin dodged the blow, and that fist crashed into the frosty ground, igniting a string of curse words.

Fin gripped a boulder, clawing his way upright. He jabbed a boot into the Rebel's midsection. Jimmy Lee grunted, his breath an audible rush.

Fin grabbed his arm, yanking him up. "Enough of this! Call a surrender."

The pop of gunfire sounded more distant and the acrid sulfur of battle gave way to scents of earth and damp.

"*You* call a surrender!" Jimmy Lee lunged forward, knocking Fin to the ground. Then he dropped to his knees, locking his arms around Fin's neck. "Call a surrender, Dabney. So help me . . ."

Fin's breath stalled. Blackness played at the edges of his vision, and a heaviness gently lured him into a hidden chasm.

Concentrate!

He pushed his arm forward, then thrust his elbow back, connecting with Jimmy Lee's ribs. The Rebel cried out, loosening the strangle hold just enough. Fin wrenched the arms away. Never had air been so precious. He crawled like a madman, slipping and clutching at the frozen ground, lunging away from Jimmy Lee's grasp. He stood at last.

Just six feet between them, they circled, facing each other like two cougars—each huffing, gasping for wind. And each figuring their next move.

A distant roar vied for his attention, but Fin focused on the man opposing him. The man he loved like a brother, but was battling with every ounce of strength. He swiped the stinging sweat from his eye, smearing fresh blood across his face and into his hair.

He would try again. He had to talk sense into him. "Jimmy Lee, I think—"

With a growl to rival a grizzly, Jimmy Lee slammed into him, sending both of them through the air. They crashed to the ground, skidding several feet through the icy mud. They rolled and pummeled one another in a tangle of arms and legs, gaining momentum across the sloping terrain.

Fin squinted against the bark and rocks pelting his face. Straining, he struggled to keep his head from striking the granite chunks that dotted the landscape. Still hurtling end over end, he threw back his head to butt his opponent's face, but gagged. Choking on blood, he spat a crimson stream that splattered across Jimmy Lee's face.

The next instant, they were plummeting in free fall.

No sounds of war. Rushing air. A muffled thud.

Blackness.

Noah pulled up hard on the reins, and his horse skidded to a halt. "It's no use, they got just enough of a head start. Wish I'd known there was only six. We could've taken 'em real quick-like in the beginning." He pulled his horse around and took a head count. All accounted for, except Fischer and Dabney. "We're gonna head on back to look for our own."

Things had not gone quite as they had hoped. After an hour-long exchange of fire, the Rebels went quiet. Five minutes later, the sound of hooves told him they had made a break for it. What was there to do but mount up and chase after?

"Spread out through these trees some as we make our way back, boys. Mayhap we'll come across some stragglers."

"You thinking there's more than just those that got away?" A gangly private from Cincinnati, known as "Stump" cocked his head to one side in question.

"No way of knowin'."

"Last I saw of the Sarge, he was wrestling one of them boys on the ground," Walter said.

"Any of you see what happened to Fischer?" Noah scanned their faces. When no one answered, he kicked his horse into a gallop, heading back down the trace.

They soon discovered a groggy Fischer slumped against a tree, cradling his head. A knife lay on the ground beside him, and blood stained the length of his sleeve.

"What happened here?" Noah dismounted. Pulling his haversack from the saddle, he squatted next to the wounded man.

"I definitely got the long end of that stick." He pointed to a prone body several feet away. "My first knife fight ever." His face went slack. "I think he's dead."

Noah worked to free Fischer's arm from his shirt. "Better him than you, soldier."

"He's dead all right," Stump said, checking the fallen Rebel.

"Hey Walter, you come over here and tend to Fischer while we hunt for the Sarge." Noah stood and checked his pistol. "Fan out. If you find him, fire a shot."

The minutes flowed into a full hour as the men looked for their leader. Noah found signs of a scuffle that seemed to continue down a hill and abruptly end at a sheer drop-off to the river below. Far below.

He hollered 'til his voice went croaky, pausing to listen from time to time.

Benzinger stepped up beside him, his face a solemn mask. "That's enough of a fall to kill a man. And if it didn't, those rapids would've swept him clean away." He pulled off his forage cap, pressing it to his chest. "He was a good man, the Sarge."

"We'll follow the river up a ways best we can. Mayhap he caught a log or rock or such." Noah turned away from the cliff. He sure had a hankerin' for a chaw just now. Anything to lighten the lead weight lodged in his belly. "Let's go!" *Lord Almighty, take care of Fin wherever he turned up. And please, let him be alive.*

PART TWO

Thou calledst in trouble, and I delivered thee.
I answered thee in the secret place of thunder.
I proved thee at the waters of Meribah.

Psalm 81:7

Twelve

T hunder rolled somewhere in the crushing darkness. Fin willed his eyes to open and his muscles to respond. *Concentrate.* His eyelids refused the efforts, so he tried to speak. A pathetic, child-like groan answered—a weak challenge to the thunder. Then gray waves drew him, sucking him back into a blissful unconsciousness.

His eyes snapped open. *Where am I?* Fin rolled to his side and gasped. Another inch and he would careen into the rushing water below. He rolled the opposite way, coming within inches of Jimmy Lee's blood-smeared face.

The fight.

He looked up through tangled brambles. They had plunged over that cliff—that was it. He watched the rise and fall of his friend's chest. *Thank you, Lord.*

Fin attempted to pull himself into a sitting position. Daggers shot from his foot to his knee. He half-expected his leg to be twisted at an unnatural angle, but it looked normal. Maybe it wasn't broken.

They had landed on a sandy ledge, no more than three feet wide and barely the length of a man. Once Jimmy Lee regained consciousness, they'd have to choreograph their movements.

Minutes or hours passed. He drifted in and out of sleep until a soft groan jerked him from his lethargy. His friend's dark eyes fluttered.

"Don't even think about trying to move." Fin's voice rasped, and he swallowed what little saliva he could work-up. "We're stuck on a soft ledge here and there's nowhere to go but down. Into the river." He gripped Jimmy Lee's arm. "You all right? Can you feel all your limbs?"

"Of all the stupid things ya ever done, Fin Dabney. This is the stupidest." He grimaced, contorting his blood spattered face into a ghoulish mask.

"Stupid? Stupid? You expected I was just gonna give myself up?"

"What I didn't expect was to ever be in a position to have to expect anything." Jimmy Lee raised his head and flinched. "One wallop of a headache." He turned his head gingerly, taking in the surroundings.

"Can't neither of us move much without the other." A rattle of branches drew Fin's gaze into the thicket above. A grackle hopped from one branch to another. The bright yellow eyes seemed to surmise his predicament, taunting him with a shake of its feathered head.

"Is there room for us to sit up?" Jimmy Lee rolled his head, trying to see over him.

"Long as we do it at the same time I reckon. But real slow-like."

"Ya wanna sit up or just lay still for now?"

"We can just lay here. Maybe 'til my head stops pounding."

"Yeah, mine too."

Obscured by the torrent below, music rode the cool mist, its tones and rhythm almost swallowed by the angry roar. Fin had always marveled at this mystery. He listened harder for the mesmerizing melody within the thunderous rush of water as it struck rock and tree and earth.

The screech of a hawk broke his concentration, and Fin's thoughts reluctantly slid back to his dilemma. "I wonder if they came looking for us? Appears it's been at least a couple of hours, near as I can figure."

"How many boys did you have up there?" Jimmy Lee ventured.

"Twelve. You?"

"Seven besides me."

Fin thought back to his goodbyes when Jimmy Lee took off to join up. The ol' boy was all palaver and so full of himself. "Was it everything you thought it would be? You know—when you signed on?"

His wry laughter answered the question before he spoke. "I wanted to be a hero. I was a fool." He took in a long breath and let it gush back out. "There's nothing heroic about takin' a man's life, feelin' his blood on your hands—the . . . the stickiness. Ya can't just wipe it off. Ya gotta wash it off. And I never been so cold in all my born days."

"I'll acknowledge the corn." The truth was not pretty, but truth it was, nonetheless. "I'd give just about anything to turn the clock back. I'd turn it back to before my mama died. Life was so innocent then, ya know? Seems this entire war has brought with it a waterfall of misery."

"I was surely surprised to find you'd joined up. But I figured if you ever did, it'd likely be on the Federal side. But I figured your pap wouldn't have it. What made you do it?"

"You want it straight?"

"I do." Jimmy Lee angled his face toward Fin.

"Evil. There is plain evil out there, and I want to stop it."

"That's a mighty broad brush you're paintin' with there, Fin."

"Tiny. The men that killed him were Confederate soldiers. Pure evil. It wasn't war, it was murder of the vilest kind."

"There's wicked men on both sides, brother. We got 'em, you got 'em."

Fin closed his eyes against the sun's rays cutting through the branches. He swallowed. "Pap's gone, died of his sickness. A while later, slave hunters killed Izzy. Hung him by the neck down by his cabin."

The grackle's purple feathers shimmered in the sunlight as it hopped closer to the men, twisting its head to eavesdrop. *How carefree you are.* A sudden wash of comfort stirred words in Fin's memory. "But even the very hairs of your head are all numbered. Fear not therefore, ye are of more value than many sparrows."

"Good to know you still got those verses floatin' around in that head of yours. Ain't no getting around needin' God Almighty with what we're asked to do."

Fin chuckled. "I just pictured the Lord looking down on us this very minute. He's saying, 'What are those two fools doing, layin' there on that ledge with nowhere to go?'" His voice scratched out the words an octave lower.

Jimmy Lee grinned. "Yep." He cleared his voice, then sucked in his bottom lip, his gaze set above. "It's real good to see you, Fin. If we don't figure a way outta this . . . well, there's no one I'd rather die with."

"I've missed your ugly mug, too."

Fin wanted to hug his arms to his chest, but there wasn't room. The cold crept into his muscles. And it would only get worse as the sun dropped lower.

"Where'd you go for training when you first joined up?" He hoped the continued conversation would keep their minds off winter's icy fingers—bound to take them both before morning.

"We trained under James Hamilton just outside of Charleston the first couple of months."

"Hamilton? From over Hawk's Nest way?" Fin never met the man, but the Hamiltons were big landowners and held a good deal of sway in the county.

"The very one. He's a good man. Kinda reminds me of your pap. He trained most of us in the first Kanawha under Colonel Tompkins. Hear tell he's over outside of Mountain Cove now, straddling the fence for all he's worth."

"How ya mean?"

"The man never committed. He's not for North or South. After Wise's retreat, when Tompkins' troops fell-in with the 22nd Virginia, he backed out of the conflict all t . . . together." Jimmy Lee let out a ragged breath that frosted the air.

Shivers rolled over Fin's limbs and claimed his middle, grabbing hold of his jaw. He clamped it tight, trying to control the chatter of his teeth. "M . . . maybe we oughta t . . .try to sit up so we can get warmer. We'll have to do it real careful-like. There's no room to maneuver here."

"All right. You go first s . . .so's you don't roll off the edge." Jimmy Lee lifted his head, trying to see over Fin's chest. "Not m . . .much margin for error, is there?"

"I'll sit up and you b . . .bend your knees so I can s...s...sit where your feet are, then I'll help you." With his arms stretched in front of him, Fin sat up slowly, leaning away from the edge. Turning his legs, he let his feet dangle over the edge. He'd never had a fear of heights, but a bundle of something stirred in his belly. He inched his way back, then Jimmy Lee rolled to his side.

A shower of dirt cascaded somewhere beneath them. A muffled *CREAK* whined like a barn door. That something in Fin's belly grabbed hold of his windpipe and squeezed the air clean out of him.

Jimmy Lee stiffened, eyes round and his mouth stretched tight.

In a gravelly *WOOSH*, the ledge gave way. Fin reached for his friend and found nothing. He plummeted, encased in an earthen waterfall. Rocks and sand scoured his body until he plunged into the roiling darkness below.

Frigid water snatched his breath away, calling every muscle in his body into frantic flailing. He kicked hard, ignoring the sharp pain assaulting his ankle. Gulping a mouth full of air, he went under again.

The wet wool uniform dragged him deeper. He pulled wildly against the water, surfacing again, straining to get a glimpse of his friend. Something snagged his coat, and he twisted, expecting a branch. Jimmy Lee gripped his sleeve, determination coloring his eyes as he drew a deep breath before the water pulled him under. Fin clutched his collar, but his hand refused to cooperate. Numbed muscles ignored his commands. He tried again, willing the stiff fingers to grip the fabric.

Long, agonizing seconds passed before Jimmy Lee's face exploded through the water. Clinging to one another, they spun through the churning water, striking rock after rock as if they were fallen leaves in the autumn rains.

At last, Fin looped his arm over a snow-covered limb, halting their journey downriver. Anchored by his elbow, he pulled Jimmy Lee closer. "Grab the branch!" His words ripped away with the torrent.

Jimmy Lee reached his free hand toward the branch. The purple fingers stirred, brushing against the bark again and again, unable to grab hold. He sputtered as water lapped over his face, repeatedly washing a crimson gash above one eye.

Resignation sparked in his friend's eyes.

"No!" The acrid taste of fear surged into Fin's throat. *Please, God!* He willed his numb, claw-like grip on his friend to hold.

In an instant, Jimmy Lee disappeared.

The current's pull threatened to snatched him from Fin's grasp. Fin looked up, choking on a surge of water. "Help me!" His desperate scream drifted into a silver sky.

Jimmy Lee resurfaced, choking, spewing water. Relief surged. Fin still had him.

He smiled that dopey smile that used to infuriate Fin.

Fin smiled back.

Like a nightmare that traps you into thinking it's real, Jimmy Lee washed away. His head bobbed in the white foam until Fin lost sight of him.

Fin's hand had betrayed him. The hand he assumed to be at the end of his arm, neither of which he could feel. He stared down stream, the numbness of his body a sharp contrast to the agony of his soul.

He could pull his arm from the limb and float down with Jimmy Lee. If ever he had courted despair, it was now—it hailed him from a place of hopelessness, urging him to give in.

"Was this Your way of helping?" He glared into the sky, finding it stark and hostile.

When thou passest through the waters, I will be with thee, and through the rivers, they shall not overflow thee.

The unbidden words enveloped his spirit like a warm blanket. He was not alone.

With renewed determination, Fin pulled his free hand up to grasp the limb, which was wedged precariously between two boulders. Working his wooden fingers and an unyielding elbow, like a giant inchworm, he made his way toward shore, praying all the while the limb would hold steady.

Darkness had pushed away the twilight when at last he found himself face down in frozen riverbank mud. The river's angry laughter grew softer and an indomitable exhaustion pulled at his eyelids.

Fin jerked awake. He scoured his surroundings. How long had he slept? A dusting of snow covered everything but the rushing water.

His stomach lurched and gave up a frothy slime. He heaved again and again until his stomach was empty. Dragging his mouth across a rigid sleeve, he forced his head upright. Moonlight glistened on the fresh snow, brightening the riverbank and the surrounding foliage.

He thought to scramble up the sloping bank, grabbing hold of the roots and thickets to pull himself along, but fire shot up his calf, and his feet and hands would not obey.

He rolled onto his back discovering a star-strewn canopy, stunned by his own smallness. *You're still here, aren't you, Lord? Just You and me?* He choked back a sob at the image emblazoned in his mind. Jimmy Lee, torn from his grip, head riding the angry white swirls as the merciless torrent carried him farther and farther downriver. Folks lose their lives to that river every year. It was a miracle Fin had survived. A miracle. But the guilt burrowed deeper into his soul by the hour.

He took in a shaky breath. Now. What do I do? I need wisdom. *You said to ask. I'm askin', Lord.* Tucking his knees beneath him, Fin inched his way to the tree line. Painful shards in his ankle strangled his breath with every movement. He settled with his back against a young willow. Were it not for his ankle, he could jog into the trees and warm himself.

To revive the feeling in his hands, he began thrashing them against his legs and sides like a fledgling fallen from its nest. He worked his good leg at the ankle, back and forth, reminding him of priming a pump. Eventually, the first faraway sensations returned to his extremities—sensations as uncomfortable as welcomed.

Besides his waterlogged uniform and boots, he had his cartridge box and powder horn. Thankfully, Pap's Bible was still snugly buttoned into his jacket pocket. His cap box hung lopsided and empty, much as he felt at the moment.

He fingered his thigh, expecting to find his knife, but the sheath was empty. He hissed a long sigh, remembering his matches and survival kit were safe and dry with Duke—a lot of good they'd do him there.

Next, he pulled his cartridge box around. The leather-covered tin box was undamaged, and though undaunted by rain, the river was no match for it. Every cartridge was soaked. But the musket tool—now that might come in handy.

Daring to hope, he fingered the powder horn. Surely the cork was tight enough to keep the gunpowder dry. He worked the leather strap over his head. Grasping the cap in his teeth, he tugged on the horn, carelessly spilling a bit of the precious black powder on the ground. *Stupid!*

If the powder was dry, he had only to gather fuel for a fire and strike a spark. He crawled a little farther and scraped snow from the ground. Shoveling with numb hands, he gathered up bits of bark and dried pine needles until a sufficient mound rose from the tiny clearing. A mound he thought to call Little Mount Hope, for it was that and so much more if he could just get a fire going.

He remembered scratching and digging at dirt and rocks as a boy. He would work a spot to serve as his own make-believe farm, complete with carved horses, cows, and pigs. It was a lifetime ago.

How he cherished the innocence and safety of his growing-up years—before death sullied his carefree life, taking from him those he cherished most.

Melinda Jane. She floated in and out of his thoughts like cotton-wood seeds on the late spring breeze. Did he cherish her? He did. Beyond a doubt, he did. And more than he wanted a fire, he wished he'd had the courage to tell her before he left. *Another bucket of regret.*

The activity got his blood pumping, prompting uncontrollable shivers. They started in his middle and made their way to his jaw. He clamped his teeth together to stop the sudden chattering. The tingling in his hands and feet had turned downright painful, but common sense told him that was better than the numbness.

He flexed his hands for several minutes, welcoming the return of feeling. Scooting on his bottom and crawling, he raked larger twigs, dead branches, and what brambles he could loosen into a pile to add to the fire.

Fin squinted, adjusting his eye to the dimming light as the moon hid behind a tree. He had collected a few different kinds of rocks. Surely one would work for the musket tool to strike a spark. Fluffing a promising mound of moss nestled among pinecones, he planned out the order he would add the tinder and which rock he would try first.

He pulled the tap from the powder horn. His hand shook so violently that he had to steady it with the other one, scattering a bit more powder over the moss than intended. Rock in one hand and musket tool in the other, he began striking the rock with the metal tool. Over and over. Trial and error. If not that rock, then maybe the next.

As much as his chattering teeth would allow, he bowed his head and prayed aloud. "Almighty Father, I don't know what You're doing here, but I know You're here with me 'cause that was Your promise. If I'm to die here and now. So be it. But if not, I'm asking You to intervene here and start this fire. In the name of Jesus, Your Son. Amen."

He picked up the last rock. Smoother than the rest, he treated it like flint and willed his trembling fingers to work one more time.

A spark.

But it missed the gunpowder. He held his breath and struck it again, harder.

WHOOSH. The force knocked him back, singing his eyebrows. Blinking away the spots before his eyes, he scrambled to add the tinder. "Thank You. Thank You." His quivering voice sounded frail and girlish, but no matter. Before long, the fire burned on its own accord, lapping up the fuel, heralding the promise of warmth. The promise of survival.

Thirteen

CHARLESTON

Melinda Jane looked up from her music as the last chord resonated. She smiled at the congregation, then shifted her gaze to Preacher Lambert before stepping from the platform.

A grin peeked through his bushy, dark beard. "Thank you for that lovely solo, Melinda Jane. Now, if you'll all stand for the benediction."

Mrs. O'Donell dabbed her eyes with a hanky and swallowed Melinda Jane in a warm hug. "Just beautiful, lass. Brought tears to me eyes, it did."

"Praise the Lord!" Widow Cox breathed the words reverently, resting a hand on Melinda Jane's arm. A velvet cape draped across her simple Garibaldi dress, with a matching hat angled to eclipse her eyebrows. "Such a lovely voice, my dear. God has surely given you a gift to use for Him."

"Why thank you, Mrs. Cox." She dipped smartly, flashing her brightest smile. A tap on her shoulder made her turn. "Why, hello Mrs. Overby."

"I just wanted to say thank you for blessing us with that wonderful song this morning. It brings my heart such joy, and there seems to be so little of that nowadays." The woman clung to the hand of three-year-old Jerome. He about jerked the poor woman's arm from her socket. She sighed and pursed her lips. "I best get this boy home." She nodded a goodbye and allowed the tike to pull her through the thinning crowd.

Melinda Jane managed a few more polite replies to heartfelt compliments while keeping an eye on Bertie. He was engaged in some animated story-telling with two other boys.

A man's voice close to her ear startled her. "I wonder if we might spend a bit of time practicing, Miss Minard. I've already checked with Brother Lambert, and he's given his permission for us to stay on here for a while and use the piano."

She looked into the hazel eyes of Anderson Price. "Well, I . . . I'm not sure." They could not practice alone, here in the church. It just wouldn't be proper. She turned to Will. The girl stood stiffly, one hand on her hip and her lips drawn in a straight line. "Will, honey, would you—?"

"Don't even ask. I'm goin' straight home."

Well, that was that. Will had made it perfectly clear that she disapproved of Melinda Jane spending time with Anderson Price. *She still holds out hope for me and Fin. Poor girl.* If she was honest, there was so much that Melinda Jane herself didn't understand. Well, she'd just talk Zander into staying with her here at the church for a little while.

"I'll be right back, Anderson. Let me just find Zander." She whirled, searching through the church-goers still milling about. A flash of blond hair caught her attention. Zander looked like a coon caught in a trap, cornered by Maggie and Lola Talbert. She caught his eye and motioned him over. Sheer relief flickered across his face. He made his apologies and pushed past the girls, making a beeline toward Melinda Jane.

"You saved me." Zander flashed a thankful grin. "I owe you one."

Perfect. "Why, yes, I reckon you do. I'd like to cash in on that right now, if you don't mind." She motioned toward Anderson.

"Anderson here would like to practice on a song for the next little while. Would you mind staying here with us?"

"I'll stay. It'll give me an excuse not to walk those Talbert girls home. If they hinted at it anymore, they might as well be ordering me around like a servant. Be back in a minute." Zander did an about-face, crossing the floor with a swagger, right back into that coon trap.

Anderson sidled up next to her and whispered, "The sacrifices a man must make."

Melinda Jane couldn't contain the giggle. "That poor boy." She glanced at the man beside her, admiring the sharp fit of his waistcoat and the shine on his shoes. He surely was easy on the eyes.

Zander sat on the front pew, hunched forward, elbows on his knees. After a time, he leaned back and tipped his hat over his eyes. Melinda Jane finished her second song, and Anderson drew out the final arpeggiated chord.

"You play so beautifully, Anderson. I wish I could play the piano."

"It's not so difficult. Come, I'll show you." He stood, beckoning her to sit on the round stool. When she did, his arms encircled her from behind, to place her hands on the keyboard. "Like this, you see."

Melinda Jane's heart raced as he pressed closer, leaning over one shoulder, guiding each finger to rest on an ivory key.

His low voice brushed her ear. "You're a natural."

She glanced at the snoozing Zander. A lot of good he was as a chaperone. Flutters in her stomach made her squirm. How she longed for arms to hold her—and Anderson's nearness only stirred up that old yearning.

"I reckon we'd best be heading back now, dontcha think, Melinda Jane?" Zander's voice boomed into her blurred senses.

Anderson stiffened and drew back his arms. "I believe that is enough practice today."

She jumped up, embarrassed. Were her feelings painted across her face for all to see? "Yes . . . yes. Quite enough." She grabbed Anderson's hand, pumping it vigorously. "Thank you for playing for me, Anderson." She walked to the pew to retrieve her bag. "Time to go, Zander." Practically marching out the door of the church, she was ten paces ahead of Zander for several yards, until he caught up to her.

"I see why you asked me to stay," he said finally.

"Why, whatever do you mean?" She lifted her chin and quickened her pace.

"He's a smooth one, that Price feller."

She huffed. "Zander Dabney, you just mind your own business, you hear?"

Fourteen

FAYTETTE COUNTY

February 1862

F in gingerly coaxed off his stiff right sock, then edged up the pant leg. He grumbled at the purple mound enveloping his ankle. Probably not broken, but it was mighty sprained. Sucking in a breath, he worked quickly to tug off the other sock.

He had pretty well dried out and thawed his extremities throughout the night as he snoozed and fed the fire. The next step was to make his way up out of this canyon so he could get his bearings. The terrain was steep, and it would be hard going with his injured ankle.

He reached for his Bible, its pages fluffed and swollen. He had taken care to fan it as it dried, hoping to salvage the precious book. The carte de visite of Melinda Jane slid to the ground. He picked it up, rubbing his thumb over the face he loved. How he longed to be with her. He would tell her of the way she rattled his thoughts and claimed his dreams. He would hold her tight, protecting her from the hurts and evil of this world.

But wasn't that what he was doing, in his way—protecting her and his family from evil? The evil that takes a man's property, that decides one human being is worth more than another. The evil that decides who lives and who dies on a whim.

No. He would finish this fight. Then he'd find Melinda Jane—and pray that she had waited for him.

After several minutes of searching, he found a sturdy branch for a crutch and doused the fire with snow. He reckoned the easiest path up from the river and set to it.

Were it spring, he could dig his fingers into the soft ground, but the snow on the frozen ground only hindered his progress. Bracing with every painful movement, he grasped roots, saplings, and brambles, ascending the steep terrain on his knees at a snail's pace.

At last, he found himself smack dab in the middle of a game trail. The arduous climb called on bruised muscles and sheer will, but he managed to follow the trail up to a clearing.

Tall, winter-worn grass lay crushed beneath the flattened snow. Up to twenty deer would bed down here come nightfall. He longed to fall into a heap right here, but he had to keep going.

The game trail switched back and narrowed, turning gravelly. The sun crawled past its zenith, but he would put the remaining hours to good use by getting up off his knees. If only he wasn't so exhausted.

The throbbing in his ankle radiated up the entire length of his leg, setting his teeth on edge. With every step, gravel slipped beneath him. He thought to crawl on his knees once again when the quivering in his thigh worsened. Stabbing, then digging his crutch into the earth, he leaned on it, pulling his bad leg forward, bearing his weight on the staff and his good leg. Stab, dig, pull. Stab, dig, pull. The going was tedious.

Finally, he could see past the trees and over the water. He leaned on the crutch, thinking how good some cool well water would taste just now.

The ground floated closer. Not the ground. It was him!

111

He swung his arm to keep his balance, but succeeded only in batting away the crutch. He saw, more than felt, the harsh earth's whirling armor of nettles and jagged rocks. Stumps. Razor-sharp ice.

Abruptly, it all stopped.

He glimpsed dull, dark eyes. And fur. The image wavered, then vanished in a gossamer haze.

Fifteen

Drawing the knife through the loaf of bread, Melinda Jane surveyed those waiting patiently in line. She placed a thick slice into a grubby hand. The angelic smile she received in return was all she needed in the way of thanks. At least today these folks wouldn't go hungry. There had to be more she could do.

Finally, her eyes found Nettie Penchant near the end of the line, one arm around Olivia's shoulder. An eager Perry jerked on the other arm. She smiled and waved. Nettie looked happier today.

When she had doled out the last drops of soup and only breadcrumbs remained, Mrs. O'Donell set out a basket covered with one of her cheerful linen napkins. Zander set a heavy crock onto the wagon bed, then wielded a wooden spoon.

"What's this?" Melinda Jane bounced a curious look between them.

"A surprise." Mrs. O'Donell slipped off the napkin. "Soap. Your friend, Sarah Young brought this by."

Zander pried the lid off the crock. "She brought this too. Bacon grease. Seems she collected it from one of the army cooks."

The treasured chunks of soap and dollops of grease transformed the day into a regular celebration. Melinda Jane led the folks in song, encouraging the children to sing out real loud and the older ones to join in. She split them into two groups to sing in a round, and the merriment swelled with the results.

Mrs. O'Donell pressed her apron to her eyes. "'A merry heart doeth good like a medicine!' Just look how ya blessed these folks, lass." She chuckled some more, wagging her head and wiping at her rosy cheeks.

Will jumped down from the wagon. "Who would've thought a simple round could wind up in such a mess?"

"Who, indeed!" Melinda Jane pulled the girl close, bumping her with a hip, matching her grin with one of her own.

An echo of thunder crawled across the sky. "We'd best pull out of here if we want to beat the rain," Zander said, pushing the pots up tight against the front of the wagon. He pulled out an oiled tarp. "I figured this might come in handy."

"That's enough singin' for today. You stay warm and dry now," Melinda Jane hollered to the crowd as they dispersed. "Nettie!" She trotted to catch her friend before she left. "You doin' all right?"

"Milo ain't been here 'bouts for some time. Mayhap he found work. Said he's a-tryin' to get on as a smithy with the Army. He's a real hard worker when there's no Devil's brew to be had." The sadness in her eyes sat heavy, but she forced a brave smile. "We be jest fine. Don't you worry none, Miz 'Linda." She rubbed her belly and one side of her lips curved. "He'll come 'round. You'll see."

Melinda Jane hugged her friend. Stooping, she pulled the children to her, planting a kiss atop Olivia's and Perry's heads. She watched as they walked hand in hand to the tiny hovel. How truly blessed she was and how much she wanted to share that blessing. She sighed. *Lord, I just need you to show me what to do.*

The list was taking shape. Melinda Jane jotted down each idea as it popped into her head. Some were not practical, some so simple she was embarrassed to have not thought of them sooner. She turned to Sarah. "How is your list coming?"

Sarah peered at the paper in front of Melinda Jane. "Not as well as yours. I'm stumped. The last thing I came up with was to offer haircuts. Not exactly a necessity. More of a nicety."

"Assuming you mean the giving of haircuts, and not us cutting off our own hair to sell, I think it's a right fine idea." They shared a chuckle. "Go ahead and read your list."

"I'll just read the ones I like, not the silly ones. First, I thought of keeping warm. Maybe we can collect a wagon of coal or wood. I just don't quite know how to go about that."

Melinda Jane clapped. "That's a wonderful idea! We can just take the wagon around town and see who can throw some in to donate for the poor. What else?"

"Well, as for keeping warm, I also thought of seeing if folks would like to donate old quilts."

"Quilts are fine, but seems to me that most folks hang onto them till they're so threadbare there's no warmth left in them anymore." Melinda Jane stood. An idea was just beginning to take shape. "What if we made them? We could just tie 'em so they'd be done real quick-like."

"Ooooo." Sarah stood too, rubbing the palms of her hands together. She crossed the room, one finger in the air. "What if we had the churches compete in a contest to see which church could donate the most quilts—say, in four weeks?" She pressed both hands onto the tabletop, a sly grin sprouting on her face. "We can appeal to the spirit of competition that has set dormant within the confines of those hallowed pews for years."

"I declare! Sarah Young, you are a conniver. I'll talk to Preacher Lambert and see what he thinks." Melinda Jane threw her arms around her friend. "I do believe we've got a good start with these ideas."

"I can keep collecting extra fat from the army mess, too. I just bat my eyes and tell them I'm Captain Young's daughter and they pretty much fall all over themselves to oblige me."

Will stomped into the room, her dramatic entrance cutting their joy short. "That Price feller is here to see you." She did an about-face like a soldier on parade and marched out.

"Me?" Melinda Jane passed a look to Sarah, fully aware of the warmth climbing her neck.

"I told you he's sweet on you." She picked up her cottage cloak. "It's time I got back anyway."

Melinda Jane followed Sarah to the front door, where Anderson waited.

"Good day, Miss Young. Miss Minard." He stood there, hat in hand, not a hair out of place.

"Hello Anderson. I'm just leaving." Sarah turned to Melinda Jane, winked, and placed a kiss beside her cheek. "I'll see you Tuesday." She nodded to Anderson as he held the door for her.

"I didn't expect to see you today, Anderson. Please, come in." Melinda Jane led him into the sitting room. "Can I get you something to drink? Tea, maybe?" Whatever could he want? She smiled politely, practicing the hostess techniques described in Sarah's *Godey's Lady's Book*.

"No, thank you, Melinda Jane. Sit down, won't you?"

She sat in one of the upholstered chairs while he continued standing. "Is something wrong, Anderson?" The lilt in his eyebrows and the way he kept fingering the bill of his derby coaxed a hundred more questions. He positively beamed.

"I've just come from the Kanawha House. Mr. McFarland is opening a room in the back with a piano and a few tables. He's looking for entertainment, and I immediately thought of you." He sat abruptly and grasped her hand. "I . . . I thought, 'How grand it would be to have Melinda Jane Minard standing there, singing for others to enjoy as they ate their meals.' I would accompany you, of course. That is, if you are interested. Mr. McFarland said he would pay one dollar each evening for Friday and Saturday entertainment."

Her breath caught. "My." Then her mind reeled. "That would be two dollars a week. Think of the fabric and food I could buy for the folks at the poorhouse. I could even take baskets down to the shanties by the river."

"I should've known your first thoughts would be of those less fortunate. Always putting others first. One of the many things that endear you to me, Melinda Jane."

She stood, pulling her hand back. "I'm feeling a bit overwhelmed at the minute, Anderson. I'll have to think on this."

He stood, amusement dancing in his eyes. "You do that. In the meantime, I'll round up some songs."

Her feet carried her toward the door in slow motion. *This must be what sleepwalking feels like.*

"Don't bother. I'll see myself out." He leaned forward slightly, then hesitated, as if he had a mind to kiss her cheek. It caught her off guard, and he seemed to realize it. A grin flashed across his cheeks before turning to leave.

Thoughts tumbled in her head like popping corn. Would they enjoy the hymns she loved to sing? What about the songs of the mountain folk she held so dear? Maybe if she learned some Jenny Lind songs—or songs from those Christy Minstrels. Oh, but what if unsavory sorts congregated there? *They'd* want some of them baudy songs she'd heard tell of.

Her mind went to Fin. And she knew why. Hadn't he always been her stabilizing force—a presence in the darkest and brightest times of her life? And here he was—in this moment of tipsy-turvy imaginings, once again, bidding her to settle her thoughts. She envied his strong, quiet ways. An anchor—that's what Fin was for her. Would he ever be that anchor again? Or was she off on a different sort of voyage, one that needed just the wind in her sails to carry her off on her own journey?

Sixteen

Mountain Cove, Virginia

T he dullest of roars swelled excruciatingly to the strongest of thunder. He willed his eyes to open, but his body argued. A sweet voice sang out an old mountain melody. He recognized the tune. The words. Melinda Jane. She was here!

He forced his lips to move. "Melinda Jane." A thick tongue faltered, his voice sounding foreign, a mere croak. He longed to kiss her lips, to quench this unbearable thirst.

The sweet music drew near.

"Don't worry. I'm here." Such a welcomed voice.

She was here. His dear Melinda Jane was here, and he needed her to be here. He willed his eyes to open once again, and through the haze he saw the tawny crown of hair that marked his beloved.

She leaned closer. "You're coming around, aren't you?"

Her lips were so near. More than breath, he wanted her. His arm lifted and his hand touched the back of her head, pressing her full lips to his own. *Ah, heaven.* Was there ever a kiss so sweet?

She pulled back suddenly.

"Melinda Jane?" He pushed the words out.

A stranger's face suspended above him.

"Oh, dear." The young woman's hand covered her mouth. She blinked several times, then cleared her throat. "I bet Melinda Jane is your wife, huh?" The voice was unfamiliar.

"Where am I?" Fin's eyes searched his surroundings, and he attempted to sit up. The thunder returned, the painful barrage racking not just his head, but other body parts.

"You're in the home of George and Nancy Hunt. My brother, Matthew, found you." The young woman bit her bottom lip, glancing nervously around the room. "I'll get Mama." She was off before he could ask her anymore.

Sleep dragged him back into its grip.

Coolness swabbed his temple, stirring him from sweet sleep. Fin opened his eyes to a comely woman, her dark hair salted with years. "Where am I?" he scratched out.

"You just lie quiet. You're safe for now in our home. I'm Nancy Hunt. My eldest, Matthew found you when he was checking his traps." She dipped the cloth in a basin, squeezing out the water. "Appears you got a nasty twist on your ankle and lots of cuts and bruises, but you'll live."

"How . . . how long?"

"You've been sleeping for two days. I bet you're mighty thirsty. Hungry, too." She lifted a porcelain cup to his lips. "Just a little, now."

The cool water soothed his parched throat, prompting a longing for more. She offered him another drink, then straightened. "I'll get you some broth. Start you off easy."

As she turned away, he reached for her arm, but his hand fell short, dropping to his side. Anvils hung from each limb, pinning him to the bed. Corralling his thoughts, he struggled to make sense of all of this.

Gradually, like a train moving coal up a mountain, car by car, his memories lined up. Jimmy Lee, the fight, the fall, the river. He moaned as images flitted through his brain. The river.

He had lost Jimmy Lee.

Mrs. Hunt returned with a cup and saucer. After propping up his head with a rolled blanket, she spooned warm broth into his mouth. His stomach protested, and he turned away.

"We'll try a little more later," she said, setting the cup aside. "Where you from?"

"Over near Gauley Bridge, ma'am. Am I still in Fayette County?" Surely he hadn't wandered so far from the ambush sight.

She nodded. "Mmm. Not far from Mountain Cove." The door banged, and she stood, smiling at a tall man about Fin's age. He had the woman's eyes and dark hair. "This is Matthew. He's the one who found you."

"Looks like you're gonna make it after all. Good to see it. You took a pretty nasty fall. If ya hadn't ended up so close to my trap line, you might still be out there." Matthew Hunt's likable chatter reminded him of Noah.

Fin's thoughts went to the scrimmage just before he and Jimmy Lee went over the edge and into the canyon. No one would find him here. He had to get back to camp. Back to his men.

He cleared his throat. "Much obliged." The man had saved his life. Mere words were lacking. He lifted his leaden hand.

"Happy to help," He met Fin's hand with a firm grasp, grinning through a neatly trimmed mustache and beard.

"The name's Fin Dabney."

"Fin." Matthew nodded and released his hand.

Another young man stood behind Matthew, just as tall, but skinnier. Mrs. Hunt pulled him close. "This is my youngest, John."

"A pleasure." Fin said, receiving a shy nod in return.

"Well, Fin Dabney." Mrs. Hunt removed the rolled blanket from his neck, easing his head back. "Why don't you try to rest a little while I get supper on. Maybe you'd like to try some more broth in a while."

"Thank you, ma'am. I'd like that."

The heaviness in both body and eyelids won out, and he allowed himself to drift again.

Voices and *shushing* woke him from a sound sleep. He listened for a time. If he didn't know better, he would think he was back home with the family around the table. The bantering, scolding, and chattering sounded so familiar, it could've easily been a Dabney family meal.

He sat up, leaning on one elbow, taking in the room. A nightstand, dresser, and washstand pretty much took up what wall space the bed allowed.

The earlier pounding in his head was little more than a tap now. Every movement, however, required serious thought, as his limbs protested each of his suggestions. His uniform sat neatly folded on a nearby chair and the drawers he wore appeared clean and not his own.

When he attempted to swing his legs to the floor, the room tilted and an invisible wildcat clenched its teeth over his lower leg. He flopped back onto the pillow before his stomach heaved, squeezing his eyes closed to stop the spinning room.

Steps padded across the floor. "You oughtn't try to sit up just yet, Mr. Dabney. Your body is weakened. You need to gain your strength back."

The voice was familiar. He opened one eye. Dark eyes, framed by escaped curls, the color of dried grass, shown with compassion. She pulled the covers to his neck, then scurried to the door.

"Mama, he's awake," her voice called from beyond the room.

She returned to his side, fairly floating across the carpet. Her cheeks glowed of health and her smile of kindness, drawing his gaze to the round eyes that beamed with an air of mischief. "I'm Rebecca. We met earlier, but you might not remember." A blush climbed her neck.

"Evening, Mr. Dabney." Mrs. Hunt swept into the room, a tray in her hands.

"Please call me Fin, ma'am."

"All right. Let's see if we can get you on the road to recovery, shall we?" She set the tray on the whatnot table beside the bed and pulled up a chair.

The cup of broth worked wonders toward filling his stomach and at last quenched his thirst. An ornery ache in his shoulder and the scrapes and bruises were nothing to keep him here. His left ankle was another thing entirely. Rainbow colors he'd never seen on a body marred the puffy balloon where his foot connected to his leg. Even if he could tolerate the pain, there would be no getting his boot on for some time.

Mrs. Hunt insisted he stay in bed. Several times a day, she would bring in a basin of green water and dip a rag in it. Wrapping the soggy rag around his ankle, she would scold, "Don't you put any weight on that foot, now. Just let it heal."

She meant well, but when she insisted Fin use the chamber pot in the room instead of hobbling out to the outhouse, he wanted to put his foot down.

Matthew sat in to keep him company in the evenings and over the next few days, Fin became acquainted with the rest of the Hunt family. Twenty-one-year-old Mark was lean like the other boys, but shorter by a couple inches and the spitting image of his brother, Luke, just a year younger. The two could have been twins.

"Where's your pap?" Fin asked one evening, setting up the board for another game of checkers. "I know it's none of my business, so you don't have to tell me."

"The Federals took him as a political prisoner a few months back." Matthew slid a checker and frowned. "Some of our neighbors moved on back to New York, so we're taking care of the Hopping's farm, besides our own."

"New York? Is that where ya'll are from? I knew you weren't from around here."

"Yeah. We've been here a long time, though. Came out to farm and such with a group of others some years back."

"Your mama said your family is neutral in this war. How do you manage that?" Fin moved a checker piece, then gulped down some water. He could not imagine these friendly folks being left unmolested for much longer.

"We've had some trouble with Confederate bushwhackers, but when we tell them our father's in a Union prison, that settles them down. Especially when we give them what they want." Matthew stared down at his clasped hands before pinning Fin with serious eyes. "Just between you and me, I think it's just a matter of time before a band of guerillas comes knocking at our door and forces the four of us boys to fight."

"What're you gonna do when that happens?" Fin admired Matthew. From what little he knew about him, the integrity and hard work ethic of the man had won him over, regardless of what side they would have to support.

"We aim to stay out of this conflict as long as we can. If we're forced to, we'll leave."

"You mean you'll run from conscription if it comes to it?"

"That's exactly what I mean. This isn't our battle, Fin."

Fin scoffed. "That's exactly what my pap used to say. I said it for a while, too. Right up until this ugly war plopped plum in the middle of my farm and took the people I love from me."

He wanted to pace the floor. The old restless spirit inside him blazed to the surface. "I gotta get back to it." He dropped his head against the pillow. "Confound ankle! I gotta start walkin' on this thing. My unit probably has me figured for dead by now."

Matthew stood. "I gotta make sure the barn's locked up. It didn't even have a lock until all this started." He headed for the door. "See ya tomorrow, Fin."

"Goodnight, Matthew." He studied the rough-hewn ceiling boards. The Hunts had a nice place here. Nearest he could tell, the log home set real secluded, tucked back into a thick grove. He longed for sounds of his own brothers and sisters. A knock at the door interrupted his thoughts.

"Come in." He scooted to a sitting position.

The door creaked open, and Rebecca entered with a tray. "I brought you some fresh water and some bread and butter for a snack later if you get hungry." Her smile brightened the room as she set the tray on the table.

"Thank you, Rebecca. That's mighty kind of you."

"Mind if I sit with you for a bit?" She pulled the chair a little closer, smoothing her skirt over her lap as she sat.

She was such a pretty thing. All soft-spoken and feminine. A faint scent of lavender accompanied her into the room and the lantern light bounced off her curls, giving them the appearance of ice crystals.

"I've been meaning to ask you, Fin." She folded her hands in her lap. "Do you like to read?"

"I do. The only thing I have to read is this Bible here." He picked up Pap's Bible from the table. "I reckon it's the most important thing a body would want to read anyway."

"Oh, I agree completely. 'Thy Word is a lamp unto my feet and a light unto my path.'" She grinned. "My mama feels that memorizing the scriptures is important."

"Your mama's a wise woman, Rebecca." He cleared his throat, chasing a strange sensation in his middle. "You'd like my family. My sister, Gus—well, her name is really Augusta, but we just call her Gus—she's a fine woman. Strong willed, but in a good way. Got the thickest, longest bunch of red hair you ever did see and a spray of freckles across her face." He sniggered at a thought. "She used to try to wash them off when she was a girl."

She laughed. "Are you the oldest?"

"I am, but only by a year. After me there's Gus, then there's Zander. He's close to your age, I reckon. That boy can ride a horse like a wild Indian. Never seen anybody with a way with horses like my little brother." Fin closed his eyes, remembering Zander as a boy, riding bareback without a shirt on a hot summer day, blond hair flapping in the wind.

"There's Will. Her name is Willamina, but don't ya be calling her that unless you're game to be on the receiving end of her ire. She's thirteen now. She's like a feisty young filly with all the breeding to make her a fine mare. Well . . . woman. Bertie just turned seven. That boy can talk a snake into a circle and make you laugh till your gut aches."

"I can tell you love your family." She covered his hand with her own, her eyes drawing his.

He smiled, finding her touch a comfort. "I lost them for a time after I found my farm with the barn burned and bushwhackers livin' in the house. Makes a body truly appreciate his family, I tell you that."

"But they're all right?"

"Yeah, I guess so. Letters finally caught up to me. Appears the barn burning was an accident. They're staying in Charleston to be safe."

Gus's letter had said James got badly burned in the fire. She was in Wheeling caring for him and others there. It would likely be awhile before he knew much more. How he missed what he could never get back. Mama, Tiny, Izzy, Pap. Would his family ever be together again? Safe, under the same roof?

"You look sad." Her voice was soft, and her eyes moved to their now intertwined hands.

He sighed. She stood, bending to embrace him. He wrapped his arms around her tenderly at first, then stronger. How good it felt to be held. How right. He closed his eyes, breathing in her scent as the warmth spread through his chest, chasing away the heaviness.

Melinda Jane's feisty grin played before his eyes. He could almost hear her scolding him, slapping his hands away from some wondrous baked concoction of hers.

Rebecca pulled away and sat back down. She smiled. "It's okay. I just felt so sad for you. Like you needed a hug."

Fin coughed and reached for his water glass. He swallowed such a gulp that it brought on a worse coughing spell.

"Were you thinking of Melinda Jane just now?"

He liked to drop the glass. "Why do you say that?" Confusion trumped his embarrassment for a second.

"When Matthew first brought you here, the first couple of days, you called her name. Quite a lot actually. Like you were dreaming about her."

He could feel warmth climb his neck. "She . . . she's a friend."

Rebecca laughed, then stood, retrieving the tray. "If I had a friend that dreamed of me and called my name in his sleep, I'd be inclined to think there was a whole lot more to our relationship than mere friendship."

He was stunned. Stunned into silence—like all those times he wanted to tell Melinda Jane what was truly in his heart for her and nothing would come out.

"Mmm. I've got four brothers, and I know that look." She set the tray down and planted her hands on her hips. *So much like Melinda Jane.*

"You best tell that girl you love her or you have only yourself to blame if she finds someone else to tell her what she wants to hear." She shook her head. "I declare. I'll never understand why God made men so dense about women. You'd sooner fight a war than tell a girl how you feel about her!"

Rebecca picked up the tray and headed for the door. Turning in the threshold, she balanced the tray with one arm. "Goodnight, Fin." She flashed a sympathetic smile and closed the door.

Seventeen

CHARLESTON

"Will!" Melinda Jane hugged the mixing bowl to her side, standing in the kitchen doorway. "Will!"

The girl skidded to a stop in the hallway. "I'm right here, you don't need to holler."

"I still have to frost this cake so I need you to make sure Bertie's got on his Sunday best." She puffed a stray curl from her eyelash. "And make sure his hands and face are clean." Her voice calmed and pleaded with a smile. "Please?"

"It's just Gus and Dr. Hill, why do we all have to get so gussied up?" She stomped toward the sitting room.

"And make sure you wear a Sunday dress, too. And tell Zander I want to see him. We need to leave in a half hour." Melinda Jane found herself talking to an empty hallway. "You hear me?"

"I hear you," echoed from another room.

"My, 'tis a pretty table you've set." Mrs. O'Donell bustled about the kitchen, fussing with the curtains and repositioning the throw rug with her feet. "Excitement is gettin' the best of me, I dare say. I've not seen the lad's face since last spring, ya know." She beamed, drawing herself up like a mother hen. "'Twill be good to have him home again. And Gus, too."

Melinda Jane turned the cake plate as she dabbed at the frosting. "To think, Gus left here to marry the banker to save the farm, but she's comin' home with James." She cast a sly grin toward Mrs. O'Donell. "Now, what do you suppose this surprise is that Gus says she has?"

"I think we both know what it is. I just hope we're not wrong in our suspicions." The woman chuckled.

"Everything has to be perfect." Melinda Jane set the cover on the cake and placed it in the center of the table. "If only Fin were here," she whispered to herself, regretting the sad thought at such a merry time. She said a prayer for him, as she had vowed to do whenever he came to mind.

Fishy odors mixed with smoke from the wood-burning engines, and black smoke belched from the tall stacks of a vessel heading away from the dock. Stewards in neat caps and vests muscled trunks and bags from a four-wheeled cart, stacking them on the boardwalk. Passengers appeared, sending the gangplank bouncing above the lapping water as they filed off.

Melinda Jane stretched her neck, hoping for a glimpse of her dearest friend.

"I see 'em! I see 'em!" Will pointed to the muddle of passengers.

"I see 'em too! Gus!" Bertie fought Melinda Jane's grasp.

"Oh no you don't. Just wait till they reach the boardwalk." She smiled as Gus lifted a gloved hand, waving to her family. Her crisp green gown and matching bonnet set her red hair off like an oil painting, and James stood tall in his Federal uniform. Melinda Jane hadn't felt this happy since before the war. So much had happened in the last year. So, so much.

She held onto Bertie's shoulders until the cross traffic of pedestrians slowed, then let him go. His hands flailing in the air, he hollered and whooped, running for all he was worth, straight into his sister's arms. Gus staggered from the force, but James steadied her, a cane in one hand.

James turned his head, and Melinda Jane swallowed hard. Dear Lord, have mercy. If the scarring was visible from this distance . . . Tears sprang to her eyes.

Will rushed to the couple next, and Melinda Jane could wait no more. She hurried forward and threw her arms around Gus, both of them mingling tears and laughter.

"I have so much to tell you that I couldn't put in a letter," Gus whispered as she held her tight.

Mrs. O'Donell's face blotched red, and she blotted her eyes and nose with not one, but two hankies. "Me dears, me dears. 'Tis so good to have ya home at last!" James wrapped her in a bear hug, a grin lighting his face, the likes of which Melinda Jane had never witnessed. He had always been somewhat sullen to her recollection, but there was a light in his eyes now, and it reflected the sparkle in Gus's own.

Melinda Jane winked at Gus. "Let's get you two home."

Zander lifted his older sister off her feet as he embraced her. "Welcome home, Gus." He extended a hand to James. "You, too, Doc." James pumped his hand, keeping a steady grip on the cane.

He leaned toward Zander. "We'll take a hansom cab." His look dropped to his leg for an instant. "I don't think I can manage the wagon."

"I'll just load your luggage in the wagon so you won't have to worry about it, and we'll meet you back at your place." Zander's lip twitched. "We're just glad to have you back. And I want to say thank you for havin' us here. Don't know what we would've done . . ." He nodded, and his smile melted into a precarious line just before turning to retrieve the luggage.

Melinda Jane set the tea tray on the low parlor table. She passed glasses of milk to the two youngest and teacups to the adults. As an act of grace, Mrs. O'Donell had consented to Coot's presence, and the dog lay with his head resting on Gus's foot.

James had removed the glove of only his right hand and his left leg remained outstretched. Shiny red skin evidenced his badly burned cheek and the area around one eye, but there was no mistaking the knowing look he exchanged with Gus.

Melinda Jane released an impatient breath. "I'm gonna bust if you don't share that surprise with us that you eluded to in your letter. Out with it. Now!"

James slipped his arm behind Gus and squeezed her shoulder. She had never seen such a brilliant smile on her friend's face.

"James and I are married," Gus said, her eyes bouncing to each family member.

"Married?" Will's mouth gaped, and Melinda Jane chuckled as she nudged the girl's chin back into place with one finger.

"Wahoo!" Bertie whooped like an Indian. "That means I've got me another brother. This day just keeps gettin' better." His milk mustache widened as he slapped one knee.

"Saints be praised," Mrs. O'Donell said softly, dabbing at a fresh bout of tears.

Mirth circled the room as Gus's hand reached down, caressing Bertie's sandy mop like an old hound.

"When did this happen, exactly?" Melinda Jane looked from Gus to James. "And who did the askin?" That brought another round of chuckles.

"I asked," James said, his fond gaze meeting Gus's.

"We wanted to wait until we were here with family, but the Sisters at the hospital felt it wouldn't do for me to be doctoring James as was needed unless we were married. So . . ." She beamed at her husband.

"We were married not long after she arrived in November." He pulled his gaze from his bride and scanned the faces in the room. "Not only did God give me a wife—" His throat bobbed. He looked down at his lap for an instant. A quivery smile spread from his mouth to his eyes. "He gave me a second chance. A chance to live the life *He* wants me to live—one tethered to *His* grace instead of my own bitterness."

"Praise the Lord!" Mrs. O'Donell's hands flew up, then smacked her knees. "Sure'n there's a God in heaven who answers the prayers of the lowly." She mopped her face some more, then patted the soggy hankies against her red skin from forehead to neck.

Melinda Jane could not wait to get Gus alone to hear those details she wouldn't share in a letter. Her heart took a little dip. Gus would be sharing her room with James, and their late night girl talks would be no more. How quickly her own selfishness had ousted her joy for her dearest friend. And how disappointed she was in herself just now.

Seeing the newlyweds so happy made her thoughts turn to Fin. He would be happy for the couple. She was sure of it.

As if reading her mind, James spoke up, "Have you heard anything from Fin?"

"We got a letter a while back. I'll go get it for you." Will jumped up and disappeared from the room.

"He's stationed at Gauley Bridge for a time. Sounds like he was worried sick when he found the barn burned and all of us gone." Melinda Jane chewed her lip. She hated to imagine the grief it must've caused him.

"He didn't get our letters?" Gus asked, concern shading her voice.

Zander set his empty glass on the tray. "Sounded like he hadn't gotten any for a long time on account of moving around."

"There's something else we need to talk about." James said, pulling his arm from Gus's shoulder.

Will dropped back onto the floor and handed the letter to Gus. "This is it."

"Thank you, Will."

James cleared his throat, scooting to the edge of his seat. "I want to talk about the barn. The truth of the matter is that I was goaded into a fight with your cousin, Carter. And in the process, he knocked down the lantern that started the fire." He looked down at his hands, his right one caressing the gloved hand.

"I can't tell you how awful I feel about it. I know your pap and Izzy built that barn. Just as soon as this war is over, we'll rebuild it." He glanced at Gus. With a wan smile, she dipped her chin to urge him on. "I'd like to ask your forgiveness."

A mouse's steps would've sounded like a parade in the stillness.

Zander spoke first. "So, not only did Carter lie about you being alive, he was responsible for the barn fire and you getting burned?"

James held up his palm. "Now just a minute. I don't argue that your cousin isn't despicable and a liar, but I do accept partial blame for the fire."

Will huffed angrily, "If it wasn't for Carter, the fire never would've happened."

"It takes two to fight. A man can't fist fight with himself. That's why I'm seeking your forgiveness."

Melinda Jane stood and stepped behind the settee, placing a hand on each of James's shoulders. "Well I, for one, am more than willing to forgive you and say I'm awfully happy you're not dead."

"I forgive you, too," piped Bertie, smearing the milk mustache with his sleeve.

Zander and Will spoke in unison, "So do I."

Melinda Jane squeezed his shoulders. "There you have it, James. And welcome to the family!"

"As of right now, that makes you my favorite brother," Will said, leaning against Zander's leg, jabbing it with her elbow.

"And I'm real glad my favorite sister's home," Zander quipped, glaring back at her.

Gus's laughter rang out as she mussed Bertie's hair. "It is *so* good to be home!"

Eighteen

The family settled in the parlor, the old familiar chatter warming Melinda Jane's heart. Will had once again moved to a bed in the big room downstairs, allowing Gus and James to take his old room. The long flight of steps had been a trial for James, but he insisted on calling it his physiotherapy.

"Zander, I am so proud of the way you've been helping the families who need it." Gus patted his hand. "I've only been gone a short time, but I do believe you have grown some. Maybe even taller than Fin now."

He grinned. "Pap always said I'd be the tallest of his boys."

Bertie stood, a pout taking shape on his freckled face. "Hey now. Pap meant well, but I do believe I will outgrow the both of yous. Ya just gotta give me a little more time, is all."

Zander grabbed him around the middle, lifting his squirming body off the floor. "I'll give you time. Till then, I'm the tallest and I don't wanna see that pouty lip, mister." He turned him over his knee. "Gus, I do believe Melinda Jane's been too easy on this young'un and he's in dire need of a paddlin'."

Bertie squalled, "Nooo! Put me down! Gus, make him put me down."

A knock sounded at the door, inciting a bark from the kitchen.

"I'll get it." Will sprang to her feet, slamming shut the book she'd had her nose in.

Mrs. O'Donell set her teacup on the table, leaning toward Zander. "Maybe it's Mrs. Overby lookin' for ya. She came by this afternoon while you were out."

Will stood in the parlor entry, her eyes drilling into Melinda Jane. "Anderson Price is here to see you." Her voice sang the words, but her lips pressed into a firm line.

Melinda Jane stood and smiled sweetly. "If you'll excuse me a moment." She lifted her hem and glided out of the room.

Finding the door closed, she immediately opened it to a perturbed Anderson standing on the chilly front porch. "I am so sorry, Anderson." She swung the door wide and stepped back. "Please, do come in." *This has got to stop! I'll have another talk with Will.*

"Am I interrupting something important? Will didn't seem to want me to come in."

"You're not interrupting a thing. Come into the parlor and meet more family." She draped his hat and coat over the hall tree. "This way."

Zander stood, offering his seat, then excused himself to see to the horses. Gus, her normal, gracious self, chatted amicably with Anderson, as did James. Will kept silent, but shot bullets with her eyes, while Bertie went to the kitchen to play with Coot.

"Price?" James asked. "Would you be Cyrus Price's boy?"

"Yes, sir." Anderson nodded, pulling on his collar with one finger.

"He's up dealing with the new state congress, isn't he?"

"Yes, sir. He spends most of his time in Wheeling these days." His eyes darted around the room a moment before straightening his vest and brushing make-believe dust from his boot. "Melinda Jane has the most beautiful voice I've ever had the pleasure to hear. She has become quite the favored soloist in church here in Charleston."

"I do believe you're exaggeratin' a mite, Anderson." Melinda Jane battered her eyes, then stopped abruptly when she caught Will's glare. "Anderson is a wonderful pianist."

"She's going to get top billing at the Kanawha House when she sings there." His broad grin matched the pride sparkling in his eyes.

The cat was out of the bag. She had not mentioned a word about the Kanawha House. Not to anyone. The right opportunity just hadn't presented itself. Now here she was.

Four pairs of questioning eyes pinned her to the chair.

"What's this about you singing at the Kanawha House Hotel, Melinda Jane?" Gus's forced smile looked natural, but her eyes were definitely not smiling.

"Since when do they have entertainment there?" James asked, lines forming on his brow.

"I . . . I haven't said yes—least not for sure . . . yet." She stared at intertwined fingers resting in her lap. "It's just me singing, and," she nodded to her right, "and Anderson accompanying me. Just for the folks to listen to in the back room while they eat."

"So folks will just be eating supper, while you entertain them with your singing? That's all?" Gus asked.

"Of course that's all. I can do some church songs and some songs like I sing for the folks down to the poorhouse." She twisted her skirt in her fingers, trying to avoid Will altogether. Leaning closer to Gus, she half-whispered, "It's a *payin'* job. Two dollars a week for two evenings on the weekends."

At last, Gus's smile appeared genuine as she addressed them all. "I think that's just wonderful. More people should get to hear Melinda Jane sing. There's not much around here to keep all us women busy. Why not?"

"'Tis a respectable place, the Kanawha House. I see no harm in the las singin' there. Not like it's a baudy house or somethin'." Mrs. O'Donell winked and patted Melinda Jane's hand.

"James? You're part of this family now. What do you say?" Gus asked. She covered his good hand with her own.

"Why not? I've never known John McFarland to be a shady sort."

Melinda Jane clapped her hands together. "Oh, thank you. I can hardly wait to learn new songs."

"I'm already collecting them for us." Anderson nodded and stood. "I best get home."

She popped up from her seat. "I'll see you out."

A soft knock at the door stirred the quiet. Melinda Jane snapped the Bible closed, setting it on the bedside table. "Come in," she said, snugging the covers up to her chin.

Gus poked her head through the door. "Do you have a minute?"

"Always for you, Gus." She scooted into a sitting position and smiled at the sight before her. Gus's long auburn waves hung freely past her waist, and stray curls escaped a single comb to frame her freckled face. She fairly floated across the floor in the white eyelet wrapper. "You look positively radiant!" Melinda Jane reached for her hands. "Sit with me."

"I'm so sorry we haven't had time for each other yet. I can't tell you how much I miss our talks." Gus tipped her head. "Now is a fine time to catch up. James is already in bed."

"I just gotta say it. Marriage looks real good on you, sister. And that smile you put on the good doctor's face? Why, I never thought I'd see the day."

"I give the Almighty credit for this smile. James walked a long, lonely road before he finally let the Lord have His way. I can't believe how God has turned the sorrow of this past year into joy."

Melinda Jane patted her hands. "Well, joy for you, least ways."

"Oh, I am sorry. I didn't mean to go on so." Gus frowned. "Why don't you tell me what's been happening here. What about this Anderson Price fella?" One side of her mouth lifted, but a smile failed to sprout.

"He's just a real nice gentleman, is all. He treats me like a lady, and he's sincere in helping me with my singing. We have fun together." *But how do you feel about that?* Gus never made a secret of her wish for Fin and Melinda Jane to strike up a courtship one day.

"What about Fin?"

"What *about* Fin?" Melinda Jane threw herself back onto her pillow. "Gus, I gave that man every hint God ever designed for a gal to show her feelin's. Every time I opened wide the door, your brother would run the other way!"

"Oh honey, I know he's a little thick when it comes to women, but you just gotta give him time." Gus smoothed her tawny curls. Her sad smile touched Melinda Jane's heart but for an instant.

"I've been patient, Gus. You know I've been patient with that boy. I've been waiting nearly ten years for him to notice that I'm not *really* one of his sisters." She sat up again and huffed. "Fin and I are good friends. Next to you, he's my *best* friend, but I'm afraid that's all he's ever gonna see me as." A tear snaked its way down her cheek.

"Do you still love him . . . like God wants a woman to love a man?" Gus's expectant gaze held steady, pinning Melinda Jane's heart to the truth.

She sat up again. "You know I do, Gus. I'd marry him tomorrow if he'd only ask. But he'll not voice his intentions toward me—not even in a letter. I reckon it's just a childhood crush that's gone on way too long." She wiped her wet face and sniffed. "Why pine for a man who doesn't return my affections? I'm not gettin' any younger, ya know."

"But, honey, he's off fighting in the war. He's got a whole lot else on his plate right now. Can't you give him a little more time?"

"If he was to send me a letter of intention, I'd wait till this wretched war ends. But, like I said. He just doesn't feel the same way I do . . . did."

Gus stood, schooling a look of disappointment. "I'll let you get to sleep, honey. See you tomorrow." She dropped a kiss on her head and floated out of the room, pulling the door shut with a soft click.

Melinda Jane twisted in her covers, then pulled at her nightgown to free up her legs. She reached for the tattered doll that stood guard by night on the bedside table and dozed in her bed by day. The doll mama made for her fifth birthday, with its faded black face and hands in a once-pink calico skirt. It was a beautiful reminder of who she was and where she came from and what was most important in this life. Hugging it to her neck, she stared at the ceiling and said the Lord's prayer in her head.

She lowered the wick on the lantern, yearning for the weariness that crept upon a body just before sleep. Flipping to her stomach, she pounded and fluffed her pillow.

As she prayed for the family and thanked God for Gus's happiness, she asked God to watch over Fin, like she always did.

She choked on a sob. It seized her throat with such force she lifted her head to catch a breath. *Why don't you love me, Fin? Have I done something wrong?* If all she felt for him was a childhood crush, too long held, why did her heart ache so?

Nineteen

FAYETTE COUNTY

F in hobbled across the yard, leaning his weight on the makeshift crutch. The swelling in his ankle was down somewhat, but even after two weeks, attempts to walk normal snatched his breath away.

If he didn't make it back to camp, the Army would take him for a deserter. By now, though, more likely they thought him dead. He could not have asked for a better family to tend to his needs these past weeks—except maybe his own. Spending time with the Hunt boys and their sister brought back some cherished recollections of his own family.

He stood on the porch of the large cabin, breathing in the crisp air, marveling at the rate new snow filled in his footprints. Far as he could see, the heavy, cottony clouds met with the white horizon in a seamless union, wrapping all of nature in a blanket of silence. He pined for the farm, then remembered the barn's ugly ruins. His pap loved that barn. It was as much the heart of the Dabney family as the kitchen.

Fin leaned on the railing until the cold air seeped into his hands. Feeling pretty useless, not being able to get out of the house and help with chores, the Hunts had allowed him to work on their tack. The fashioning of a couple of studded bridles helped ease his guilt for being a burden to the family. He still hadn't written any letters as to his whereabouts since no one had ventured into town, but that was about to change.

Mark and Luke, sons two and three, were heading in to the post office tomorrow, and Fin had two letters to write. One to Colonel Moor and one to Melinda Jane. Rebecca left the paper and envelopes on the nightstand a week ago, but as he was prone to do, he had put it off. But he best get to it.

Working his way through the front room, Fin stopped to admire an elaborately framed portrait. Two, maybe three-years-old, the picture of the Hunt family served as a reminder. This war had altered their lives, too, like his own family's. Few folks in these parts managed to avoid its awful touch in some way.

He tried to imagine his pap in prison instead of dead. A fierce protection sparked and anger stirred at the idea. That spark was just what he needed to pull him from the brink of this depression weighing him down. He would pray for healing, write those letters, and get on out of here as soon as he possibly could.

The letter to Colonel Moor was short and to the point. If only he could do the same with Melinda Jane's. He'd prefer a pencil instead of a pen, but the ink and quill was what he was given.

He closed his eyes, pretending she was sitting right there in the room with him. That was no good. *Lord, I may sound a fool, but I need your help here.* He dipped the pen. "Dear Melinda Jane." *No. I should've written "My Dearest Melinda Jane."* Because she was his dearest. But he had already written the salutation.

Several inkblots, a handful of doubts, and a bucket of regrets later, he finally sealed the envelope. He addressed it to the Charleston address as best he could remember.

Two weeks later, Fin found himself with Matthew and Mark heading toward Mountain Cove on a winding trace. His spine relaxed as he rode the borrowed gelding. It felt good to be in the saddle again. Was Noah taking good care of Duke?

"I appreciate this friend of yours being willing to help me get back to my unit."

"He's happy to do it," Matthew said, twisting in the saddle. "I wanna thank you for the leather work you did for us. You do fine work."

"Don't seem so much like work when you're laid up, fixin' to go stir crazy."

They rode in comfortable silence for a time until freezing drizzle started pelting their hats.

"We're nearly there," Mark hollered, ducking his head against the onslaught. "What say we pick up the pace?"

"Let's." Matthew leaned forward, urging his horse into a gallop, and the others followed.

Halting at a nice-sized barn, Matthew dismounted and slid open a tall, railed door. He motioned for the other two to enter, then followed with his own horse. "Just tie the horses to that board. We'll throw them some hay. There's a barrel of water over there."

"Must be pretty good friends of yours if they don't mind you making yourself to home." Fin looped the reins over the stall rail.

"Folks around here are pretty close-knit. That's one of the reasons there's been such heartache with this war. One family and all their kin takes a side, and the family next door and all their kin take the other. Draws a line right down the middle of the church congregation." Matthew slashed through the air with his arm. "Union on the left. Confederate on the right. And let me tell you—ne'er the twain shall meet. Folks like us are barely tolerated."

"Is that why you had me wear your clothes instead of my uniform? Afraid I won't make it out of Mountain Cove alive?" Fin joked, but he knew it was no laughing matter.

"Don't you worry about a thing. James will see you safely to your unit."

The rain let up some, turning more liquid than ice as they ducked under cover of the wide porch. The two-story clapboard house reminded him of his own, back in Gauley. Before they could shake the rain from their hats, the door swung wide and a sandy-headed man of medium build ushered them in. "Come in boys. Looks like a warm fire is just what you need. Did you put the horses up?"

"Yes, sir. Thank you." Matthew shook the man's hand. "This is the stranger I was telling you about, James."

Fin felt a little like the fatted calf for a minute as the man looked him over. Fin offered his hand. "Sergeant Fin Dabney, sir. I was separated from my unit."

"Pleased to meet you, Mr. Dabney. The name's James Hamilton. I'll leave off your military rank for now. It's safer that way."

"Wait. Did you say James Hamilton?" Fin remembered Jimmy Lee talking about the man.

"The very one."

"I . . . ran across my old friend, Jimmy Lee Campbell, with the Mountain Cove Guards. Said you trained men for the Confederacy up near Charleston." Feeling somewhat perturbed all the sudden, Fin didn't try to hide his confusion.

"Why don't you boys come sit by the fire and warm up. I'll get you some coffee."

Fin pulled on Matthew's coat sleeve. "I thought this man was a Union sympathizer. Is this some sort of setup?" His knees went weak as a rock settled in the belly.

"No, Fin. Just listen to the man. He'll explain himself." Matthew sat and motioned for Fin to do the same.

Here he was—no gun, no horse of his own, wearing borrowed civilian duds—possibly surrounded by Rebels. Feeling like three kinds of a fool, he took stock of the furniture and weapons within reach. Aside from the poker and coal shovel beside the parlor stove, there wasn't much he could make use of.

"Here we go, gentlemen." Mr. Hamilton set a tray on a low table and handed each man a steaming clay mug of coffee. "You boys sit long enough to warm yourselves, then I bet you can make it back home before dark." He took a sip, letting out a low whistle. "Careful, it's a mite hot."

"We're much obliged, James. Fin here, he's a good sort." Matthew grinned at Fin, nudging his arm.

"Yes, uh . . . Mr. Hamilton. Thank you for the coffee," Fin said, still taking in the room details. Exits included.

"Boy, you look like a rabbit in a snare. Let me set your mind at ease some. I did not exactly train Confederate Army men, per say, I trained militia and other boys for Colonel Tompkins from Gauley Mount. Once the militia officially became tied into the 22nd Virginia Regiment, I bowed out. And not without some consequences, I might add." He set his coffee down and pulled a tobacco pouch from his coat pocket and a pipe from his vest.

"What kind of consequences?" Fin asked, intrigued by the man's story.

"You hear of the alien enemy act?" Fin nodded as the man pinched tobacco and deposited it into the bowl of his pipe. "Well first, the Confederacy is sending marshals to arrest you if you don't swear allegiance to the Old Dominion or get out in forty days."

He packed the bowl with a finger, before adding more tobacco. "Then the Federals got on board and it seemed private citizens had to leave their home or swear allegiance to one side or the other."

He pressed once more, then struck a match, holding it to the bowl, puffing on the stem with a scowl. Satisfied with the draw, he smiled at Fin, the crinkle of his eyes reminding Fin of Ol' Izzy for a minute—the singular happiest man he had ever known.

"Not wanting to take sides necessarily, mind you, wasn't easy. I've had Confederates warring across my lane, and Union soldiers camped out on my front lawn. To Union officers, I was a man yet to declare my loyalty—and to the Confederates, I was a dis-loyalist who dealt with the enemy.

"Long about last October, I finally swore an oath to the United States." He puffed a few of times. "Mind you, if I lived up north or way east of Charleston, that might've settled all my problems. But since my land straddles the James River and Kanawha Turnpike, I'm in a sensitive predicament—the way this area keeps changing hands." He leaned forward, his eyes sagging as he took the pipe from his mouth. "I hear there's been nearly eighty civilians taken prisoners by both sides just from this county."

Fin caught Matthew's eye. "Sounds like it's only a matter of time for your family. For you and your brothers."

"I've accepted that, but I don't think my mama will."

"We trust in the Lord and don't lean on our own understanding." James addressed Matthew and Mark. "Isn't that right, boys?"

"Yes, sir."

"Well, if you boys are warmed through, it's best you get back to your mama before it gets any later. You give her my blessings, you hear. Could be your daddy will be home before too much longer. I hear tell they're releasing some of the political prisoners."

"I sure do hope you're right," Mark said, standing.

"Take your extra horse back with you, I've got one for Mr. Dabney, here." James turned to Fin. "We'll head out first thing in the morning."

Fin nodded, looking at the Hunt boys for the last time. "I can't hardly tell you how appreciative I am for all you've done for me.

147

If you ever need anything, you can find me at Gauley Bridge with the Twenty-eighth, or with Colonel Lightburn." He extended his hand and Matthew pulled him into an embrace.

"You keep yourself alive, you hear?" Matthew nodded, and Mark clipped Fin on the shoulder.

Fin decided then and there that just as soon as this ugly war was over, he would make his way back here for a visit.

Twenty

CHARLESTON

March, 1862

Melinda Jane waved hello, straightening her bonnet as the wheels ground to a stop. An odd little man gimped toward the wagon at an impressive clip, flogging the air with a crushed bowler. She returned the greeting. "Morning Mr. Howard. How ya gettin' on?"

"Well sakes alive, if it isn't my favorite folks! Come to ease this day's unpleasantries?" His grin showed more space than teeth as he wiped his hands down the front of his filthy britches and squinted. "Well, I'll be! If it ain't the doc! Mighty fine to see ya again, Doctor Hill."

"Good to be back, Mr. Howard." James gingerly climbed from the buckboard seat, unsuccessfully hiding a grimace of pain.

"Well, uh . . ." The man growled, started to spit, but swallowed instead. "We appreciate yer sacrifice. Indeed, we do, sir." His head bobbed, fingers mangling the old hat against his chest.

"Thank you, Mr. Howard." James retrieved his medical bag while Will started wrestling crates of food and other donations to the rear of the wagon bed. "Anyone particular I might take a look at today?"

Melinda Jane interrupted, "I can take you to check on Nettie. I brought her some winter carrots from Mrs. Overby's root cellar. Gotta keep her and that baby healthy."

James smiled, putting a hand on her shoulder. "Lead the way."

Gus began sorting clothing and dry goods into piles. "Will and I will get to handing out the food and donations." Folks meandered toward the wagon, many with empty tin cans.

"Got any of that bacon grease today?" one lady asked, flashing a toothless smile.

"We do, indeed." Gus pulled the lid off a clay crock and plunged in a wooden spoon. "Would you like some potatoes and gravy first?"

"Yes'm! Please and thank you." The old lady's eyes lit. She hopped a circle, dancing a jig of sorts. Holding out a tin plate, she lifted her face to the sky. "Good Lord in heaven, thankee for this bounty!"

"Amen!" Gus chuckled as she dished up the offerings.

Melinda Jane slowed, waiting for James as they neared the tiny hovel. She shooed Olivia and Perry out of the room. "Ya'll go fill those bellies now. And tell Will I said to give you a surprise." One of those crates had to have something for them. Quite a few folks were sporting the mufflers and caps she had made. Hopefully Will would find a special treat or toy for the two children.

"Nettie, I hope you'll let Dr. Hill here check you over. Just to make sure that babe is doing all right." She offered a reassuring smile, squeezing her friend's hand as she led her to one of two chairs in the room.

"Oh, that ain't necessary. We's doin' jest fine." Nettie blinked at the doctor and shook her head. "I do appreciate your thoughtfulness though. I surely do."

James removed his hat, dipping his head. "I'm happy to meet you, Nettie. I'd like to check you over a bit. Melinda Jane can stay right here with us." His gentle voice coaxed her as he set his bag on the roughhewn table.

"It's for the baby's sake, Nettie. You want this young'un to be healthy, don't you?" Melinda Jane remembered her friend's words—that Milo wanted this baby gone. Over her dead body! "Milo's gone now. You have nothing to be afraid of."

Nettie sank into the chair, resigned to their suggestions. James pulled the stethoscope from his bag and proceeded with the exam.

"You've no call for concern, Nettie." James glanced around the meager home. "The best thing you can do for that little one is to eat well and stay away from anyone that seems to be doing poorly. It wouldn't do for you to get the influenza or some other disease." James snapped the black bag closed. "Do you have any questions for me?"

The pink blush on the woman's face had faded, and she swiped at her eye with a finger. "I'm real grateful for your concern and your help. I . . . I ain't got nothin' to pay you with."

"You just did, Nettie." He patted her shoulder. "Now, why don't you get out there and get some hot food."

"I've got something special for you, too." Melinda Jane helped her up from the chair. "And bring a cup for bacon grease. I expect you to help me sing today if the weather holds a little longer." She pulled the frayed shawl around her friend's arms, making a mental note to knit her a new one.

Just as Melinda Jane finished the last verse of *Old Folks at Home,* icy drops of rain began pelting the crowd. "I reckon that's that," she said, jumping from the end of the wagon. She touched her palm to gray little faces and waved to others as they rushed for their homes. "God bless ya'll!"

"See ya next week!" Will yelled, her hands cupping her mouth as the rain came harder.

Gus lifted the tarp in the back of the wagon. "Quick, crawl under here."

Laughing like children, Gus and Melinda Jane squeezed in next to Will, propping the tarp over them like a giant umbrella. Their shoulders collided as the wagon lurched forward, spiking another round of giggles.

"Poor James and Zander." Will said. "Sitting out in the cold rain."

Gus's eyebrows shot up. "Why, Willamina, that's real considerate of you."

Will sat taller. "Can't a girl consider the welfare of her brothers at a time such as this?"

Melinda Jane stifled a choking sound, then rolled her eyes at Gus. "Why, yes. Yes, she can. And so can you, Will." Will's eyebrows knit in confusion, and suddenly Gus broke into *Camptown Ladies,* urging them to join in.

In no time at all, it seemed, they were in the kitchen, warmed by the furnace and sipping hot cocoa. "That's what we could do. Take the children cocoa for a treat sometime." Melinda Jane blew steam across the rim of the cup. Her mind played through the scenario. They'd have to get a farmer to donate the milk.

"Sarah Young has contributed so much to our brief forays among the needy. Why doesn't she come with us? It's so rewarding." Gus stirred a dash of cinnamon into her cup.

"Her pap won't allow it, so she helps however she can. She's the one that thought up the quilt contest between the church ladies."

"Is that so? It's such a clever idea." Gus leaned forward. "Never underestimate the competitive nature of church women." She winked and chuckled. Setting her cup down, she grew serious. "So, have you ever asked Anderson to join you at the poorhouse?"

Rattled, Melinda Jane gulped her drink, then grimaced against her scalded tongue. "I asked. He's just busy is all."

"I see." Gus wrapped both hands around the cup, sipping the cocoa slowly. "Maybe invite him again sometime."

She would give him another chance. Mayhap he would be free to go. "I'll do that. I'll see if he wants to join us next weekend."

Voices rose as Melinda Jane rushed down the stairs, repositioning a comb to smooth back her wayward curls. Swinging around the newel post, she spotted Will. "Whatever is all the shoutin' about?"

Will batted her eyes, fanning herself with an envelope. Her voice sang, "You've got a letter, you've got a letter."

Melinda Jane held out her palm.

"Nuh uh . . . guess who it's from, first."

She reached for the envelope, and Will yanked it back. Stretching her neck like a chicken, she scowled. "Guess!"

"It's from the post office." Melinda Jane eyed the letter so she could snatch it away.

Will turned and danced through the hall into the kitchen. She waved the missive singing, "You got a letter from Fin. You got a letter from Fin."

Just as the girl reached the table, Melinda Jane grabbed the letter. With a victory hoot, she lifted her skirt and raced back up the stairs. Laughter faded behind and disappeared altogether when the door slammed shut behind her. She dove for the bed.

Setting the letter on the pillow, she pressed it with her fingers, drawing out the emotions that bombarded her. She was eager and scared all at once. Hope and fear stirred-up together.

After a minute, she jumped up to retrieve a letter opener from the small secretary. Her fingers trembled as she slid the sharp edge beneath the thin paper.

February 23, 1862, Mountain Cove, Virginia
Dear Melinda Jane,

153

I am happy to tell you that I am alive. In the process of hunting bushwhackers, I happened upon Jimmy Lee. It was truly good to see him, safe and unharmed. It pains me to say we found ourselves in a harrowing situation and he was lost to me. This rebellion, in all of its ugliness, begets wickedness and enemies where none lay before.

A good family has found me injured and I am recuperating in their home and will return to my unit in Gauley Bridge as soon as I am able. My time here has given me ample opportunity to think on things, and as I gaze at your picture often, my thoughts are of you. I find myself longing to talk to you, to see your sweet smile. I am oft riddled with concern that I am no longer the same man you once knew, for dark days and deeds can afflict a man's soul.

You know me better than almost anyone, Melinda Jane, and yet I cannot find the words to tell you what is in my heart. I have determined to hold back no longer. When next we meet face to face, I will make my feelings known to you and hope, nay, pray that you return them in kind.

I covet your prayers and send you my fondest affections. — Sgt. Phineas Dabney, 4ᵗʰ Virginia Volunteers, United States Army

She read the letter twice, then carefully folded it, slipping it inside the cover of her Bible. A smile attached itself, like the stickiest, sweetest honey, to her lips. Drawing up her knees, she wrapped her arms around them. If only she knew when she would see him again. She had been patient. For years, she had been patient. Gus was right. She would wait a little longer.

Twenty-One

MOUNTAIN COVE, VIRGINIA

Thanks to the drop in last night's temperatures, Fin and Mr. Hamilton would have to ride out across a blanket of white. Fin scowled at the tracks in the snow. "This fresh fall is a double-edged sword. Keeps us from riding into a trap, but makes us easy prey if a body's looking to cause trouble."

"You're right about that. Best to keep a steady lookout. Confound snow quiets the sounds of approach nearly altogether." He pivoted his head. "Least ways there's no wind blowin'. Makes for a nice ride."

"That it does."

"Dabneys of Gauley Bridge, huh?" Mr. Hamilton snugged his hat lower on his brow. "That'd make you Jonathan Dabney's boy. Am I right?"

Fayette County wasn't so big. So, no surprise this man would know his pap. "Yes, sir. He passed last summer."

"Sorry for your loss. He was a fine man."

"How'd you know my pap?"

Mr. Hamilton scrubbed his sandy beard. "I'm pretty sure *my* pap was the one who surveyed the land for your farm when I was just a schoolboy. We got to know one another through some meetings at the courthouse over the last ten years or so."

Fin nodded as a measure of peace settled in, replacing any misgivings he might've still had about the man.

They rode in silence, their senses alert to every snap of the frozen limbs. Before too long, Mr. Hamilton pulled up his horse, putting one finger to his lips. He dismounted, signaling Fin to do the same. "Smell that?" he whispered.

Fin had just picked up the smell of a campfire when they stopped. He nodded, patting the revolver the man had loaned him. "We gonna check it out?" Remembering he was not in uniform, Fin decided he'd lean on Mr. Hamilton's judgement. A little reconnaissance couldn't hurt.

After tying the horses to a young maple, Fin followed Mr. Hamilton's lead as the man angled off the path. *Not much of a breeze, but I do believe this is the same direction I would've thought to take.*

From a crouched position behind a boulder, no more than sixty yards ahead, they spotted a group of men taking breakfast. And they did not look in any hurry to leave. They seemed to enjoy the fire and camaraderie.

This was not the usual bunch he'd become accustomed to. Some were older and better dressed. Their duds were neither the buckskins of the trappers and mountain men, nor the bedraggled work clothes of the poorer folk. A few of the horses brandished silver buckles on their halters.

Fin surveyed the campsite, spying a couple of high quality saddles. He counted eighteen, and he figured there might be two or three out of sight. He swung his gaze in a complete circle, searching for any sign of a lookout.

When a young man stood at the fire and turned their way, Mr. Hamilton's scowl deepened, and he backed away from their hiding spot. Fin followed in retreat and rode in silence until they had covered a hundred yards farther down the path.

"I could tell you recognized those men," Fin said, his typical patience settling on curiosity.

"Sure did. That guerilla band's lieutenant is E.D. Thomison. The old coot was Sam Fox. Owns a good deal of land over in Greenbrier County. Done plenty of business with him over the years."

Fin let out a low whistle. "I'll be! We been warned to keep a lookout for that bunch. And me without my men. You know Thomison?"

"I knew his pap better. That boy's got a mean streak." Mr. Hamilton shook his head, reached for the pipe in his pocket, but came up with a disappointed look instead. "Sad thing. Real sad. The way they figure it, they're just protecting the land from invaders." His hand dipped toward that pipe again, then fingered the reins instead.

They had ridden twenty minutes in silence when the unmistakable crunch of hooves quickened Fin's heart rate. He and Mr. Hamilton exchanged wary looks. They reined their horses around, looking back over the meandering trail of hoofprints. They had deliberately avoided any kind of regular trace or deer trail, so the sound of horses could only mean one thing—someone was following them.

"Circle back and meet here?" Fin danced the horse back and into a tight turn. At Mr. Hamilton's nod, he launched into a gallop, veering off into the trees.

Trotting when he could, Fin picked his way through the trees in a wide circle, taking his bearings from a tight cluster of three Aspens. If the riders didn't split up and follow their tracks, there would be no cause for concern. If they did—well, then there'd be serious cause.

Approaching the old trail, he paused. The kicked up snow told him there were at least twenty-five riders. He scanned the area for any sign of Hamilton and before he could start off again, a shot rang out.

"Stop right there or the next one's finding a resting place between your eyes." His Colt already drawn, Fin held it up in surrender.

Lacking the local color, the voice resonated with a more western accent. Optimism tapped on his brain as he turned his head. When his eyes landed on a blue uniform with a unit patch, relief surged, and he smiled. "Twenty-third Ohio."

"What of it?" A private stepped closer, a skeptical look on his boyish face and a tight hold on a rifle.

Hands still in the air, Fin drawled, "Sergeant Fin Dabney, temporarily assigned to Colonel Moors' Twenty-eighth Ohio." If you look in that saddlebag there, you'll see my uniform.

Another soldier stepped from behind a tree and edged toward the saddlebag, his pistol trained on Fin. He tugged out the rolled uniform, letting the pants drop to the ground.

The soldier stared at the Union trousers, a rumpled pile in the snow. He passed a knowing look to the private wielding the rifle, then reached for Fin's gun. "I'll take that nice and easy."

Fin's mood scooted from relief to irritation. "You don't believe me?"

"How do we know you didn't take this off a dead body?"

They had a point. What proof did he have? Even the Bible was no proof that he didn't just assume someone's identity.

A knife sliced the rope and a Federal let the pieces fall to the ground. Rubbing the rope marks on his wrists, Fin muttered, "Thanks."

"Can't be too careful, Sergeant." The private replaced the knife in its sheath, passing a sheepish look to his captain.

"If Mr. Hamilton vouches for you, it's good enough for me." Captain Maguire removed his hat, tipping his head to examine the sky. "Now, I suggest you put that uniform back on and lead us to where you last saw Thomison and his band."

"Yes, sir." Fin grabbed the wadded uniform. "I'd appreciate the use of weapons and a horse, sir. Just until I get back to Gauley Bridge. Mr. Hamilton here has been more than generous."

"Of course, Sergeant Dabney. We'll round these bushwhackers up and get you back to Colonel Moor as soon as possible."

"It's here." Fin motioned up ahead just before Hamilton came into view. He pulled up, and Captain Maguire signaled his men to wait.

"I reckon this is where we part ways, Mr. Hamilton." Fin extended a hand. "Thank you for all you've done for me. I won't be forgettin' it any time soon."

"It was an honor, Fin. God keep you from harm and return you to your family when this rebellion is brought to an end." Mr. Hamilton nodded to Captain Maguire, then cantered away, the extra horse tethered behind.

Just as Fin hoped, Thomison's men hadn't bothered to move their camp. Since the Federals outnumbered them, the troops would just surround the guerillas and force a surrender. But first, they would quietly take out any sentries. The captain ordered Fin and four others to advance.

Two pickets succumbed to the butt of a rifle, and the Twenty-third moved into place.

The officer's voice boomed. "Tell your men to surrender nice and easy, Thomison. This is Captain Maguire of the United States

Army. My men have surrounded you and your sentries are taking nice long naps."

The panicked guerillas armed themselves in a flurry of activity. Thomison was the only one looking to not have a care. He pulled a knife from his boot and went to cleaning his fingernails, never rising from his sitting position on a downed tree.

"Mayhap you think you got us dead to rights, howsomever we ain't done nothin' wrong. We just been havin' us a nice camp-out, delightin' in the good Lawd's creation here." Thomison's words strung out, biding his time. "Just zactly what is it you think we's done, here, Cap'n? We're peaceable, fair-minded men. Why dontcha show yerself and we can talk?"

"Not until every man among you drops his weapon."

Tension hung in the air as Thomison examined his fingers, admiring his handy-work. He leisurely replaced the knife in his boot. In one motion, he dropped for cover, pulling his pistol, igniting a firing frenzy. The bushwhackers scramble for cover, shooting a barrage into the trees.

Fin took aim on a leg protruding from behind a boulder, rewarded with a scream and gush of expletives. One guerilla caught a direct shot to the head, and his lifeless body crumpled over a log.

"Cease fire." Captain Maguire roared. Several more shots rang out from the camp as heavy smoke settled, eclipsing the Rebels. "Move in."

Fin and the men of the Twenty-third moved forward, daring the bushwhackers to try anything short of surrender.

Thomison rose from his position. He hawked and spit. "Don't look too good for us right now."

"No," the captain grunted, stepping forward. "It sure don't."

Guns fell to the ground. Federals plucked knives from belts and boots. In no time at all, soldiers threw bound prisoners over their own horses—destined for the stockade at Gauley Bridge.

❦

More than a month had come and gone. Never in his wildest dreams did Fin think he would be happy to be back in camp with the Twenty-eighth. The weariness in his bones measured every hour since setting out from Mountain Cove at dawn.

Darkness had long since shrouded the path through the countryside, but Fin could have led the Twenty-third here blindfolded. They slowed at the Gauley River's familiar voice. Its dark waters rushed beneath the bridge, welcoming him home. Finally complete, the new suspension bridge was high style. Quite an "engineering marvel" they called it. He would take a better look in the morning.

The sentry stepped forward. "Who goes there?" Torches burned on either side of the broad, dirt path in the middle of a field.

Finally. A friendly face! Fin grinned. "Are you gonna let us pass here, Private Fischer?"

The man's jaw dropped. "Sarge? That you?"

"Sure is, Private."

"Well, I'll be." He stepped back, lowering his weapon. When he noticed the captain, he stood at attention and saluted smartly. "Go right ahead, Captain, sir."

Fin pointed out the way to the stockade, then he led the captain to Captain Schubert's tent. He did not relish waking the man from a dead sleep.

He rapped on a wooden brace next to the door. "Captain Schubert, sir. It's Sergeant Dabney." He waited, considering another knock, but a stirring in the tent stayed his hand. He nodded to Captain Maguire, figuring the man's presence would spare him a reprimand for disturbing the officer's sleep.

The door flew open and a blurry-eyed Captain Schubert blinked, then grinned and slammed a powerful hand onto Fin's shoulder. "Good to have you back, Sergeant." He turned to Fin's guest. "I'm Captain Carl Schubert, Twenty-eighth Ohio."

Captain Maguire introduced himself and in a matter of minutes, Fin was released to turn in for the night. His step picked up, despite the weariness, as he wondered if he should wake Noah. He grinned as a few cruel antics came to mind. But by the time he reached the tent, all he wanted to deal with was the cot and some warm blankets.

Maneuvering in the dark, he dropped to his cot and removed his boots. He stretched out, pulling the covers over his clothes. *Humph.* No pillow. No matter. Leg muscles jerked as his body settled. *Thank you, Lord.*

He thought to pray—as he did every night when the clamor of the day finally settled and his body found rest. But precious sleep pulled him under before his mind could have a say.

Twenty-Two

F in's cloudy breath rose and then vanished in the crisp March air. His men stood at attention, lined up like little boys waiting their turn at a rope swing over the Gauley. He had received as warm a welcome as any man returned from the dead. This morning, he hoped for a day to regain his bearings, replenish gear, check on Duke, and maybe get a letter off to the family. But it was not to be, as now he expected new orders at any moment.

Colonel Moor, a smoldering cigar in his teeth, paced stiffly, a telegram in his hand. His eyes scanned the unit. "Men, a particularly troublesome problem needs to be nipped in the bud, shall we say." His German accent turned the words with an abrasion, and he scowled as he continued. "Every day we've seen telegraph wires cut, and our Federal couriers are being taken out at an alarming rate—some in a most insidious fashion. I want you to find the devils responsible." He halted, and yanking the cigar from his teeth, used it to punch the air in rhythm with his words.

"There is one thing preventing complete Union Army control of western Virginia—Confederate guerillas. They have wreaked havoc in these hills long enough. They care not for fair play or protection of innocents." The colonel resumed his pacing. "This unit, I am proud to say, has acquired somewhat of a reputation for its success in thwarting this human blight. Why, even your fearless leader, recently raised from the dead, returns to us with prisoners."

He nodded to Fin. "Captain Schubert has the map. He will point you in the right direction. Godspeed, men."

The rising sun already promised a clear day as Fin and his unit moved out. The snowmelt had ignited early spring scents, and coppery green sprouts of new life poked out from gray, crusty patches across the ground. Surely there could be new life for him as well. The last month had given him a second chance—if not a kick in the pants—to get his priorities straight.

Why was it he could draw down on an enemy, jump into a fray, look death in the eye, but he could not bring himself to deal plainly with Melinda Jane? But that was going to change. Yep. He was a different man now. God had given him a second chance. He had no intention of wasting another minute hog-tied by his tongue or party to a cowardly retreat in the face of the woman he loved. No sir.

Noah's eyes scrunched into slits as he leaned in his saddle, appearing to examine Fin. "I'd be plum crazy not to wonder at what it is you're thinkin'."

Leave it to Noah. Never missed a thing. "Maybe I'll share with you later."

Riding like this, alert to what lay not *only* ahead, but all around—including up in the trees—afforded little chance for talk. He would talk to Noah later, though. His friend tended to speak his mind, and he had a way of pulling a person's thoughts right out through their own mouth—all without raising their dander. He had a way with the truth and people. No doubt Fin could learn a few things from the old boy.

The day slipped by without so much as an unexplained sound from the woods—until close to dusk. The report of a rifle. One. Two. Three shots rang out.

In silence, they walked their horses through the heavy undergrowth a ways, then tethered them to the bushes, continuing on foot. Soon, voices drifted through the woods. Fin signaled Fischer and Walter to scout the flank as he moved forward.

Raucous laughter and curses filtered through the brush. In a tight clearing, four Union soldiers guffawed and swayed. A body lay on the ground, unmoving. Another man stumbled about with a grain bag over his head, hands tied behind his back. He fell mercilessly to the ground.

"Get back up here and dance for us some more, Johnny Reb. A body as ugly as you ain't good for nothing else but our amusement." The big-bellied soldier swayed, then fired his pistol, hitting the dirt mere inches from the prisoner's head.

Another soldier, this one scrawny, his beard straggling to a point, jerked the Rebel to his feet. "Dance and maybe we'll make it real quick. Not like we done yer friend here."

Fin retreated to his men and moments later surrounded the soldiers and their prisoner. He would make himself known, but he'd be a fool not to expect trouble seeing how things were. Not trusting their judgement, he'd holler rather than surprising them outright. The one private seemed mighty free with that pistol of his.

"Hello to the camp." Fin intentionally broke off a few branches as he moved forward, half expecting a shot to ring out.

"Who . . . who'd that be?"

"Sergeant Dabney, twenty-eighth Ohio." Fin stepped into the clearing, his men waiting for a sign to do the same. "You boys lost your unit?"

"Umm. No, Sergeant. They lost us." For some reason, the lot of them thought that was a real funny answer.

Fin indicated the man on the ground, most likely dead from the looks of it. "What happened here?"

"We found us a couple of bushwhackers, Sarge." Big belly kicked the motionless foot on the ground. "This one didn't want to play nice." Another round of coarse laughter.

"Where'd you find the bark juice?" Fin asked, stepping a little closer.

"Found us a still just over thataway." Scrawny beard motioned, nearly losing his balance.

Fin signaled his men to come into the clearing. "Seems to me it'd be best if we take that prisoner off your hands."

Noah squatted on the ground, checking on the sprawled man. He stood. His hard eyes flitted to Fin, then to the four men. "You cut this man's ear off?" He growled out the words and took another step closer. "You tortured this man?" Noah's hand opened and closed like it itched to pull the Colt from its holster.

"Makes no never mind. He was just a dirty bushwhacker." Big belly spat on the ground, at once a bit more sober and a lot more mean.

"Who is your commanding officer?" Fin stepped closer and his men did the same.

Scrawny beard holstered his gun, standing a little straighter as he seemed to just now take in the number of new arrivals. "Colonel Crook, Sergeant. He don't want us to take prisoners, so we can do what we want with these snakes."

"I'm relieving you of this prisoner, Private." Fin turned to his own men. "Get them something to dig with and give that prisoner some water." It galled him to no end to think how the enemy was less than human in the eyes of some. And it bothered him most that he stood on the same side of the line with the likes of these. "You boys will bury this man proper."

Fin went about searching the soldiers' saddlebags.

The prisoner slouched against a maple tree while Fischer cut the cord from his neck and yanked off the bag. "You should be thankful we came along. What outfit you with?"

The man cursed. "None of yer business!"

Noah uncapped his canteen and handed it to the bushwhacker. The prisoner poured some of the water across his muddied face and scrubbed it with his sleeve. Noah hissed a low whistle. "Well dutton tat tear ya for a duster? A face only a mama could love, and one I'm not quick to forget." He wagged his head as the man took a long draw of water. "What outfit you with again?"

"I didn't say." The prisoner took another long draw, emptying the canteen.

"Uh, Fin? Yer not gonna like this." Noah turned, colliding with Fin's iron hand, shoving him aside.

There was no mistaking the stringy gray hair, the puckered face, the soulless black eyes. Every muscle, every sinew of Fin's body quivered with a barely controlled rage. He spun around, stomping off toward Duke at a clipped pace.

For the third time in a year, murder filled his heart, propped up by a venomous hatred he had known only for this man. He detested it. And it shamed him to lose restraint with its sway. This man, this monster, had escaped twice before. This time, make no mistake—Fin would see him through to the authorities.

Boots kicked at the ground behind him. "You all right? You wanna let me in on this little secret the two of you got going on?" Noah's voice was soft, cautious.

"That . . . that man—and I'm thinking that's too good a reference for him—killed a friend of mine back home." Fin cleared his throat, straining to make himself heard. "My friend, Tiny. Knew him most of my life. He was the biggest man I've ever known. Probably the kindest heart, too. Had a little blacksmith shop. Only thing anybody ever had against him was the color of his skin."

"When all this happen?"

"Just before the war started. That piece of dung over there—what he did to Tiny. That ain't no man sittin' under that tree. That there's a demon." Fin slapped his hat against his leg and raked quivering fingers through his hair. "You just might have to stand between the two of us if he gets ugly. I don't like to admit it, but I'm afraid of what I might do. Vengeance belongs to God. It's not for me to shovel out."

"I'll keep an eye on both of ya." Noah gripped his shoulder. "Once the body is buried. What do we do with Crook's boys?"

"Pour out the rest of that moonshine, take down their names, and leave them be. I don't expect there's any more to come of it, but just in case, we've done our part. We still have some ground to cover. Let's just hope our prisoner is as cooperative as he is ugly."

Fin and his men followed a winding trace higher and higher through the dimming woods. At last, the sinking sun painted a blazing, tri-colored sky. Only a rhythmic *clip clop* rose above the silence until the unmistakable buzz of insects grew louder with every step. An odor any farmer would recognize guided Fin off the path. He motioned for Noah and Walter to follow.

The buzzing and odor intensified. The horses shied.

"Uh, Sarge?"

Fin followed Walter's gaze. There, lashed to a tree, a headless body slumped, naked and riddled with bullets. It was a wonder a bear hadn't taken notice.

"Lord, have mercy. How long you suppose he's been there?" Noah dismounted. He tied his kerchief over his nose and Fin did the same.

"Two, maybe three days." Fin stepped closer, intercepting a tumbling piece of paper with his boot. He bent to pick it up, then pointed to another. "There's more over there."

Noah handed him three letters. "By the looks of things, I believe we found us a Federal courier."

"Poor soul. I hope he met his end real quick." He was sure to see this image in his dreams for some time to come. "Walter, grab some help. We'll bury this soldier right here. Wish there was a way to identify the body."

Fin cautiously stepped, covering the area, eyes scanning the ground.

"What are you thinking, Sarge?" Noah searched also.

"I'd say three horses."

"Uh . . . where's the . . . head?"

"Not here."

Noah nodded. "Right. We're losing light. Where you figure on making camp?"

"There's a holler not far."

A joint effort made quick work of the burial. Fin led in the Lord's prayer, his mind distracted, wondering if a sweetheart somewhere waited for the soldier's return. His mind flitted to Melinda Jane, imagining for a moment his own still body, covered with fresh-turned soil.

He smacked his thigh with his hat, then crammed it back on and swung into his saddle. "Best get."

Fin had risen to stir the fire twice during the night and each time the smoke from another fire drifted on the air—barely detectable, but he was certain of it. As the first berry-red hues shone on the horizon, he kicked Noah's foot, then Fischer's, Benzinger's,

Stump's, and Dill's, a new private from Cleveland. "We're going on a bushwhacker hunt, boys. There's a campfire off to the east, and we're going to find it."

Minutes later, Fin nodded to the sentry, another recent recruit from Ohio he knew only as Nelson. "Get the others up, but keep them quiet till we get back."

Walking was slow going since darkness still shrouded most of the undergrowth. Their steps faltered as they climbed the first steep hill, slippery from the snowmelt. They pushed ahead through mud, following the waft of smoke. Just as Fin suspected, less than a quarter mile to the east, a smoldering fire glowed. Three Union soldiers were fixing to break camp.

"Hello to the camp." Fin emerged from the trees, followed by all but Fischer, who held back in case of trouble. A smart safeguard, which Fin had learned early, when you didn't know what you were walking into.

The three soldiers stood stock-still, a look bouncing between them until the shortest one mustered a smile and half a salute. "Where'd you come from, Sergeant?"

"We camped last night just over that rise. How about you boys come back with us and have breakfast? You can fill me in on any activity hereabouts." Fin stepped closer. Something was not right here. "Any objections, Corporal?" He directed his gaze to a short private, who responded. The corporal stood wide-eyed and silent.

"Mighty nice of you to offer, Sarge, but we're headed out. Uh . . . per orders," the short one said.

"What direction you headed?"

"West."

"Well, that is a coincidence. Our camp is west of here and right on your way. Grab your gear."

"Uh . . ."

Noah piped up, "You got horses?"

"No, we don't."

"Follow us. Benzinger, bring up the rear." Fin kicked dirt over the fire. "Let's go."

Fischer guided the train of nine men through the treed landscape, over a ridge and down the steep incline toward the camp.

Fin hung back, waiting for Noah. "You see the bullet hole in that uniform?"

"I did. Something fishy about those boys."

Fishy, indeed.

By the time the men filed into camp, odors of coffee and boiled sowbelly brought a rumble to Fin's stomach. His men were dishing up breakfast, having already packed their gear. They had taken to calling their sack-headed prisoner "Snake" since he wouldn't give his name. Hands still bound behind his back, he gnawed a piece of hardtack. Fin did not miss the subtle look of recognition that flashed in Snake's eyes as the three new soldiers filed in. *Curious.* The prisoner's lip curled in a brief sneer as he chewed.

"Why don't you boys have a seat here? Walter, get these boys something to eat with." Fin practically pushed them onto the ground. "How come you boys don't belong to the same unit?"

The short one looked up, a smile spread wide across his face. "What was that?"

"Your uniforms. One has a different unit patch. Two of you with Crook and one with Milroy."

Fin pulled his Colt. His men were quick to follow suit. "Lay your weapons on the ground, gentlemen. Dill and Benzinger, tie up our guests."

"Y . . . you're making a big mistake, Sergeant. This ain't what it seems. Ya hafta believe me. Ya hafta," the short one pleaded, and the sincerity of his voice nearly gave Fin pause.

Fin motioned for Private Dill to collect the guns on the ground. "Hicks, take a few men and look around the woods near their campsite. See if you find a body in need of a uniform."

"Sure thing, Sarge." Noah rounded up a search party and headed off on horseback.

Fin walked over to Snake, kicking his boot. "These friends of yours?"

"I ain't telling you nothing."

"Not even your name. I guess you prefer the nickname the boys gave you instead."

The man squeezed his eyes into dark slits. "You look familiar."

"That so?" *Familiar?* Well, *his* face was emblazoned on Fin's nightmares and the darkest corner of his heart. "Your twisted mind probably doesn't recall a big burly blacksmith you killed in Gauley Bridge last year."

The dark eyes sparked. "Just as we was leaving. You rode up. I remember now. That Negro had it coming. He needed a lesson in respect is all." He threw back his head, a maniacal laugh curdling his voice.

Fin's hands flew to the man's throat. He squeezed, aching to watch the life drain from this scum. Hatred blazed through his veins, through his fingers. Better to snap his neck and end his retched life. A powerful hand gripped his shoulder.

"Not this way, Sarge." Benzinger pleaded louder. "Sarge, stop!"

He stared at a stranger's hands strangling the life out of the now-blue prisoner. *His* hands. He pulled back, standing upright, blood pounding in his ears. He turned, striding into the woods. Deeper into the trees. His legs wanted to run, his voice wanted to howl out his anguish. Who . . . *what* had he become?

An hour and a half later, Noah and his detachment returned with three horses. "Well, they was lying about having horses. You're gonna wanna see the goodies they got in their packs."

Fin loosened a buckle on one saddlebag. Sure enough. No mistaking the evidence. These three had taken out at least one Federal courier.

Noah dismounted, stepping closer. "We, uh, found another body. Stripped of a uniform. Buried it where the boy lay. Fischer found this haversack a several yards from the body. Still got all the trappings inside. Least ways we can identify him."

Fin fingered the worn bag. This worn bag was all that remains of a brave man. Were there letters from a wife or sweetheart? Maybe even children? He would make sure the contents made it to this man's family. What was in his own haversack? What would he leave behind? Right then and there, he decided to write a letter to each family member just as soon as he got the chance.

"Good work, Noah." Fin hugged the sack to his chest. "I'll take care of this."

Twenty-Three

CHARLESTON

"Not too tight now. I still have to breathe. Why, some of those women wear theirs so tight, I don't know. I do believe their innards are just crying out from overcrowding." Melinda Jane steadied herself, hands on the back of a sturdy chair.

Gus laughed. "You are so dramatic! Like you even need this restricting thing! God gave you a perfect hourglass figure even without a corset." She pulled the laces bit by bit, keeping the ends even. "Is that too tight?"

Melinda Jane took a deep breath. "It'll do, I reckon. I'll not be one of those swooning types. I declare, just because I'm a mite short, men think I'm fragile."

"You ready for the crinoline?" Gus gathered the fabric, bunching it around the hoops, working the whole contraption into a disk before placing it on the floor.

Stepping into the center, Melinda Jane pulled the opening up so her friend could secure the ties. "I don't know how Sarah wears one of these things every day. It's nice to get all gussied up now and then, but give me my calicos for comfort."

"This blue brocade is so striking." Gus lifted the skirt over her friend's head. "And the ivory jacket will have folks taking you for a fancy business woman."

"I do feel pretty in this."

"Honey, you are pretty no matter what you wear. It's just something you've never been able to help."

"You remember what Izzy used to say?"

"Nothin' so perty as a soul set free, wearing robes that been washed in de blood of de Lamb." They recited the beloved words as one. Throwing their arms around each other, they chuckled at the memory and Melinda Jane brushed away tears.

"How I miss Izzy." Gus pulled back, her eyes shimmering with wetness. "And Pap."

"Many a time I close my eyes and it's like I can see them together—sitting at the feet of the Lord. Talking about old times along with your mama and mine." Melinda Jane clasped Gus's hands. "But I'll have me some joy again. The Lord whispered it in my ear as I was laying in my bed praying one night. I heard His voice with my ears. 'Daughter,' He said, 'I will turn your mourning into dancing, and your tears into joy.'"

"My sweet sister, you will have joy again. I never thought I'd marry and have a family of my own. Now look at me."

"God has truly given you the desires of your heart, hasn't He? Did you say family? As in —"

"No. Not family exactly, yet." A rosy glow crept into Gus's face.

"It won't be long. You'll see."

Gus ushered Melinda Jane over to the dressing table. "Now then, let's see about your hair."

Will barged into the room just as Gus positioned the last hatpin. "Anderson's here and he looks pretty spiffy. He's got one of them shiny type vests on. Spats, too." She paused for a breath, looking up from the book in her hand. Her mouth gaped. "Look at you! You're all fancified. You must really like this Anderson fella if you'd go to all the trouble to dress like that." Will plunked down on the bed, her lips pulled off to one side in consternation.

Melinda Jane stood and lifted Will's limp hands in her own. "I am dressed up for my singing debut at the Kanawha House, not for Anderson."

"Oh."

"Come downstairs with me?" She tipped her head, trying to draw Will's gaze.

"Oh, all right." Will stood, pulling her hand back. But I get to announce you. She shot out the door and Melinda Jane and Gus followed.

In her exuberant way, Will's announcement echoed through the entire house. "Her lady, Melinda Jane Minard, recently of Gauley Bridge and guest of Doctor James Hill, and heir to the Minard fortune." She bowed with a flourish as Melinda Jane arrived at the newel post.

Anderson stepped forward, taking her hand in his. He bowed, pressing a kiss to the back of it. "Milady. You compel the brilliance of spring roses to fade in your presence."

She didn't mean to giggle. Why couldn't she just be sophisticated and accept his compliment? She smiled politely. "Why, thank you most sincerely, kind sir."

Will rolled her eyes and pivoted, striding toward the kitchen.

"Shall we?" Anderson threaded Melinda Jane's hand over his arm.

She nodded as she had seen so many fancy women do—raising her chin, then tipping her head forward in a smooth, graceful movement. "We shall."

Stars sprinkled the velvety sky by the time Anderson lifted Melinda Jane from his buggy. She had a shiny silver dollar in her reticule—the first dollar she had ever earned at one time. Anderson had been a wonderful escort. His encouragement helped her through the first couple of songs as her stomach did flip-flops when the tables began filling with patrons. Some folks ate their meal, but many filtered in with a wineglass in hand. By the time Anderson started in on the fourth song, she had made up her mind to enjoy herself, and the rest of the night went smoothly.

"Did you have fun tonight?" Anderson guided her up the walkway, patting her hand as it rested on his arm.

"I did. I very much did. Will we do the same songs tomorrow night?

"If that is all right with you. I shall try to work up some others for next week. Is there a day we can go over them?"

"Let's meet at the church on Thursday." Melinda Jane turned to face him.

"I have an idea. Why don't you come to my house to practice. I can pick you up after lunch on Thursday."

She'd much prefer to practice at the church. "That would be fine. I can bring Will or Bertie with me. I'm sure they'd love to see your home."

His lips pressed into a line for an instant before curling into a smile. He took both her hands in his. "That will be perfect. I'll pick you up for tomorrow evening at the same time."

"Until then, Anderson."

He placed a chaste kiss on her cheek and smiled. "Goodnight, Melinda Jane."

She spun to the door and fumbled with the knob. Stepping across the threshold, she caught her toe on the hem, teetered off balance, and grabbed up her skirt before shutting the door behind her.

Her left hand touched her cheek. He kissed her! Just how had that happened? She'd always thought her first kiss would come from Fin. A hoedown in her belly told her things were different now. A strange sadness bowed to excitement and a host of emotions do-si-doed inside, sending her running up the stairs, bunching up the voluminous dress as she ran.

Chairs lined the kitchen wall, one hosting a stack of four neatly folded quilts. Melinda Jane leaned over a colorful crazy quilt spread across the tabletop, an ancient melody sporadically creeping from her thoughts to her lips.

She snipped yet another thread, tying the ends in a double square knot. "This feels like working in a factory, the way we're all working our own jobs to do this real fast-like." Snip, tie.

Mrs. O'Donell guided a needle and thick thread along the length of one end of the quilt. Across in one direction, then back the other, following the rows of the colorful pieces. Gus was a row behind her, snipping the thread, then tying the knot. Sarah and Melinda Jane mirrored their actions at the far end of the quilt.

Mrs. O'Donell stood upright, stretching her back. "Mores the pity the piecin' of the quilt top wasn't as quick. We've done a good bit o' work here, ladies."

"Thank you so much for all your help, Mrs. O'Donell." Sarah closed one eye as she threaded her needle. "I've been thinking. Maybe we can contribute two of the quilts to the Methodist and two to the Episcopal church. That way we won't tip the scales one way or the other."

"That sounds fair to me," Gus said.

"Well now, such a thought never crossed me mind, but I like yer idea just fine, Sarah." Mrs. O'Donell poked the needle into the pincushion with a flourish. "There now. I've earned me cup o' tea. Ladies?"

Snip. Tie. "Almost done here. That sounds delightful, Mrs. O'Donell. Thank you," Gus cut another thread.

"Yes, please. You worked so fast, Mrs. O'Donell. I still have two rows." Sarah pulled the thread through the colorful fabric like she was mending delicate lace. "Or maybe I'm just slow."

Melinda Jane snickered. "Sarah, it's not that you're so slow. Mrs. O'Donell just does pretty near everything faster than all of us." Snip. Tie.

"That's not true!" Mrs. O'Donell measured the loose tea into an oversized porcelain teapot. "'Tis me years on this earth responsible for the sewing and the cooking, but 'tis the same years responsible for slowing me down and the like."

"You can talk real fast when you're in a tizzy." Will sat in a corner on the floor arranging quilt blocks.

"Will!" Gus's voice scolded.

"It's the truth. You shoulda heard her when she burned a pie last week. I couldn't understand a word, they were flying from her mouth so fast."

"Don't be hard on her, Gus. She speaks the truth." Mrs. O'Donell handed Will a cookie and turned to the others with a wink. "I think we'll be having cookies with tea."

Melinda Jane hesitated. How to answer Gus's question about the Kanawha House? "Well, this weekend was a little different from the first because this one gentleman requested a song I didn't plan to sing. I mean Anderson and I hadn't rehearsed it."

"Did you sing it anyway?"

"Yes, but then another gentleman requested another song and that one I knew, but I just wasn't going to sing it. It was one of those songs you hear the men a-singing when they're coming from the saloon."

"You did the right thing, Melinda Jane. Don't you compromise your convictions for anyone." Gus pulled her friend down beside her on the bed. "Now, tell me about Anderson's house. You've been there twice to practice already, and I haven't heard one word about it."

"Oh, it's real fancy. And big. He's even got a cook and a manservant. I don't know if you call him a butler, but he kind of does all sorts of stuff around the house." Never had she been in such a fancy house. "You should see the piano. It's square, of all things. And the finish on it is smooth as glass."

She wouldn't tell Gus about the little disagreement she'd had with Anderson over the two songs he had wanted her to practice. He had smoothed it all over though, in that charming way of his, and all was well.

"Did you ask him about coming to help deliver the quilts to the poor next week?"

"He said he was busy with more important business." Those were not his exact words, but it's what he meant.

Twenty-Four

The ribbon of dirt changed to mud beneath hooves as cold raindrops pelted the ground. Fin leaned back in his saddle while Duke carried him down another slick, sweeping hill. The sticky mud wasn't much of a bother on flat land, but a real nuisance to horse and rider in this terrain of undulating ground. He had the safety of the string of men behind him to think of.

Once again on level ground, Fin pulled to the fringe of a wide clearing awaiting the last man. Hooves plopped and sucked to the churned-up mud, which now banked a rivulet of brown water down the center of the trace.

"We'll be taking a little break. I'm hoping this rain lets up some." He pointed to a stand of maple. "Head over there." *No sign of lightning yet, so the trees it is.*

They had all just reached the center of the wide clearing when a volley of shots rang out, echoing through the hills.

"Make a run for it!" Fin pulled his Colt, spinning Duke in a tight circle. He searched the edges of the meadow. They were sitting ducks, all of them—until they could make it to the tree line.

Another volley.

Unless those Rebs were sharpshooters, he figured his boys stood a decent chance. Even with the wash of rain, a telltale haze hung in the trees to the south. He fired into the wooded haze, bringing up the rear of the frantic entourage. By the time he reached his men, clustered in the trees, the firing ceased.

"Hicks, Walter, Fischer, Dill, with me!" Fin guided the men through the scrub until a glimpse of activity gave him pause. From the sound of the shots, he figured there to be only six or seven Rebels. Movement caught his eye—the glint of a barrel, its aim intent on Noah.

Fin fired.

An agitated whinny. A barrage of hooves pounding through the mud, breaking through the undergrowth. Several seconds of stillness.

Noah found the victim of Fin's quick action. "He's still alive, Sarge."

The boy was young. Real young. A butternut jacket bore a growing black stain under one arm. Fin took a knee, offering up his canteen. "Take it easy, son. We'll take care of you."

The soldier coughed, pulling away from the canteen. "Was supposed to be the other way around, only in a less-chartable sense."

"Why'd the rest of your unit keep going?" Noah asked.

"Our orders were to evade patrols and carry out the new marital law."

"What new martial law?"

The boy coughed again. He tipped his head forward for another drink. "President Davis declared martial law. We were ordered to set to blazes every moonshiner still we could find and arrest any Union sympathizers we come across. Something about not engaging the enemy this time out."

"Ya forgot about that last part, I guess." Noah stood, grimacing as his knee popped. "*Tsk, tsk.* So much for following orders."

"Can you stand?" Fin capped the canteen. The boy grew more pale by the second. His head drooped and Fin patted his cheek. "You've lost a lot of blood, son. What's your name?"

"Si . . . Silas, sir." His voice croaked, little more than a hoarse whisper now.

If this was Zander sitting here, dying . . .

"Have you taken Jesus as your Savior, Silas?" Fin chose his words carefully.

Noah knelt on the opposite of the boy, his sad eyes connected with Fin's and he nodded.

"I was born again when I was young. But I'd surely appreciate a prayer, Sergeant."

Fin grabbed his hat and crushed it to his chest. "I'll say the words, but you're the one that has to pray, son. Are you repentant of your sins?" The boy soldier nodded as tears tumbled down his cheeks. Fin continued, "Lord Jesus. I'm praying for my brother Silas, here. Thank you that you died for him so he wouldn't have to suffer in hell. In your mighty name we are asking You to forgive his sins, save his soul, give him peace, and take him into your kingdom. Amen."

"Amen."

Noah leaned forward, his ear to Silas's mumbling lips. "A letter?"

The boy's only response was a placid countenance as his head lolled to one side.

Noah maneuvered the haversack from the boy's shoulders. He dug through the contents, producing a letter, and handed it to Fin.

"Silas Archer. Looks like he doesn't live that far from here—just over towards Hawks Nest. Letter's addressed to his mama, I guess. Looks too young to be married."

He tucked the letter back into the sack. Another bright light he had personally snuffed out. And another piece of Fin Dabney left right here on this piece of blood and water-soaked ground.

A familiar boulder pressed into his middle. What a miserable path for a man to trod on this earth. A spark of envy surprised him. At least young Silas Archer wasn't on that path any more.

"What say we take a little side trip on the way back? Confederate or no, Silas here deserves a decent burial and his mama deserves to know how he died."

❧

Fin knelt next to their prisoner, Snake, and slit several inches up the bottom of the sticky pant leg. Fischer had offered to tend the man's wound, but Fin had grabbed the field kit to take on the job himself. Somehow, he knew he had to do it. *Love your enemies.* Love. What he thought of this lowlife couldn't be further from *love.* He'd act on it because that's the way he was raised. And that was all.

"Looks like it's your lucky day, Snake." He flipped open the kit's canvas flap.

"Clawson," the prisoner said, his voice gruff. He tossed his head, trying to throw a hank of scraggly gray hair off one eye. "The name's Clawson."

The purplish scar covered one side of the man's face—no doubt from Tiny's forge when his friend was fighting for his life. Loathing. Fin swallowed it down. In silence, he wrapped the wound. Judging by the ragged tear in the flesh, he figured the bullet had passed right on through.

The rain was a mere splatter now and the roll of thunder echoed from a respectable distance off. Fin had always loved the sound of thunder, but this time it surprised him. There had been no lightning here. But if not here, then farther along or behind, but thunder followed lightning, even if it stayed in the clouds. What a mercy—when lighting kept to the clouds. Nobody gets hurt, no fires ignited.

As the others mounted, Fin yanked Clawson to his feet. "Time to go."

Clawson cursed. "You can't expect me to manage with my hands tied."

"Hop." He gripped his upper arm, jerking him forward.

Fin hoisted the prisoner into a saddle. Noah's curious expression caught his attention, and he motioned for Hicks to help tie Clawson to the saddle. He wrenched hard on the rope, taking pleasure in the spark of pain that flashed in the Rebel's eyes.

Clawson sneered, then spat in Fin's face. "I enjoyed every minute earning this here scar, thanks to your big friend." His eyes boiled black. "He cried for his mama . . ."

"Gag him again!" Fin strode over to Duke. He sucked in a breath and willed away the tightness in his chest. Running his hand over the glossy withers of the bay gelding, he whispered, "Peace. Be still." He longed for peace—to calm this raging storm within.

"Head out!"

After a stop for directions, Fin and his men halted in the bare yard of an unpainted single-story house. The porch sagged, sad and bare but for a branch rocker. Blue print curtains hung in the lone window. A woman stepped onto the porch, her gray hair slicked back into a knot at the base of her neck.

"I ain't got no more food for you boys. You done took near everthin' I had." Her hand kneaded her back as she talked.

"Are you Mrs. Archer, ma'am?" Fin dismounted and approached her, with Noah close behind.

The woman nodded as her eyes rested on the blanketed form draped over Noah's horse. Even from a distance, Fin could see the color drain from her face. She reached for the arm of the chair to steady herself.

"I'm Sergeant Dabney, ma'am. This is Corporal Hicks." Fin removed his hat.

The woman gestured to the body, working her chin for a time. "You bringing me my boy, aintcha?"

"Yes, ma'am."

"I had a knowin'. Bring him into the kitchen." She turned and disappeared through the door.

Fin and Noah carried the remains of Silas Archer into his home and to the table, where they laid out the wrapped body. "I'll get his things," Fin said, leaving Noah with the woman.

When he returned with the haversack, she was shaving soap into a basin. Her quivery voice hummed a tune he recognized from the church hymnal back home.

"Excuse me, ma'am. This belonged to your boy. Silas. We got your name from the letter inside. That's the only thing we touched." He swallowed. How to tell her the rest. She seemed a strong woman. Hopefully strong in faith. *Lord, help me.*

"'Twas you, weren't it?"

"Ma'am?"

"'Twas you that kilt my Silas." Her voice was calm, not accusatory. "Why else would a Union Sergeant bring a mother the body of her boy? Whoever heard of such a thing?" She lifted watery eyes to meet his.

"Yes, ma'am. He was about to shoot my Corporal, here. I . . ." He wanted to say he had to. What mother could hear such a thing? What would a mother want to hear?

"He asked me to pray with him before he died. You raised a fine young man, Mrs. Archer. He was right with the Lord when he passed." Fin looked at the floor, twisting his hat in his fingers. "I . . . I thought you'd want to know that."

A hand lighted on his shoulder. "This War of Secession has brought many a mama grief. Ain't no one person to blame, less'n it be the devil hisself. My Silas kilt a mama's son. He told me 'bout it.

It tormented him something fierce. Now he's at peace. No more torment." She wiped a single tear from her face with the back of her hand. "Thankee for bringin' my boy home, Sergeant."

Fin dipped his head and followed Noah to the door. Spent, body and spirit, he could say nothing more. The pile of regret kept mounting, but he would steel himself against it, or he could never face his men.

"Sergeant?" The woman's voice turned him from the doorway. "I forgive you."

The voice of an angel. A salve for his aching soul. The sweet aroma of grace. He turned back, forcing words from a puny voice. "Thank you, ma'am."

Noah blew out a long breath as they stepped from the porch. "Lord o' mercy, I nearly broke down and wept."

He shook his head and strode to his horse, leaving Fin standing alone with his thoughts. When he lifted his gaze from the ground, the stony eyes of Clawson drilled into him and his scar folded into a sneer against the gag in his mouth.

Horses clattered across the suspension bridge over the Gauley, as the detachment inched its way to camp. He had added four men to the stockade. If only the courier problem would disappear now. Best to give his superiors a chance to interrogate the three in Federal Uniform first.

Fin turned to Noah. "Let's check in with command before heading to the stockade. I don't want to see this day drag out any longer, but I'm not holding my breath."

"You got the map with the gravesites marked?"

Fin fumbled in his pocket. Now, where did he put that? Oh, yeah. "I remember putting it in my pack. Guess I'm feeling a mite road weary."

"You ain't the only one. Covered a lot of ground the last few days."

Colonel Moor and Lieutenant Colonel Becker detained three of the prisoners. Thankfully, Fin could hold off his debrief with Captain Schubert until the next morning. He considered walking the rest of the way to his tent—until he realized how bushed he was.

"You mind taking Clawson over to medical, then to the stockade? He'd have a better chance surviving the trip if you take him." What did he care if the vermin lived another minute, let alone another hour? Fin fought the inclination to look at the prisoner.

Noah scrunched up his mouth. "He's one ornery cuss—fowling the air with that whopper jaw of his every time we pulled that gag off for watering. I'd be plum delighted to walk him to his fate."

Walter handed over the reins of Clawson's horse to Noah. "Good riddance to this one," he muttered, then headed toward the corral.

Fin trotted up beside Clawson, pulled his knife, and cut the gag. The man worked his jaw and wet his lips. "You ain't seen the last of me, Dabney."

"If this war doesn't kill you, I'll see you hang for murder, Clawson." Fin ground his teeth, then stared the man in the eye. "You'll give account for every wicked thing you ever did come Judgement Day. There's nothing I'd like more than to see you pay for what you did to Tiny. It's beyond my comprehension, but God is willing to give you a chance—right up till you breathe your last. If I ever see your ugly face again—"

Fin trotted off toward the corral, swallowing the bile rising in his gullet.

Twenty-Five

April 1862

F in's dreams had been a crazy tumble of headless apparitions, soulless eyes, and Melinda Jane's sweet face. He groaned and flipped to his stomach as reveille sounded. Why couldn't he dream of fishing, or skinny-dipping in the Gauley? An image of Melinda Jane jumping into the water in her bloomers warmed his middle.

Sitting up, he scoured his face, needing to get that image out of his mind real fast. The days were hard enough without entertaining such thoughts. Remembering his meeting with the Captain, he swung his feet to the floor. He'd need to double-time it to the command tents.

"Fine work out there the last few days, Dabney. From the sound of things, those three you brought in were the primary force behind the disappearance of our couriers. I suppose it is just a matter of time before they are replaced." Captain Schubert blew over the rim of a clay mug. Swirls of steam puffed into the air.

Fin sipped the hot brew. "Thank you, sir. Uh . . . what can you tell me about Davis enacting some kind of martial law around here?" Silas Archer's words made little sense.

"I guess you're due for some catching up, Sergeant. President Davis has suspended the writ of habeas corpus. Thus, he has declared Martial Law in Fayette, Greenbrier, and eight other counties this side of the mountains. They've got their own brand of military police trying to impose and enforce all manner of fabricated laws on the locals."

"Civilians?"

"That's right." The captain took a careful sip, then a long draw from his mug. "Mark my words, so much as a hearsay of northern sympathies will send a family man or woman to a Confederate prison. If that is not enough, Governor Letcher and the Confederate congress have issued a proclamation officially sanctioning guerilla warfare. They called partisans to organize and, I quote, 'strike where least expected.'"

"I thought the CFS high command was trying to discourage partisan warfare. What happened?"

"As is oft the case, the politicians are not listening to the field commanders. It is my understanding that some of those bands are nothing more than a refuge for deserters. They wreak their own brand of havoc—as likely to take on Rebels as Yankees."

The captain tossed a folded paper on the table in front of Fin. "This came yesterday. Seems you'll be leaving us, Sergeant Dabney."

Fin unfolded the telegram. For the first time in months, a chord of exhilaration vibrated through him. He was going to Charleston. He glanced at the captain with a grin plastered across his face.

"I thought you'd be pleased. That's where your family is, is it not?"

"Yes, sir. It sure is."

Captain Schubert stood, extending his hand. "You have done fine work here, Dabney. Not only did you train men, those men have trained others in a unique skill set. We would welcome you back to us gladly. Enjoy your time with family."

Fin saluted, then pumped the man's hand. "Thank you, Captain."

"Dismissed, Sergeant."

Fin returned to his tent with a lift to his step and his heart.

Noah sat on a bench outside the tent, rubbing grease into his boots. "Well now"—he dipped his fingers into a tin cup and massaged the gray goo into the leather—"don't you look happier than a pig in the sunshine!"

"Colonel Joe has ordered us to return to Charleston right away." Fin fanned the air with the piece of paper. "I can just about smell home cooking."

"You reckon you might could share some of that home cookin' with this soldier? I did save your life so's your kin didn't have to read your name off a list."

Fin laughed, feeling his insides bounce—something he had forgotten how to do.

"Fin! Fin Dabney!" Four riders approached.

"Well, I'll be. Is that the Hunt boys I'm looking at?" Fin raised a hand in greeting. "Good to see you boys."

"You weren't as hard to find here as we thought. I asked for you by name back at the gate and the guard said, 'So you're here to see the *Dragon Slayer.*'"

"How's that?" Did he hear right?

A snort erupted from Noah. "Yeah . . . uh . . . I was gonna tell you 'bout that. Seems you gone and earned yourself a nickname around here."

Of all the ridiculous . . . Fin wagged his head. "Somebody's got mush for brains." He stepped closer to Matthew. "This is Corporal Hicks. This here is Matthew, Mark, Luke, and John Hunt."

"Happy to meet your acquaintance. I'll spare you my jokes concerning the four gospels. Matthew, you must be the one what found my Sergeant here near frozen. Mighty kind of your family to take him in like you did." Noah made like he was looking behind them. "Don't suppose you brung that pretty sister of yours. Rebecca?" He wiggled his eyebrows.

Matthew's eyebrows dipped.

Fin slapped a hand on Noah's shoulder, shoving him aside. "Never mind him. He's just being his natural flamboyant self. Why don't you boys water your horses, then come sit a spell—tell me what brings you this way?"

A dark cloud puffed itself up like an angry porcupine while the Hunts tended their horses. Fin boiled up a pot of coffee, keeping one eye to the sky.

Minutes later, Noah ducked into the tent and pulled off his hat, letting water drip on the floor. "Too bad this rain has us cooped up in here. Least ways ya had decent weather till now." He handed the four borrowed tin cups to their guests.

"What brings you boys to Gauley Bridge, Matthew?" Fin emptied the coffee pot into the last cup.

"No good, that's for sure." Matthew took a sip, then grimaced. "The Confederates passed a Conscription Act. Unless we leave home, we'll be forced to join up with the Rebel cause. You know we're not about to do that, Fin."

"Did you come here to join up?" Noah asked.

"Naw. We're just passing through and thought we'd stop and see if you were here. We're heading to Ohio until this business plays out."

Fin groaned. "Boy, this has gotta be hard on your mama. You got neighbors looking out for her and Rebecca?"

"I think they'll do all right—so long as neither of them gives those Bushwhackers any cause for harm. The neighbors know we're gone."

Fin set his cup down. "Noah, here, and myself are heading to Charleston first thing tomorrow. How 'bout you boys ride along with us? We'll keep to the turnpike. Doubtful we'll run into any trouble with six of us together."

Matthew conferred with his brothers, then smiled. "Sounds like a good plan to me."

Noah lifted his cup in a toast. "We can feed you and put you up tonight, then head out in the morning. It'll be right hospitable-like."

Matthew grinned at his brothers, nodding. "We'd be much obliged."

Twenty-Six

CHARLESTON

"It's just perfect!"

Melinda Jane ran her hand over the raised calligraphy lettering on the sign. "Oh. This paint is so thick and the color so bold. Why, any church would surely be proud to earn such notoriety and post this sign. Proud in a respectable way, I mean."

Sarah playfully slapped at her friend's shoulder. "I know what you mean, silly. You really like it?"

"It looks real professional. Now all it needs is the winner's name filled in." Melinda Jane set the lyre-shaped wooden plaque on the table. What a reward, to see their idea come around full circle like it did. And now it was all coming to an end. But there would never be an end to the needs of the poor, would there?

A lyrical tune drifted into the kitchen, followed by a red-faced Mrs. O'Donell. "It's nearly warm out there today." She patted her brow with the corner of her apron. "I thought I'd get a start on the garden. I'm planning on a big one this year, since I've a bit of help to see to it." She stopped at the sight of the colorful plaque. "What you got there, darlin's?" She dropped into a chair, fanning her face.

"Do you like it, Mrs. O'Donell?" Sarah asked, waving her hand over the sign in a presentation.

195

"'Tis fancy, for sure. But you've not filled in the winner." She scowled.

"It will be filled in soon enough." Sarah produced an envelope from her dress pocket. "*This* holds the winning church." She leaned down in a conspiratory fashion. "Can you keep a secret, Mrs. O'Donell?"

"Aye! Can I keep a secret? These lips will go to the grave for want of a tellin' that ne'er been told." She turned an invisible key to lock her lips, drawing laughter from the women.

Sarah dramatically worked open the envelope. "And the winner of the first annual Quilts for the Needy Contest is . . . by two quilts . . . St. Michael's Episcopal Church."

"Saints be praised!" Mrs. O'Donell's hands fluttered in the air. "If these feet didn't hurt so, I'd dance a jig."

"Now you can't even whisper the results. Not yet." Sarah eyed both women.

"We'll notify all the pastors of the results, and they can announce the winners—and losers, I guess—in church this Sunday," Melinda Jane said.

Sarah took the seat next to Mrs. O'Donell. "And I'll finish the plaque and take it over to the Episcopal parsonage on Saturday."

"When will we distribute the quilts?" Mrs. O'Donell pulled a hanky from her apron pocket and pressed it to the back of her neck.

Melinda Jane sank into a chair. "Why not go the very next Monday? The sooner the better."

"And we can invite the church ladies to help distribute them. If I see my father before then, I will utterly beg him to allow me to come, too."

Mrs. O'Donell placed a spotted hand on Sarah's. "You've a good heart, lass. All the work you do for the poor and yet yer deign to see the look of joy upon their faces when they receive the blessings.

A word of warning to ya—don't be disappointed if nary a one of the church ladies agree to visit the poor. It's the way of it, is all."

Sarah's eyes fell to the cornflower-drizzled tablecloth. "I know, Mrs. O'Donell. What others choose to do is between them and God. I am doing this so those poor people will have warm blankets. As long as they receive them, I won't be disappointed."

"I understand what you're saying—about the need to learn new songs, Anderson. I'm just not comfortable with all the ones we practiced." Melinda Jane set the music pages on the smooth piano top.

"But your audience wants to hear these songs. Folks are already singing some of the war tunes."

"It's just that some are just so sad, and that one song sounds like a drinking sort." She crossed her arms, hugging her elbows.

Anderson rose from the piano stool, and standing beside her, he squeezed her shoulders against his side. "How about we compromise? You pick which verses you are willing to sing, and we will just do those." He smiled that adorable dimpled smile of his.

"All right. I guess I can do that." There was that look in his eye again—the one he got right before he kissed her cheek a couple of weeks ago. Her stomach quivered. And why not? She smiled, and he leaned over, placing a light kiss on her cheek. The scent of Macassar oil floated in the air and she breathed it in, memorizing the unique aroma.

"Can we go yet, 'Linda Jane. I'm hungry." Bertie snapped his reader shut. "And I read all I was supposed to—and then some." His shoulders drooped with the impatient attitude of all seven-year-olds.

"Yes, Bertie, we can go now." She turned to Anderson. "Please, say you'll come with me to hand out the quilts to the poor. It just warms a soul clean through to see the joy on their faces."

Anderson gathered the sheets of music. "I don't have time for such things, Melinda Jane. My father has requested I join him in Wheeling. Voters have approved a constitution for the new state."

She would not show her disappointment. "And they'll call it Kanawha?"

"No. It seems the votes favored the name *West Virginia* for our great new state. I'll be leaving Sunday."

"How exciting!" She drew her cloak from an upholstered chair. "Gather your things, Bertie. I'm ready to go."

Anderson picked up a silver bell from a petite carved table. He rang it twice. "I hope you don't mind if I have Sheldon drive you home. I have some things to tend to."

"Why, I don't mind a bit. You'll come for me this evening?" She tipped her head, meeting his eyes. Something was different about him. She couldn't put her finger on it, but something had changed.

"Same time as usual." He bowed, touching his lips to the back of her hand. "Milady."

Why did his silly gestures make her want to giggle like a schoolgirl? She held up the sheet music. "I'll be sure to practice these."

Never in a month of years had she imagined herself in such a lovely conveyance, driven by a hired servant of all things—and getting paid to sing for other folks. God had a strange way of mashing things together in her life. She had so much.

Still, her spirit deflated.

In Fin's last letter, he said he would share his heart. He signed it, "*with fondest affection.*" There it was again—that ache and yearning—not for some-*thing,* but some-*one.*

Twenty-Seven

The sun warmed their backs as Fin, Noah, and the Hunt boys followed the James River and Kanawha Turnpike towards Charleston. Spring scents stirred a longing in Fin to break up the ground for planting. Springtime on the farm meant tending to the new calves and sometimes piglets. It was the foals kicking up their heels in the pasture, then making a beeline to their mama for a quick meal.

Every now and then, a fish would jump and land with a splash in the shallows of the Kanawha River that flowed along beside the pike. It brought a smile to his face. Fishing sounded real inviting.

Melinda Jane's sweet smile was inviting, too. He had been rolling words around in his head, summoning the courage to wade in and ford the river of their relationship. He'd be charming, yet bold—direct, but not demanding.

"Ya got that dopey look on yer face again, Fin. Just thought you should know. Kinda hard to keep yer thoughts private when they're written all over yer face." Noah clucked and the Hunt boys snickered.

"My sister said you got a gal in Charleston, that right?" Mark Hunt asked, guiding his horse a little closer.

The words that stormed into Fin's brain were none too kind. He'd like to keep what's private, private. *Courage, man.* "That's

199

right. The prettiest, perkiest little gal you ever laid eyes on."
There was a freedom here. He could do this.

Noah spoke up, "He was living with her under the same roof before the war." He shot an exaggerated wink at the Hunts. "Ain't that right, Sarge?"

Courage. "That's right. She shared a room with my sister. Known her since she was a little tike, too."

"Sounds like you know her real well then," Matthew said.

"How come you're not already married?" Mark piped up, pulling a long piece of new grass through his lips.

"Are you married already in the eyes of God?" John, the youngest of the Hunt boys was full of surprises.

"John!" Matthew scolded.

"Well, they lived under the same roof." John retorted. "Paw says that temptation and women go together."

Courage. "It was sort of a slow-moving relationship between us. And that's the end of the discussion."

Noah laughed, calling forth more of the same from the Hunts. Fin passed a stern look to each of them, hoping to squash the entertainment, but it only served to send Noah into such fits—he had to wipe water from his eyes.

Charleston

Fin nudged Duke's head from the watering trough. "You can have a little more later, boy." He turned to Matthew Hunt, who was adjusting the cinch on his saddle. They had been ready for a break, but these boys, especially, needed to stretch their legs before the long trek northwest to the Ohio border.

"It was real good to see you and your brothers again."

"We're grateful for your company on the road, Fin. I want you to know I'll be praying for you. You and Noah both." Matthew shook his hand, then motioned for his brothers to mount up.

"I appreciate that. I hope you all find jobs where you're going."

"We don't need much, but it'd sure be nice to send some back to Mama and Rebecca."

"Well," Fin drawled, "if you're ever in Gauley, there's a hot meal for you. All of you." Noah and Fin made the rounds, shaking the hand of each of the Hunts.

"Godspeed!" Fin lifted a hand in farewell as the horses kicked up dust, heading out of town.

"Nice family, those Hunts," Noah said. He tucked in his shirt, adjusted his galluses, and threw back his shoulders. "You ready to report to the Colonel, Sergeant Dabney?"

"Yes, Corporal, I am." Fin brushed off his hat and hitched up his britches.

They had only a short walk up the block. A small, unpainted house looked to be squished up against a good-sized warehouse. Beside the door, a blue banner read: FEDERAL COMMAND OFFICE.

Pushing through the door, Fin removed his hat at the sight of a young woman sitting at a paper-piled desk. She rummaged through a stack of telegrams, then, as if she had not heard the door open, jerked her head up in shock. "C—can I help you . . . Sergeant?"

"We're here to see Colonel Lightburn, ma'am."

Her piercing blue eyes fixed on Noah, as if Fin wasn't even in the room. She touched the spectacles perched on her nose and lowered her eyes, suddenly shy.

Noah's mouth gaped, then snapped shut. He snatched off his cap and stepped forward. "I'm Corporal Hicks, ma'am. I am truly pleased to make yer acquaintance."

The woman smiled and met his gaze. An awkward stillness fell over the room.

Fin cleared his throat. "We're here to see Colonel Lightburn." He turned from her to Noah. How they both managed that same silly look, he would never know.

She leapt to her feet, bumping the desk and scattering the stack of telegrams. "Yes. I'll let him know."

She was taller than Melinda Jane, and there was more of her, too—especially on the top half, which looked to be a mighty burden for her tiny waist. Fin felt guilty for noticing such a thing. She disappeared through a door.

Noah sighed. "I think I'm in love."

"Have a little guide of yourself, Corporal—and suck those eyes back into their sockets."

The secretary reappeared with a demure smile and held open the door. "The Colonel will see you now."

Col. Lightburn stepped around a heavy walnut desk. "Sergeant Dabney and Corporal Hicks. The promotions suit you. Have a seat, men. It's real good to have you back under my wing."

Fin pulled a chair closer to the desk and waited for the colonel to sit first. "It's good to be back, too, sir."

"Yes, sir. We're happy to be back with our regiment." Noah sat down, following Fin's lead.

"Sounds like you boys have been worth your salt battling the guerilla bands east of here. Even making quite a name for yourselves."

"Just doing our job, sir." And it was just that to Fin, too—a job ridding his home of the thieving, murderous bushwhackers who'd just as soon use the war as an excuse to ravage innocents.

"I'd say you boys have a gift, and I'd like to spread that gift around. By week's end, the Fourth Virginia Regiment will be moving down the valley to our new base camp at Top Mountain. Our mission is to combat the growing guerilla trouble in the eastern counties of the soon-to-be new state of West Virginia. You will begin training men of the Fourth for this task tomorrow."

"Sunday, sir?" Fin was at a loss for words. Col. Joe was a God-fearing man and took the day of worship real serious.

"Training will begin at noon, after the morning service. I fear the task before you"—he indicated Noah—"both of you, is monumental."

"I was hoping to visit a spell with my family here in Charleston, sir." Fin's hopes slid precariously downward.

"Check in with the orderly sergeant and quartermaster for anything you need to get set up for your time here. You can take leave for the evening and report back here at nine o'clock. Will that give you time for a visit?" The colonel rose from his chair.

"Yes, sir."

"Corporal, you are dismissed. Sergeant Dabney, a word."

Noah headed out, raising an eyebrow to Fin in passing.

Col. Joe gripped Fin's shoulders and squeezed. "You've been through quite a lot the last few months, Fin. Sit down and talk to me." He turned the chair Noah had vacated so it faced Fin's.

Where to begin? "What have you heard?"

"I got a letter from Colonel Moor, lauding your efforts and successes. He also informed me of the situation with your farm. I'm sorry. That must've been difficult for you."

"Yes, it was." He ground his back teeth together. "But my family is here in Charleston for the time being, and they're all safe. I'll get that barn built back after the war, though it could never be as grand as the one my pap built."

The colonel nodded, a knowing sadness passing over his features. "And what of this run-in with the river and your injuries?"

Fin related the story, along with the details of some of the missions, emphasizing the Federal courier threat.

The colonel seemed to sense Fin's thoughts straying to the family visit. "I'll let you get going. We can catch-up some more over the next few days."

After checking in with the quarter master and orderly sergeant to secure quarters and a few training materials, Fin headed to the barbershop. Bold red lettering listed the services on the large window: SHAVE 10¢, HAIRCUT 15¢. He washed up in the back room, then waited impatiently as the man in the white coat vanquished months of uneven whiskers and overgrown hair.

Fin rubbed the short, even beard, feeling like a new man on the outside. He would change into his other uniform, which was a bit less rumpled and stained. Mayhap he could find some flowers too.

He tipped his head in polite greeting to passers-by as he rode down Front Street, but scowling faces turned away. Now and then, he would glean a respectful nod.

The steamboat landing housed several steamers. Two of them puffed black smoke, preparing for departure. He headed away from the river on Summers street and spied a tall, brick building at the end of the block. Fancy signage read: KANAWHA HOUSE HOTEL.

He turned the corner onto Back Street, thinking to ask at the hotel for directions. Just before dismounting, he spotted another sign farther up the street: LAIDLEY'S DRUG STORE. A bucket of bright yellow daffodils set on a bench in front of the store window. Perfect.

Fin tied Duke and headed toward the store. A merchant tugged on his apron, attempting to smooth it over his ample middle. Fin stepped closer. "Pardon me, sir. Can you direct me to the home of Dr. James Hill?"

Sour lemons couldn't have puckered his face more. The man stood taller. "What business you got there?"

"My family's there, sir."

"Family? You related to Miss Minard?" The man cocked his head, as if daring Fin to pick the right answer.

"In a way, sir." What could he say? "She lives with my family, sort of a . . .a sister to me." Now *that* was not true. "We grew up together."

The man relaxed his stance and a trace of a smile, more just a pleasant expression, crept over his face. "Well, I'd be obliged to help you out then, son. Even if you are a Yankee." He pointed east. "Head on down a little farther and take a left on Cox's Lane. It'll be up on your right a ways, past Mercer Academy. Can't miss the shingle on the front porch."

"I'm appreciative. I'd like to buy some of those yellow flowers you got out there, too."

The man actually smiled. "Miss Minard will like those real fine. Lovely flowers for a lovely lady, eh?" He chuckled. "Voice like an angel, that one."

As anxious as he was to see his family, Fin walked Duke along the dirt road at a slow pace. He rolled over and over in his mind just what he would say when he came face to face with Melinda Jane.

"These flowers are for you and that hanky I picked out special. I love you, Melinda Jane." That wouldn't do. You can't just up and tell a woman you love her. Can you? Maybe he'd pull her to him in a manly but gentle way. He'd say, *"I'm finally claiming you as my own, Melinda Jane."* No. That made her sound like property. She'd buck at that for sure. What words could he use that a woman like her would take to heart? *Oh Lord, I could sure use some help here.*

He was more comfortable in a firefight and giving orders than spilling his guts to the woman he loved, and that was the sad truth. It was no foundation for a marriage, and he knew it.

A high-dollar black buggy passed him, heading the opposite direction, and he took notice of the dandy seated beside a woman in the interior. A fancy blue hat cocked over her forehead shadowed her face. He would make sure Melinda Jane had a fancy carriage like that one day. And fancy clothes, too. After the war. After he built the farm back up.

Twenty-Eight

M elinda Jane removed the long hairpins from her hat, careful to protect the feathered netting that dipped over one eye. Such an extravagant thing, but she had purchased it plain blue, and,with Gus's help, fancied it up to match her best dress. She handed the hat to Anderson, who stood patiently with her cape draped over one arm.

"The room is already nearly full." He grinned and turned toward the cloakroom.

She scanned the space. It seemed each time she arrived at the Kanawha House, something had changed. Now there was a lovely green velvet scarf draped over the piano top, its graceful fringes framing the beautiful piece of furniture. Weren't there more tables in here? It seemed . . . cramped.

Couples sat here and there, still finishing up supper. That was different. A row of empty chairs lined one wall this evening. In one corner, several men sat at two tables playing cards, tendrils of cigar smoke circling above their heads. She frowned at the decanter of amber liquid on a low table, then noticed that some of the men had small glasses in front of them. The men played cards at only one table last week, but this week there were two card tables—liquor as well. What would next week bring?

A waiter glided across the floor, setting an empty glass on the green piano scarf.

Her insides pressed against her outsides. She had never intended to sing before an audience of gamblers and drinkers. She had merely wanted to share her music with others—to bring some levity to folks during this time of the turmoil. A verse from Colossians squeezed into her mind. How did that go? *Whatsoever ye do in word or deed, do all in the name of the Lord Jesus.*

She startled at the touch of Anderson's fingers on her arm. "Are you all right?"

"I'm feeling a mite all-overish. Every time I come here, the audience is different. Last week there was just two soldiers, now there's a half dozen." Keeping her back to the audience, she whispered, "And there's two card games—and *whiskey!*"

Anderson pulled her closer, one hand on her arm and the other on her back. "Not to worry, Melinda Jane. They all love you. Word is just getting around town about the lovely young lady that sings. That's all." His hazel eyes sparkled in the glow of the gas lights, capturing her attention. "I will protect you from any ruffians or fowl play, milady." He bowed, pressing his lips to her hand, his spade beard brushing over her fingers.

She giggled. "Maybe I am being just a little silly about this." She pulled a folded piece of paper from her beaded bag. The list of songs contained a couple of new ones. They had agreed on songs that were neither Northern nor Southern in sentiment, but hopefully neutral. Oh, how she hoped there would not be too many requests tonight.

Anderson played a series of arpeggiated chords and the room fell quiet. "Ladies and gentlemen, the lovely Miss Melinda Jane Minard." He started right in on the introduction of "Camptown Races" as people applauded politely.

Folks clapped to the rhythm when she followed with "Oh, Susanna." She paused for a drink of water and continued with "Comin' Thro the Rye." She sang the sad ballad of "Barbara Allen," squashing the fleeting pain as she told the sad story of Will and Barbara, whose love lay unrequited until death. Images of Fin bounced through her mind, and she stumbled on the words for a moment.

A hush fell upon the audience as she sang of the rose that grew from poor Will's heart. From Barbara's grew a briar, which wrapped around the rose in a lover's knot. She quelled a sob as she ended the last note.

A man crossed the room to place a heavy coin into the empty glass. "A request, please. 'My Old Kentucky Home.'" He nodded politely. A grumble emanated from the soldiers.

"I'd be delighted to, sir." Melinda Jane passed a look to Anderson, who simply encouraged her with a smile as his fingers began the song. The requests continued, leaving her pining for the songs on her list. More folks filtered in, soon filling not just every table, but all the chairs along the wall as well.

Anderson stood. "Miss Minard will take a brief break and be right back with some newer songs." Energetic applause filled the room.

"Let's hear some dancing music!" one of the card players shouted. His tablemates joined in, sounding off in agreement.

Anderson walked Melinda Jane to the cloakroom. "Are you doing all right? You can't let those rowdies get to you."

"Oh, I know. Just so they don't get out of hand. You're sure about these new songs, now?"

"If you're ready, I think they will be well received."

She took a deep breath and let it out, willing her mind to focus. "I just hope I remember all the words."

Moments later, Anderson played a chord, and she began acappella: "Do they miss me at home, do they miss me? 'Twould be an assurance most dear, to know that this moment some loved one were saying, 'I wish he were here.'" Even the gamblers stilled, and one woman dabbed at her eyes with a hanky. Melinda Jane almost missed her entrance when the piano joined in on the second verse. How heavy her heart felt. *Yes, you are missed, Fin.*

She sang "The Vacant Chair," and the brand new, "Tramp, Tramp, Tramp." Each at the request of a soldier in blue. A yellow-haired soldier stared at her in a most curious way, much to the irritation of his well-endowed guest.

Next she would sing the slow George Root ballad she had worked on—"Just Before the Battle Mother." My, but the room seemed to dim, reflecting the mood in her heart. Sniffles dotted the subdued audience.

One of the card players crammed a dollar bill into the request glass. "The Southern Soldier Boy." It was more of a command than a request. Melinda Jane shot a panicked look at Anderson. Immediate disapproval arose from some in the crowd, and the volume of discord grew.

Anderson stood, his hands urging the crowd to calm. "We are happy to take requests, but we ask that you choose those songs which are neutral in sentiment."

Another man stood to his feet. "You sayin' the suffering of a Southern soldier ain't worth singing about?"

"It's not that . . ." Anderson stepped away from the piano.

"You and her are Yankee lovers, aintcha?"

"We don't need no trouble here." The yellow-haired soldier stood. "Sing whatever you want to, Miss." He nodded to Melinda Jane.

"She wants to sing, Dixie. Dontcha young lady?" A gray-bearded gentleman stood and his wife jerked at his sleeve, trying to yard him back to his chair.

"Yeah, sing Dixie!"

Chairs scraped against the floor as more folks stood. Bickering escalated into shouting matches—until the smack of a fist clipped the tension, followed by the collision of a Union soldier's face with a chair.

Anderson jostled Melinda Jane into the cloakroom, shoving her hat and cape into her arms. "Let's get out of here." He guided her through the mayhem, skirting what was now a brawl in the middle of the room. A gaggle of fussing, weeping women tried to crowd through the door at once.

"My belly couldn't hold another bite, Mrs. O'Donell. Thank you. Those beef dodgers were real tasty and the brown betty plum filled me all the way up." Fin patted his middle. What a feast compared to camp food.

"The dodgers were me own, but the brown betty—now that 'twas Melinda Jane's doin'."

"Speaking of . . . she'll probably be here any minute, Fin." James stood. "Can I get you some more coffee?"

Fin was trying to get used to the severe scarring on his new brother-in-law's face. The pain must've been horrific. Maybe still was.

Mrs. O'Donell rose, shooing James back. "You sit down. I'll bring out the pot."

"Thank you, Mrs. O'Donell. The coffee is real tasty too. You wouldn't believe some of the stuff they call coffee at the mess." Fin glanced again at the mantle clock. He noticed the fireplace was all set for a fire, but a small, coal-burning parlor stove warmed the house instead.

"Can you come back tomorrow?" Gus asked, patting his hand. "Melinda Jane will be heart broken if she misses you."

"Yeah, well, you can tell her I was disappointed too, I reckon." All his plans dashed. His speech, the flowers, her gift. More than his patience was getting trampled on as he pictured her with some

211

Anderson fella, singing in front of who-knows-what type of men. And women, he supposed. He was trying not to get keyed up.

"You hear about the vote and the new state constitution?" Zander asked.

The boy met him eye-to-eye when he opened the door earlier this evening. He had grown into a man, it seemed, in no time at all. "I heard. I still don't think they should be calling us 'West Virginia.' Seems like we're just still an extension of the Old Dominion that way."

"Yeah," Zander said, rubbing his hands on his knees, "I think they could've done better with that too." He glanced at the clock, then shrugged. "Melinda Jane's not the only one that's found a job. I been picking up work from some of the families missing a husband off to war. Got myself a list of regulars—chopping wood, shoveling coal, and odd jobs."

"Why, you're real enterprising, Zander. How's Rampart doing? No pasture and all. Probably mighty hard on him."

"I take him out every day. I'm keeping him shod with the money I make. Plus help out around here with food and such."

Fin squeezed his brother's shoulder. "I'm proud of you. Real proud."

"What about me?" Bertie asked from the spot he had claimed at Fin's feet.

"I'm proud of you too, little brother." He scrubbed his head and patted the blondish cowlick with his hand.

Fin passed his gaze around. Hard to get over the idea of Gus and James being married. Might be he would find himself an uncle one of these days soon. He smiled. Yeah, he liked that idea. *Uncle Fin.*

Will seemed tamer somehow, without the countryside as her playground. When had she grown into a young woman? Such a difference without that old hat and overalls he was used to seeing her in. No doubt she was sure missing the barn. Gus, too, for that matter. The farm was in their blood. Every one of these Dabneys.

Just as Fin glanced at the clock again, Coot bounded for the door with a short yip. He whined, then plopped down, his nose to the doorjamb.

"That surely means Melinda Jane's home." Bertie jumped up and headed for the door.

James grabbed his shoulders, turning him toward the kitchen. "What say we all make our way to the kitchen—or to bed. Somewhere that's not in here." He caught Gus's eye, and she wasted no time pulling Will to her feet.

Melinda Jane breathed in the lingering aroma of spring blossoms that positively permeated the night air. "Too bad this beautiful evening had to be spoiled with such bawdy behavior." She turned to Anderson before putting her hand on the door. "I think I'm through at the Kanawha House. I can't believe I practically incited a riot."

"It was hardly you, Melinda Jane. It was a handful of men just looking to vent their frustrations. You handled it all magnificently."

"I should've listened to that little voice inside me. I felt uncomfortable the minute I saw those gamblers with their whiskey. What was I thinking?" She scolded herself on the inside, too. Next time, she would trust her instincts. No. Not her instincts. She would listen to the Holy Ghost. That's what Izzy would've told her to do.

Anderson sighed. "What if I talk to Mr. McFarland and request he have a couple of men there. Just in case something like this ever happens again."

"It won't happen again because I'm not singing there anymore." She crossed her arms.

"The card playing surely is a picayune affair. Think of all the good you're doing with the money you've earned. The hungry are no longer as hungry. You mustn't be selfish, Melinda Jane."

Her back went rigid. *Selfish?*

"What I really want to say is . . . don't you think God provided this opportunity so you could help those folks?"

Anderson pulled on one hand until she assented, then folded it in his own. He smiled that charming smile of his. "If. *If* I get Mr. McFarland to agree there will be no more alcohol served while you are performing, will you agree to give it another shot? And . . . we'll say no more requests. Surely that would make you happy."

Happy? What would make her happy is if she never sang any of those sad songs again. They only made her heart ache more for Fin.

True. She had helped folks so much more with what she made at the hotel. Did she genuinely want to deprive them because she was uncomfortable?

"And no more smoking either." She would make the sacrifice.

"Done. I'll speak with Mr. McFarland tomorrow . . . or Monday."

"And I pick all the songs. I don't want to sing anymore about boys dying in the war or love lost."

He chuckled. "You drive a hard bargain, Miss Minard. I'll see what I can do." With one hand still holding hers, he cupped her shoulder. "See you in church tomorrow?"

"I'll be there."

He pressed a chaste kiss to her cheek.

Fin pulled the hanky from his shirt pocket and smoothed the wrinkles. Snatching up the flowers now in a vase, he headed for the front door, brushing Coot out of his path. His heart thumped like a galloping horse and already his palms were moist. Now, if he could just remember what to say.

He turned the knob and jerked the door open, relishing the burst of surprise on her face. His breath caught.

There stood Melinda Jane and some dandy, with his paws on her. And he was kissing her!

She jerked back, her mouth agape and eyes wide with shock. "Fin!"

An invisible mule kicked him in the gut.

He slammed the door. Stumbling over Coot, he grabbed up his hat and bolted for the back door. Fin yanked the reins from its ring and vaulted onto Duke. He squinted into the dark, squashing with all his might the roar that belted his insides. What was he thinking? He had been three kinds of a fool!

Melinda Jane fumbled with the doorknob. "I have to go." She slammed the door behind her, leaving a confused Anderson on the porch. "Fin, wait. It's not what you think!"

James and Gus stood in the kitchen doorway, fear etching their faces. Gus stepped forward. "What just happened?"

Yellow daffodils littered the entry. Melinda Jane reached down to pick up a white hanky with fine lacy edges. Across one corner, the most delicate embroidery spelled her name. She choked back a sob. "Where is he? Where is he, Gus?"

Her friend wrapped her in a caring embrace. "He's gone, honey. He waited for you as long as he dared."

"But . . . but what he saw . . . it wasn't what he thinks." Her chest heaved and great tears rolled down her face. "Oh Gus, I've lost him!"

Twenty-Nine

F in stood in his stirrups, shifting his weight to stretch out a cramp. Ah. Clean air at last. Back in Charleston, the smell of industry wafted on the breeze. Just another reason to be clear of that town.

Ten companies of the Fourth Virginia Regiment snaked along the Kanawha and James River Turnpike. Tucked into the tight formation of dedicated Unionists, it was good to be a part of something bigger again. Fin preferred to rely on the line of command under Colonel Lightburn, as opposed to deciding life and death issues for his own small band. He didn't mind leading when he had to, but right now, this felt better. In the next few days, they would meet up with General Cox and head to their new outpost at Flat Top Mountain.

Hours ticked off at a snail's pace until a rider galloped from the front of the ranks and pulled up next to Fin. "You're Dabney, right?"

"That's me." Fin glanced around for anything out of the ordinary.

"The Colonel wants you and your Corporal up to the front." The man spun his pony and galloped back up ahead.

Noah scowled. "Now what could that be about, you suppose?"

"Guess we'll find out in a bit." Fin reined Duke to the side of the column and trotted forward.

"Just when I was starting to feel things were gonna get easier, now the big man wants something from us. Just you wait. 'Dabney, I want you and Hicks to do such and such.'" His voice deepened as he mimicked their commanding officer.

"You're treading on thin ice there, Hicks."

"I didn't mean nothin' by it. Truth is, at least when we're scared silly trying to stay alive, I'm not bored." He grinned, tipping his head to one side. "True enough?"

"Definitely not boring." His motivation to make it home unscathed had gone missing. Try as he might, he couldn't get the image out of his thick head—that dandy kissing Melinda Jane. Some men would take comfort in strong drink or even another woman, but that wasn't his way. His pap would tell him to stay the course, do what's right. So. Right is following orders, trying to rid his beloved Virginia hills of those bent on taking them for their own.

"Ah, Sergeant, Corporal. I want you to pick a half dozen men and ride on ahead. A scout tells me some of Spriggs' Rangers have been sighted." Col. Joe scratched his beard. "I was hoping for an unremarkable journey."

"Yes, sir, Colonel." Fin and Noah turned back. Each picked three men and within minutes took off ahead of the column.

They had gone less than a mile when a Federal rider galloped toward them and Fin pulled up. The scout yanked his horse to a stop. His chest heaved, and he surveyed the detachment. "You the advance unit?"

"We are. What do you have?" Fin eyed Noah. The boy was a little shaken.

"I saw them. Spriggs' Rangers. They didn't see me, but I'm real sure that's who they are. They're walking through the trees real slow-like." He swallowed hard. "I'll show ya."

"Lead on, Private." Fin took his men off down the pike, pulling up real easy when the soldier pointed into the thick growth of trees.

Thirty minutes of looking, and sure enough, there they were. Looked to be about a dozen men on horseback picking their way through the trees. In a short time span, Fin and his men surrounded them.

Noah fired a shot into the air.

Fin called out, "You are surrounded by the Fourth Virginia Regiment. Put down your weapons, and we'll take you in peaceably. If not, you're outnumbered, and we won't be peaceable." The outnumbered part was a falsehood. He would ask forgiveness later.

The Rangers halted, every eye scanning the surrounding woods. They looked to a stout, orange-bearded man. He scowled. Just as Fin thought he was going to come peaceably, the man opened fire into the trees, igniting a firefight.

Fin took careful aim. His bullet hit the man's gun hand.

The red-beard growled. "Hold yer fire!" By the time the smoke settled, two of the Rangers lay on the ground. Only one moved.

Yep. Nothing quite like the familiar smells of home. Fin pointed ahead. "You're really gonna like the new bridge, Colonel. Corporal Hicks and I watched them test that thing with near every piece of artillery and able body at the camp. Quite a sight."

"A thing of beauty, that's for sure. Kind of makes those pontoon boats obsolete at this point." Col. Lightburn returned a salute to the guard as the column marched across the bridge. They would quarter here tonight, then head to Flat Top tomorrow.

Fin saw to the prisoners before making his way to check in with Fischer, Walter, Benzinger, and the rest.

Noah beat him to it. He was already jabbering about the young woman from the Charleston command office. Fin was sick of hearing about her. Let someone else listen for a change.

Hicks had talked her into having supper with him, and they ended up in some brawl in an eatery of sorts. To hear him tell it, he had saved her from the entire War of Rebellion.

"Did you hear the news, Sarge?" Fischer said, dropping to the ground, offering Fin his cot.

"What news is that?"

"Lieutenant-Colonel Becker is soon to be acting commander of the twenty-eight Ohio. Colonel Moor is being reassigned to Cox's Second Brigade. We'll be seeing you boys up to Flat Top sounds like."

"Well, what do you know?" Noah grinned. "Maybe we'll just have to get the old band back together, huh?

Fin grunted and stood. "Good to see you boys. I'm beat. Gonna find my bedroll."

"Night, Sarge."

Noah followed him out. "I sure wish you'd let me in on whatever's got you all melancholy. Something happened when you went home. You can tell ol' Noah."

"Not gonna happen." Fin strode out ahead, putting distance between them, hoping the pie-eater would take a hint.

"Sergeant Dabney!" Col. Joe waved him over, closing the gap at a clipped pace. "I was in need of some leg-stretching. I've got some information you may be interested in."

"Sir?"

"There was a wounded prisoner you brought in before leaving for Charleston—Clawson, I think the name was. Moccasin Rangers ambushed the transport of prisoners, and he escaped. Colonel Moor thought you would want to know."

Like a festering wound, loathing bubbled up all rank and ugly. Would he ever be rid of that man? He cleared his voice, willing his throat to relax. "When did this happen?"

"Day before yesterday, he said. I can see by your reaction this news pains you. Why is this prisoner so special, Fin?" The colonel relaxed his stance, folding his hands in front of him. He had a way of inviting a sharing of confidence, wooing a man to let down his guard.

Fin studied the top of his foot, then squinted into the distance. "Sir, that man killed a real close friend of mine last summer. He and his men murdered him, leaving him with a hot iron tine in his chest—all on account of his skin color, I reckon." Fin swallowed down the bile as Tiny's maimed face flashed in his mind.

"And still you brought him in, alive, when you could've just as easily exacted your vengeance, no questions asked." Col. Joe's scrutinizing gaze drilled into his soul.

"That's something I recognized in you, the first month you were in my unit. You have a keen sense of justice, but you don't count yourself the judge. Takes a strong man to live that way." He gripped Fin's shoulder. "God will bring justice to that vermin—either in this life or the next, maybe both. And God will reward your integrity. I wish I had more men like you, Fin. Men I could trust. We are in a war, yes, but it needn't strip a man of his humanity or God's favor."

"Thank you, sir." He did not feel so strong at the moment.

"Get some sleep, Sergeant. We head out at seven o'clock in the morning."

"Good night, sir." Fin scuffed the sole of his boot along the ground as he neared the campsite. He would truly welcome the opportunity to kill Clawson. What kind of man had he become, to regard murder in his heart that way?

He inhaled through his nose, filling his lungs before snorting it out like a goaded bull. *Give me the strength to leave it in your hands, Lord.*

Thirty

CHARLESTON

Melinda Jane squinted as sunlight poked over the rolling landscape. How she loved the Easter sunrise service. Back at Gauley Bridge, the congregation would meet down by the river on this most glorious of mornings. Sometimes there would even be a baptism. Here in Charleston, though, they held the service indoors. What a waste of a new day's beauty.

On this Resurrection Day, her heavy heart yearned for newness and a resurrection of her own spirit.

"You're looking mighty pensive for an Easter morn, Melinda Jane." Gus threaded her arm through hers. "I can see where your thoughts are, sister. You pray for a chance to set things straight with that brother of mine, and you'll see—he'll come around."

"I don't know. I waited so long for this spark to flame brighter and when it did, I stomped right on it, snuffing it to cold, charred sticks." She shook her head, patting Gus's hand. "I can only trust God to make this right now. He knows my heart and He can work on Fin's. If it's meant to be, it will." Such sadness pushed on her insides. She swiped at a tear. "If it's not meant to be . . . well then, I'm asking the Lord to make it clear to my stubborn thinker real soon so I can move forward."

"But you still love him?"

"I do. Oh, I certainly do. Why else would this hurt so?" She forced a smile, then pulled Gus close as they entered the church.

"Miss Minard. Mrs. Hill." Preacher Lambert greeted them with two outstretched hands. "He is risen!"

"He is risen, indeed," the two women replied in unison.

"I wonder. If you ladies are going to minister to the poor this afternoon, might I accompany you? I was planning on an afternoon service there on this most holy of days."

Melinda Jane exchanged looks with Gus. "That's a wonderful idea, Preacher. The folks will be so pleased!"

"I'm looking forward to it. I'm also looking forward to the choir's presentation this morning, Melinda Jane." He smiled, then turned to Mr. and Mrs. Talbert, greeting them next.

Melinda Jane waved her hands in the air, partly directing and wholly encouraging the audience's exuberance. Standing in the wagon bed, she lifted her declaration to the heavens on a melody that burst from the very depths of her soul.

What a glorious day! Ragged folks, weary of each day's dregs, raised their voices with such passion. "Christ the Lord is risen today," they sang. A few quivery hands raised in praise of a God who would send His son to die for them. "Raise your joys and triumphs high!" Tears brimmed in her eyes as she quieted her own words to listen to the sweet sound ascending to the throne room. These folks searched for and found joy—choosing to believe that somehow, they truly had triumphed over their meager lot.

Nettie smiled through her words, hugging Olivia and Perry to her side. The unseen child beneath her skirts was making himself known to others now, and Melinda Jane wondered if Nettie's husband, Milo, had been around to notice. No bruises on the young woman's face. A blessed sign of the man's absence.

Brother Lambert preached an impassioned sermon of the Good News, urging folks to keep their eyes on Jesus and the promises of the next life. How the crowd responded!

Standing beside Nettie amid the crowd, Melinda Jane listened. She focused on bringing back her thoughts from soldiers whose lives were in danger today. She remembered the names and faces of those she knew from Gauley Bridge, when soldiers were at the farm, using the barn as a hospital. *Please be with them, Lord.* And for the hundredth time, her heart clutched at the thought of Fin, cold and still somewhere on the ground. *Heavenly Father, please!*

"How have you been feeling, Nettie?" James's voice tugged Melinda Jane back to the present.

Nettie rubbed a hand over her belly. "I's doin' jest fine, Dr. Hill."

"Remember, have someone come for me if you encounter any problems with the pregnancy, you hear?"

"I most surely will, Doctor." She rubbed Perry's head. "Thank you."

Melinda Jane pulled Olivia into a hug. "I have something for you, little lady." She pulled two ribbons from her dress pocket.

"They's so purty, Miss Minard! Yellow and green!" The girl fingered the smooth pieces. "For me? Just me?"

"This most special day of the year deserves something special. Just as God gave his Son as a gift, I'm celebrating by giving you a gift. You might even want to share one with your mama on occasion."

Oof! The girl's body crashed against Melinda Jane's hip and spindly arms squeezed her middle, forcing the air out of her.

"You are a gift to us, Melinda Jane." Nettie pulled her close in a hug.

Will skipped up, her hand swinging in rhythm, attached to the hand of a girl who was a head shorter. "Do we have time for a game of knuckle bones before we leave?"

"I'm sorry, sweetie. We're about to head out."

Will frowned and turned to her friend. "Let's play hopscotch for a few minutes then."

The girl pulled on a ratty braid, puffed with tangles of flaxen hair. "All right." Her voice was nearly a whisper, but her enthusiastic smile warmed Melinda Jane's heart. If only she could do more for these people—to bring joy to their lives every day, not just on the weekends.

Thirty-One

FLAT TOP MOUNTAIN, VIRGINIA

Fin inhaled the crisp air, detecting the familiar scent of campfires as they neared Flat Top. The lengthy column of soldiers scattered, with the Fourth's ten companies ordered to various locations for quarter. Thinking to look around the area before a church meeting that night, Fin and Noah headed off to the east of Camp Flat Top in search of a higher viewpoint.

Surely there was no land on this planet more alluring than the scene before them. Visibility was good—thirty to sixty miles of undulating country. Fin imagined the waves of tall spring grasses that would prompt this magnificent landscape to life in just a few short weeks. Some of the highest points of the Blue Ridge rose like dark clouds in the distance. Smaller mountain spurs dissolved into rolling hills nearer the Alleghany range.

Noah let out a slow whistle. "Brings a tear to yer eye, such beauty."

"That it does. Our Creator wields a mighty fine idea of what pleases a man's eye in nature."

Noah elbowed him. "That include women? I mean, you did say nature, and ain't women part of God's creation too?"

"This moment was real pleasant right up until you had to go and let your mind take a gander."

"Just can't seem to get that little gal in Charleston out of my head." Noah turned his horse around. "Think I'll head back. Get cleaned up for that meeting the boys were talkin' of."

Fin followed, but now his mind wandered too. He could see Melinda Jane taking in this sight. She'd most likely toss her bonnet, if she wore one, and spin in a dance, her arms outstretched. He'd always loved her free spirit and the easy way she shared it with others. She was strong in ways he saw himself weak—or at least used to.

He was discovering new things about himself. Some he liked. Some he didn't. He'd considered that maybe his whole infatuation with the girl was for the purpose of teaching him something. But, what? What was he supposed to be learning from all this? If there was a lesson to be learned here, it was an insufferable one.

Fidgeting soldiers crowded into rows of crude benches in a semblance of order. Fin followed Noah, sitting behind the benches on felled trees forming three more makeshift rows, flanking a center aisle. A church in the wilderness, with a pieced tarp stretched over a portion in the front.

Men sat on the ground or reclined, eventually filling available space all along the sides. A few even found a seat among tree branches. The subdued hum of conversation seemed almost reverent. Even the air hung in anticipation, its freshness unsullied by sour cigar smoke or pipe tobacco.

From what Fin learned, this prayer meeting, started by a few faithful, had grown over the weeks and now he looked at almost a hundred men. He scanned the crowd, noticing that many had army-issued Bibles in hand. He glanced down at the one in his own. Gus had given him Pap's Bible the day he left home. The very one that held the picture of Melinda Jane. He stopped himself before he pulled it out. *Not now.*

The sweet croon of a harmonica brought a hush to the crowd. Fin thought of Sergeant Mallory, stationed at the Dabney barn last year. Never had he heard a body play with such passion and skill. But this music? He tipped his head right, then left, stretching his neck to see the gifted musician. Off to one side, up near the front, stood Mallory, the stocky, graying sergeant who had been James's right-hand man. A wave of nostalgia twisted a knife inside him. So much had changed in his life since he first met the sergeant.

A spectacled man in his early thirties, sporting a Chaplain's patch, stepped to the front. His clean-shaven face wore a welcoming smile as he began leading the men in *When I Survey the Wondrous Cross.*

Fin sang out, letting the words sink deep into his hungry spirit. *Love so amazing, so divine, demands my soul, my life, my all.* How good it felt to be among this throng of believers. Men of the Twenty-third and Thirty-fourth Ohio mingled with his own Fourth Virginia, some voices singing the lyrics in German.

A medium build man with a dark spade beard stepped to the front, gripping the chaplain's shoulder in greeting. "I'm Lieutenant Colonel Hayes of the Twenty-third, and I'd like to welcome the Fourth Virginia to Flat Top. We are honored they've brought with them a man I call friend, and one they respectfully refer to as *Colonel Joe.*" The men of the Fourth clapped rowdily, then quieted at a motion from Colonel Hayes.

"I've invited the *Reverend* Joseph Lightburn to speak to you tonight." He took two long steps, greeting Col. Joe with one hand and pulling him forward with the other. They shared some quiet banter and a laugh before Col. Joe took his place, front and center.

"What an honor it is to be among this congregation of fighting men as we celebrate the resurrection of our Lord." Bible in hand, he fanned away the splattering of applause. "Jesus did battle as He walked this earthly soil. His weapons of war were not the wood of the musket stalk, but the wood of a splintered cross." He paused as a few scattered *amens* floated through the air.

"His weapons were not the iron of a gun barrel, but the iron of Roman nails." A few more *amens*. The colonel smiled and nodded. "He recognized two sets of rules in war: worldly rules and heavenly rules. He chose the latter."

He balanced the opened, worn Bible in one hand as he stepped closer to the men. "In the second chapter of Hebrews, the second verse tells us that for the joy that was set before Him, Jesus endured the cross, despising the shame. I offer to you a few heavenly rules for this fight we wage here on this soil right now."

"From Romans chapter twelve, beginning with verse seventeen: 'Recompense to no man evil for evil. Provide things honest in the sight of all men.' I say to you, let even your enemies recognize you as a man of integrity, doing what is right and fair in God's eyes rather than the very deed your enemy would set upon you." He strolled to one side at the front, his demeanor that of a wizened father, counseling a diffident son.

"And verse eighteen: 'If it be possible, live peaceably with all men.' The key here is the word 'possible.' If you can resolve a situation without bloodshed, by all means, do it. Now I know that some in command would tell their men to take no prisoners." He stopped his slow pacing and faced the congregation. His chest expanded with a deep breath.

"I have made up my mind to spare a life if the opportunity presents itself. You might think all butternuts deserve death. But may I remind you that every one of them boys is somebody's father or brother or sweetheart. And may well be sitting this minute in a meeting such as this—singing and praying to the same God we do this night." The colonel cleared his throat, massaging his eyes with thumb and forefinger.

"The third rule of this battle is here in verse nineteen: 'avenge not yourselves, but rather give place unto wrath: for it is written, Vengeance is mine; I will repay, saith the Lord.' Now, you cannot take that any other way. I've known many a soldier that thought himself to be jury and judge. A soldier is an instrument, whether of a government or the army or God, but only that, an instrument. God is the one to see to the vengeance."

He resumed his slow steps across the front. "Many of you have clashed with these renegade bands that seize our state of war as an excuse for all manner of atrocity and senseless harm. This sinful indulgence is nothing less than barbarism. It is a tool of Satan himself to tear apart this country which was founded for the sake of religious freedom. Tear it apart clean down the middle." He bowed his head, pulling his hand across his mouth in slow motion.

"The last two rules separate the god-*less* from the God-*fearing*. In verse twenty: 'if thine enemy hunger; feed him. If he thirst, give him drink.' What man among you would not minister to the most fundamental physical need of a human being?" He held his Bible above his head with an outstretched arm. "Matthew twenty-five, forty. 'And the King shall answer and say unto them, verily I say unto you, inasmuch as ye have done it unto one of the least of these my brethren, ye have done it unto me.'" He lowered the tome and a keen silence settled over the men.

Fin glanced at Noah, whose chin sat on his chest, his yellow hair shrouding his face from view. A sniffle sounded here and there. In his own heart, Fin felt a pang of conviction. Oh, he had tried to demonstrate a sense of fair play in his dealings with the enemy, but there was always more he figured he could have done to honor God. Foremost in his mind were the murderous thoughts he had entertained for the Rebel Clawson. He had fought that giant, like David, and he thought he'd won, too—until hearing about the escape.

"In second Samuel, chapter twenty-two, David is on the run from his enemies and Saul is looking to kill him." Colonel Joe continued, his voice lower now. "He cried out to God, saying, 'In Him I will trust; He is my shield, my deliverer, the horn of my salvation, my high tower.'" A soft *amen* grew to several, one after the other, growing in strength of numbers and volume.

"'My Refuge. My savior'." More *amens*, and now some stood.

"'I will call on the Lord, Who is worthy to be praised!'"

"Hallelujah!" Noah rose abruptly from the log seat.

"'In my distress I called upon the Lord, and cried to my God: and He did hear my voice out of his temple, and my cry did enter into His ears.'" Col. Joe waited until a hush settled. "And did God answer David's plea?"

"Yes!" voices shouted in unison.

"He answered David's plea all those years ago, and He *will* answer yours today, men. He will answer just the same—for our God is the same yesterday, today, and forever."

"That's right!"

"Amen"

"Yes, He is!"

"Verse fourteen: 'The Lord thundered from heaven, and the most High uttered his voice.' The Lord what?"

"Thundered!" Deep voices shouted in unison.

"That's right. God Almighty *thundered* from heaven. Now if you are a student of science, you know that thunder follows lightening. Lightening is a powerful, fearful force of nature. It is the *lightning* that sets aflame. It is the *lightning* that brightens the sky making the darkness as mid-day."

His voice grew softer again, and Fin could feel the men lean forward, straining to hear the next line. "Listen for the thunder, boys. That thunder tells you God has heard your heart's cry. It tells you He has already put His answer into action. Honor God in the battle and seek His help. You *will* hear His thunder!"

The colonel stepped to the side, shaking the hand of the chaplain. "Thank you for that word, Colonel Lightburn. Let us take this time now to seek God, as the Colonel said. Beseech Him to help us fight the good fight. Cast our cares on Him. Listen for the thunder that is His response to our heart's cry.

"You are welcome to come forward for prayer or stay where you are, men. Bare your hearts to the One who holds your life in His hands. Pray for your brethren, sharing their burdens." He nodded to Mallory and the smooth harmonica music lead the men in song.

Fear not, I am with thee, O be not dismayed,
For I am thy God and will still give thee aid;
I'll strengthen and help thee, and cause thee to stand
Upheld by My righteous, omnipotent hand.

Night had long since descended by the time soldiers made their way from the prayer meeting. Sergeant Mallory had continued with his music, playing hymn after hymn, through worship and prayer until only a few remain. Fin had not remembered the man as religious. In fact, he seemed on the rougher side, as men go.

He lingered, waiting to greet Mallory, when a hand clamped onto his shoulder.

"'Tis a mighty fine way to end a day—comin' upon an old friend."

Fin grinned and spun on his heel. "Seamus McLaughlin!"

The burly man with the copper beard wrapped Fin in a bear hug, lifting him off the ground. "I ne'r thought to see a Dabney again. Come, sit with me. Tell me how the family is." Fin followed Seamus to a spot near men circled around a fire. They settled on the ground, and Seamus leaned back on his elbows, his long legs outstretched. "Spare me no news."

"I heard you were burned in the barn fire." Fin tried to remember just what he had heard.

"Sure and I was, but I was back to the medical after a month. Mostly it was the smoke that got to me." He held out his hands. "My palms and my knees kept me in bed a couple of weeks. I took no care for meself, but it were James and your Gus that scared me most. It took months, but I finally learned James made it through. I thought he was gone for sure when they transferred him up to Wheeling. When I left the house, Gus was unconscious." He slapped Fin on the knee. "Here, now. I'm doin' the talking, and you've not told me a word."

They jawed for an hour, just catching up. He had always been comfortable with Seamus. How good it felt to be with someone from before. Before life reared up on him and bolted off, out of his control.

Seamus laughed at the news of Gus and James's marriage. Seemed he had that match figured out long before they did.

"Let me tell you something, Fin. I am not the man I was last year. I've turned more than just half me heart toward the Savior. He's got me whole self now. E'n in the midst of this bloody war, I have ne'r felt a keener sense of peace. The hospital is slow for the staff they have here, so I've had ample time to read me Bible. I've prayed for James. Such bitterness he carried inside, and not a once would he let on about it."

"I hope you can see him again. He's a changed man, Seamus. He's found peace, too, it seems." Fin looked up, trying to make out the stars away from the glow of the fire. "You know my sister. She' never would've married him less'n he was godly."

Seamus grinned, then dropped his head as a yawn commandeered his face. He stood, lending a hand to Fin, pulling him upright. "I best be finding me pillow. Early shift in the morn." He slapped a hand across Fin's shoulder. "Tickles me fine to know yer here." He turned, heading into the darkness.

"Goodnight, Seamus."

Fin picked his way between tents and dimming fires, remembering to count the tents when he came to the fourth row. He'd look for Mallory tomorrow and find out if he knew any other men posted here.

Peace. The tangles and twists had smoothed enough to calm his spirit, and he'd rest in that for now.

Thirty-Two

May 1862

"Who would've figured us meeting up like this again?" Fin brushed the moist dirt from his britches and tugged his gun belt to one side. It had taken a couple of days to finally catch up with his old friend. "I thought after your Ironton Cav mustered out you'd go on back home. Retire all nice and peaceful."

Mallory harrumphed. "Retire? Me? I'd rather be cold in the ground." He poked a twig into the sticky mud, leaving it upright. "When you left that early morning last fall, I said to myself, 'Now there's a man who's got a reason to fight.' And look at you—got your sergeant stripes already." Mallory shifted to his knees before standing. "The creaks and cracks, they come a-plenty these days." Fin offered a hand, but the man shooed it away.

"When I found what those bushwhackers did to the home place, I added another reason, real fast-like." Fin grinned. "And when I heard that harmonica playing, I figured it had to be you. Your music brought a sense of . . . tranquility to that old barn."

The sergeant harrumphed again. "Weren't my music, Fin. It was the Spirit of God, called down by Ol' Izzy, the saint that he was."

Fin let the silence settle comfortably for a time. He called back his thoughts, swiping his forage hat against his leg. "Didn't see

Seamus last night at the meetin'. I think I'll go see what he's up to."

"Be seeing you around, *Sarge.*" The man nodded, one corner of his lip curled in half a smile. He turned and strolled off, the soft remnants of a song trailing after him.

Fin needed to stretch his legs. Leaving Duke to graze, he set out for the mile and a half hike down to the tableland of Camp Jones. He stuck a blade of tender grass between his lips and quickened his stride, remembering the long walks he would take with his pap as a boy.

He and Pap made a game of guessing what his mama would have ready for supper when they returned. His pap would come up with notions such as coyote steak with polecat gravy. Love for his family warmed his middle. Truly, he had been blessed. He'd hold that feeling of blessedness close to his heart for when he would need to draw on it.

A tall, thick figure with a red beard and a bloody apron tossed a pan of brown water into the scrub brush. He waved at Fin. Sure enough, Seamus was working, just as he suspected.

"I missed you last night," Fin said, nearing the hospital tent.

"Been a bit busy here. Those Flat Top Copperheads ambushed several of the Twenty-third's boys. Did some damage, they did—till enough reinforcements arrived and sent them guerillas running all the way to Princeton."

"Do tell."

"Set fire to the town first, they did. All to keep Rebel supplies from our hands. But Colonel Hayes's boys saved most of the town, then took one of the houses as a new command post."

"Seems I'm missing all the action these days."

"Be thankful for that. Sure'n you'll be busy again before long." Seamus wiped at his thick eyebrows with the back of his hand. "I've got me some bandages to change."

Fin tipped his chin in a farewell. "See you when things slow down again." He headed back up the rise, not in any hurry to resume his garrison duties.

❧

Charleston

Melinda Jane settled another can next to the sack of flour, jostling them to make room in the crate. "I think we can fit one more in this one."

Sarah pressed on the sack of cornmeal, flattening it into a square to tuck into the allotted space. "It pains me to see these portions get smaller and smaller. With the prices climbing up, I don't see us doing more than staples come next month. Why, tea is nearly five dollars a pound!"

"We'll just pray the Lord increases what we do give to the needy—just like the loaves and fishes." Melinda Jane plopped a bag of dried beans into the last crate. That's the last of the donated items. Is the coal already in the wagon?"

"I believe so." Sarah stomped her foot. "I do wish Daddy would allow me to accompany you and your family!" Her bottom lip protruded in an exaggerated pout. "When Edgar and I are wed, we will tend to the needs of those poor dears, side by side."

"Did that boy ask you for your hand?"

Sarah turned away, as if to recheck the empty crate on the floor. "Well, no. Not yet. But he will." She folded her hands together, pressing them to her heart. "He will." Her face very nearly glowed.

"Until then, you just mind your pap and don't give him a reason to say you can't help at all. I couldn't do this alone, Sarah." She hugged her friend, then smoothed back shiny dark hair from her eyes. "Thank you."

Sarah grinned, attempting to lift a heavy crate from the tabletop. "It is purely my pleasure."

"Let's have Zander haul these crates out to the wagon."

The crunch of rocks fell silent beneath the wagon wheels as Zander pulled the horses to a stop. Melinda Jane jumped down, unwilling to wait for Zander's help. She had spied Olivia and Perry Penchant huddled outside the door to their tiny hovel. *Strange.*

She waved to James and Gus in the carriage, just coming to a halt behind the wagon. "I'm going to check on Nettie." Lifting her hem, she bustled toward the two children.

She called out to them as she neared, and Olivia raised her head. They ran to Melinda Jane, and she wrapped them in a tight embrace, alarmed at their tear-streaked faces. She held them close, setting free a torrent of tears.

"Shh . . . hush, now. I'm here." Her voice may have been calm, her heart cried for God's intervention, for she had some idea what lay beyond that door—and she figured Nettie was not alone.

"What's wrong? Melinda Jane?" Will stepped up, massaging Olivia's shoulder with her hand.

Melinda Jane ushered the children toward Will. "You children go with Will now. She'll take good care of you and find you a little something special."

A quick glance at Will, and she turned, racing to the door. She jerked it open. Nettie sat crumpled in the corner, her knees drawn up to her chest, one hand protecting her head and the other clutching her legs.

"I'm sorry!" Nettie sobbed.

A broken chair teetered in the air, held menacingly by muscled arms. Milo roared, about to bring the chair down on his wife.

"No!" Melinda Jane screamed and lunged at the big man, yanking on his arms.

"Get out of here. I told you before. This be none of your bizness." He jerked his arm from her grasp, and Melinda Jane staggered.

She grabbed at the chair leg. "Stop it!"

He brought the chair down on her head. She crumbled to the floor.

Pain seared her head, her neck. The room tilted, and her stomach lurched. Nettie's screams. A dark stick struck Milo once. Twice. It stabbed into his lower back. He screamed out and turned. The hammer cock of a revolver. Her vision dimmed.

"Get out now and don't you ever come back!" Growled a voice. It quaked with rage, the likes of which she had never before heard.

The darkness consumed her, and silence with it.

Thirty-Three

FLAT TOP MOUNTAIN

F in walked another wounded man into the hospital before returning to help with the stretcher. Outside the tent, more of the wounded reclined, scattered across the grounds.

Something told him his boring days of garrison duty were about to come to a halt. Col. Von Blessing's men had been ambushed outside of Princeton. Then soon after, Federal soldiers had to flee the town, outnumbered by Rebel reinforcements. The casualty count was still unknown as more wounded trickled into Camp Jones.

Fin lifted bodies, hauled water, and emptied bloody basins. He learned long ago how to take on the inglorious tasks necessary in doctoring. Several hours of chaos finally lulled to a quieter, more organized tending to the injured and dealing with the dead.

"What a night." Sergeant Mallory leaned against a tree, palming his harmonica.

"I don't think Seamus will be getting any sleep tonight." Fin dropped to the ground, feeling relief to the soles of his feet.

Mallory flipped over a bucket and sat down. "Word has it those German conscripts of Von Blessings helped themselves to a wagon of Confederate whiskey, and that's how the Rebels took them in that ambush."

Fin let out a low whistle. What could he say? Today, the love of whisky got men killed and maimed. Somebody's head was gonna roll—if that somebody was still alive.

Seamus stepped out of the tent, his apron brown from the evening's work. He plucked a dipper of water from the barrel, then another. "'Twas a necessity having yer help tonight." He stood at Fin's feet. "The last count is twenty-three dead and sixty-nine wounded. They're thinking at least twenty-one missing." His voice cracked with exhaustion, and he ran his hand through his thick, coppery hair.

"I recognized a few of the dead," Mallory said. "Boys that came to saving grace in the meetings."

Seamus's shoulders seemed to sag in the darkness. "Well, me boy-os, I best be seein' to me charges."

"Godspeed, Seamus," Fin stood. "I'm gonna head for bed."

Mallory hauled himself up from the bucket. "Me too."

They walked their horses to the edge of camp, then loped most of the way back, under strips of murky clouds and a waning moon.

Noah snored softly on the other side of the tent, his cot creaking now and then as he shifted. Fin's body lay weary and his eyes heavy, but his thoughts shot this way and that like popcorn in a hot kettle. Finally, he lit the lantern. Turning it low, he pulled out paper and a pencil nub.

Camp Flat Top, May 18, 1862

Dear Family,
I am well here at this beautiful camp. It is good to be with Col. Joe once again, as he is both mentor and

encourager to me. He is a godly man who treats his men with respect and kindness.

A prayer meeting has been going here among the men for some time now. We meet every night and it has been growing in numbers and interest. There are over two hundred meeting in one accord. Chaplain Kern is an engaging leader and often Col. Joe will address the men. On occasion, General Cox has also spoken and led us in prayer. It has been good for me. Some of the men confess they had not enjoyed religion of late, but desired to renew what they once knew as faith. Others say their "feet had well-nigh slipped" but they have gained encouragement and strength, choosing to persevere to reach old Beulah Land. Many a powerful testimony has been reported among the men of answered prayer and the saving grace of our Lord. Among our assembly is a number of Germans and often our meetings are carried out in English and German. We are of various denominations and I find it no less than wonderful that we all seem to travel the same road and have need of the love of God to light our way. I think of the verse in Psalm 133: "Behold, how good and how pleasant it is for brethren to dwell together in unity!"

I am happy to have met some old friends here. Among them are Seamus McLaughlin and Sergeant Mallory, whom I know you well remember. They ask me to extend a greeting to James. Seamus is working at the Camp Jones hospital, very busy of late with the casualties from our loss of Princeton. There is much excitement in the camp at the news of our new state of West Virginia petitioning to join the Union.

I know not when or if I will see you again, my family. Please know I dwell in the arms of our loving Savior and will strive to do that which honors Him as long as He allows. I think of you all often.

Your loving brother—Phineas Dabney, 4ᵗʰ Virginia Regiment

Melinda Jane tipped her head back, eyes closed as Gus's voice read Fin's words. No message to her alone or even her name mentioned. She touched the scabs on her cheekbone, feeling more than a little sorry for herself. Here she was, battered and bruised, without the hope of Fin's love. Ever since she was ten years old, she had held out for that boy's attention. For his love.

"Well now," Gus folded the missive. "It sounds like our Fin is in fine hands, and it sounds like he is growing in faith." She beamed at James.

"It does indeed. He didn't say specifically whether Mallory and Seamus are attending the meetings. I hope they are. They're both good men." He stood, lifting the tea tray from the low parlor table.

"*Tsk, tsk, tsk.*" Mrs. O'Donell shook her head. "Sure'n that man will carry the tea tray to the kitchen when he's old and feeble." Her rosy cheeks rounded in a broad smile. "Just one of the things I love about him."

"I'll have my wife carry the tea tray when I grow up," Bertie declared, a yawn snatching the last word from his lips.

Gus pulled on her little brother's hand, leading him from the parlor. "It's nigh past your bed time young man."

"O . . . kay." He drawled the word in unusual submission.

"Is he feeling all right?" Will asked.

Zander tossed a book onto the table. "Check him for a fever. He's not himself." He grinned at Will, and she bumped him with her elbow.

Melinda Jane rose from the settee. Her muscles still ached from Milo's attack. She had awakened at the house and begged James to go back and get Nettie and the children. Gus said they tried, but she had refused. James had examined Nettie and said the baby seemed fine.

It was days before Melinda Jane learned the truth—James had come to her rescue. He seemed such a different man in those moments, although the entire event was a bit hazy in her mind.

She took the steps up to bed, one at a time. Gus waited at the top, her arms outstretched. Seems her friend was reading her mind again. Melinda Jane melted into the embrace, fighting back the tears.

"I'm sorry, honey." Gus squeezed her shoulders. "You put this in God's hands and let Him take care of it. What is that verse in the Psalms? 'Delight thyself also in the Lord and He shall give thee the desires of thine heart.' That's your verse right now, you hear?"

Melinda Jane smiled a tired smile. "Thank you, sister." She kissed Gus on the cheek and shuffled into her room. Her eyes fell on the old doll. Fin had found it and brought it to her right after Izzy's murder. She clutched it to her chest and dropped onto the bed, turning to her side to let the tears wet her pillow.

Melinda Jane snapped shut the book and tossed it on the parlor table. A second turn of the doorbell told her the caller's impatience matched her own as she pushed herself up from the brocade chair. "Coming," she called out, nearing the door.

Behind a bouquet of tulips, Anderson Price grinned like a schoolboy. "Good morning. I saw these colorful beauties and a voice prompted, 'Take me to Melinda Jane'."

She smiled at his attempt at levity. "Now aren't those just the prettiest. Just what I need to brighten this dreary morning." She gathered the flowers in her arms. "Won't you come in?"

Stepping back, she swung the door open wide, inhaling the rain-washed air. A storm had moved across the valley during the night and the thunder had fairly shaken the house, robbing her of sleep she dearly coveted these days.

Anderson snatched off his brown Derby and stepped inside. "I can only stay a moment." He worked his fingers around the edge of the felt hat. "The Minstrel show is finally coming through Charleston. I know we spoke of it before, but I needed to be sure you still wanted to attend."

She moved at an ant's pace, closing the door behind him, ignoring the frown that wrinkled his forehead.

He covered her hand with his own and pushed the door shut. "I see you are still in pain. Will this incident convince you to cease your forays to the poorhouse and shantytown at last? You cannot deny there is danger there for a lovely woman such as yourself."

"My entire family was there, Anderson. James took care of the matter just fine." Did this man not recognize the good she was doing? First, he had used her work with the poor to goad her into continuing at the hotel. Now he urged her to quit.

He fidgeted, and as if reading her mind, apologized. "Shall we plan on the minstrel show, then?"

How could she say no to that boyish grin? She dipped in a half-curtsy. "I'd be delighted, sir."

"You've made me a happy man. I'll be out of town for a few days, but I'll be back to collect you Friday night, if you feel you are up to it."

Her body would be ready, but would the rest of her? "I'd like one more week of rest, if you don't mind, Anderson. Can we make plans for the next week?"

"Certainly. Let's practice some songs after the weekend. I'll let Mr. McFarland know." He donned his hat, reaching for the doorknob. "Rest up, Melinda Jane—and please, consider what I've said."

"Thank you for the flowers, Anderson. Good day." She closed the door and returned to the chair. A minstrel show. At last, she would see a minstrel show.

"Where's Will?" Zander sauntered out of the kitchen, a letter flapping in his hand. "She's got a letter here. Looks to be from the Dortons."

Will skipped in from the downstairs sleeping room. "A letter for me?"

"Now why is it you can hear a body mention your name from another room, but I have to work to get your attention when it comes chore time?" Melinda Jane asked, her head cocked off to one side.

"Guess my hearing comes and goes," the girl said with a shrug.

Zander held the letter over Will's head, laughing at her antics as she jumped to reach the envelope. He lowered it at last just enough for her to snag it. Plopping onto the settee, she pried it open.

"Mamie says Fin came by a few months back to check in on them. She says the bushwhackers took most of their livestock. And they're working hard to plant an extra big garden this year so's they have plenty to hide and save for the winter, cause they were eating mostly shriveled vegetables and bread as the spring came on." She read some more silently, her eyes scanning the page. "Says her mama is making her do school at home and she doesn't get to visit with other children because her pap says it's too dangerous. She says she hears gunshots sometimes, and it scares her 'cause she doesn't know where the Rebels are."

"Kind of makes you thankful to be here in Charleston, doesn't it?" Melinda Jane sighed, her thoughts shifting to the farm.

"I know I'm thankful to be here. I heard tell some of those bands are forcing young men into service whether they want to go or not." Zander turned on his heel, heading out the back.

Melinda Jane chewed her cheek. She was thankful to be here, too. Charleston was a refuge, of sorts, for her family after the losses of last year. But she felt a keen new loss, too. The loss of her childhood protector and the love she had held close all these years, reserved for a day of declaration and satisfaction.

She would write Fin again. This time she would bare her heart.

Thirty-Four

Nicholas County, Virginia

June, 1862

R oad weary, Fin stretched out his legs on the borrowed cot. Movement of troops in and out of Summersville allowed him this luxury for tonight only. He had spent the last two days escorting a wagon of prisoners up to Summersville, and now he would head down to Hawk's Nest as a courier. And more than happy for the opportunity to stop off at the Dorton place and Gauley.

He had committed a new verse to memory, and he mulled it over: *Cease from anger, and forsake wrath: fret not thyself in any wise to do evil. For evildoers shall be cut off, but those that wait upon the Lord, they shall inherit the earth.* After some time in prayer, he had decided to forego a visit to the farm. A visit to home would *not* help him forsake wrath. He dozed again, unwilling to rise before dawn if he didn't have to.

The morning light glowed on the walls of the tent, coaxing his eyes open. Surprised to see Noah up already, Fin tried his voice. "Mornin'."

"A real pleasant read to start yer day." Noah tossed a newspaper onto Fin's chest. "It's that paper the Forty-fourth Ohio prints in Lewisburg."

Fin swung his feet to the floor, rubbing his eyes into focus. The headlines read, UNION VICTORY AT LEWISBURG—CROOK DEFEATS HETH, and LORING REPLACES HETH.

"Says here they finally captured Spriggs in Greenbrier County. He'll be hung as a guerilla by Federal Authorities for the burning of Sutton, back in December, and 'acts against the Union,' it says. Makes me wonder how many more of those Rangers are still wreaking havoc." Fin read some more, then tossed the paper onto the other cot.

Noah dangled a gray cotton poke. "The camp baker was generous with the biscuits this morning. Said we could help ourselves. I grabbed enough for both of us."

Fin sniffed. "I can smell them from here. Let me get some coffee and we'll be on our way."

The morning's mugginess pressed against the summer heat. Fin had started out with his coat rolled-up and tied to the saddle, and already he was turning up his sleeves and seeking out the shady side of the trace.

"Great day in the morning!" Noah leaned forward in his saddle.

Fin squinted through the blinding shade, trying to make out an approaching rider. A young woman sat astride on a sorrel mount, her red dress draped across the horse's back. She smiled as she neared them, her dark hair swept up into a fancy bonnet.

"Good morning, soldiers." She pulled up close, stopping two feet in front of them.

Noah doffed his hat, slicking back his yellow hair with one hand. "Ma'am."

"It's *Miss*," she said, batting her lashes the way Fin had seen women do.

He eyed the trees as his right hand rested on the Colt's polished handle. "Are you all alone, Miss?"

Noah backed his horse a couple of steps, turning sideways. He craned his neck, looking over the road behind them.

"You have nothing to fear from me, gentlemen. I'm simply in route to visit with a friend of mine up in Summersville. And yes, I am alone."

"It ain't safe for a young lady such as yerself to travel in these parts, Miss. I'd escort you myself if we weren't heading in the opposite direction." Noah replaced his hat, a sunken smile across his face.

"And where would you brave men be heading this fine day?" Her blue eyes pinned Fin's, and his insides warmed. My, but she was pretty.

"We best be heading on. Do you have a weapon on you, Miss?" He calculated how much time he'd lose if they did, indeed, escort this young woman to Summersville. He would willingly give up what time he had planned for the Dorton visit.

"The woman patted a small blanket roll nestled in front of her. I have protection right here, so no need to concern yourselves with me. My . . . uh, friend instructed me quite well in its use."

Her gaze never wavered from his, and he could feel the heat seeping into his ears. She licked her lips and an impure thought hammered his mind.

"I could use a drink of water, if you can spare one," she said, bringing her horse alongside his. "I've been riding since first light, and I'm afraid mine is empty."

Fin fumbled for his canteen and handed it to her. If there were any proper words to be said, they had all up and run off. She took the canteen, brushing her fingers across his, never breaking her locked gaze.

He fidgeted as she sipped and then wiped her lips with the back of her hand.

"I've got some more if you need it, Miss," Noah blurted.

She capped the canteen, giving it back to Fin. "I'm much obliged, Sergeant."

His tongue must've glued itself to the roof of his mouth, for all the good it did him.

Her voice seemed to drop lower. "Enjoy your day, men. And, thank you for your service." Noah's eyes followed her back down the trace.

Fin scanned the trees. This was unnatural. "Don't you think that was a mite odd? Her being out here all by herself?"

"Likely an angel sent from heaven to ease us weary travelers." Noah turned back all starry-eyed, a smitten grin plastered across his face.

"Yeah, well, Satan himself can transform into an angel of light, ya know." Fin leaned forward, his knees urging Duke into a faster walk.

Unsettling, that's what that was—and about the oddest encounter he'd ever made. Shame dug at him for the thoughts that swirled in his mind, and he scolded himself.

Charleston

Melinda Jane adjusted the new spoon bonnet, setting it forward a bit, then moving it back again. She sighed and pulled the yellow ties into a crisp bow. Never had she spent so much time primping and playing with her hair, taming her curls into something entirely new.

The butterflies in her stomach had only grown more agitated as she dressed for the Minstrel Show. Anderson would be here any moment, and here she was, reconsidering her entire ensemble. Such frivolity! This was not like her.

She startled at the turn of the doorbell and spun from the hall tree mirror. "How do I look?"

Gus's fingers brushed a stray curl from her cheek. "You are beautiful inside and out, as always, honey. I'll get the door."

Anderson stepped into the foyer, a corsage of tiny roses in one hand. He snatched off his tall top hat with the other. "My, but you are pretty this evening, Melinda Jane."

The butterflies danced a jig. "That's most kind of you to say so, Anderson."

He handed her the corsage. "Lovely flowers for a lovely lady." He clicked his heels and bowed.

"They're so pretty. Thank you." Now what? She threw a look at Gus that brought her friend scurrying to the rescue.

"I'll pin it on for you, sister." She fidgeted with the flower, positioning it just so, pinning it below Melinda Jane's lace collar on one shoulder.

Melinda Jane whispered a thank you.

"Shall we go?" Anderson offered his arm, and she threaded a lace-covered hand through.

For so many years, she had yearned to see professional musicians perform and finally her time had come. Something inside her whispered, *This night would be a night she would never forget.*

Anderson escorted her to a place in the line forming outside the theater entrance. The muggy air, warm, even for June, foretold of a coming rain shower before the night's end. Before long, the crowd of folks began shuffling forward and Anderson pulled her close. Too close.

What grand seats they had—only four rows up and right in the center. Her heart raced as the lights dimmed.

"Are you excited?" Anderson asked, a grin lighting his face.

"Oh, yes." she whispered. "Never in all my days did I expect to be sittin' here like this."

With the theater's darkness complete, a shiver ran the length of Melinda Jane's arm. The tinny roll of the curtain pulled her forward as the draped fabric opened to a piercing musical fanfare. Glittering stairs supported rows of chairs with a center aisle and musicians sat in bright uniforms, filling the back two rows. Brass instruments and banjos shot sparks of reflected light into the scene as the musicians moved with the brisk music.

Men danced down the stairs, two by two, singing and waving their hands to the rhythm. Colored men. No. She gasped, covering her lips with her hand. White men with black-painted faces. They wore white gloves and white shirts with black suits. Thick white paint lined their lips. She had read about this, but it hadn't even occurred to her this would be one of *those* kinds of shows.

The spirited dancing brought applause from the audience as one familiar melody smoothed into another. A short, chubby man sang an unfamiliar song, then the music softened. It continued through one silly riddle after another.

"Say, what's the difference between a schoolmaster and an engineer?" one performer asked.

"I don't know. What *is* the difference between a schoolmaster and an engineer?" another responded.

The first performer faced the audience, his hands outstretched. "The difference between a schoolmaster and an engineer is that one trains the mind and the other minds the train."

The audience laughed and clapped. Melinda Jane smiled politely, but something critical and nagging, shrouded any mirth. A yellow-suited, black-faced man poured a bucket of sand across the floor and danced, his feet scrubbing a mesmerizing rhythm to the music. A few folks in the audience stood, clapping and shouting encouragement.

The players reorganized themselves, leaving two of the actors on the stage, one on a soapbox, gesturing broadly to the crowd, presenting pun after pun to the audience—some of which poked fun at slaves. Poked fun at mammies and field workers.

Indignation rose within her. She wanted out of here. Caught up in the *entertainment,* Anderson laughed and clapped with the rest of the crowd. She glanced to her right and to her left. She was boxed in.

At last, the curtain closed, and the house lights rose. A man, dressed as a provocative woman, his skin slightly darkened, stepped onto the stage in an extravagant red organza dress, its bust ridiculously enlarged. He strolled across the stage with a sign that read: JULIUS SNEEZER. The audience clapped and hooted as the curtain opened once again.

An outlandish mockery of the classic play followed. A pillow-stuffed man portrayed a mammy pulling a white-faced man's head onto her bosom. The mammy shushed him like a child as he smiled and winked at the audience. The people roared with laughter. Dirty. She felt dirty just sitting in this audience. She sank into her seat.

It lasted less than a quarter hour, then the stage crew spread a sheet of pale blue fabric across one side of the stage. An actor—now a dandy in fancy vest, spats, and a tall hat—sat in a chair, clutching a fishing pole, dangling it over the blue patch on the floor. *He's dressed just like Anderson.* She sat a little straighter, leaning her body away from her escort, but not so much as to draw his attention.

"Well, now. It sure is a nice day for fishing." The dandy talked to the audience, and another actor stepped up behind him, peering at the blue-covered floor.

"Watcha fishin' for, Frank?" the second one asked.

"I'm a fishin' for something big today, Arthur."

"Something big, huh?"

"Yep, that's right." Frank dipped the pole several times.
"Looks like ya got a big 'un there!"

At that moment, a disheveled, black-faced man with ratty clothes appeared. He stumbled onto the blue fabric and grabbed the string hanging from the fishing pole. He flipped and twisted. The audience erupted in hoots and howls.

Bile rose in her throat.

"I sure got me a big one, I did. Could surely win some contest with this one." The dandy said. "Why, just look at those big eyes and fine fat lips. This buck surely has got to win me some ree-ward."

Something akin to rage overflowed and leaked from Melinda Jane's eyes. She stood, pushing her way through the row of people, muttering, "excuse me, excuse me,"—all the while thinking she needed no excuse. The audience grumbled as they stood to let her pass. She did not care one whit about their inconvenience or even if Anderson followed her out. Capturing a sob, she yanked her skirts from the last obstacle in the row and ran up the darkened aisle, clutching the sides of her dress in trembling fists.

Outside the theater, her chest heaved. Rain sluiced off the building's overhang, spattering her skirt as she leaned against the brick wall. The theater door burst open, and Anderson gaped, a look of horror on his face.

"Whatever is the matter, darlin'?" He stepped toward her, his hand outstretched, but she recoiled.

"You . . . you found that atrocity in there entertaining?" She wiped at her face with a new lace hanky. Gus had crocheted the trim just for this occasion.

His jaw went slack. "Atrocity?"

"Yes! That . . . that *Minstrel* show that folks were laughing at—including you."

"Now, just a minute. You wanted to come to this. We've been planning it for weeks, and now you stand there calling it an *atroc-*

ity? I don't understand what you're saying, Melinda Jane." He scowled. She figured more from irritation than confusion.

"All that poking fun at colored folks, portraying them as dim-witted and lazy. They came right out and said a happy Negro is an enslaved Negro!" She drilled him with her glare and balled her hands into fists.

This was a nightmare. Cruel people were everywhere, true—but to mock and laugh at such things?

Anderson smiled in that charming way he had about him. He reached for her hand. "Now darlin' you're just all out of sorts. Nothing wrong with having a little fun. It's not like they were making fun of real people. Not white people."

A loud *SMACK* pierced the night air as her palm struck his cheek. How could she have been so deceived by this . . . this person?

He grabbed her wrist. "Now what was that for?" His eyes flashed in the dim light.

She ground her teeth, despising the hot tears that streamed down her cheeks. She dropped her eyes to the place on her wrist, painful from his grasp.

"So what if they poke fun at some darkies. They're not poking fun at you."

There it was. She glared at him, her lips trembling with rage. She had no more to say to this man. This man she *thought* she knew—who she had grown fond of.

He squinted, then pulled his head back, inspecting her, head to toe before releasing her wrist. His eyes grew wide. "Are . . . are you . . .?"

She smoothed her skirt and lifted her chin, holding his gaze, refusing to blink.

"I . . . um. I'll send a conveyance for you. I need to get home." He turned away, heading off toward the buggy, his long strides carrying him out of her life forever.

Good riddance!

The thumping of her heart finally slowed until it matched the rhythm of the *plop, plop* of raindrops striking the stony ground.

Thirty-Five

NICHOLAS COUNTY, VIRINIA

July, 1862

"Spread out. Look for tracks that veer off," Fin told his men as he guided them down yet another hill. Any time now, he expected signs of riders headed out through the trees for cover.

"Here, Sarge!"

Sure enough, the tracks of maybe a hundred horses left their mark a few at a time, over a wide area, angling off to the north. His unit of twenty Federals followed at a good clip, dodging branches and skidding down the steeper gullies.

"Hold up!" Fin reined Duke to a sudden stop. Trampled brush evidenced that a second large group of riders had joined the first. "We got a serious something happening up there." The tracks were only two hours old, best as he could figure.

He led his unit as fast as the terrain would allow, praying this chase wouldn't end in an ambush. His men would not stand a chance against such numbers, but he couldn't abandon the trail.

It emptied onto the trace leading into Summersville. Plumes of black smoke rose in the air above the town. A lead weight landed in Fin's belly. They were too late. He kicked Duke into a run, pulling up at the edge of town, taking in the sight. Three buildings blazed, and a half dozen bodies lay prone in the dirt. A wounded man, caught fast in suffering, called out, and a soldier rushed to his aid.

"Where is Colonel Starr?" Fin asked the private, who was now sitting in the dirt, the wounded man's head in his lap.

"They took him. Him and Capt'n Davis."

Flattened by dozens of hoof prints, a wide area of mud and grass fanned out toward some of the buildings. "What happened here?"

The man stared down at the wounded soldier, whose head had lulled to one side, his eyes fixed on eternity.

"I'm sorry." Fin cleared his throat and dismounted. He glanced around, looking for a wagon, seeing none. "You, and you," he told two of his men, "gather the dead in one place—and cover them. The rest of you bring the wounded to that building." He pointed to a log structure that appeared intact.

The private rose to his feet. "It was Confederate Cavalry. At least four companies. Rode in here about daybreak and surrounded our sleeping quarters. Strangest thing though . . ."

"What's that, Private?"

"Seemed more intent on taking our commissary stores and supplies than wiping us out. Completely ignored Company F and took pretty near all the men from Company A. Burned their quarters, too. Left here with upwards of sixty prisoners—marched 'em out on the double quick. Couldn't have been here more than an hour."

Noah galloped up, jerking his horse around. "Appears the telegraph office has been destroyed. No sign of the government operator. Near as we can tell, they made off with a goodly amount of blankets and clothing from the stores. There's not a horse, mule, or wagon to be found."

"Sergeant Dabney, over here!"

At the edge of a clearing, in a patch of tall grass, one of his men bent over a Union soldier. A vicious chest wound had turned his jacket purple. Fin knelt, offering the man a drink from his canteen. "What's your name, Private?"

"Jeremiah Hayman, Sergeant. Company F." The man gulped another swallow.

"Easy. Go slow, now. You want to tell me what you saw?"

The man battled sleep, but forced his eyes to focus on Fin. "They knew. The Rebels knew where everything was. They knew ahead of time. They had to." He coughed and Fin tipped the canteen once more.

His raspy words continued. "There were voices outside and I started pulling on my boots. Our orderly sergeant said he'd see to it. Next thing I know, those voices were talking about Company A, and they took off on the double quick to Company A's quarters."

He closed his eyes, then pried one open. "When I asked the sergeant what was goin' on, he rallied us up, saying Company F was safe for now. Something about his cousin. I didn't understand until I seen him halted by a Reb later, and they let him run. That was when I got shot."

"Sarge." Noah pulled Fin's attention to the trees. One after another, soldiers—likely Col. Starr's men crept from the trees. Relief sparked on each face as they seemed to realize they were not alone.

A lieutenant limped from the tree-lined cover. "Fall in, men."

Fin approached the officer and saluted. "Sergeant Fin Dabney, sir, Fourth Virginia. We've been tracking these Rebels, but it seems we're too late."

The lieutenant holstered his Colt. "Lieutenant Anderson, F Company. Good to have you here, Sergeant. Sorry you missed the excitement. They captured our Colonel, Captain Davis, and Lieutenants Stivers and Ewing."

"Some of the wounded are saying there was someone on the inside." Fin said.

"It was Nancy Hart. I saw her leading them in, then she vanished. We housed her for a couple of weeks in our jail, until she killed one of my men and escaped." He spat the words, anger sparking in his dark eyes.

"I've heard about her. Do you have a sketch so we can go after her?"

"In my quarters." He stepped out, limping hard.

"Do you want me to take a look at that?"

"It's just a sprain."

Lieutenant Anderson shuffled through the mess of papers strewn across his cot. "Ah, here is one." He turned, handing the paper to Fin.

Fin stared, feeling like a fool. It was her—the woman on the trace a couple of weeks back. Why hadn't he thought to interrogate her more? He had been duped. All he knew was the name, but not the face.

"I see you recognize her." The lieutenant squared his shoulders.

"I came across her a couple weeks back. She was dressed all fancy-like, said she was heading to visit a friend in Summersville."

"Very likely she told you the truth to some extent. She's managed to ingratiate herself with some folks hereabout. Oh, she's a sly one, that she is. A she-wolf of a Rebel spy."

"Mind if I take this picture?" If he could pass it around among his men and get it to Colonel Joe, he figured they stood a good chance of finally apprehending the woman.

"Certainly." The lieutenant fumbled with some of the other papers, then started for the door. "We need to send a telegraph immediately."

"The lines are down and the office destroyed. I can ride for you—deliver it to the nearest outpost to send on by wire."

"I heard mention of Salt Sulphur Springs. That's probably where they're headed with the prisoners. It will be slow going on foot for them." The lieutenant massaged his temples as he thought aloud. "If we can gather the manpower, maybe we can catch up to them before they make it that far."

The ridges carved in the lieutenant's forehead relaxed. "I'll write it out. Give me an accounting of the survivors, if you will, while I pen the message. And ready your men to ride. I'll need to notify General Cox that the Rebels have taken Doctor Rucker also. We'll need to include him in the prisoner exchange."

"Doctor Rucker? He was here?"

"Unfortunately, yes. Now that they have themselves a legendary *Union spy*, no doubt those Confederates mean to make an example of him.

Fin flopped a second sock over the tree limb to dry in the hot summer breeze. Next, his winter drawers, still dripping from the wash in the river. They slithered to the dirt, and he growled, "That's it, just add another thing to my list of blunders."

"Don't take it out on your drawers, Sergeant."

He started at Col. Joe's voice. "Yes, sir . . . I mean, no, sir." He fumbled to switch the muddy wad to his left hand so he could salute.

The colonel laughed. "At ease, Sergeant. I thought we might have a little talk." He eased himself to the ground, resting his back against an ancient elm tree.

"Sure thing, Colonel." Fin flipped the drawers over a branch and sat down on a wide root spreading its tentacles across the grass.

"I see how you roll your thoughts around in that head of yours. This is your home, and while you don't see a problem with protecting it, you wonder if the boys you're fighting aren't just thinking the same thing. Am I right?" The colonel plucked a long blade of grass and popped the end between his lips.

"Reckon you about said it." He looked down, his finger tapping the cool ground. "I'm not a coward, Colonel. I just gotta have a good reason for doing what I do, else it just doesn't make sense in my mind."

"Understandable."

"My best friend since we were babes. I looked him in the eye and couldn't shoot him. If that makes me a coward, well, then maybe I am, but it's not *my* definition of a coward." He waited, considering the irritation that squeezed his chest. "I hauled my neighbor in to the stockade, wondering how his wife was gonna make it through the winter without him." He had gouged a hole in the dirt, so he wiped his stained finger on his pant leg.

Col. Joe pulled the blade of grass through his lips. "I fought the Mexicans for five years. A long ways from here. An enemy with a unique language, a different look. It was easy to tell the wrong from the right—your enemy from a friend. It's different this time, fighting right here in our own back yard—against the very same boys we played mumblety-peg with."

"Exactly what I'm saying" He appreciated this man. His easy way—not condemning.

"I'd lay odds you're the oldest. Am I right, Fin?"

"Yes, sir. How'd you know?"

"Because I know the way of the oldest, blazing the trail for the others, always bearing the weight of setting a proper example, feeling all protective."

Fin started back to his digging. "Yeah. I reckon so."

"I've got four younger brothers. Now, I suppose you know two of them."

"Yes, sir. Captain and Lieutenant Lightburn. Everybody knows your brothers."

"I reckon so. My youngest brother, Ben, he's at home. Too young for warring. I'm thankful to the good Lord for that."

"I know what you mean. My youngest brother won't see this war, but I fear for my other brother, Zander. This war goes on much longer, he's likely to find himself in uniform."

"And which uniform would that be, Fin?" The colonel looked up, a question shading his eyes.

"Why, Union, of course."

Col. Joe let out a slow breath. "Of course."

"There are rumors, sir."

"And you want to know if they're true. Yes. They are. My brother John is fighting for the Confederacy."

"I'm sorry." Fin lowered his eyes. What to say?

"Life was sweet, back in Lewis County. Running the family mill, farming 600 acres with my brothers and pap. Real sweet. Right up until my best friend got accepted into West Point instead of me. Both our families ran mills. Wasn't even much difference between us, but they picked Thomas over me." He tossed his blade of grass and picked up a new one. "Now, why do you suppose God allowed that?"

"Can't say, sir."

"I just figured the Almighty knew something I didn't. So I carried on, fought the Mexicans like a good citizen. Only ten years ago I left the warring—just a sergeant like yourself, Fin. Married my Harriet, and we had our family. Finally got my license to preach, thinking I got it all figured out, and God's finally letting me into His confidence." He laughed dryly. "Then along comes the states with a mind to secede, and this whole upscuddle takes off."

Fin's thoughts ran to Melinda Jane and his middle warmed. "Sometimes I lay awake at night, wondering if I'd be married right now if it hadn't been for this war."

"No sense spending much time wondering. God's ways are most certainly not ours. From this end, it seems that just as soon as you think things are going along one way, they change on you."

An easy silence settled between them. The scent of the mud from the soaked drawers on the branch sailed past Fin's nose. When he looked up, a chickadee was sitting on the wet clothes, pecking at the fabric. He felt like those wet drawers—heavy with the weariness of war. Dirtied by the blood on his hands. And pecked on by duty.

But he was determined to have it all make sense in the end. Just as those drawers would eventually get washed again in the river water, then dried in the sunshine. Only God could see him through this ugliness.

"Not a day goes by," the colonel said, breaking the silence, "that I don't wonder if I'll be responsible for the death of my brother, John, or my friend, Thomas."

"Jackson, Sir?" Fin had heard of his commanding officer's ties with the Confederate they called "Stonewall" Jackson.

"Yep. We played at Indian wars as boys. He's just nine months older than me to the very day." He chuckled. "We used to try to convince the girls we were brothers, but too many folks knew us back home." His smile disappeared. "Many a fine man is fighting for the Confederacy, Fin. Some we know by name. Others we know by the way they exemplify the kind of man God implores us to be."

"Sometimes it's easy to forget that the officers feel the war that goes on in here, too."—Fin thumped his chest—"It's wearisome."

"It is that." Col. Joe stood, brushing off his britches. "I've got a baby girl I've only seen twice. I figure I've got plenty of men under my command who share my predicament. The Psalmist says, 'With the merciful thou wilt shew thyself merciful, and with the upright man thou wilt shew thyself upright.' I need God's mercy, Fin. We all do. And I'm just gonna keep trying to walk upright."

Fin stood to his feet. "Thank you, Colonel. For the talk."

Col. Joe stretched out a hand to him, grabbing his shoulder with the other. "You're a respectable soldier and a fine man, Sergeant Dabney. One foot in front of the other. Keep walking upright, you hear?"

"Yes, Colonel."

Fin watched his commander climb the hill to camp. The sun had hidden itself behind a dark cloud at some point, and he had not even noticed. One drop, then more splashed onto the tree limb as he wrestled with the muddy drawers. He jerked his socks from the limb and hustled up the hill. Just when he thought he would finally get his laundry done today, God had another plan.

Thirty-Six

Charleston

August, 1862

"But what about Nettie's baby?" Melinda Jane dropped to the settee, her thoughts on the woman and the danger she and the children could be in.

James exchanged a look with Gus before answering. "We'll stay until the baby comes and leave for Wheeling soon after. If all goes well, I don't expect we'll be gone more than a month."

"Would you like us to take Will and Bertie with us? Should I ask them?" Gus sat beside her friend, squeezing her hand. "I feel I've already asked so much of you, watching over them these last few months."

"First off, they're my family and you don't have to ask me to watch over them. Second, if you were to take those two with you, they'd be bored to tears after the first week, making your whole trip a trial."

Surely Gus would see the sense of it. Being surrounded by family was the only thing keeping her from a pit of lonesomeness.

Gus pushed a lock of tawny curls from her friend's cheek, searching her eyes. "Are you sure?"

"I'm sure. I have Mrs. O'Donell to help me and Zander minds himself. Whatever would I do without Bertie's misadventures or Will's caterwauling?"

"That brother of mine just doesn't understand the jewel of a woman he's letting slip through his fingers."

"Don't be blaming Fin. He's got too much on his shoulders just now to think about the future—whatever that looks like to him." There she went, sinking lower in her spirit. She forced a smile. "Now, you two take advantage of this time together. Think of it as a second honeymoon."

James chuckled. "Right. The first one was in the hospital and this one will be too. Not much of a honeymoon when the groom is bedbound, dreaming of holding his chosen without the needles of pain."

"James!" Pink climbed Gus's neck.

"Will this surgery to remove scar tissue help with the pain?" Melinda Jane hoped it would, for both their sakes.

"That's the idea. At the least, it will give me more mobility in my leg." He stepped closer to his wife, his warm gaze drawing Gus's own.

The love between them was something a body could almost touch, the way it traveled through the air. She studied the right side of his face. No scars. He was a handsome man, indeed. How she wanted what they had. She wanted the kind of love that left her speechless when a man looked at her a certain way.

"Melinda Jane?" James chuckled. "I know that look. I used to see it on Gus's face before the fire." He pulled his wife up by the hand, then wrapped his arms around her waist, gazing into her eyes. "He hath made everything beautiful in His time."

"Ecclesiastes," Gus said, her eyes held fast to his.

Melinda Jane stood. "I think I'll leave you two alone and see if Mrs. O'Donell needs anything." Their soft laughter trailed behind her, rankling her as she entered the kitchen. Ecclesiastes.

"Humph." *A time to love, and a time to hate.* She cringed at the rest of the verse . . . *a time of war and a time of peace.*

In the last year, she had learned to hate. She didn't think she had it in her, but the evil she had witnessed demanded nothing less. The war. She was powerless to stop it. But she would pray to the One who could stop it. Then she would beg God with all her being for a time of peace and a time to love.

Fayette County

Fin tossed another crate of ammunition into the wagon and yanked his kerchief from his back pocket to wipe the stinging sweat from his eyes. The Gauley Bridge supply depot buzzed with activity as soldiers loaded armaments and stores for General Cox's departure.

General Lee pressed north, accelerating the Rebel threat against Washington. For this reason, Cox's forces were being split. Of the fifteen thousand Union troops in the Kanawha Valley, General Cox would take with him two-thirds to join General Pope's Army of Virginia in the East.

Earlier this morning, Fin stood on a granite cliff watching keel-boats, heavy with supplies, horses, and wagons heading up from Kanawha Falls. A five-man crew guided each of the sixty-foot boats, using long poles to push the boats against the river's flow. The line of rocking arks floated like ducklings, their burdens bound for Maryland and parts northeast to help preserve the Union. A train of men and supplies also snaked its way up the Weston-Gauley Bridge Turnpike.

In just a couple of days, Col. Joe would assume command of the Kanawha District. The sergeant from the Mexican War would command the entire state of West Virginia. Fin shook his head.

Only God could orchestrate that one. Likely, this new post would bring the man to his knees—wearing armor, seeking God's direction.

Row upon row, blue-clad troops lined the parade ground, shoulders back, eyes trained forward. Fin wiggled his eyebrow against a trail of sweat creeping down his brow. The clouds, heavy with rain, added to the muggy air causing their skin to itch and shirts to stick fast to their bodies. He glanced across the sea of men, seeking out familiar faces. A movement up front caught his eye.

Colonel Joe stood at attention as General Cox read the command notice aloud. "Brigadier General J.D. Cox hereby turns over to Colonel J.A.J. Lightburn, Fourth Virginia Volunteers, the command of the Kanawha District."

The formal change of command ceremony lasted only a short time, after which soldiers were released unit by unit to resume their duties.

Later that evening, a private Fin didn't recognize handed him a note, calling him to a meeting with Colonel Lightburn.

"Well, aren't you just the teacher's pet." Noah plopped onto the cot, pushing his forage cap over his eyes. "I smell a promotion comin' for *Sergeant* Dabney."

He stuffed the note into his pocket. "I doubt that. It's probably just a meeting to update us on the reorganization of troops." He donned his hat, then swiped some dust off the tops of his boots.

Officers stood in a semi-circle, and Fin realized he was the only Sergeant in attendance. He discreetly stood in the back of the small crowd and waited. When the tall Colonel approached the table, silence fell, and they stood at attention. Colonel Joe saluted. "As you were, men." He spread a map across the table.

Several of the officers pulled out small notebooks, some touching a whittled pencil to their tongues. Why didn't Fin think of that?

"I wanted to fill you in on some of the new placements due to our downsizing." The colonel smiled directly at a few of the men and nodded. "Colonel Siber's Thirty-fourth and Thirty-seventh Ohio regiments will be stationed at Raleigh Court House with two companies of infantry to guard trains at Fayetteville. Colonel Gilbert's Forty-fourth and Forty-seventh Ohio regiments, along with two companies of Virginia Cavalry, will stand post just ten miles east of here, at Camp Ewing."

He looked up from the map, scanning the faces, then continued tapping the map with a finger. "Summersville will be garrisoned by Major Curtis and two companies each of Nine Virginia Infantry and Second Virginia Cavalry. Other companies will be stationed at established points between here and Charleston. Pulling troops from some of our outposts may very well serve as an invitation to General Loring, but we will be ready should that prove to be the case."

He looked across the assembled officers, rolling the map into a tube. "Questions? There will be an informal notice posted tomorrow morning."

"What if Loring makes a move?" one captain asked.

"Then *our* next move depends on when and where the Confederates make *their* move." The Colonel's lip rose on one side. "That is all, men."

Fin turned to leave, but Colonel Joe called out his name. He waited until the bulk of the officers had left. "You wanted to see me, sir?"

"Yes. I'm sure you noticed you were the only non-commissioned officer here."

"I was wondering about that."

"I have a special plan for you, Fin—to use you as both courier and scout." He tapped the rolled map against one hand. "You know this land better than anyone here, but no doubt some of Loring's men know it just as well. I want you and Hicks to remain here in Gauley during my command, ready to leave on a moment's notice."

"Yes, sir." *But why me?* Fin wanted to ask, but he held his tongue.

"I know I can count on you, Sergeant Dabney. Dismissed."

Charleston

Joy—the only thing in this harsh world that lifts a spirit to the throne of God. It filled her and overflowed her eyes with welcomed rivers. Melinda Jane squeezed warm water from the cloth and brushed it across the newborn's wrinkled arms, marveling at the tiny fingers as they flexed. Unfolding the cloth, she let the water drip across his bald head. Amazing how blood pulsed through his umber skin, a life force holding this child fast to this side of heaven.

"Oh, Nettie, he's beautiful. Just beautiful." Melinda Jane's tears ran unabated.

"Can I hold him?" Nettie strained to sit upright.

"Just another couple of minutes. We'll finish up here, then you can hold this healthy son of yours." James grinned, winking at Gus, who stood at Nettie's shoulder.

Melinda Jane sang softly, rocking in time to an old Scottish tune of her mountain heritage, cradling the infant in her arm. His mouth stretched into a little "O" as he yawned, and his curled fists punched the air. She laughed as more tears fell. "You best hold him soon if you want to catch him awake, Nettie."

James nodded to Melinda Jane, and she handed the baby over to his mother.

Gus ran her hand around the back of Melinda Jane's waist. "Do you want to stay with her until evening? I can send Zander to get you before dark."

"That would be wonderful—if you're sure Zander won't mind fetchin' me."

"If he's busy, I'll come for you," James said, snapping his medical bag closed. He passed his eyes over the little hovel. Stepping closer, he whispered, "Maybe you can talk her into coming to the house for a few days."

"I'll try."

"Nettie," Gus said, touching the woman's foot. "Would it be all right with you if Olivia and Perry came to our house? Just for the afternoon. We'll bring them back when we pick up Melinda Jane."

Gus looked at James, who flashed one of his smiles. The kind of smile Melinda Jane figured said, "I love you," as good as any words.

"That'd be a special treat for my young'uns for sure. Let them see the baby first." Nettie motioned to the two children huddled on the floor, playing with carved animals.

After meeting their new brother, Melinda Jane hugged the children one last time and sent them off with Gus and James. She turned to Nettie. "Now then, you feeling like a cup of tea?"

"I'd like that. You mind puttin' this one to bed?"

Settling him in a dresser drawer lined with threadbare curtains, she covered him with a soft blanket she had knitted some weeks back just for this occasion. She stuffed a rolled blanket behind Nettie, helping her sit up.

Returning with two steaming tin cups, she handed one to her. "I put some honey in it for you. I thought to grab some before I left home."

Nettie blinked as tears brimmed. "I ain't never knew a white woman so kind as you been to me, Miss Melinda." She sipped the hot brew.

Melinda Jane blew on the cup, sending the steam tumbling off one side of the rim. "We're not so different—you and me." She considered this woman, and only love filled her heart. "No, not so different."

"You a white woman, Miss Melinda. No disrespect, but what you know of my life? You wear that purty dress there and your hair all fancy. You don't gotta wonder what you gonna eat come tomorrow."

"Things aren't always as they appear, my friend." She lifted Nettie's hand, matching her warm ochre fingertips to her own. "My grandpappy Izzy was born a slave in Kentucky."

"You joshin' me!" A dribble of tea splashed onto Nettie's blanket as she sat a little straighter.

"I am not. His master sired him, but when the master found Jesus, he up and set all the slaves free."

"And yo granny?"

"Meemaw was a mountain woman. Her and Izzy married under God. Izzy went to glory only last year." She stroked Nettie's hand, staring at the white nail beds. "You see, Nettie. We're not so much different. No difference at all in the Lord's eyes. Izzy taught me we're all born into bondage. It matters not a whit what color a man's skin is or the color of his horse or house—we're all in shackles and only Master Jesus holds the key."

Nettie's eyes sagged sleepily, but she smiled. "That story warms my heart, missy. All right with you if I name this here man-child after your grandpappy?"

She swallowed around a lump in her throat, swiping at the start of a fresh round of tears. "Why, I'd be honored, Nettie."

"Mayhap he'll grow to be the kind of man your grandpappy was."

"We'll pray it so, Nettie. We'll pray it so."

৵

Gauley Bridge

Fin found himself once again standing among officers, anticipating news. News that had provoked Col. Joe to pace back and forth, an unlit pipe in one hand. He walked over to the map-covered table. What had carved the man's face with such worry lines overnight?

"These raids of Jenkin's have been just successful enough to pull our attention from our biggest threat, men." The colonel frowned, poking a pipe between his teeth and jerking it out again. "That threat is General Loring's numbers—twice that of our own. That is the threat we must focus our efforts on."

General Jenkins's Rebel raiding parties were encircling the Kanawha Valley and boldly engaging Federal Forces at Salt Sulphur Springs.

"I'm concerned for the safety of our flanks and rear, currently unprotected." He turned his attention on the map, leaning over the table and pulling his finger across the paper as he spoke. "Colonel Siber's forces will fall back from Raleigh Courthouse to Fayetteville. Colonel Gilbert's men will fall back to Camp Tompkins on Gauley Mount."

Colonel Joe shook his head, his lips forming a tight line. His finger tapped the map. "Summersville seems a likely target." He lifted his head, his face rough with concern. "Colonel Gilbert, you will send six companies of the Forty-seventh to reinforce that point."

Standing to his full height, he scanned the group of observers. "Quartermaster. Ready stores for shipping on to Charleston. I'll have a list for you shortly."

To Fin's way of thinking, a howling storm was working its way across the land, and this was the Union Army's way of boarding up the windows and hunkering down. With only five thousand Federals left to defend his home, this storm of Loring's ten thousand troops threatened to blow down the door. And this new state of West Virginia, birthed from this entire Confederate tempest, would huddle again, terrified of yet another storm.

Bile worked its way up his throat, and he swallowed it down. He had lived here all his life, and this much was certain—when the thunder rolls, the waters rise. This time, it threatened to wash away all he held dear.

Thunder. God's voice is in the thunder. *Lord Almighty, help us.*

Thirty-Seven

GAULEY BRIDGE

September, 1862

"We're heading out again," Fin kicked Noah's foot. "Get your sorry hide up and dressed. We leave in ten minutes."

Noah groaned and rolled out of bed, landing on his knees. "Where to this time?"

"Just up to Tompkins farm." Fin stepped into the morning chill. Not quite summer and not quite fall. A sense of excitement lingered in the air. The last few days had been a scurry of activity. Colonel Joe had him and Noah riding from one post to the next, bringing news of each unit's progress in anticipation of an invasion from General Loring. Despite the hot, clear days, storm clouds of war seemed to build higher each day, billowing dark and ominous. Sure enough, the rivers would rise and the thunder would roll, driving every soldier to their duty.

A couple hours later, Fin tipped his canteen, filling it with frigid spring water. Shade from a patch of elms called to him, so he reclined there while he wet his throat. Men of the Forty-fourth labored at felling trees, and hauling them to the Lewisburg pike.

They blockaded the road and cleared some timber, giving them a clearer shot at the Rebels should they attack at this site.

"These boys seem a mite stirred up. They're like cackling hens frettin' about a rat in the chicken coop." Noah took a long draw from his canteen.

"They've every right to be frettin'. Loring would be plum stupid not to take advantage of our diminished numbers. That disaster up at Manassas last week's been hard on morale. Last report I saw said nearly ten thousand Federal casualties." Colonel Joe's friend, Stonewall Jackson, had been instrumental in that one—helping Lee push Pope all the way to Washington.

Noah whistled. "Ten thousand casualties! You're right. That surely do send the fear of God into a man, don't it?"

"That it does." Fin capped his canteen. "What say we get back and report the progress of these boys?"

Noah stood, shaking one leg, then the other. "Leg fell to sleep." He motioned toward the soldiers. "Looks like the second shift. They'll likely be done before dark, I s'pect."

Conversation hummed, floating through the camp anew as Fin and Noah dismounted. Fin knocked on Colonel Joe's tent. The man burst through the opening, his eyes sagging from lack of sleep and dark with concern.

"There you are." The Colonel handed an envelope to Fin. "Rush this to the telegraph office. General Jenkins has placed a Confederate flag on Union soil in Ohio."

Did he hear right? Ohio? "Yes, Sir," he sputtered. He strode to the log hut, his chest tight—real thankful to be a lowly sergeant right now.

Charleston

"You just sit right down now and drink your tea. I'll finish up here." Melinda Jane bustled Mrs. O'Donell toward the table and pulled out a chair as Will set a plate of cookies on the pink tablecloth.

"You can sample my new recipe, too." Will slid the cookies closer to the teapot.

Mrs. O'Donell lowered herself to the seat, one eyebrow tipped. "*You* tried a recipe?" Her gaze dropped from Will's face to the cookies. Tucks of skin drew her mouth in an "O" and she cautiously picked up one and took a bite. She smiled as she chewed and promptly poured a cup of tea and drank.

"How do you like it?" Will hovered over the woman. "It's my very special recipe. I call it cinnamon snaps."

"Is it, now?" Mrs. O'Donell sipped more tea.

Melinda Jane broke off a piece and popped it into her mouth. "Mmm. Quite . . . *creative* of you, Will."

"I'm glad you like it. I tried to make your Molasses Crinkles, but I used extra cinnamon instead of molasses. They sure look good." The girl took a big bite and the more she chewed, the more her eyes bulged. She ran to the sink, pumped a glass of water and gulped it down.

Mrs. O'Donell chuckled, shaking her head. "First rule of cooking—sample it yerself afore offering it to some poor, unsuspectin' soul."

"How much cinnamon did you put in that batch anyway?" Melinda Jane wiped a tear from the corner of her eye with one hand, the other still on her shaking belly.

"I can't believe you ate that and didn't say anything!" Will wiped her wet chin with a sleeve. "I love cinnamon, so I figured if I put a half cup in, it'd make it that much better."

"A half cup?" Melinda Jane walked over to the cupboard, pulling a tin down from the shelf. She lifted the lid, peering inside. "No more baking for you, missy! Cinnamon's getting expensive."

"Fine by me. I only made 'em because Zander was teasing me about not knowing how to bake proper."

"What'd I do, now?" Zander ambled into the kitchen, Bertie right behind him.

"Cookies!" Bertie dove for the plate on the table, snagging one in each hand.

"Bertie." Melinda Jane planted her hands on her hips.

The boy halted, sheepishly looking up. "Um . . . may I puh-leez have some cookies?"

Will covered her mouth, muffling a snicker.

"You may have all you'd like." She didn't mean to be cruel, but some lessons come at a price. She honestly should tell him right up front that Will made them. That would stop him in his tracks.

Zander passed a questioning look at Melinda Jane, then to Will. He started to help himself, then drew back his hand.

"Ach!" Bertie ran to the sink.

Will handed him the rest of her water. "You're gonna need this."

Zander plopped down in a chair, his raucous laughter sending him into a coughing spell.

Will glared at her older brother. "It's your fault, you know."

"Not my fault you can't bake worth a hoot."

"All right, you two." Melinda Jane patted Bertie on the back. "Next time, don't shove the whole cookie in your mouth."

"I'm gonna tell Gus you tried to poison me," he said, pumping more water into the glass.

"She's not here, and I didn't try to poison you. I tasted them too. Just made an error in judgement is all." Will sank into a chair. "How long are Gus and James gonna be gone?"

"James said it'd likely be a month or so." Zander drummed his fingers on the table. "If'n they're gone too long, I might miss them before I leave."

"What do you mean, 'before you leave'?" Melinda Jane asked, a sudden weight flattening her stomach.

"Lincoln has called for three thousand more men aged eighteen and up."

"Well, you're not eighteen for another couple of months. Maybe the war will burn itself out by then." She worried her lip, imagining the boy in a Union uniform. The ache of watching his older brother ride off on that sad morning squeezed her throat, sending a burn rising behind her eyes. "Let's not discuss this right now." She wiped her hands on the towel, needing to be alone just now.

Melinda Jane headed for the stairs, halting at a sudden banging on the front door. Whoever could that be? Most polite folks rang the doorbell.

More banging.

Zander beat her to the door. "Let me get this." He situated himself between her and the door. He cracked the door open a couple of inches, then swung it wide.

"Oh, Miss Melinda!" Olivia Penchant fell into her arms, eyes red and chest heaving.

"Honey, did you run all this way?" She fell to her knees, folding the child into a protective embrace. "What's the matter, child?"

"It's Pap, he come for mama . . ." The girl gulped and swiped at the tears rolling down her cheeks.

"Oh, dear Jesus, we need you," Melinda Jane whispered, trying not to imagine the worst.

Zander put a hand on the little girl's shoulder. "Just take a deep breath and tell us everything, Olivia."

Anger flashed in his eyes. How much like his brother he was at this minute.

"He come for Mama … say he gonna kill baby Izzy … say Mama gonna get what's comin' to her for not doin' what he tell her."

"Where is your mama now?" Zander fingered the knife he kept lashed to his thigh.

"She hidin'. I's the only one in the house when Pap came. Mama and baby Izzy and Perry were down to the river. The neighbor be hiding them now. Mama sent me for you, Miss 'Linda." The girl sniffled, then turned to the door. "Come on. We gots to get 'em."

Melinda Jane exchanged a wary looked with Zander.

"What ere ya waitin' for. Go!" Mrs. O'Donell stood in the hall, her hand on Bertie's head and Will standing beside her. "You get that lass and wee ones and bring them here."

Will stepped forward. "Olivia can stay here with me."

Zander shot out the door. "The wagon is already hitched." His words trailed behind him.

She passed Olivia to Will. "You wait here, honey. We'll get your mama and brothers and be back shortly. Don't you worry, now. You just ask Jesus to watch over them, and He will." She kissed the girl's brow and rushed out the door.

"You doin' all right back there?" Melinda Jane twisted on the buckboard seat, lifting the edge of the blanket to check on Nettie and the children. They had located them without running into Milo, and for that, she was forever thankful. She shuddered to think how all of this could've played out had there been a confrontation. Zander had worked up a head of steam preparing, but he was no match for Milo.

"Where we going, Miss Melinda?" Nettie's voice had calmed since being bustled into the wagon.

"I'm taking you to James's house. You'll be safe there."

"Oh, no. You can't do that. Milo, he know the doctor stopped him last time, so he be lookin' there for us."

She hadn't thought of that. Melinda Jane passed a look to Zander, a silent plea for counsel in her eyes. He frowned in that way he did when he was thinking.

"What about Preacher Lambert?" He raised his eyebrows in question. "Maybe he knows a place where they'll be safe for now."

"Yes. We'll go straight to the parsonage. Surely, he will know of somewhere they can go." She turned to Nettie. "Don't you worry about a thing. We'll see you and yours to safety."

Twenty minutes later, they followed Brother Lambert down the dark stairs into the church cellar. "It's not as damp down here as you might think. You can keep your things here, but you're welcome to spend your time upstairs when there's no parishioners about. The fewer folks know you're here, the better—for your safety."

"Thank you, Preacher," Nettie said for the tenth time. She snuggled the baby to her chest, taking each stair step carefully. "We won't be here long. Just till Milo be gone again."

"I'll be by every day to check on you and bring you food and water. Don't you be worrying about a thing, Nettie. The Lord is providing for your family and keeping you safe." If only Melinda Jane could soothe her friend's fretful state.

"I've got to get back to the house," Brother Lambert said. "Widow Cox has asked for a meeting." He said it with a sigh, and his shoulders drooped a little. He turned to Nettie. "Remember what I said about the fewer folks that know you're here, the better." He smiled and squeezed her hand. "You're in the Lord's care, Nettie. Trust in Him." He tipped his hat, then headed up the stairs.

Zander scrubbed Perry's head with one hand, meeting the boy's round eyes with a smile. "I'll be waiting in the wagon." He bounded up the steps.

A lone shelf held canned jars, probably donated by the church ladies for the needy. She scooted around a few chairs and an old table. "There. Just make yourselves to home. I'll be back over in a while with Olivia. She'll be mighty happy to see ya'll. I'll bring you food, blankets, a slop jar, and something to haul water in." She glanced over the dingy room. "And some rags for cleaning."

"We be jest fine, Miss 'Linda. We don't need any more than what we got." She patted the tied clothes bundle . But that was all they had with them, and they needed so much more.

"Your milk doin' all right?" she asked Nettie, thinking about the possible need of oatmeal and mashed potatoes for the infant. And fresh water daily for his mama.

"I's doin' fine. He's a good eater, my little Izzy. He's growin' real fast."

"Good." She hugged Nettie and Perry once more before lifting her hem to scurry up the steps.

Thirty-Eight

FAYETTE COUNTY

September 10, 1862

C hest pounding, Fin hovered both reins over the pulsing neck, giving Duke his head. The whine of a Minie ball split the air. Another near miss. He glanced behind. Noah kept up, his attention focused on the trail.

Sharpshooters had taken to the trees, attacking the Federals' flank just four miles south of Fayetteville. Command needed to know Loring's main body of troops was preparing to attack from the turnpike. He sucked in a quick breath, tasting dust.

Noah hollered, motioning up ahead.

They had arrived. Just two miles before Fayetteville, three companies of Federals hid in the thick trees on either side of the pike, battle ready. A captain stepped into the road, and Fin pulled Duke to a jerky halt. The horse pranced, lather forming around his mouth.

"They're right behind us."

"We'll be ready," the captain said. "You best keep riding."

Fin saluted and raced ahead. He'd have to rest Duke soon. Noah's horse didn't look any better.

284

Musket fire popped in the distance behind. Sure enough, the Rebels had reached the troops they'd just warned. He transferred a rein and wiped one eye with his kerchief. Sweat rolled from under his Forage cap, disappearing with the swift ride, but dust clung to his eyelashes. Fin squinted, watching ahead for the laurel that hid another unit of Union soldiers.

Another half-mile and he spotted it. Undetectable in the dense thicket, Federal soldiers lay in wait for Rebel forces. Fin and Noah reined their horses around to the back of the bushes and dismounted. Their horses pranced, heaving and black with sweat.

"How far?" A sergeant asked, handing his canteen to Fin.

"Thanks." Fin wet his kerchief and wiped his face. "A mile and a half. We heard skirmishing. There's no stopping them. Just too many. The force coming down the pike is over five thousand strong." He poured water into his cupped hand, offering it to Duke, who slurped it dry. He repeated the process.

Noah walked his horse in a tight circle. "We need to rest these mounts."

"I'll send a man to Colonel Siber," the sergeant said, before jogging off.

"We'll stay on here for a bit." Fin welcomed the respite, and now that he was stationary, the heat enticed his weariness. He led Duke into the shade, lobbing the reins over a section of laurel.

"Loring's got enough troops to run clean over us." Noah secured his horse to a sapling.

"That he does. But we're not going to let him do it without a fight."

Before long, the sound of musket fire rent the air. Fin and Noah scrambled ahead for a view of the pike. Union troops were drawing back to Fayetteville pursued by the Confederates. Fin double-checked his carbine, preparing to return fire. The advance column converged on the pike and Federal lead poured into the

Rebel ranks. A deafening shower of Minie balls produced a great cloud of smoke, obscuring much of the thicket.

The Rebels brought up two artillery pieces. Noah shot a panicked looked to Fin. There was bound to be a slaughter if they stayed.

"Fall back!" The order repeated again and again.

Fin and Noah stayed low, making their way through the thick smoke to the horses. Duke's eyes, wide with fear, flashed as Fin reined him sharply, springing into the saddle and lunging into a run to circumvent the town. Spotting movement in the hills, he halted, and reached for his binocular case.

The Confederates were rapidly repositioning through the woods, covering three hills and effectively surrounding Fayetteville in a flanking maneuver. He handed the field glasses to Noah. "See for yourself."

He let out a low whistle and returned them to Fin. "Don't look too good."

Fin crouched next to Noah, suddenly wishing for a field musket. His carbine was useless at this distance. Another ball flew past, splintering a tree. The staccato of fire echoed across the field and smoke sank in the stale, hot air. For the second time, Colonel Siber's men charged the knoll held by the Fifty-first Virginia infantry.

The thirty-fourth was fearless, charging up the hill, some of their number falling with every attempt. Hours ticked by, stretching the nightmare as bodies littered the field. One of those bodies writhed in pain, a limp hand waving in the air, pleading for help. Fin would rather dodge death fighting than watch this.

Noah elbowed him, drawing his gaze. Two Ohio drummer boys, each with a half-dozen canteens slung across his back, made their way in a trot, zig-zagging across an open section of field. They fell to their knees when they reached cover, passing the water to the soldiers. Fin caught sight of Mallory, taking a swig from a canteen, then tossing it to another soldier. The men rallied for a third assault on the knoll.

"The Johnnies are low on ammunition. Just like last time, they're waiting till our boys are closer before they shoot," Noah tossed his head to indicate the rise.

"I see what you mean." Fin pulled out the field glasses again. He watched Mallory, his mouth contorted in a soundless rally cry, charging fearlessly up the hill—

Fin's heart plummeted. He bit back a yell.

Noah grabbed his arm. "What's wrong? What'd ya see?"

"Mallory." He lowered the field glasses. He had seen enough. His friend would not be going home to Ohio. But he would be going to his true home, of that much Fin was certain.

"Sorry," Noah mumbled. "I know he was a friend of yours. The Thirty-fourth has taken more losses than anyone."

Mallory's sweet harmonica music drifted through his mind. He remembered it from the Dabney barn last year. How beautifully his friend had played for the prayer meetings just a few months back. There would for sure be harmonica music in heaven tonight.

War didn't allow time to grieve. He figured the grieving would come by the bucketful once this all ended.

"We need to get back to Colonel Joe." Fin hauled in his druthers and tucked away the ache for another time. "We'll have to stay off the turnpike, it's most likely under Rebel control by now." He backed out of the scrub brush. "Let's go."

༄

Fin and Noah drew some fire skirting the turnpike, but they made it to the command post unscathed. Just as Fin had suspected, the Rebels commanded the pike from Fayetteville to the Kanawha River. A smart move as it prevented Federal trains from passing, and it cut off Col. Siber's retreat.

After Fin helped round up the remaining officers at Gauley, Col. Joe ordered three companies of the Fourth to advance to Fayetteville. Then he positioned five companies of the Forty-seventh Ohio on top of Cotton Hill to assist in the event of a retreat.

Turning to the quartermaster, the colonel barked, "I want the troops to pack up everything they can and destroy the rest. This depot carries the stores for the entire region, and I'll not have it falling into the hands of the Confederacy." The officers scattered in haste to carry out the orders.

Col. Joe waved over Noah as he scribbled on a piece of paper. "Corporal, I want you to high-tail it up to Camp Tompkins. Tell them to strike tents and pack them up. Have them burn whatever commissary stores they cannot haul and head back here to await orders." He handed the crumpled note to Noah. "Godspeed."

"Yes, sir, Colonel." Noah saluted and shot out of the tent.

"Sergeant Dabney. You know which families are Union sympathizers. The information I have tells me they will not be treated kindly by Loring's troops. Please inform as many as possible to take refuge in Charleston immediately. I want you back before dusk."

"Yes, sir."

Fin struck out for Duke once again. At least the poor boy got something of a break. He mentally figured what homes he needed to contact, planning his route. Many of the Gauley Bridge residents with Union sympathies were still gone from all the trouble last fall. He would spread word through town first, like Paul Revere—then he would head up Gauley Road.

Most of the townsfolk found more levity than fear in the news of the Rebel invasion. But Union families hitched their wagons and readied their escape. Fin continued on to the Dorton place.

Silence hung heavy in his neighbor's yard as he rode in. He hollered once, then dismounted. He jogged to the front door, hitting the porch in one step.

"Hector! Maude! It's Fin Dabney. Anybody home?" He walked around to the back of the house. A short figure stepped from the cornfield, a musket leading the way. Hector halted and his wife stepped up beside him.

"It's me, Fin Dabney, Hector." Fin strode toward the field, his hands raised, just in case the man's eyesight had gone bad.

Hector lowered his gun and stepped forward. "Good to see ya, Fin."

"I've got bad news. General Loring's got more than five thousand men heading this way and the Union army is backing out. You need to get your family out of here, Hector."

The man's eyes dropped to the ground as he scrubbed the lengthy gray beard that brushed against his chest. "I reckon I'll just hold my own, like I been doing, but thanks just the same for the warning."

"You don't understand. This is a mass of Confederate Regulars, not bushwhackers. Even the Union Army is fixin' to run from them if they make it to Gauley. Please hear me. Pack up your family and head on to Charleston right now." How could he make this man understand the danger he was putting his family in?

Maude stepped up just then. "Listen to Fin, Hector." She pulled their twin boys to her.

"If we go to Charleston, I can visit Will!" Thirteen-year-old Mamie, with the same exuberance as his little sister, bounced on her feet. The innocence of youth.

"You don't want to stay here. Gather food for a few weeks and what you need for a makeshift shelter. Mayhap this will turn around for us in not too long." Fin turned to leave.

Hector grabbed his arm. "If your family was still here, would you have them leave?"

"I most surely would." Fin met the man's eyes, catching a glimpse of fear. "Yes, sir. I would. And right now." He pulled away. "I've got more riding to do. Pass the word along, will you?"

Fin strode off, wishing he could stay and help see them off so he would know for certain they'd made it. But he had his orders. He figured he had at least three more stops and the sun wasn't waiting for him.

Thirty-Nine

An eerie amber settled over the turnpike, the last remnants of a scorching sun, now snugged beyond the horizon. Fin patted Duke's withers, raising dust from the coppery coat. The gelding had covered a good many miles already, and though the day was near a close, somehow, Fin knew he would need even more from the old boy before his work ended.

Fin road with Col. Vance's men, keeping to one side of the pike as they advanced to Fayetteville, allowing the oncoming civilians to pass. They appeared in bunches at first—some on foot, others in wagons heaped with household goods. A few families even towed their livestock behind. Eventually, a solid stream of refugees flowed up the turnpike from Fayetteville.

Assorted citizen tales of incidents along with the state of the Union Army grew in horror. Some folks claimed they had been surrounded, and that a slaughter of sorts had commenced.

"What do you make of these reports, Colonel?" Fin grew more uneasy as they neared the town. He could sense the soldiers' wariness, their eyes scanning the trees for Rebel muskets. A poor time of day to be needing a clear view, that much was certain.

"I'll take these stories with a grain of salt, Sergeant. Folks tend to get a mite het-up when they feel their lives are in jeopardy." Col. Vance turned in his saddle, motioning to a captain to join him.

Fin squinted into the dark woods. "This area was heavily guarded by Rebels earlier today. I can't see them just letting us ride into town unmolested."

"My scouts haven't reported anything. Let's hope it's because there is nothing to report."

"That would surely be a blessing." Occasional shots rang out in the distance, too far to figure their whereabouts.

It was after nine o'clock when Fin rode into Fayetteville with Col. Vance's men. The brightness of the moon in the clear sky eased his mind some, and the sounds of battle had long-since ended. But he refused to relax his guard. He had known a false sense of security to kill many a soldier.

Fin stood in the back of the large room, half-expecting to be sent off with a report for Col. Lightburn. He strained to listen as Col. Siber briefed Col. Vance.

"We've held our positions the duration of the afternoon, and it seems things have at last quieted for the night." Col. Siber paced the floor, his voice bold and clipped like many of the Prussians. "Ha! That one-armed Reb came looking for a fight today, and by God's grace, we gave him one! A single Federal regiment and six companies, supported by four howitzers and two six-pounders, successfully defended against a force of five thousand Confederates with sixteen artillery pieces."

Col. Vance clapped a hand on the colonel's shoulder. "One for the history books, indeed!"

A sergeant pushed past Fin, rushing to the front of the room, a folded paper in one hand.

Col. Siber took the missive from the sergeant, frowning as he opened it. "Our count is currently thirteen killed and eighty wounded." He looked at Col. Vance, his face drawn and pale in the lantern light. "It could've been so much worse."

Fin's thoughts went to Mallory. A man's life on this side of heaven was, indeed, a vapor.

"What now?" Col. Vance asked.

"We'll prepare the wounded for transport, then wait until after midnight to evacuate. That will give your men a chance to rest up and the Confederates time to settle in for the night." Col. Siber dropped into a chair like a rag doll. "Perhaps an hour of sleep first."

Col. Vance propped his hand on the hilt of his sword. "I'll leave you to it." He strode toward Fin, signaling for him to follow.

"Yes, sir?" Fin asked, half expecting to be herded out the door.

"When the bulk of our regiments leave, I want you to ride on ahead to Cotton Hill and let them know we're coming. You've had quite the day of it. Grab a little rest."

"Yes, sir."

Minutes later, Fin's legs stretched out in the straw of the stable floor. Head resting on his saddle, he finally let sleep take him.

Muted voices. Urgent voices. Fin roused, rubbing his aching eyes. Duke stomped, incited by the flurry of activity as men led horses out into the open air and the smell of smoke drifted into the dim stables. Time to go.

Fin scrubbed across Duke's back with a handful of straw, smoothing the sleek coat as he went. He shook out the pad, threw it onto the horse's back, followed with the saddle, and tightened the cinch. He shushed Duke, sliding the bit back into the horse's mouth. "Sorry to do this to you again, boy. At least you got a little break. Only God knows when we can rest again."

Heavy smoke shrouded the darkness as commissary stores dissolved in flames. Agitated horses snorted, adding to the commotion of loading the wounded into wagons. Infantry fell into a tight column while cavalry ordered ranks, preparing to leave Fayetteville to the Rebels.

Within the hour, Fin headed out into the night alone, just ahead of the Federal troop withdrawal. Once again, the Confederacy raised a fist in victory, tightening its stranglehold on Fayette County. *His* home.

He rode by the light of the near-full moon, the stillness void of coyote calls. Even nature cowed to this impending storm. Would Melinda Jane still be in Charleston if and when he made it that far? Was his family trapped there?

Jenkins' Raiders had taken points west of Charleston, posing a threat to strategic strongholds. Now the Confederate Army was poised to squeeze the Kanawha Valley like a vice.

Fin's brief nap felt like days ago as he joined the Thirty-seventh Ohio on Cotton Hill. Col. Joe had planned well, sending these boys here early on. Colonels Vance's and Siber's troops would be happy for the reprieve.

As the first rosy hues glowed on the horizon, Federal troops from Fayetteville arrived on Cotton Hill.

Col. Vance looked out over the valley. "We made it through, quite unmolested until the end, when the last company of the train took fire from the trees." He frowned and pulled a brass telescope from a leather holder. "The Rebels wounded three men and captured a supply wagon."

He sent Fin to retrieve Col. Siber and when he returned, an ominous sight awaited. General Loring's army, with colors flying in order of battle, was deploying at the base of the mountain.

Col. Siber turned to the officers standing on his right. "Push the main body to continue the withdraw. I want four—no, five—companies of the Thirty-seventh to remain behind. Give them a detachment of artillery. That should slow Loring's advance." Several of the officers jogged off, relaying orders.

An explosion in the distance echoed across the green hills, luring all eyes to the west. "That would be the powder magazines at Kanawha Falls," Col. Vance said.

Fin followed the troop movement with his field glasses. Something wasn't right. He turned to Col. Siber. "Excuse me, sir?"

"Sergeant?"

"The Confederate force is splitting. My guess is General Loring is sending maybe half his men along the Fayette road."

Col. Vance swore. "I agree. The other half is headed straight up this hill along the turnpike."

Col. Siber barked orders, which werer hastily passed on. Breastworks would be constructed as quickly as possible to afford some small advantage.

"Shall I ride on to Gauley, sir?" Fin asked.

"Yes. Report the situation here to Colonel Lightburn. Tell him we will continue our withdrawal down the valley."

"Yes, sir." He was off again, making a note to refill his canteen from the spring before he headed for Gauley Bridge.

So many troops and civilians to evacuate. His mind spun. *How many could escape the Confederates' maw?*

When he rounded the crest of the hill, an extra weight hammered his chest. The entire valley, spanning a distance of probably two miles from the falls to the bridge, was enveloped in smoke. Smoke from the burning of millions of dollars in Federal supplies. He pushed on to board a ferry at the river crossing, passing the panicked crowds. Civilians and soldiers alike clogged the pike, all with a single purpose—to stay ahead of Loring's army.

Duke stomped on the ferry's wooden floor. His eyes shone white, and he snorted into the smoky air, uneasy with the wake of the river water. Fin soothed him, crooning words of comfort to himself as well as the horse.

Bodies crowded around him, black and white alike, some with only children in tow, others laden with bundled belongings. He blocked a pushcart from ramming into Duke's hind legs as the ferry bumped the shoreline and bobbed to a halt.

Another mile farther and he found himself pressed against wagons and human traffic, crossing Gauley Bridge. He could not help but notice the fuse line and gunpowder barrels—awaiting a match.

The grand covered bridge he'd grown-up with was burned only last year, the glow from its fire seen even from his farm. A fitting memorial to the way life at Gauley had been before all this secession trouble. Hadn't he watched the construction of this suspension bridge just this year? And here it was, sentenced to a fiery death once again.

Several log buildings smoldered and smoked in various stages of incineration around the camp. Soldiers had struck half of the tents and scurried like rats, collecting whatever they could. They tossed supplies and extra arms onto already full wagons as a second wagon train made its way out of camp.

After passing on the report of the Confederate troop movements and Col. Siber's plans, Fin accompanied the Forty-fourth Ohio back to Morgan's Ferry. They aimed to block Loring's advance by positioning themselves on the riverbank, while the rest of the troops retreated towards Charleston along both sides of the Kanawha.

Fin pulled his kerchief over his nose. The stifling heat, thick with smoke, called sweat into his eyes. He blinked away the sting, then grabbed one of his good kerchiefs from a pocket, wiping his wet eyes. Once at the ferry, he joined the battle line with the Forty-fourth along the bank. They would cover the frantic retreat of the rest of Siber's men from Cotton Hill.

He pulled out his field glasses, scanning the wooded slope of Cotton Hill. Men, scurrying like rabbits from a hunter, made their way down, slipping and jumping over the brush. Some fell, and others stumbled over them. Even at this distance, the panic was evident. Men tossed haversacks and even laid down arms—anything that impeded their progress.

"They're coming fast," Fin said, checking his Colt. He pulled his carbine from the scabbard. Three ferry boats waited for the men.

The first bedraggled soldiers collapsed into the front of the ferry. "They're right on our tail," one said, heaving for air. "We held them as long as we could."

A sweat-soaked private guided his horse onto the ferry. A barely conscious officer slumped behind him. "Blasted sharpshooters! We lost two of our officers. I went back for the captain, here."

"Tend to that wound immediately!" Fin barked, watching a dark stain spread rapidly across the officer's sleeve.

More men trotted onto the ferry, disheveled and bloodied, many with no gear. The Rebels materialized and soldiers from the Forty-fourth shoved the last of the Cotton Top troops onto the crowded ferry. As it left the shore, a group of Rebels broke off, taking a line along the near shore in pursuit of the main body marching down the river.

An order sounded and the Forty-fourth opened fire on them. Fin ducked under the trees, braced his rifle on a branch, and took a clean shot, taking out one Rebel. He reloaded, repeating his success.

The Forty-fourth's cannonade provided a considerable distraction for the pursuing Confederates, and precious time for the retreating Federals to escape. As the enemy recovered, Fin pulled his pistol and held his position on the line.

Minie balls and grapeshot rained down on the Rebels as they scuttled toward the river. They first dropped with regularity, then dashed into the trees for cover. The cannonading continued, preventing further advance from Loring's men.

Here and there, Fin picked off a man foolish enough to make a run toward his line. The hour and a half of cannon fire felt like an eternity. But it afforded a fair amount of grace by allowing the army and civilians that much more of a head start in this wild race out of the Rebels' clutches.

At last, the order to fall back sounded. Fin galloped to the rear as infantry retreated on the double-quick. After everyone had safely crossed the river, they placed a cask of gunpowder on the empty ferry and ignited it. The boat erupted into a rush of hot flames.

Confederate cannon fire from Cotton Hill thrashed the trees just off of the bank, sending men scurrying for cover. When they finally stepped from the trees, again, the ground exploded, hurling a man to the dirt, clenching his head in his hands. Fin raced to his side and turned the wounded man over. A cry guttered and the mangled face froze.

Col. Gilbert trotted up beside them. "We'll take him back. You best get on to Gauley."

"I'm sorry, sir." Fin laid the man's head back, folding his lifeless hands atop his chest. Only a monster could say you get used to this. He stood, wiping his hand across his thigh, leaving a streak of fresh blood.

"I'll take him, sir." A thick-armed private squatted next to the dead man, lifting him like an infant.

"Thank you, Private." Col. Gilbert pressed his lips into a firm line for a moment, then barked out orders to continue the retreat.

Fin rode on ahead to Gauley. It was the last time he would cross the magnificent bridge, only months old. Cannon fire detonated a loaded wagon, propelling wood splinters into the air. He turned his face away, shielding it with his arm. Duke's muscles tightened as the horse pranced and snorted.

He found Col. Joe stuffing a trunk with papers alongside a tall major whose black beard dripped with sweat. The colonel stood and looked at Fin. "Well?"

Fin coughed hard. The colonel poured water into a tin cup and shoved it at him. He drank deeply, savoring the water's sting as it drenched his parched throat. His stomach threatened to hurl it back.

"The last of the Forty-fourth has crossed the river. Set fire to the ferry. They should be coming across the bridge real soon." He set the cup down, trying to steady his breathing.

"Good. I have men set to blow it. Let's go."

A horse skidded to a stop just outside the tent. "Corporal Hicks reporting, sir!" Noah saluted, and practically jumped from the saddle.

"Go ahead," barked Col. Joe, securing the latches on the trunk.

"The Forty-seventh got cut-off falling back from Summersville, sir. They burned their train and took to the mountain traces. Reckon we'll meet up with them at some point, but no telling where."

The colonel nodded, then turned to the major. "Load this trunk. And I want you to personally stay with it. Hicks, Dabney, you're on scout." He mounted, jerked his horse around, then headed to the bridge.

"Ain't he going the wrong way?"

"No doubt he wants to make sure the last few companies make it over the bridge before it's blown. He cares more about the last man in line than he does himself." He gave in to a rack of spasms again, coughing himself ragged. "We'll fill canteens and water the horses then head out."

Forty

Charleston

"Thank you, Zander. I surely do appreciate your help with all this." Melinda Jane frowned, studying the three crates setting on the cellar floor as the dust settled. "I hope I didn't forget anything on my list."

She checked her pockets, exasperated. "Now where did I—?"

Sarah dangled a folded piece of paper in front of her.

"Oh." She glanced at the list, then stuffed the note and her concerns into a skirt pocket. "Sarah brought several things from her home, too."

"My, my, Miss Melinda, you brought us near all your stores." Nettie shot a stern look at Perry, and he snatched his hand back from exploring the contents of a crate. "I never seen so many goods in one place."

Melinda Jane wrapped one arm around Nettie's frail shoulders. "I was just trying to think of what I might want if I was hidden away down in this musty old basement."

"It ain't so bad. We go upstairs at night, and I let the children run till they be tired-out."

"Are you staying warm? Do you need us to do anything while we're here?" Sarah asked, looking over the dank cavern.

Zander bent to look Perry in the eye. "If your mama says it's okay, I brought you and your sister a treat." He pulled two pepper-

300

mint sticks from his pocket, laughing as the boy's eyes grew round. His little hand reached up to take one, but Olivia gently slapped it away.

"Can we, Mama? Can we have a stick of candy?" She pled with a mountain of six-year-old sincerity with her hands clasped beneath her chin, as if praying for the right answer.

"Zander, you spoiling my young'uns?" Nettie smiled at Perry, whose chin sagged and lower lip seemed to creep farther and farther over it. "I reckon my chillin deserve some spoiling."

Sporting a grin as big as the childrens', he handed each a candy stick.

"Thank you so much for your help, Zander." Sarah said, snugging her light shawl around her shoulders. "I really need to be heading home. Papa was going to come for supper, but there's something happening, and he had to cancel. I do hope it's nothing serious. I often don't find out there's been any threat until it has passed. That Confederate General Jenkins and his bunch are giving our boys fits, coming this far west and all. Maybe that's why Papa has to lead his men off."

"I've gotten kind of use to the peace here in Charleston the last few months. You be careful, Sarah, and get yourself home before dark. Hear?" Melinda Jane hugged her friend. "Least ways Nettie and the children will be safe right here in the church basement, no matter wherever else there's trouble." She turned to Zander. "I'll be along shortly."

"No hurry." He tipped his hat to Nettie and Olivia, then winked at Perry. "I know from experience, if you eat that too fast, you're liable to get a bellyache."

The little boy smiled, sliding the sugary treat in and out of his mouth, a rim of red already forming around his lips. He nodded to Zander, his eyes bright, then he stuck out his hand like a tiny old man.

Zander shook it, failing to push back a grin. "See ya soon, Perry." He headed up the stairs, taking that good-natured chuckle with him.

"Well, now. Let's see what we got here." She set a stack of clean nappies on the rough table. "I figure I'll just keep doing these up for you since there really isn't any place around here for you to dry clean ones. It's gotta take two days or more for them to dry down here with all this dampness." She unloaded a can of kerosene and two blankets, a sack of biscuits, and a bundle of dried beef. "I figure it'll be easy enough for you to make some gravy with this. And I put in two tins of milk."

Nettie bowed over the larger crate on the ground. "My, oh my. Look at all them cans of food."

"Zander left more wood up by the stove for you. He's been asking around to see if anybody's seen Milo. So far, nobody's seen him." Melinda Jane set a bucket of soiled diapers near the steps. "I don't want to forget these."

Nettie patted little Izzy's bottom through the sling that snugged him to her chest. "You are truly a blessin' from God. If it weren't for you . . ." Tears crowded her glistening eyes.

Melinda Jane hugged her and the babe. "How could I do less? I just want you and your precious little ones safe from the meanness in this old world. The good Lord wants us to help one another and love one another. That's all I'm doing, Nettie. I'm right proud to call you my friend."

Nettie's tears soaked the shoulder of her dress. *Oh Lord, what is your plan for this child of Yours? Please, please Lord, keep this family safe from harm and help these little ones to grow to know You and Your love.* This was her sister. Just like Gus was her sister. Did they not share the same Father? Doesn't that same Father hurt for us and love us the same? Her whole life tumbled together, sifted down, and shrank into that single realization.

"Behold, what manner of love the Father hath bestowed upon us, that we should be called the sons of God." Melinda Jane spoke softly, letting the scripture seep into her soul.

"That from the Good Book."

"That's right." She pulled back, setting her gaze on Nettie. "God loves you so, so much, Nettie. And He loves your children more than you do."

"I feel that love. I surely do, Miss Melinda. And He sent you as His angel."

"I'm no angel, Nettie. I'm just one of His children. No different than you. No different than Sarah or Zander." Melinda crouched down, pulling first Perry, then Olivia to her. "You take good care of little Izzy, now. Ya hear?"

"Yes, ma'am." Olivia said, echoed by Perry.

She stood, grabbing up the bucket of diapers. "I'll be back sometime tomorrow."

"God Bless you, Miss Melinda. He's already a-blessin' me and mine."

September 12, 1862

Melinda Jane fussed to herself over all the duties to prepare for Sunday—and here it was Friday, already half gone. Anderson had wasted no time leaving Charleston for Wheeling after their impasse. Now she had taken to practicing with Mrs. Vandyke at the church on Fridays after choir practice.

She pushed the lace curtain to one side, peering out at the street. A bit more traffic than usual, but everything seemed peaceful. Why, then, did she have a note in her hand saying that choir practice was canceled for today because of "the possible threat"?

News had filtered around town that Fayetteville had fallen into Confederate hands. What about Gauley Bridge? Was her home once again under Rebel control?

Her mind flitted about like a summer butterfly, unsettled and disquieted.

She had a scheduled solo the week after next and still needed to practice with Mrs. Vandyke. The woman had a stiff way of playing that made her almost wish for Anderson again, with his smooth way on a piano. A mixture of hurt and anger dug at her. Hadn't Izzy always warned her about a root of bitterness and how easily it could take hold in a person's life?

"Mercy, but folks have gone mad." Mrs. O'Donell's voice carried from the entry, and Melinda Jane rushed from the parlor to meet her.

"I'll take that." She took the heavy bag from the woman's arm. "Now, what are you goin' on about?"

"Folks are downright rude, they are. Pushing and grabbing food right off of the shelves."

"Now why would they be doing that?"

"They're panicked I suppose . . ."

"Melinda Jane! Mrs. O'Donell!" Will's body followed her holler from the kitchen.

"You oughta see it, Melinda Jane! There's every kind of boat you can think of." Bertie trotted in and pushed around Will to stand at her side. "Some are just rafts made of logs."

The women threw questioning looks at Zander, who followed the children. "It's true." He removed his hat, wiping his forehead and neck with a kerchief. "The river is crowded with folks heading toward Ohio on flat boats and skiffs. So many folks, looks like a parade going down Front Street. Talk says Loring's Army is heading this way."

"I'm sure we'd be told to evacuate if there was any real danger to Charleston. Those are folks from Fayette County, likely." Melinda

Jane twisted the sack in her hands. "We best be thinking about what all this means for us. With Gus and James gone, we need to have a plan if it comes down to leaving here. We'll talk about it tomorrow."

"But where would we go?" Will asked, suddenly sounding half her age. "We're running out of places to go." She worried her lip, glancing frantically from one adult to the next.

Zander set a hand on her shoulder. "Don't worry, I won't let anything happen to you and Bertie."

Bertie hugged Melinda Jane's waist. "I don't wanna leave. Coot don't wanna leave neither."

The old hound poked his head through the kitchen door, inciting laughter from Mrs. O'Donell and Melinda Jane.

"Coot doesn't look too concerned about it all." Melinda Jane squeezed the boy to her. "We'll do like we always have and trust God to take care of us. These store goods aren't gonna put themselves away." As she walked into the kitchen, the butterfly that flitted in her head sailed down to her heart, stirring up the peace she had worked so hard to hold on to.

The muggy night dampened Melinda Jane's nightgown as she lay in the darkness. At last, the curtain stirred with a wisp of air. Somewhere in the distance, thunder rolled. Could Fin hear it too? Could he hear the way it growled and rumbled, interrupting the lives of even those foolish enough to ignore it?

Forty-One

September 13, 1862

"We'll have to take to the hills if we want to make better progress." Fin veered off the pike to follow a game trail with Noah close behind. "There's a trace up yonder that cuts over toward Charleston."

Sweat stained the horses' hides as Fin and Noah pulled up for a rest. "Woowee. Will ya looky there?" Noah gazed over the valley. "Mighty nice view from here."

Rumored to be over thirteen miles long, the Federal baggage train advanced at an impressive clip, transporting all manner of military stores, supplies, and armaments. Drivers whipped the horses, forcing the wagons forward, nose-to-tailgate, as the train made its way from Gauley Bridge toward Ohio, where the threat of the Confederacy had yet to truly materialize.

Like ants streaming from an anthill, Unionists and freed slaves joined the train. Folks toting children and bundled belongings, carts and wagons heaped with food stores and household goods worked their way up the narrow spaces beside the wagons.

Farther to the east, the staccato of musket fire echoed. Fin and Noah exchanged strained looks. Most likely Rebels picking off the troops bringing up the rear of the train.

They pulled around and continued on toward Charleston, winding higher into the hills, resting with the nightfall. The morning sun offered a view of the Kanawha Valley.

"Looky there." Noah pointed to a pass, allowing a view of the south side of the Kanawha River. "They're passing on both sides."

"That'd be my own family if they hadn't moved off last year." Fin stood in his stirrups, stretching as he watched. Had the Dortons changed their minds?

"Bet you're real glad they're in Charleston."

"Real thankful. If need be, they'll just load up and cross the Elk River and head up to Point Pleasant. James will look after them." He needed to concentrate on other things right now, not worry about his family.

That old familiar regret banged on the door of his heart. He would never find another Melinda Jane. The gaping hole left there was shaped just like her shadow. One and the same. He rubbed his eyes. The want of sleep tormented his entire body. "We best get going."

They rode on, pushing their mounts harder. Other Federal soldiers streamed toward Charleston across the backcountry. Already cannon fire sounded in the distance.

"Not much farther," Fin said, leaning into Duke's long strides. Fire streaked from Rebel Parrot guns over on the river. The house where Colonel Joe had set up temporary headquarters came into view. Men scrambled near the log barn behind the house, rearranging rails to attempt some type of defense.

The ground exploded beside Noah's horse. It shied over into Duke. "Easy there, boy." Fin tried to calm the animal, spun him once and kept on with Noah just a couple of yards behind.

They raced for the barn and dismounted. Men rushed to set up a smooth-bore cannon to return fire to the aggressive batteries on the river's edge. With a grave disadvantage—a mere drop of blue to a river of gray—Federals scurried to load the big gun.

Splinters flew as a section of fence exploded. Another burst of dirt propelled a man into the air. Noah raced toward him, but another blast knocked *him* back. Noah staggered onward.

Kneeling next to the downed soldier, Noah's shoulders slumped. He raised his eyes, passing the sad message to Fin, then jogged back to the barn. Another blast and another before the cannon was ready to fire.

More assaults echoed from the east. Was it in the town? Another explosion, this time stifling a horse's scream. Fin's heart leapt, and he spun toward Duke. The gelding stood strong, his coat quivering in ripples across his neck. As if in consolation, he turned his head and his enormous eyes met Fin's.

The fire crackled and popped as she rubbed her hands together, willing the warmth to spread to her arms, her body, her legs. She smiled into the golden hazel eyes she'd so long admired. The fire crackled and popped again, louder. Fin frowned, and those eyes blackened. Another pop. Had she angered him? A loud SNAP. "Melinda Jane?" *It didn't sound like him.* "Melinda Jane?" Someone shook her. "Wake up!"

She forced open one eye. Another *POP!* She sat up. "What was that?"

Prancing like a filly, Will's frantic voice wobbled. "Zander says there's fighting on the edge of town." A *CRASH* rocked the house, and she jumped onto Melinda Jane's bed, clutching the pillow to her chest.

Bertie whipped around the doorframe and lunged at the bed, smacking his chin on Will's knee. "What was that?" With eyes round as walnuts and shimmering with unspent tears, he dug through the covers for Melinda Jane's hand. "Are we in the middle of the war?"

She struggled to free herself from the blankets and the children. Her pulse raced as she threw back the window curtains. Folks trickled past the house, heading toward Cox's hill. Parents struggled to keep children together and the anxious expressions made her wonder if even they knew what was happening.

"Where are they going?" Will asked, her voice sounding so like a little girl just now.

"I reckon they're heading up to higher ground." The high point of town, Cox's hill was the best place to view most of the area.

"I'm scared." Bertie clung to her waist with both arms now, his fingers locked in a desperate grip.

Melinda Jane hugged them both tight. "We'll just ask the Lord for peace and direction." She prayed three quick sentences and dropped a kiss on each of their foreheads. "Now, we must all be brave and responsible like adults today." She turned them around, herding them toward the door. "You two get yourselves dressed and in the kitchen just as soon as you can."

They took off running. When Will did not argue, she knew the girl was pretty shaken.

She splashed water on her face, then swiftly plated her hair, winding it into a spiral on the back of her head. Surely, Mrs. O'Donell was already up, but no warm breakfast smells seeped into the room. She glanced at the carpetbag poking out from beneath the bed, already making a mental note of important items she'd pack if it came to leaving.

Empty crates littered the kitchen floor, a stiff reminder of their hasty flight from the farm not even a year ago. Bertie sat at the table, shoveling oatmeal into his mouth. Coot stood commiserating with his head in the boy's lap. Mrs. O'Donell appeared at the back door, another crate in her hand. "'Tis the last of them I'm afraid." She flashed a weary, knowing smile at Melinda Jane.

"So it's come to this, you think?"

"It's just a knowin' for now, but Zander went out for news." Mrs. O'Donell dropped the crate and crossed to the stove. Musket fire rattled in the distance, tightening her grim expression. She picked up a spoon and stirred a pan on the stove.

"We've got a lot of work to do then." Melinda Jane pulled a bowl from the shelf and dished out oatmeal. "Eat up, Bertie. This may be your last meal till supper."

"Oh." Will stood in the doorway, her mouth drooping. "We're gonna have to leave again, huh?"

"Most likely. Get yourself a dish of oatmeal and sit down. We need to make some plans." Melinda Jane set her bowl on the table and ruffled Bertie's straight mop of sun-bleached hair. Before he could shake her hand loose, Zander burst through the door.

"Federal troops came through during the night—crossed over the Elk. Folks say the Rebels are coming from two directions and closing in." He dished up a bowl of oatmeal. "We best not wait too long to head out of here. You should see the Kanawha! You can purt near walk across it. There's flat boats, jerry boats, jollies—even canoes. I saw a woman sitting in a rockin' chair in the middle of two rafts strung together.

"Folks are still filing down Front Street too, heading across the Elk River bridge. Lots of freed slaves from the looks of things." He shoveled several spoonfuls of oatmeal into his mouth, then set the dish in the sink.

Every eye shifted to Melinda Jane. Why was she the one to make these decisions? The weight of it drove her to action.

A plan. She needed a plan.

She stood and crossed to the sink, setting the dish down. "This is what we'll do." She whirled around. "Zander, you hitch up the buggy and the wagon. The rest of us will pack one bag each and fill these crates with food and whatever else we might need."

"Just as soon as we're loaded, Mrs. O'Donell can drive the wagon and I'll drive the buggy. We can't load much into it, but anything gets left here will be taken by the Confederates for their own use, so we might just as well take it."

If only Gus and James were here. What about Fin? Was he nearby? Or had he been ordered back east by now?

Will and Bertie trudged up and down the rickety cellar steps hauling store goods and recently canned apples, blackberries, and corn. Melinda Jane made several trips upstairs, returning with armloads of quilts. The weather could turn cold any day now, and only the Lord knew how long they would be gone.

She had packed her clothes in a rush and dropped them onto the floor next to the quilts. "Will, you best see to your bag. Throw a few things in there for Bertie too, please."

Mrs. O'Donell arranged sacks of cornmeal and rice into a crate, arranging them to pad glass jars. Bertie stacked cans into another crate.

"We mustn't forget the coal oil," Mrs. O'Donell said, standing upright, her hand to the small of her back. "I think that's about all we can fit—oh, dear!" She scurried over to the cabinet and pulled a white sack from the shelf. "I nearly forgot the salt."

Zander strode through the back door. "Teams are hitched, and I threw what was left of the dried corn into the wagon." He looked over the chaotic kitchen and let out a low whistle. "This is gonna load down that wagon pretty heavy. So long as we don't have to make a run for it, we'll be fine I guess." He hoisted the closest crate and headed back out.

"Thank you, Zander." Melinda Jane pulled the door closed behind him and looked around. This certainly was a good deal of food—more than they had brought with them from Gauley Bridge. But back then, they knew where they were heading. This time there was no telling where they would end up or for how long. What if they never came back? The notion was silly. Or was it?

"Do you have your things packed, Mrs. O'Donell?"

"I packed me things soon as I heard the racket this mornin'." She mopped her brow with her apron and smiled. "All will be well, lass."

Would it be? The cannon blasts had increased, pecking a hole in her peace like a woodpecker on a tree trunk. She imagined this house, broken and pillaged.

"We need to get out of here." Melinda Jane lifted a crate and shifted it to her hip, heading out the door. "Let's help Zander load up the wagon."

"Remember to leave a spot for Coot!" Bertie hollered, half dragging a carpetbag across the kitchen floor.

Melinda Jane grunted, shoving crates aside, trying to fit them all in. Bertie nestled behind the seat with Coot curled up beside him. Will sat on the buckboard seat. Each of the children held a carpetbag on their lap and still there was not enough room in the wagon's bed.

"There's still two more crates. I guess we'll just leave out one with food. We surely can't leave the cooking pots."

"What good is the food if we've nothing to cook it in." Mrs. O'Donell clicked her tongue. "Sure's the pity. Hate to see the food go to the Rebels."

"Mayhap they won't even go into the houses left empty," Zander said, his forced smile giving up his sarcasm. They all knew it. Everywhere the Rebels had settled for a time, they made themselves to home in the empty houses. But so did the Federals, for that matter.

"Good thing you're getting out of here." Mrs. Overby stood at the edge of her yard. Little Jerome clung to his mother's hand, a finger digging into one ear.

"I take it you're not leavin' then, Mrs. Overby?" Mrs. O'Donell asked.

"You know my Charles is fighting with Mr. Patton. Folks are saying they're right outside town. I'll be safe all right." She looked down at her son, then back up. A sad smile darkened her normally bright demeanor. "I won't be hating. There's good people on both sides of this awful war. You and yours—you're good folk. I want to say thank you for being such fine neighbors."

Melinda Jane strode across the yard, enveloping the woman in a hug. "You've been a fine neighbor too, Mrs. Overby. I hope we'll be back one day." She did not want to think about tomorrow or the next day. *For the morrow shall take thought of the things of itself.* Isn't that what the Good Book says?

Tears glistened on the woman's face. "I heard folks talking. They say General Loring's intent on hanging every citizen Yankee found in the Kanawha Valley." She pressed a finger to her lips and her throat bobbed. "I don't believe any such thing. Just rumors most likely."

"Let's hope they are that." What a ghastly thought. Melinda Jane glanced at the wagon, hoping the children hadn't overheard. "God bless you, and I truly do hope you have a pleasant visit with your husband, Mrs. Overby."

"Godspeed."

Melinda Jane loaded the crate of cookware into the wagon while Zander returned a crate of food to the house. Within minutes she was trailing behind the buckboard, following Zander out to Cox Lane, gingerly easing the buggy onto the road against the flow of people headed for the hill.

A cacophony of voices, the pop of musket fire, and the occasional cannon blast stirred up an anxious fear that even the black mare could sense. Melinda Jane struggled to keep her to a slower pace, concentrating on not causing some sort of accident.

When she dared to look up from the street, pillars of black smoke caught her eye—one to the south, down by the river, and another just a few blocks to the west. The smoky air had grown stifling.

She pulled to a stop, waiting as Zander and Rampart stepped into the crowd on Back Street, attempting to clear a path for Mrs. O'Donell to turn onto the thoroughfare. Zander threw a look at Melinda Jane, urging her to keep the buggy close to the wagon.

"The Federals are burning everything!" Shouted a male voice, causing a bigger stir among the evacuating Charleston citizens. Curses and accusations fouled the street, and she wondered how much of what she heard was really true. Why would the Federals burn the town?

People stood on both sides of the street, watching the parade. "And don't come back! Loring's gonna push old Abe back where he belongs! . . . Good Riddance . . . Ain't no room for you Yankees here anymore!"

Taunts and slanderous accusations railed from folks she had waved to, sang for, worshipped with. How quickly a body can turn against another.

She wrinkled her nose against the acrid smoke, noticing the way a haze veiled the sun.

"The church is burning! The Methodist church is on fire!"

Nettie! Melinda Jane gasped at the thought. How could she have been so selfish, so shortsighted, so forgetful?

"Zander! Zander!" No use. He was too far ahead and the milieu of the crowd too loud.

The ground erupted in front of her horse. It reared. She dug heels into the buggy's floor, letting the line go slack, then pulling with all her might as she felt the two left wheels leave the ground. The conveyance landed with a thump and the horse calmed. She pulled over to the side, almost colliding with a hunched-over man leading a donkey.

"Melinda Jane. You all right?" Zander reined Rampart up and reached out, grabbing the side of the buggy.

"I'm fine, but I have to get Nettie!" The look on his face reflected the panic in her chest.

"I'll get her, you keep going."

"No! You make sure Mrs. O'Donell and the children make it out of here safely. I'd never forgive myself if something happened to them." Nor would she forgive herself if anything happened to Nettie and her little ones. "Now go! Do as I say!"

Anger sparked in his eyes and his mouth turned to stone, but he nodded. "You be careful. See you up the road."

She cut across someone's yard and headed north on Alderson Street. Her mouth went dry at the sight. Billows of black smoke funneled from the church steeple. She snapped the reins. "Get up there!" Her heart pounded in rhythm with the hooves on the hard ground, faster and faster.

PART THREE

The adversaries of the LORD
shall be broken to pieces;
out of heaven shall he thunder upon them

1 Samuel 2:10

Forty–Two

"Oh Dear Lord, help!" Melinda Jane hooked the reins around the brake and jumped to the ground. Hitching up her skirts, she ran, the blood pounding in her ears with every footfall. "Oh Dear Lord, help!" the words spilled from her lips, a deluge of constant prayer, a plea, an admission of her own powerlessness.

Several bystanders looked on, their mouths agape, as she rushed up the steps and through the door. "Nettie! Nettie!"

"We're here!"

Melinda Jane took the stairs as quickly as she dared, descending into the musty, but smokeless, basement. She slipped down the last few, landing on her bottom.

"Oh dear!" Nettie rushed to her side with little Izzy at her breast. "Are you hurt?"

Melinda Jane gasped for breath. "We . . . we need to get you out of here. The church is on fire." She struggled to her feet.

"I was just so scared with all the ruckus outside. Did you say fire?" Nettie's free hand fumbled with the buttons on her shirtwaist.

"We've got to leave Charleston. Now come on. The Rebels are coming."

Nettie's eyes grew round, and she clamped her mouth into a thin line.

"Olivia, you head up to the front door, I'll take Perry." Melinda Jane bustled the girl toward the steps, then pulled Nettie's arm. "We have to go now!"

Perry whimpered. Even in the dim cellar, Melinda Jane could see the glisten of tears ready to spill over onto his fleshy cheeks. She calmed her voice. "It's all right, Perry. God's gonna see us to safety." She grasped the boy's hand and followed the others up the stairs.

She threw her carpetbag onto the floor of the buggy and held the baby as Nettie climbed in. "We'll have to squeeze."

Fewer folks traveled the streets now. Even the spectating crowds had thinned, no doubt chased indoors by the heavy gray air that now drew coughs from her passengers.

Turning onto Back Street, she headed toward the Elk River, the town's border to the east. "We'll be out of town in just a little bit." A reminder to soothe herself as much as the others.

A cannon ball struck a house as they passed. It sent Olivia into hysterics and brought wails from Perry, who shared his mother's lap with little Izzy, the calmest of them all. The infant rested against his mother's breast, trusting eyes heavy with sleep as Nettie comforted the other children.

The lack of traffic in the streets allowed Melinda Jane to push the mare as she neared the bridge. Was the sound of muskets louder now? People trickled back to their homes with solemn vestiges. Shutters banged, doors slammed. One man led his horse into his house. Three Federal soldiers trotted across the street, stopping directly in front of her.

One held up his hand to halt the carriage. "I'm sorry ma'am. We've cut the cables on the bridge. You'll have to turn around."

"T . . . turn around?" She couldn't turnaround. She had to catch up to her family. But that would never happen unless she crossed that bridge. *What now, Lord?*

She looked at Olivia, then Nettie with her arms around the boys. A fierce sense of protection rose within. She was a lioness, and these were her cubs. In that instant she knew she would take them to her den, protecting them with her very life if need be. She lowered the reins, backing the horse, then headed home. There was nowhere else to go.

Fin pulled his kerchief over his nose to block out the thick smoke. From the Ruffner place, it looked like the whole town was going up in flames because the few buildings that burned threw up enough black smoke to darken the sun. It reminded him of something biblical.

A Minie ball whizzed past his head. He ducked lower, pressing Duke harder, knowing he and Noah were among the last Federals in town. They had been caught up in a scrimmage down at the Kanawha, and he had heard enough from the Rebel shouts to conclude that the bridge over the Elk had been dropped into the river. There would be no easy way out of this.

Where was Hicks? Fin lost sight of him just after that last turn. In the frenzy, he wasn't sure where he was, but now he recognized the street. James's house was only a couple blocks from here. He pulled his mind back just in time to lean forward as Duke leapt over a body in the street.

"There's another one!"

He pivoted in the saddle, taking aim with his Colt. Two mounted Rebels pulled up short.

His heart stopped. *That horse.*

The rider took aim with a carbine, then hesitated.

"Well, what are ya waitin' for? Shoot!"

Time slowed for a moment as Fin's finger wavered and Jimmy Lee Campbell squeezed the trigger.

Fire seared Fin's arm. He wrenched the reins. Duke reared. His arm hung limp as he willed his legs to squeeze tighter. His body crashed against the hard ground, and blackness sucked away his vision.

❧

A horse's snort. Voices. Here, then gone again. The sounds, so distant at first, grew closer. Fin's eyes refused to open. Pain radiated. Was it his head? His chest? A quagmire of senses held him fast.

He had been shot. Thrown from his horse. Charleston. How long had he lain there?

At last one eye obeyed his command, then both. His mind lurched, and clarity took hold. Lying still, he looked and listened. They had assumed he was dead. It was the only reason they had not taken him prisoner.

To his right, a blur of color danced forward, then back, at the edge of his vision. It stopped. Hooves struck the ground. One horse. It faded. If he moved too soon, they would spot him. If he waited too long, they would load the dead into wagons and discover him. *Show me what to do, Lord.*

Strange how helpless a body could feel. Without knowing what lay beyond what he could see without moving, he had no way to calculate a decision. It was his weakness—not trusting in what he couldn't see straight out.

You see what is all around me, though, Lord. Please, go before me and make a way out of this. Didn't God bring him out of those waters last winter? Hadn't Pap taught him that God's not the one who changes, but it's us puny men. And how puny he felt right now—and how big he needed God to be.

He'd just wait right here and trust God for the unction to get up and go. *Go where?* He would make his way to James's house, that's where. *Then what?* One step at a time.

After what felt like hours, finally, long moments went by without a sound. Fin turned his head to one side, then the other. Ignoring the fire in his arm, he rose, scurrying across the street to the north, hugging the side of a house as he slipped around to the backyard. A blacksmith hammered on an anvil inside his head, and his palm felt sticky as he opened and closed his hand.

If he could just make it there without being seen.

Chuckling to himself, he imagined following Jesus, saying to Him, "You go first, Lord." His stomach pitched, and he swallowed down the nasty taste. He hugged the shadows when a bald man with a long gray beard stepped onto a back porch. He struck a match on the porch railing and lit a cigar. No one could spot him. Likely, the only folks choosing to stay were Confederate sympathizers. And didn't most of Col. Patton's men come from this area?

Waiting in the shadows proved challenging as his body grew heavy, pulling his limbs closer to the ground. Blackness swirled again. He leaned against the house. How desperately he wanted to sink to the ground, but the movement could be his death sentence. The trees across the way turned rubbery, undulating like a reed in the water. He blinked, willing vigilance.

At long last, the man snuffed the cigar and went back inside. Fin stepped out, staggering now, every step a deliberate action. Mercifully, he eyed James's house and ran for it. He pushed through the back door and it crashed against the wall as he stumbled into the kitchen. Dropping into a chair, he let his forehead fall to the table. The *drip, drip* of blood on the floor faded away.

Melinda Jane grasped the old pistol she had packed in her carpetbag. It was now her only means of protecting herself, Nettie, and the children as they huddled in the cellar near the coal furnace. A crash brought a squeal from Olivia. Nettie placed a finger to her lips and rubbed a slow circle on the girl's back.

Musket fire echoed farther away now, off to the west. The cannon fire in the town had stopped some time ago. But now something crashed upstairs. What if the Rebels are going from house to house? She forced a smile, but hugged the gun tighter. "Probably just the wind."

"I don't remember no wind," Nettie whispered.

Melinda Jane sprang to her feet. The paralyzing fear she had felt only a moment ago evaporated, and somehow she knew she had to go upstairs and investigate. "I'm going upstairs. You stay right here."

Nettie snagged her arm, pulling her back down to the floor. "No! It's too dangerous."

"I'll be fine. Do you trust God to watch over us, Nettie?"

"I . . . do. But I figure He don't watch over fools, and it's a foolish thing you're fixin' to do."

Melinda Jane set down the pistol and put one arm around Olivia and the other around Perry, pulling them to her. "There's a verse in the Psalms my mama made me memorize when I was your age, Olivia: 'There shall no evil befall thee, neither shall any plague come nigh thy dwelling. For He shall give His angels charge over thee, to keep thee in all thy ways.' That's a promise from God. This is our dwelling, right here, and God's got angels watching over us as I speak. And God always keeps His promises."

Olivia's eyes grew round, the whites glistening in the cellar's dimness. "Angels? Truly?"

"Truly." Melinda Jane gripped the pistol and stood. "Now, don't you come up until I come and get you."

Nettie nodded. "We just sit tight right here with them angels."

She should be frightened, but she wasn't. Cautious maybe, but not scared. She pushed open the cellar door, creeping into the kitchen, pistol in her hand. A Union soldier sat in a chair, slumped over the table. A pool of blood spawned a narrow rivulet that flowed off, coaxed by the uneven floor. She hurried over, setting the pistol on the table.

Fin! Her heart surged, racing, threatening to burst through her ribs. She dashed to the ragbag on the back porch and returned, throwing several onto the table. Ripping one into two pieces, she rolled one half into a thick pad and pressed it into the arm wound, securing it with the second piece.

She removed his hat and traced his jaw with a finger. How could she not love this man? She placed a kiss on his temple, tasting the salty dust. She caressed his unshaven cheek and tenderly brushed the hair from his brow. A purple, duck-sized lump stretched the skin at his hairline.

Darkness had fallen swiftly on the town with the canopy of smoke snuffing out the sunlight. She would need Nettie to hold a light so she could see to his wound. He had lost a lot of blood.

Lord, don't let me lose him again.

She stirred up the cold coals from this morning and set a kettle of water to boil. With the kitchen in the back of the house, she felt safer using any lights, so she'd work on him here.

She opened the cellar door, calling down to Nettie, "I need your help. It's Fin. He's wounded."

"*Your* Fin?" Nettie herded the children into the kitchen.

"He's not *my* Fin, not yet, anyway. Please, find what you can to cover the windows. The neighbors think we've left. I'm going to round up the medical supplies I need."

After sewing up the gash in his arm, Melinda Jane managed to move Fin to a bed with Nettie's help. The bullet had dredged its way through the muscle, missing the bone, and coming out the back of his arm. So many times, she had assisted Gus in stitching up a body. But how hard it was for her to plunge that needle into Fin's arm. She had the chloroform ready to use if he roused, but he slept deeply, oblivious to even the efforts of the two petite women dragging him to the bed.

Nettie hefted a basket holding a sleeping Little Izzy. "I'm a-gonna see what I can cook up for supper. I figure best to do our cookin' at night so's not to be noticed in the daytime."

"Thank you, Nettie. I'm so glad you're here with me." And she was, too. However could she have managed this without her?

Nettie tipped her head, eyes searching. "You surely do love that man, don't you?"

Melinda Jane's throat closed. Tears stung the back of her eyes. "I surely do."

Forty-Three

Musket fire had long-since quieted on the edge of town and the strange silence brought only questions. Melinda Jane's mind told her the Rebels would pound on her door at any minute, but her spirit fought back, whispering, "*Peace, be still.*" Fin lay on the cot, motionless, his breathing steady. She laid her head on his chest, casting prayers heavenward, watching for him to wake as her eyes grew heavy.

Dawn broke, but the covered windows deceived her senses and she slept on in exhaustion. She startled awake, alerted to the late hour, when Perry patted her hand. "Oh! Oh, good morning, Perry."

"I told you not to wake her." Nettie bustled into the room, turning the boy around and guiding him out the door.

"It's all right, Nettie. It's past time I was up."

"Just look at those dark circles under your eyes. You need your sleep, Miss 'Linda." She motioned to the bed with her chin. "Has he been awake at all?"

"No. Not even a twitch." She stared at his eyes, willing them to open, willing the lips to smile in recognition. Lines spurred off from the corners of his eyes. Lines that had not been there just a year earlier. And his beard seemed fuller, thicker. She thought of shaving him. But what if he woke suddenly? Imagine the scar a razor could leave. She pressed her palm to his cheek and leaned close, her breath brushing his face. "Please wake up."

"I'll bring you in some breakfast. Just what I saved from supper last night."

"Thank you, Nettie." She was too exhausted to argue.

The next morning saw no change, nor the next. Melinda Jane's knees grew tender from her prayer vigils and doubts assailed her like bats. She would swat one away, and here'd come another. She looked for advice in James's books, but they read like a foreign language with their big words and strange references to who knows what. If only he were here. Even Gus would know better what to do.

A groan drew her attention and her heart flip-flopped. Fin's lashes fluttered and at last she glimpsed those eyes she'd loved since she was young. He squinted, seeming to focus his eyes. His lips curved in a smile.

"Am I in heaven?" his voice graveled a whisper.

Melinda Jane laughed, then covered her mouth as tears flooded her cheeks.

He frowned. "My head hurts. Must not be heaven."

"*Shhh.* You're injured. You've been unconscious for days now."

He narrowed his eyes, confused. His gaze roamed the room, then a flame sparked in them. "Why are you here?" His voice was louder, angry even. "You were supposed to evacuate." He raised his head, then dropped it back to the pillow, pain pulling at his features. "Where's the rest of the family?"

Rest of the family? Is that what she was to him—family?

She wiped away the tears with her apron, along with t her joy. "They escaped just fine."

"But why are you here?"

"I got held up some and missed my chance." She stood. "I can give you something for that headache if you want."

"Of all the aggravatin'ist—You can't be here, Melinda Jane. You can't. There's Rebels . . .unless . . . unless you think that Anderson feller is gonna protect you."

If blood could boil, hers was surely fixing to. After all she had done for him, he throws that in her face.

He tried to lift his arm. "Ow."

"I stitched up your arm. Lucky for you I didn't have to dig the bullet out." She would've waited until he could feel it! "It tore up the muscle pretty good. It's that knot on your head seems to be the bigger problem." She gathered up the tray of dishes Nettie had brought in. "I'll bring you something to eat now that you're awake."

She turned to leave.

"Don't bother. I'll just rest a while, then I'll be on my way," he grumbled.

Her heart must've fallen clear through to the cellar, as bruised and battered as it felt.

That woman! How could she be so dense? Didn't she understand what those Rebels would do to her if they found her here alone? A beautiful flower like that? He oughta throw her over his knee and paddle her like he had back when she stole his hat. He smiled at the memory.

What was he thinking, being all owly like that? He loved her and he was scared for her. That's all. How was it he could track a man across rough country, live off the land, and fight an enemy hand to hand, but stumble so miserably through the overgrown backwoods of relationship—of bearing his heart to the woman he loved?

Hadn't he decided once before to be done with all this tomfoolery? But that was before that Anderson fella. Boy, did he hit a raw nerve when he brought that up.

Melinda Jane returned with a tray, her steps deliberate and loud. Her eyes were red and puffy like she had been crying, and guilt kicked him in the gut because he knew he had been the cause. He itched to touch her.

She set the tray on the low table beside the bed, then fidgeted like she was trying to decide whether to stay or leave.

"There's water with some laudanum for your head if you want it. The big glass is plain water. You need to be drinking as much of that as you can." She glanced at the empty chair, then back to the tray. "You'll need to get some of that soup down too, to get your strength back."

Just do it. He took in a deep breath and reached for her hand. She startled at his touch, then her eyes softened. "Sit down beside me," he said, hoping she wouldn't argue. She didn't.

He held her hand and stared up at the ceiling. "I'm sorry."

"I know." She covered his hand with hers.

His heart raced at her touch, and he started to hide it like he had for so long. Too long. His gaze caressed her hair, her face, her chin, savoring the effect it had on him.

"I want to explain about Anderson," she said calmly, but he felt her stiffen.

He would rather take another bullet.

"What you think you saw was not how it was. Anderson was a friend, nothing more. He was simply one to give a lady a kiss on the cheek quite freely. It was just his way."

"He *was* a friend?"

"Oh, I guess he tried to woo me . . . but we came to an impasse—of sorts."

Uninvited thoughts ruffled his new determination. He knew the way of men like that. He could figure the rest out all on his own. *Hold steady, man.* He pulled his hand back. "What kind of *impasse?*"

"Let's just say we have different opinions about people . . . and the color of their skin."

He chuckled as his heart took flight, a bird freed from its cage. He knew better than most anyone how Melinda Jane felt about the color of a person's skin. She guarded her secret from the world, but it fueled her passion for all of God's children, no matter their color. He reached for her hand again, pasting a stupid grin on his face. He felt like a schoolboy. No, not a *boy.*

"Come here," he whispered. His head throbbed. "Come here."

She bent over him, concern marring her beautiful eyes. "What is it? What's wrong?"

He pulled her to him, his hand on the back of her head. This was not the way he had planned it, but it had to happen. It had to. He'd waited too long already. Their lips met for a moment in a kiss that only left him wanting more.

She smiled. "You must be feeling better." The look in her eyes buoyed his heart. It shouted of years of pent-up love and unspoken words . . . and forgiveness.

"Not really, my head is pounding, but I'd never forgive myself if I waited another minute to do that." He squeezed her hand. "I'll take that laudanum now, nurse."

She chuckled, and joy swaddled him as she held his head while he drank the medicine.

Melinda Jane breezed into the kitchen, a song in her heart and on her lips. She was a child at Christmas—the wonder of the Christ child, the mystery of the Star, and, of course, the gifts. She'd just received permission to open the most lovely of wrapped packages beneath the tree. It had waited for her there, year after year.

"You look like you just about to burst with happiness, Miss 'Linda." Nettie dropped a rag into a pan of water. She lifted a naked Perry with a towel and carried him to a chair. She tickled his feet, then his neck, and he giggled like all four-year-olds do.

That will be her someday. The thought of having Fin's children brought her goosebumps. "You're a good mama, Nettie."

"What brought that on?"

"Oh, I was just thinking. I'd like a whole litter of young'uns. The boys will look like Fin and the girls like me." Such silliness.

A voice in the back of her mind warned her against such happy thoughts. This war had changed so much for so many. Husbands and fathers not coming home. Families ripped apart forever for so many reasons. Homes burned. She had heard of freedmen captured and forced into slavery even. This old world was a mess, sure enough.

"The next time Fin wakes, I want him to meet you and the children. He thinks I'm here alone. He'll feel better knowin' I'm not."

Fin awoke long enough for soup and introductions to Nettie and the children. When Melinda Jane introduced him to little Izzy, she was sure his eyes grew misty. She practically forced a glass of water down him before he dozed off again.

She watched him sleep for a while before falling to her knees. First, she poured out her thankfulness to her Heavenly Father. Then she assailed the gates of heaven for this man before her, casting aside the burden of knowing he would soon return to his unit.

Fin awakened to a room washed in gray because of the blanket-covered window. The pain in his head had faded to a dull throb now, and he could lift his head, taking in the room. He was downstairs, just off the parlor. Of course. The two women would've never been able to carry him up the stairs.

His clothes set folded on a chair across the room, no doubt clean by Melinda Jane's hand. *His clothes?* He lifted the blanket, suddenly aware he was bare-chested, then let out a breath when he saw he had on drawers. But they were not *his* drawers. The thought of Melinda Jane bathing and changing him like a child brought heat to his face.

The door opened a crack, then wider. Melinda Jane's face lit a dozen candles in his heart.

"You're awake." She fairly floated across the floor, setting a tray of cornbread and milk on the table. "Feelin' up to something besides soup?"

"I could eat just about anything right now." He sat upright, and she pulled his pillow, fluffed it and stuck it behind his back.

"Just a minute." She looked around the room. "We packed most of the quilts in the wagon. Sure could use some right now." She left the room and returned with two pillows from the parlor. "These should help."

He sat back, enjoying the change of scenery. She sat in the chair, but he snatched her hand before she could pick up a spoon. "Thank you."

"You are very welcome, Mr. Dabney." She batted her eyes, teasing him like she had done for years. The desire that sprung to his chest was frightening, and what he wanted to do with that desire would have to wait for another day. Most likely another year. Blast this war!

"How is your head today?"

"Better."

An awkward silence cut through the moment like a knife separating them. She shyly pulled her hand away and poured the milk over the cornbread. "Do you want to feed yourself?"

"I believe I can do that much."

She tucked a yellow napkin under his chin and handed him the bowl and spoon. He balanced the bowl on his injured arm and shoveled in a bite.

"Is that coffee I smell?"

"Well, your nose is working just fine." She chuckled. "It's nearly the last of it, I'm afraid. We packed all but this dab into the wagon."

He shoveled the cornbread and milk into his mouth like he was starved—or rather, just like Zander. He handed her the empty bowl. "I'll take some of that coffee now please, miss."

"Why, certainly, sir." She grinned, batting those eyes again, exchanging the bowl for the steaming cup. Her eyes were on him as he took the first drink.

"Ahhh. I haven't had coffee this good since I don't know when."

She sat with her hands folded in her lap, a soft smile lighting her sweet face. There was so much he wanted to tell her. So much he wanted to say. He emptied the cup. "Don't suppose there's just one more cup of that?"

She rose, taking the cup. "Maybe just one. I'll be right back."

He watched her leave, her skirt rocking back and forth beneath her hips, her step choppy and sassy, just like her. All that was good and right with this world—that was Melinda Jane. He felt her love for him as sure as he knew he adored her. But they were not children anymore. Times were complicated.

She returned with another cup and he took it, letting the steam moisten his face.

"You're smiling," she said, settling into the chair.

"Am I?" He grunted, making her laugh. He needed to tell her. "It was Jimmy Lee."

"What about Jimmy Lee?" Her eyebrows dipped with concern.

"He's the one that shot me. He's alive, Melinda Jane. Jimmy Lee's alive."

She blinked several times. Her mouth flew open, closed, then opened again.

"I thought he drowned in the river, but he's here. In Charleston."

"But he *shot* you. Maybe you've got some kind of brain injury." She stood to feel his forehead, and he grabbed her wrist with one hand, passing the cup to her with the other.

He pulled her next to him. "Sit here, I want to talk."

The worry lines relaxed, and she settled onto the bed, turning to face him.

He caressed her hand. "Jimmy Lee is as good a shot as I am. If'n he'd wanted to kill me, he would've. If he didn't shoot, the other guy would've. It's God's providence that I was thrown and ended up unconscious in the dirt like a dead man."

Her chin quivered and she nodded, taking in the truth.

"I'm not the same man you knew back in Gauley, Melinda Jane." He dropped her hands and stared at his own. "My hands are stained with men's blood. Some of them good men. Men with families and dreams. Men who worshipped the same God as you and me."

She enveloped his hands in her own. "There's always been war of some kind or another, Fin. Been good men on both sides. I can't wrap my head around the particulars, but I know God sees your heart." Her eyes grew red and tears settled on the rims.

"You're a fine man, Fin Dabney. This I know with everything inside me. And beneath all that hurt and regret lies the boy—the man I have loved for such a long, long time." The tears over-flowed, dripping from the edge of her jaw.

He wiped them away, and she leaned her cheek into his hand, raising a warmth in his middle and a fire in his heart. He wanted so much to protect her. To make her proud. But—

"Forgive me, Melinda Jane. Forgive me for taking so dadgum long. Forgive me for doing what I have to do. And forgive me for telling you how very much I love you."

He took her face in his hands and pressed his lips to hers. She leaned into him as embers flamed. He tasted the passion he had suspected simmered beneath the flirtatious bantering he had tried so hard to ignore. He ached for her like nothing else, and it scared him.

He pushed her away, holding her gaze captive, keenly aware of the way their quickened breaths matched. Several seconds passed.

She sat up, pink flushing her cheeks. "I've waited so long for that. I'm not lyin'." She grinned before covering her mouth.

Fin sighed, pulling the damper on the furnace that still heat-ed his insides. "There is nothing I want more on this entire earth right this minute than I want you."

There. He'd said it. If something happened to him, he want-ed her to know she had been loved. Loved the way she needed a man to love her. He wanted to be that man. But the war . . .

"You're leaving. I know." She tipped her head, eyes strained with sadness.

"I have to get back to my unit."

She sat straighter and pulled back her shoulders. "Well, how's that gonna work with all these Rebels in the town?" Tears brimmed, and she squeezed them back. "Take James's mare. She's in the barn. If you don't take her, the Rebels will."

"If you can get me a Confederate uniform—at least a hat and a jacket—I can sneak out of town during the night."

Lines crowded her brow. "Let me think on that." She scowled, then a smile blossomed. "Mayhap Preacher Lambert can help. He's a respectable man, Fin."

"You sure you can trust him?"

"He's our only hope, lessin' I woo a Confederate soldier and—"

He hauled her close, raising a cry from the bedsprings as she bounced onto the mattress with a gasp. "If there's to be any wooin', I'll be the one doing it." He kissed her soundly. "Let's pray the pastor can help us."

Forty-Four

"I can't thank you enough, Brother Lambert." Melinda Jane wrapped the tattered Rebel slouch hat and butternut jacket in the tablecloth she had brought. "However did you find these?"

"I'll pretend you didn't ask me. Let's just say I now have something in common with the thief on the cross." He lowered his head, looking over his spectacles. The spattering of gray in his black beard had spread in the few months she had known him, but his eyes had not lost their luster. There was a silent strength to this man whom she had admired from the moment they met.

"Well, I'm sure you don't intend to venture further down this sinful road. I do apologize for my part in it."

"I have already repented, my child." He turned her toward the parsonage door. "Now, off with you."

She snugged the brim of her bonnet over her brow, hoping to avoid any attention. What if someone discovered her with the stolen uniform? The thought sent a chill through her bones.

With just one block to go, she rounded the corner, quickening her steps.

"Well if it ain't Melinda Jane Minard!"

She gasped. Her knees went weak. She had known that voice all her life. *Dear Lord, I need You.* She painted on a cordial smile and turned toward the street. A tall black horse stepped up close as Jimmy Lee Campbell plucked a stick from his lips and flicked it away.

"Why, what are you doin' here, Jimmy Lee?"

He cocked his head off to one side, putting on that womanizing grin of his. "I think that's pretty obvious. What are you doing here? In Charleston? Most the Unionists have moved out." He dismounted. "Can I carry that for you?"

She hugged the bundle to her. "No, thank you. I don't have far to go." Why did she say that? What if Jimmy Lee discovered where she lived and came snooping around? She scrambled to move the conversation ahead.

"We came here when things got pretty bad at the farm." She pulled at her bonnet as two soldiers walked past. "I'm real happy you're safe and all." This was so awkward.

"I'll walk with you. Not every Confederate is the gentleman I am."

She laughed. "Same old Jimmy Lee." She strolled along, taking her time. She needed to think of some way to get rid of him.

He nodded to a passing soldier. "You hear anything from Fin lately?"

Her steps faltered. *Lately?* "Well . . . I . . .did get a letter a few months back. In fact, he told me he'd met up with you." She had to stall. She stopped and turned to him. "He thought you were dead."

"Thought I was *dead*?

"What I mean to say is that in his letter he said he had lost you. I assume he thinks you're dead. He sounded like it hit him hard."

He scanned the street. "Yeah, well I guess God had other plans for me."

Never in all her days had she heard him speak of the Almighty. "God?"

"It's a story for another time." His eyes narrowed. "Why didn't you evacuate, Melinda Jane?"

"I . . . just got too busy and didn't make it out of here in time."
She walked on, her steps slow and short.

"Is Gus with you?"

"No. No, she and James are up in Wheeling." He had always
taken a shine to Gus. Of course he would ask about her.

"And the rest of the family?"

"Oh, they went off with Zander."

"I swear, it's like pulling quills from a hound's snout trying to
get answers out of you."

"Well, you can't blame a girl for gettin' a little rattle-brained
when she's being interrogated by a Rebel soldier, now can you?"

He laughed long and hard. "Now that's the Melinda Jane I
know."

"Don't you have more important things to do than escort me? I
appreciate it, I really do, but I'm nearly there, so I free you of your
chivalrous duty, Officer."

He snickered. "You think that 'officer' bit will get rid of me?"

Still three houses from home, she turned to him and smiled.
"It's been real nice to see you again, Jimmy Lee." She swallowed,
remembering the skinny boy who always tagged along with Fin.
She motioned toward a nearby house. "I'm here now. Thank you."

He mounted and tipped his hat. "Any time, Miss Minard. Any
time." He turned his horse, trotting back down the road.

She watched him turn the corner, hitched up her hem, and
sprinted to James's house.

It was his own face in the mirror, but he wore enemy butternut.
The mirror told the truth, all right. The only difference between
the two sides was the color of the uniform. Fin straightened the
Confederate hat. He would toss it the minute he was out of town.

Chances were, no one would stop him this time of night. Melinda Jane had found an old saddlebag in the barn for him to carry with his Federal uniform tucked inside.

She slipped her hands around his waist and hugged him to her, pressing her head into her back. "I'm so selfish. I don't want you to go."

He squeezed her hands. "You don't have a selfish bone in your body, honey."

He turned to face her, then wrapped his arms around her, relishing the feel of her body against his. "I love you," he whispered into her hair. The flyaway curls tickled his nose, and he smiled, pressing his face harder against her head.

His shirt grew damp. He pulled back to look at her. "I never could stand to see you cry."

Her eyes pleaded with him to stay.

He kissed her wet cheek, tasting the saltiness of her tears. He kissed her temple and felt her melt into his arms. How he longed to stay with her, to never leave her side, to protect her. Her breath passed over his neck, then he found her lips and their sweetness left him dizzy.

She whispered, her lips touching his, "You best be leavin'."

"I know," he grumbled. He drew her by the hand to the kitchen, where Nettie sat with the children at the table. "Thank you for the food, Nettie."

"Oh I didn't make yer food, Mr. Dabney, sir. It were Miss 'Linda. She insisted on cookin' everything for you herself."

He grinned at Melinda Jane. "You did that for me?"

She opened her mouth to speak, then clamped it shut. An inner struggle tarried on her face as tears brimmed again.

After checking his pistol one last time, he fitted a blanket roll over one shoulder and threw the saddlebag over the other.

They stepped onto the back porch, and Fin pulled Melinda Jane to him in the darkness.

"I'll be prayin' for you. Prayin' without ceasing." She clung to his jacket and sniffled.

"I'll be back for you. I promise. Will you wait for me?"

She slapped him playfully on the chest. "Daft man. I been waitin' for you half my life."

He kissed her one last time, then opened the door. "I'll be back."

Ghostly clouds shrouded the moon, but still, its pale glow stretched across the sleeping town. Fin moved through the shadows, leading the black mare along the side of two houses. He crossed the street at a brisk pace, wincing at the clip of hooves on the packed dirt.

Something glinted in the darkness off to his left. He stole behind a burly oak tree, waiting. The hair on the back of his neck told him he wasn't alone. He eased his Colt from his belt and stepped away from the tree. A silhouetted figure leaned against the corner of a carriage house, one knee bent with a boot against the siding, not forty feet away.

Had he been spotted? After several minutes, he said a quick prayer and moved between the trees into the shadow of a house. He glanced at the figure. The man stepped into a patch of light—not just any man. Jimmy Lee met his gaze. The corner of his mouth ticked up. He nodded once, turned, and walked into the night.

Forty–Five

October, 1862

Melinda Jane had yet to venture out since Fin's departure, except to the backyard during the night. The house, pleasant as it was, had become her prison.

She slumped in the kitchen chair, watching Perry roll an empty thread spool across the floor. "I wish these children could play in the fresh air. It pains me to see them trapped inside like this."

"Don't you mind about that now. Least ways we're safe." Nettie wrung out a clean nappy.

A knock at the back door sent a jolt through Melinda Jane's heart. Her eyes darted to Nettie. Springing from her chair, Nettie lifted Izzy's basket from the floor. She put a finger to her lips and motioned for Olivia and Perry to follow her down the stairs to the cellar. Melinda Jane set the bucket of nappies on the cellar step and glanced around the room for anything else she would be hard up to explain.

Oh dear Lord, protect us! Melinda Jane smoothed her skirt and crossed the enclosed porch to the outside door. She pulled back her shoulders and nudged the curtain aside. Mrs. Overby stood on the step, one hand dangling little Jerome's spindly arm and the other looped through a basket.

Whatever will the woman think? Melinda Jane was not supposed to be here. She painted on a smile and took a deep breath as she pulled the door open. "Why, Mrs. Overby, what a pleasant surprise."

The woman glanced past her, into the house. "May I come in?"

"Of course you may." She stepped aside and followed Mrs. Overby through the porch and into the kitchen. Melinda Jane cringed when her eyes fell to the thread spool on the floor.

"Please, have a seat. Would you like some tea. I'm afraid I am out of coffee." She bustled over to the stove, her mind working up explanations for the questions that were sure to come. Silence fell on the room as she pumped water into the kettle. She set the fresh water to boil and measured the tea leaves sparingly.

Mrs. Overby ignored Jerome as he rolled the little spool across the floor, chasing after it with all of his toddler energy. She glanced around the room and removed a paper from her basket, laying it on the table. "So where is everyone else?"

"Oh, they all made it out of here just fine before the bridge went down, " Melinda Jane said, taking a seat.

"But why are you left here? Alone, I assume?"

"I . . .I forgot something and returned for it. When I headed back out, the bridge was down."

"Oh dear! What was it?"

"What was what?" She stared at the kettle, willing the steam to rise from the spout so she could jump up and make the tea.

"What was it you forgot? What was so important that you had to come back for it"

"My . . . I forgot my heirlooms. Yes, I forgot the precious jewels that are an inheritance." Melinda Jane smiled, feeling her shoulders relax a little. "Why, I just can't imagine what I was thinking. I could never go off and leave something so precious behind."

Mrs. Overby smiled. "I know you're trying to hide out, Melinda Jane. The only way I knew you were still here is that I saw you peek out the window when I was leaving the house yesterday."

"Well . . . I'm just not sure what's happening out there."

"You needn't be afraid, dear. I brought you this newspaper so you can catch-up on all that's going on in town."

Melinda Jane picked up the paper, surprised at the banner across the top: *THE GUERILLA, Devoted to Southern Rights and Institutions*. "Wherever did you get this?"

"The Confederacy took over the printing press at the *Kanawha Valley Star*. Now they're printing their own paper every afternoon." She leaned forward, lowering her voice a bit. "And if you have any Cincinnati newspapers around here, they've outlawed them. Best to burn them if you got any."

Melinda Jane stiffened. "Thank you for the warning." She jumped up, rescued by the wisps of steam rising from the kettle. She poured water into the teapot and placed the tea service tray on the table.

"I also stopped in to see if you'd like me to get you some salt?"

"Salt?" What a strange thing to ask about. "I don't have the money to spend on salt, Mrs. Overby. I'll just make do without it for a while." A *long* while. With salt at five dollars a bushel, it would wait a good long time.

"But the Army captured wagons of salt and is offering it to citizens for just thirty-five cents a bushel!"

"You're toying with me."

"Not at all, dear. The Federals dumped a monstrous amount into the river so the Confederate boys couldn't get their hands on it, but there are still wagonloads to be had. My Charles says there's been wagon trains of salt being transported to the East and parts south."

"Your husband? Did he come home, then?" What was she thinking—keeping this woman talking? She needed to escort her out, but surely she could spend the money for salt.

Mrs. Overby leaned back in her chair, a smile lighting her face. "Charles was home for a whole week, but he's gone now. He left to serve under General Floyd, with the Virginia State Line. He traded the two years he had left for one. It was so nice to have him home for a bit. Why, Jerome hardly seemed to know him at first, but he surely knows his daddy now."

Melinda Jane sat with fidgeting hands in her lap as Mrs. Overby went on about the party atmosphere around town the first week after the occupation. Such merriment throughout the town with the return of Colonel Patton's Kanawha Riflemen. She assured Melinda Jane no harm would come to her were she to venture out. Some stores had closed, but were now urged to reopen—on the condition they do business with only Confederate graybacks.

"I best be on my way. We are walking to the Presbyterian church to ride with some others over to get the salt." She frowned. "The Army's been in need of horses and wagons and such, so I'm without transportation, like most folks in Charleston I guess."

Melinda Jane thought of the carriage in the barn, thankful she had Fin take the horse. If only she knew for sure he had made it out of here all right. "Oh, your money."

Melinda Jane stood on tiptoe to pull a small clay jar from the corner shelf.

"I hope to see you out getting some fresh air soon." Mrs. Overby chased down little Jerome, grabbed his hand, and headed for the door.

"I'm sure I will. Thank you so much for the visit." Melinda Jane handed her the coins. "And for the salt. You won't have to carry it to your house, will you?"

"Certainly not. Mr. Upton has offered to deliver it for the women who live alone."

"Good. I'll try to watch for it and come over to your place to get it." She bent to look Jerome in the eye. "Goodbye, Jerome." He grinned and wiggled his fingers, mimicking Melinda Jane's wave.

"Thank you for the tea." Mrs. Overby nodded and slipped out the door, tugging the boy along behind her.

She waited until the woman stepped through her own back door, then she scurried over to the cellar door. "You can come up now, Nettie."

"Wasn't that a neighborly visit." Nettie brought up the rear of her brood, closing the door behind her. "Sorry you had to lie for us, Miss 'Linda. I don't like being the cause of such."

"Why, I don't know what you're talking about. I didn't lie."

Nettie lifted one eyebrow and put her hand on her hip. "You forgot your jewels? Your inheritance?"

"These little ones are precious jewels." She grabbed Olivia's arm, wrapping her in a bear hug. "The Good Book calls children an inheritance of the Lord. I did not lie one bit!"

Nettie laughed. "No, I guess you didn't. You one smart woman."

Melinda Jane settled at the table with a cup of hot water, reading through the *Guerilla* newspaper. "Listen to this, Nettie: 'Hundreds of people who, two years ago, were the quiet possessors of large farms are now driven away from home in a condition bordering on destitution. Unable to remove their farm stock, they are obliged to leave behind them what they depended on for subsistence during the coming winter.'

"That was us just a year ago, and now all these poor folks have been driven from their homes."

"These is mighty hard times for them folks." Nettie lifted little Izzy to her shoulder and thumped his back.

Melinda Jane continued reading: "'Arriving at Gallipolis, or elsewhere, most of them have to seek a charitable home among strangers.' I been wondering and praying for the children and Mrs. O'Donell. No telling where they are. I wrote a letter to James and Gus care of the Wheeling Hospital, but wasn't sure how to get it into the mail. If what Mrs. Overby says is true, I can walk into town later and ask about sending it."

Nettie squinted. "You sure you wanna venture out there with all them Rebels about?"

"I have to try to get some word out, don't I?" She read aloud again: "'The North seems fully aware of the great loss they have sustained'"—She slid her finger along, moving her lips silently.— "'They are bitter against their government for having withdrawn the troops, and acknowledge that we have destroyed in a week what it took millions in money and an army of fifteen or twenty thousand men fifteen months to accomplish. They have no hopes of attempting to retake it this season, at least, as they are now in need of every available man in Kentucky and Maryland.'"

"No hopes? Oh Nettie, I am so sorry I didn't get us out of here in time."

Nettie reached across the table, laying her hand on Melinda Jane's. "Now don't you be sorry about us. We's thankful as can be that we here with you and safe for now. God will be with us. He got his angels watchin' over us right now." Olivia had sidled up to her, and Nettie wrapped an arm around the girl. "Ain't that right, child?"

"Yes ma'am." Olivia bobbed her head, her brown eyes sparkling with childhood sweetness.

How could she have been so caught up in her own doings that she almost left Nettie and the children in the church? *Forgive me, Lord.* But if she had made it out, what would've happened to Fin, being injured and all? And he never would've finally told her he loved her. She blinked back tears, but one escaped, and she swiped it away.

"Read us some more," Nettie urged. "Go on, now."

Melinda Jane scanned the paper. A lump caught in her throat. "Thank you, Jesus." She read on, tears blurring the words.

"What's that? What are your reading?" Nettie leaned forward, tapping the table with a finger.

"Oh, Nettie, listen to this:

> "'Lincoln seems to be getting to the last stages of infamy and despair. Baffled and defeated at every point, he is now writhing under the punishment he promised us. In the last Cincinnati papers is published his fiat, giving notice that he will, on the first of January, 1863, cause to be emancipated all slaves, or persons of African descent, who shall then be in the employ of any person residing in any State still in rebellion against the United States; and that all officers of the Army and Navy are commanded to show proper respect to the negroes, as freemen, and that they are to assist them in all their endeavors to throw off the shackles of slavery.'"

Nettie pulled a rag from her pocket and wiped her nose, shaking her head. Her wet face glistened. "I didn't get all them big words, but I reckon I got the gist of it. I don't know what to say, my hearts a-poundin' so hard."

Melinda Jane whisked Perry up off the floor and plunked him on her lap. She wiped her cheek against his bristly head. "I can't imagine the rejoicing in heaven. I'll bet Ol' Izzy's dancin' a jig to make a Scotsman proud!" She laughed aloud.

She wanted to shout out her joy. Her relief. Her thanksgiving. "Thank you Jesus!" It was the echo of her heart, ringing over and over, like a call across the hollers of her beloved mountains.

⸜⸝

"If I have to spend one more week in this camp, I'm gonna bust. Every day's the same." Fin stripped another piece of bark from the twig in his hand. Without a mind to make something of the piece of wood, he kept pushing his knife down the length of it, stroke after stroke. He thought of Duke in the corral with the other horses. He oughta take a ride, that's what he oughta do.

"Quit yer pinin'," Noah said, cleaning his pistol for the third time without shooting the thing.

"I'm not pining, I'm bored."

"Yer pinin' away worse than I ever seen a man."

"Did I tell you how much I appreciate you hanging onto Duke for me?" After Fin's fall in Charleston, the horse had simply caught up to Noah outside of town and been with him ever since.

"Yeah. About five times."

"Oh."

The first week after leaving Charleston, Fin had found his brothers and sister and Mrs. O'Donell in Ripley. They were beside themselves with worry about Melinda Jane, and Zander was blaming himself. It took a heap of convincing from Fin to lift the weight from the boy's shoulders.

He patted the button-down shirt pocket over his heart. The other thing he had done that first week was to buy a necklace for Melinda Jane at Point Pleasant. A shiny gold locket, as perfect as she was. He'd even had it engraved.

A red-headed private strode across the grounds, his attention on Fin. "Sergeant Dabney?" Fin nodded and the soldier handed him a folded paper.

Fin opened the note and his mood changed. "Thank you, Private."

"Something interestin' I hope." Noah stood, brushing the dried grass from his britches.

"Looks like we're going scouting, old son. Let's load up."

Forty-Six

M elinda Jane's head swiveled left and right, taking in the *new* Charleston. It had transformed in such a short time. Smoky campfires dotted the town, no doubt cooking up the soldiers' noon meals. The flashy green of Kanawha Riflemen stood out among the gray and butternut garb of the other soldiers meandering through the streets. The only businesses open were those willing to deal in Confederate currency.

She had hurried past crumbled black remains of buildings—Mercer Academy, the Bank of Virginia, and warehouses near the river. So much destruction. Several houses had suffered from the spreading flames as well.

A single wall of the Kanawha House Hotel remained. The charred skeleton mocked her somehow, announcing her regretful choices to everyone. The debacle of her last performance niggled at her, prompting her to switch direction. A broadside in a store window caught her attention, and she bustled across the street.

She scanned the papers nailed to the siding: VISITORS REQUIRED TO REPORT TO MAJOR THOMAS SMITH, PROVOST MARSHALL. Below that, a Recruiting Office ordinance required young men to join the Confederate Army.

How thankful she was that Zander was out of harm's way. She'd heard tell of boys being yanked into service against their will on the threat of their family's lives.

A large notice read: TO THE PEOPLE OF WESTERN VIRGINIA. She skipped to the bottom. It was a rather long statement by General Loring. "Humph." She covered her mouth hoping no one had witnessed her disdain. . . . *come among you to rescue the people from the despotism of the counterfeit State Government imposed on you by Northern bayonets.*

The Confederacy sure had a strange notion of a rescue. Why the Martial Law then? More like she and Nettie and others like them were the prisoners who needed rescuing.

. . . Your country has been reclaimed for you from the enemy.

Why, how nice of them! Melinda Jane wiped the sour look from her face and glanced around. She folded her arms across her chest for an instant, then dropped them to her sides. She stared at the doorknob at the Provost Marshall office and took a breath to squash her trepidation and bolster her courage.

Now, to find out if she could mail this letter somehow.

October 14, 1862

Fin looked out over the Kanawha River valley, his mind on Charleston. General Loring's troops had trickled out of the area over the last couple of days, leaving General Jenkins's Cavalry to keep watch in the town. Loring could have just pushed on through the city when he had the chance, taking Lightburn's forces in a sweeping victory. He for sure outnumbered them. The Rebels could have had half of West Virginia under their control in a short time.

Colonel Joe was probably right—the Confederates were only after the salt works. They got what they came for and now, just maybe, they would leave the valley for good.

Was this a retreat or a ruse? That was his mission. He had seen with his own eyes the vast number of Confederate troops camped at Kanawha Falls.

"You think General Cox's troops have made it to Charleston yet?" Noah coughed, then spat an entire chaw of tobacco onto the ground. "I don't know how a body gets used to this. Some figure I'm less of a man 'cause I can't stand the stuff. I try and try, but it just don't agree with me."

Fin shook his head. "I don't like it either, but I'm not dumb enough to keep forcing it on myself. And to answer your question, let's just head on back and see about General Cox and his troops for ourselves."

"Mighty good plan."

They had kept to the cover of the trees and game trails, criss-crossing the terrain to get the best view from the higher hills. The going was slow and the chilly fall weather called for a fire at night, so they took turns at watch.

Two days later, as they looked over the James River and Kanawha Turnpike, they spotted Confederates heading toward Charleston. A sizable formation traveled down the pike at a fast clip. General Loring's troops were heading in the other direction now. So who was this?

Fin and Noah raced back, circling north of Charleston, reaching Point Pleasant road-weary and hungry.

They entered the command tent and Col. Joe looked up. "Yes, Sergeant?" He said, pulling off reading glasses Fin had never seen him wear.

"A hefty unit of Confederates will be entering Charleston by morning, Colonel."

"Ah. That would be General Echols, I'm afraid. We've received information that General Loring has been ordered to Richmond and has handed over his command to Echols. If he is this close, I assume he will re-occupy Charleston." He pulled at his beard and lifted an eyebrow. "I don't believe he'll be too happy about General Cox's arrival. It's just a matter of time before our numbers will be such that we can push them back to the Old Dominion."

"Happy to hear that, sir." He could not get back to Charleston soon enough—where his heart was holed up in a house under Rebel occupation.

"Fine work, Sergeant, Corporal."

Once dismissed, they headed off to find their tent. Sleep called to Fin and by the time they turned out the horses, he was getting punchy. Noah must've felt the same because they landed in their beds without a word.

October 27

The dreary morning seeped through the walls of the water-soaked tent. Lightening had flashed throughout the early darkness as Fin battled sleep. He sat up, throwing his legs over the edge of the cot. "You awake, Hicks?"

A groan from the other side of the tent was his reply. Hicks pulled the blanket to his chin and grumbled, "It's Bubba's turn to milk, Maw." He stirred and ground a fist into one eye.

Fin jerked off the blanket, wrestling it from Noah's grip. "Rise and shine, boy. We got big things to do today."

Today they'd head out with an advance unit. General Cox's troops were within ten miles of Charleston, and it was a good day to see just what General Echols and his Confederate force would do about it.

Capt. Green led the advance unit of seventy men into the pouring rain. Progress was slow, with mud glommering onto hooves. They left Point Pleasant, then angled south on the Ripley Road.

Fin's spirits glided a little higher with every step closer to Charleston. Raindrops splashed off his oiled gum blanket, and pewter clouds swirled in the angry sky as if warning the Confederates of their impending doom.

Bring on the fight. Today he was invincible.

His stomach grumbled, folding in on itself. They had stopped for a meal around three o'clock, but that was six hours ago. The next time they pulled off, it would be for the night. A long, wet night.

Gray day receded into black night. Dividing into groups of eight, they combined their tarps, each group fashioning a shelter of sorts with a vent for smoke. It afforded the opportunity for a filling meal and a warm enough night's sleep.

The moonless sky flashed. The ground beneath shivered with the roll of thunder. Fin lay awake, counting the seconds between the lightning and thunder, his mind racing ahead to tomorrow, hoping to enter Charleston. Agitated whinnies mixed with the howling wind.

A loud *CRACK* of a tree limb brought him upright. He waited for the tree to come crashing down on their heads. The tree smashed. Wood splintered. Lightening flared. Heavens collided with earth and a resounding rumble vibrated the ground, lifting its angry roar to new levels. He covered his ears.

A private named Barnes sat up. "That was a bad one!"

"Yeah, it was. Good thing thunder can't hurt ya." Noah leaned up on one elbow. "I didn't hear anybody holler when that tree came down, so I guess it didn't land on any of us."

"I'm gonna try to get some sleep." Fin flipped to his stomach, hugging his Haversack for a pillow.

Dawn crept upon them like a timid child, apologizing for the sky's behavior the night before. The sun refused to press through the heavy clouds, but they enjoyed a few hours without rain.

Mud sucked and spattered as the Federals trotted on, watching for General Jenkins's Cavalry or any pickets set to sound a warning. North of Charleston now, the captain guided them higher for a view of the surrounding area. By noon, they reached high ground and stretched their legs, letting the horses graze on weeds and wilted grass.

Fin pulled out his field glasses, scanning the valley. "Captain, I think you should see this."

Captain Green slipped a field scope from a leather holder and adjusted it to his eye. He smiled. "Now isn't that a pretty sight."

Fin handed the field glasses to Noah, who whistled at the view. "A purty sight, indeed."

Wagon trains and several companies of infantry filed down the turnpike, snaking along the Kanawha River. "No doubt General Echols decided he was finally outnumbered," Fin said.

Noah returned the field glasses to Fin and turned to Capt. Green. "What now, Captain?"

Captain Green flashed a broad, yellow-toothed smile. "We rest a bit longer, then we head into Charleston from the North, past the cemetery."

"Easy, now." Fin leaned back, jarring as Duke's hooves slipped in the gumbo. Water carved ruts in the trace they followed that zigged down in tight switchbacks into the valley. Lightning flashed in the east. The horses' ears twitched as thunder swelled in the distance.

A shot rang. Fin pulled his carbine and galloped into the cover of trees as the others pulled off the trail. Another shot, this time splintering tree bark not five feet away.

The men of the company wasted no time forming up a battle line of sorts along one edge of the trace. Most dropped behind trees, leaving their horses.

He motioned to Noah, and they rode along behind the line of men. If only he could get a look at what they were dealing with here. Was it two men or twenty? Were they all in one spot, or was the enemy working on surrounding them?

Another shot rang out, this time returned with a Federal volley.

Fin and Noah picked their way around several yards behind the unit, searching for any sign of movement. Fin jerked his head down at the rush of a Minie ball. Another one raised a scream from Noah's horse. It reared.

"Easy!" Hicks worked to calm his mount, but the horse took a hit, and there was no telling how long it would remain on its feet.

Another shot. This time, it lured Fin's eyes to a pistol barrel in the crook of a tree. He fired, and a scream from the tree told him he had hit his mark. He traded the carbine for his Colt, searching more trees.

Another exchange sounded from back by the trace. He shot a look in Noah's direction. Had his mount gone down? A Rebel stepped from the undergrowth into the open, a rifle fixed on an oblivious Hicks, struggling with his horse.

That hair!

Like a hot iron, the realization seared Fin's gut.

Clawson smirked. He fired.

"Noah!" Noah plummeted to the ground. His horse staggered, falling against a tree. Fin turned his Colt on Clawson. The man deftly reloaded and looked up. Just as recognition contorted his face into a malevolent grin, Fin pulled the trigger.

The bullet struck him in the chest. He took a choppy step, then lifted his rifle. Fin fired again. Clawson glared down at the red stain on his chest, and fire flashed in his eyes as he stepped forward, aiming again. A third time, Fin fired into the Rebel's chest and he dropped to his knees.

Fin approached him for a fourth shot, his vision tunneled. It was just him and Clawson. Against all of his training, he ignored his surroundings, stepping closer, his raging obsession focused on one thing.

The Rebel teetered on his knees for several seconds, until the weight of his pack pulled him backwards, and his body dredged the ground behind him. Vacant eyes stared into the rain.

Justice had finally been served.

"That's for you, Tiny," Fin rasped.

A clap of thunder brought him up, alert again to his situation. He scanned the trees, turning in a circle. Noah lay unconscious, half of his face mud-coated. Fin dismounted and sprinted to him. *Father, please.* He lifted his friend's head and lowered his ear. The cacophony of rain was deafening. He strained to hear, to feel breath.

He was alive.

Fin lifted Noah's gum blanket, tearing at his jacket, looking for the wound. Blood oozed from one side of his belly. Tugging off his kerchief, Fin wadded it, pressing it into the wound. Reaching into his pocket for another, he added it to the first. Struggling with icy fingers, he unbuttoned Noah's braces, then tied them around his body to hold the wad in place.

Fin whistled for Duke. The gelding tossed his head, snorting his apprehension as he neared the dying horse just a few feet away. "It's okay, boy. Let's get Noah out of here." He hoisted Noah onto the saddle, then climbed up himself, settling his friend in front of him. Holding him upright with one hand, he steered Duke back to the unit.

Forty-Seven

CHARLESTON

C aptain Green led the company into Charleston, and Fin trailed behind with Noah. General Cox's men had claimed the city, and Union troops filled the streets. The captain galloped toward him, pointing off to the west. "The medical is set up over there."

Fin steered Duke toward a house with a sign in the window that read HOSPITAL. Cox's men wasted no time, that much was sure. He threw his leg over the saddle, then slid Noah off, letting him fall over his shoulder. Merciful thing he was unconscious because, try as he might to avoid it, the wound was pressing against Fin's hard shoulder.

He kicked open the door. "Medic!"

"I hear ya. I hear ya." The voice came from the back room. A red-bearded angel, standing over six feet, rounded the doorway, drying his hand on an apron.

Fin sighed with relief. "You're a welcome sight."

Seamus blinked in shock. "Fin . . . what? Well put that man down here. Is that Noah?"

"He took a hit then fell from the horse." Fin laid him on the bed. Seamus caught his head, settling it onto the pillow.

Seamus ran his hand through Noah's hair, checking the back of his head. He sat him up. "Help me get this off." Fin held

Noah while Seamus removed the gum blanket. He chuckled at the makeshift bandage. "I see you learned a few things about field medicine."

"Is he going to be all right?"

Seamus gathered a pan of water and a cloth, then bent over the patient, removing the blood-soaked kerchiefs.

"Well, the bleeding's stopped. Even if the bullet is still in there, from the looks of things, the wound is too distal to hit anything major. I'm more concerned about that knot on the back of his head."

"What can I do?"

"Not a thing you can do, boy-o. Just let me do me job, and we'll trust the Lord to do the rest." Seamus slapped a meaty hand to Fin's shoulder. "You did a fine job of getting him here. Stop back in a few hours to see if he's awake."

Fin nodded. A kind of numbness teased at his mind. What are the chances he would find Seamus here, and the wound would not be serious? *Please, touch this boy, Lord. He's an odd sort, but I'm pretty fond of him.* He nodded once to Seamus and turned for the door.

Pivoting, he dug the necklace from his pocket. He stalled, turning it over and over in his hands. "It's for Melinda Jane." Heat climbed his neck.

Seamus clapped him on the back, chortling. "Sure'n it's about time, Sergeant Dabney!"

Why did he get the feeling he was the last one to figure out God's plan all along?

He guided Duke up the block and over, then up two more streets to James's house. Despite the chilly wet day, the windows were all opened, likely for the first time in six weeks. He turned the bell on the front door and it flew open.

Melinda Jane threw herself at him, stealing his breath away. "Fin, you came!"

He soaked up the love and spunk that was his Melinda Jane. Had he ever felt so loved, so wanted? She kissed his cheek, then pulled him into the house. He closed the door behind him and held her again, kissing her soundly, enjoying the warmth that flooded his body.

He pressed his cheek to hers. "You waited for me."

"Where was I gonna go?"

"I mean, you waited for me. For so long." He was lightheaded at the thought of it.

"I did that. Indeed I did." She smiled, her doe eyes luring him, enticing him to thoughts of—

He dropped to one knee. "Marry me, Melinda Jane." He fumbled with the button on his pocket and produced the tiny box. His fingers trembled as he opened the lid and removed the delicate gold locket.

She gasped, covering her pink lips with perfect fingers. Fresh tears sprang to her eyes.

She frowned. "I may need some time to think about it."

"Wha—"

"I'm done. Oh, Fin, of course I'll marry you." She lifted her hair, turning so he could put it on her. He fumbling with the tiny clasp, distracted by the graceful lines of her bare neck.

She turned and fingered the locket. "It's just perfect."

"I thought we could put our wedding picture in it."

Her finger caressed the engraving on the back. "'He hath made everything beautiful in His time.'" She looked up at him with tear-flooded eyes. "Yes, He has."

Please Review

If you enjoyed this book, please,
leave a brief review wherever you
buy your books.
This encourages authors and helps readers
discover great books!
For more places to leave your review,
go to https://kendypearson.com

Thank you!

WANT A SNEAK PEEK?

**Keep reading for a Peek of the next book in this
captivating series by KENDY PEARSON.**

West Virginia: Born of Rebellion's Storm 3

IN

TEMPEST
WINDS

KENDY PEARSON

*H*eart
of
*i*story
an imprint of
PEAR BLOSSOM BOOKS

IN TEMPEST WINDS

CHARLESTON, WEST VIRGINIA

April 1864

C antankerous weather or not—that finish line was his!

Zander Dabney laughed as mud pelted his cheek. Leaden skies spat great drops, and a frigid wind showed spring the door—but no matter. He tucked his head lower, squinting against the hair that whipped across his eyes.

Settling the reins against Rampart's pulsing flesh, he yielded to the roan gelding's instincts. The shouts of rowdy spectators disappeared, trampled by thrumming hooves with a rhythm as smooth and familiar as his own heartbeat. The horse skirted the ancient sugar tree in a graceful list, kicking soggy turf high into the air as he angled back toward the finish.

"Atta boy," Zander crooned. "Patience, old son, patience."

Throwing a quick look over his shoulder, he gauged the trailing challenger's distance. Just a mite closer. Come on, Crowder. Closer . . . that's it. Now!

Grit salted his smile as he squeezed his knees and shifted his weight. Rampart's powerful legs stretched and his speckled withers quivered with anticipation. The sheer rush of an all-out sprint—horse and rider as one, skimming across the ground, airborne, yet tethered by the brief touch of hoof to earth.

A raucous crowd of soldiers and civilians amassed near the finish line where Paul Skanks waited. His long beard whipped with a gust as he flailed a yellow kerchief in the air.

Zander paired his breath with the cadence of the gelding's chugs as the last few seconds ticked by. One hand raised in victory, he slipped past Skanks and tugged twice on the reins to grab Rampart's attention. The gelding shook his head and slowed to trot a wide circle. He knew just what to do. He always knew.

"Dabney wins again!" Bass shouted joyously, swiping dark curls out of his face. "Collect your winnings, men. A bout of bad luck for one Private Crowder. Maybe next time. Great courage there—going up against the undefeated Private Zander Dabney of Fayette County!"

The boy could sure handle a crowd, Zander would give him that. Henry Bassoom would've made a better city hawker than a German baker. But here he was, stuck in the Fifth West Virginia Cavalry, right along with everybody else.

Zander threw his leg over the cantle and landed on both feet. With a broad sweep of one arm, he bowed to the audience and Rampart deftly extended one front leg and bowed in tandem. The crowd laughed and clapped.

When he turned his back, the great chestnut head butted his shoulder. Zander feigned ignorance with a shrug. After a third nudge, he rewarded Rampart with a bit of biscuit, saved in his pocket for the occasion.

"Wish my woman was that well behaved!" blustered a bystander.

"If she was, she'd ne'er tolerate the likes of you." A gruff voice sailed over the merriment of the crowd.

Zander remounted, walking Rampart through the dispersing onlookers. He patted the wet, sleek shoulder. "Good boy. I knew you could beat him." The horse responded with a contented whicker.

He complimented the horse on a job well done every which way he could think of. It wasn't the words that mattered, after all. It was more that he needed to talk, and he was pretty sure Rampart needed to hear his master's voice.

A broad-shouldered man in a velvet derby approached, admiration sparking in his eyes. "A race well run, son." He ran a hand along the horse's neck. "Fine piece of horseflesh you got here. Don't suppose you would consider parting with this steed?"

"Rampart's not for sale, sir." How often had he fielded that question?

"Humph. You can't blame a man for asking now, can you?"

"No, sir. Nothin' wrong with asking."

"Dabney, huh? Where have I heard the name?" His brow wrinkled and his grizzled mustache jerked like a dying frog.

Here it comes.

"Ah, yes . . . you related to that guerilla fighter Dabney? What do they call him?"

Again.

"Dragon killer . . . something like that."

"Dragon Slayer, sir. And yes, that would be my older brother, Fin." He dismounted and swiped his kerchief across his face so he was no longer looking down on the man.

The gentleman clapped Zander's shoulder. "Well, you must be proud. Bet you can put those bushwhackers in their place yourself. Probably shoot as well as you ride, too."

"No, sir, I don't."

"And you'll likely be joining up with those Blazer Scouts real soon, too, I expect."

"No, sir. I won't be."

"And—" His chin disappeared like a turkey's. "What's that?"

"I won't be joining Captain Blazer's men, sir. If you'll excuse me, I've got some things I gotta do." Now that was a record. A whole three minutes after winning a race before somebody reminded him—he was just Fin Dabney's little brother.

"Dabney! People are waiting to tell you congratulations." Bass pointed out a gathering of soldiers. "And to say thank you for making them some money."

"You thank them for me, all right? How much did we make?" Zander pulled a hoof pick from his pocket and lifted Rampart's front foot. He dug out a wad of grass. "Mmm?"

"You made thirty dollars." Bass collected a fist full of coins and bills from his hat.

Zander raised an eyebrow and studied the forage cap. "You sure you ain't dipping outta there?"

Bass sputtered, and Zander pounded him on the back. "I'm only funnin' with you." He chuckled. "You shoulda seen your face. You don't close that mouth, a wasper's gonna fly in."

His friend frowned. "You are not as funny as you think you are, Dabney."

"Just take your half and put mine in the bag." Zander started for the paddock with Rampart close behind.

He figured Bass was too serious to be the thieving sort, and that's why he trusted his friend with his savings. Some would call it winnings, but that sounded a touch shady. The money was his savings, so he called it such. Four months so far, and the funds for his future were accumulating nicely.

Rampart nibbled at his sleeve. "Not paying enough attention to you, am I boy?" He hadn't meant to keep his meanderings to himself. Most days, he would ramble on and on to his four-legged confidant. Horses didn't compare you to your brother. They merely nodded their understanding and agreement to your plight. Yes, sir. And their soulful eyes spoke a measure of wisdom that was hard to ignore. Better company than most humans, too, no doubt about it.

Zander turned out Rampart after a thorough brushing and set out for the stables. Tomorrow he would request a furlough. It wouldn't do to be this close to his family and not even share a meal with them. And it wouldn't do for any of them to hear about his racing. Some things a body just knows.

The dark clouds had scooted farther east, settling for the evening over the Alleghenies. Blinking into the clearing sky, he smiled with a keen satisfaction. A day well spent, all in all. As much as he hated making the occasional enemy of a disgruntled loser, his racing was just a means to an end. Wide blue skies and all the land he could claim waited for him out West, and he was not letting anything get in his way.

Let that limelight shine on Fin for now. Zander would make a name for himself, too. Soon as this war was over, he would earn himself a reputation as the best horseman west of the Ohio. Then folks would talk about Zander Dabney, the horseman—long after his brother went back to being a nobody farmer, just fighting off critters in the crops instead of Rebel guerillas.

Orders.

Zander dropped onto his cot and stared up at the hut ceiling, hopes of visiting his family trampled to dust. Second day here, and his furlough was denied because of orders. Four long months of garrison duty up at Cumberland, a sudden order to Charleston under General Hayes, and now . . .

Bass looked up, his hound dog eyes flashing with excitement. "Maybe they will send us to a different garrison. Maybe Gauley Bridge. You would like that, ja?" He dug through his saddlebags, his frustration evident until he finally dumped the contents onto his blanket.

Skanks plopped onto one end of Bass's cot, sending the other end to bouncing.

"Ach! What do you think you are doing, Skanks?"

"Same as the Union Army's doing to us. Upsottin' your stuff. I, for one, was thinking on going into town this evening to the Kanawha House for a fine meal and entertainment." He stroked his sparse whiskers right down to the wiry hairs resting on his chest.

Zander rummaged through his saddlebags for paper—paper he had saved to write all the letters good intentions never quite seemed to get to. "The Kanawha House? You don't want to go there."

"I don't?"

"It burned to the ground."

"When?"

"The second year of the war, when General Loring took Charleston." Zander touched the stub of a pencil to his tongue. "Anybody got ink?"

"Well, no wonder we got orders. If'n I'd made plans to do something normal, like playing cards, we'd stay put. Just wish I'd known is all."

Bass looked up, his mouth agape. "Skanks, I sometimes wonder how your mind works."

"Taps" sounded and Zander shoved the paper and pencil back into his pack. Another loss for good intentions. Hopefully, his family would be more understanding than the Fifth Cavalry.

AUTHOR NOTES

I taught the American Civil War many times in my years of teaching school. Three thoughts caused me the most angst: What would it be like to have my home, town, or county become a battlefield? 2) What would it be like to fight my neighbor, perhaps even a relative? 3) What would it be like to send my husband or sons to fight this kind of war? I address each of these considerations in the first three books of this series. I chose western Virginia because it was the most contested piece of real estate in the U.S. at that time.

When writing historical fiction, I first immerse myself in research for several months. After a time, ideas emerge for the foundation of a novel. I then weave fictional characters through a maze of factual events on a historical timeline. The characters undergo their various journeys inspired by accounts of people who lived during that period. I have taken fictional liberties when portraying real historical figures. While you will find numerous recounted historical events and genuine personalities within the pages of *When Heaven Thunders*, here are just a few:

- The execution. People engaged in authentic conversations about the reason for a new state—and yes, they considered "Kanawha" an option. Sarah Young was indeed a real person in Charleston, in love with Edgar, an Ohio soldier. (Ch 6)

- The accounts of the extreme violence of (Federal) Colonel Crook's men are of historical record, including the woman in the burning bed. The testing of the new Gauley Bridge—a bridge which was burned, rebuilt, and burned again in 1861-1862. (The town of Gauley Bridge, at first Southern in sympathy, was taken and retaken three times). (Ch 7, 9)

- The Alien Enemy Act details. James Hamilton, whose land changed occupation several times. He also trained militia for Col. Tompkins of Gauley Mount (a militia later tied to the CFS 22nd Virginia Regiment). He also later pledged allegiance to the Union. (Ch 12,19, 21)

- The Kanawha House, owned by Mr. McFarland, burned during the war.(Ch 15, 18, 28, 33)

- The biography and circumstances of Nancy and George Hunt are of historical record, including the flight to Ohio by their four sons (whom I named). (Ch 16)

- E.D. Thomison's band of CFS guerillas and land owner, Sam Fox. (Ch 21)

- The headless body found by Federal soldiers. The Federal courier problems. (Ch 22)

- CFS President Davis did suspend the writ of habeas corpus, declaring Martial law in much of western Virginia. (Ch 25)

- Civil War era songs and lyrics are public domain. (Ch 28)

- The account of the Flat Top prayer meetings; (future U.S. President) Col. Rutherford B. Hayes's presence. (Ch 31)

- German conscripts under Von Blessing did indeed imbibe in Confederate whiskey, resulting in an ambush attack. Minstrel Show details were taken from published reviews recounting shows of that era. (Ch 33, 34)

- The account of the Summersville attack with peculiar circumstances. Doctor Rucker was a Union spy taken prisoner from the Summersville raid in July 1862. Nancy Hart was one of West Virginia's women spies. (Ch 35)

- The vivid recounting of (CFS) General Loring's attack on Fayetteville and subsequent movement of his forces down the Kanawha Valley to Charleston. Two Ohio drummer boys aided soldiers during the battle, crisscrossing the battlefield, providing water. (Ch 38, 39)

- Details of the massive Federal retreat toward Ohio from Loring's forces. The subsequent celebration of Charleston citizens at the return of CFS occupation. The return of Charleston back to Federal control. (Ch 41-45)

Throughout the book, I followed the 4th Virginia Regiment's postings and movements. The biography of Col. Joseph AJ Lightburn and friendship with "Stonewall" Jackson is of historical record, as is the layout of historic Charleston. Discover more gems from my research and historical novels by signing up for my newsletter at kendypearson.com.

I sincerely hope I have sparked your interest in this tumultuous, heart-wrenching era of our nation's history. Unfortunately, this subject is no longer commonly taught in public schools. At one time, I had a large sign on the wall of my classroom:

THOSE WHO CANNOT REMEMBER THE PAST ARE CONDEMNED TO REPEAT IT.
—George Santayana, 1905

ACKNOWLEDGEMENTS

I am indebted to many people who deserve much credit. This series, "West Virginia: Born of Rebellion's Storm" has been a labor of love. Foremost, I am thankful to Jesus Christ, my Lord, and Savior, Who reminds me He chose me to bear fruit (John 15:16). For over a decade, writing has been fruit-bearing for me. I want to thank the following for helping me bear that fruit:

Present/past members of my critique group, The Encouragers, who have faithfully offered support and true encouragement over the last ten years. A special thank you to Melody Roberts, my ever-vigilant critique partner throughout three novels.

My hero husband who advised me on a variety of technical issues and sacrificed many a home-made meal while I worked away on this book. And to my four (now adult) children, whose tastes in entertainment spurred the viewing of a plethora of war movies over the years. (It's a guy thing.)

Kara Starcher of Mountain Creek Books LLC for her lovely book cover, expert recommendations, regional guidance, and patience with my unending questions.

Sarah Forster and Joan Anderson—proof-readers extraordinaire. Rachel Williams, Publicity Assistant extraordinaire.

Terry Lowry, historian at the WV State Archives Library for his expert recommendations and sharing numerous maps and images with me.

Donny Jones, reenactor with the 13th West Virginia Infantry (aka "The Uniformed Historian") for his expert advice and answering many questions.

West Virginia State Historic Preservation Office for answering a myriad of questions.

RECOMMENDED READING – Fiction

D o you enjoy clean and Christian Historical fiction set during America's Civil War? Here are some books I'd like to recommend:

- *A River Between Us, and* "Heroines Behind the Lines" Series by Jocelyn Green https://jocelyngreen.com

- "Refiner's Fire" Series by Lynn Austin https://lynnaustin.org

- The "Belmont Mansion", "Belle Meade Plantation", and "Carnton" series by Tamera Alexander https://tameraalexander.com

- These three novels by Tara Johnson: *Engraved on the Heart, Where Dandelions Bloom,* and *All Through the Night,* https://tarajohnsontories.com

- The "Accidental Spy" and "Ironwood Plantation" Series by Stephenia H. McGee https://stepheniamcgee.com

- The "Rescued Hearts of the Civil War" series by Susan Pope Sloan: *Rescuing Rose, Loving Lydia,* and *Managing Millie,* https://susanpsloan.com

RECOMMENDED READING – Non-Fiction

If you are interested in further reading, I recommend these books to learn more about the Civil War in West Virginia:

- *The Civil War in West Virginia*: A Pictorial History: Cohen, Stan

- *Bullets and Steel*: The Fight for the Great Kanawha Valley, 1861-1865: Andre, Richard, Cohen, Stan, Wintz, William D.

- *The Atlas of the Civil War*: McPherson, James M.

- *Civil War in Fayette County West Virginia*: McKinney, Tim

- *The Coal River Valley in the Civil War*: West Virginia Mountains, 1861 (Civil War Series): Graham, Michael B.

- *A Banner in the Hills*: West Virginia's Statehood: George Ellis Moore

ABOUT THE AUTHOR

When Kendy Pearson discovers a pocket of American history omitted from the schoolbooks, she enjoys digging in and turning that pocket inside out. Her novels merge fictitious characters with historical events, timelines, and personalities—and she always includes a romantic thread to warm the heart. Every story is a journey through tragedy, secrets, regrets, and God's undeniable grace. Her books have received eight literary awards to date.

Kendy is a veteran high school teacher, accomplished musician, worship leader, bluegrass fiddler, and Civil War reenactment enthusiast. She also enjoys public speaking and teaching writing workshops. Her favorite things include ice cream, snowy days, fireplaces, and maple trees. Kendy is the mother of four grown children and lives with her sweet hubby and two amusing miniature dachshunds.

Subscribe to her newsletter to learn more about upcoming books, freebies, and insider nuggets at **kendypearson.com**.

Find Kendy on Social Media:

- facebook.com/kendy.pearson.author

- goodreads.com/kendypearson

- instagram.com/kendypearson

- threads.net/@kendypearson

- twitter.com/kendypearson

- linkedin.com/in/kendy-pearson